The band was starting up, a slow dance. He was still staring at her, drinking her in. Those green eyes darkening, going black with desire. She had the sudden feeling that he might jerk her to him and kiss her hard, without ever saying a word.

"Would you like to dance?" she said softly. I'm playing with fire, with something I don't understand, she thought suddenly. And in that instant she realized that she was frightened. Her heart began to pound violently. It was as if those green eyes spoke to some part of her that was buried deep beneath the surface—and that part was screaming "danger" at her. Some instinct older than civilization was telling her to run, to flee.

She didn't move.

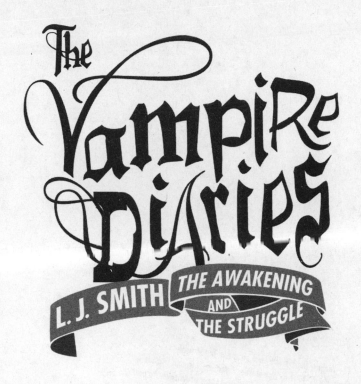

The Vampire Diaries

L. J. SMITH

THE AWAKENING AND THE STRUGGLE

HARPER TEEN

An Imprint of HarperCollins*Publishers*

HarperTeen is an imprint of HarperCollins Publishers.

Library of Congress Catalog Card Number: 2007925202
ISBN 978-0-06-114097-6

Typography by Jennifer Heuer

❖
First HarperTeen paperback edition, 2007
        16 CG/RRDC 40 39

To my dear friend and sister, Judy

A special thanks to Anne Smith, Peggy Bokulic, Anne Marie Smith, and Laura Penny for information about Virginia, and to Jack and Sue Check for all their local lore.

CONTENTS

THE AWAKENING

September 4

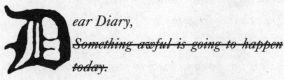
ear Diary,
~~Something awful is going to happen today.~~

I don't know why I wrote that. It's crazy. There's no reason for me to be upset and every reason for me to be happy, but . . .

But here I am at 5:30 in the morning, awake and scared. I keep telling myself it's just that I'm all messed up from the time difference between France and here. But that doesn't explain why I feel so scared. So lost.

The day before yesterday, while Aunt Judith and Margaret and I were driving back from the airport, I had such a strange feeling. When we turned onto our street I suddenly thought, "Mom and Dad are waiting for us at home. I bet they'll be on the front porch or in the living room looking out the window. They must have missed me so much."

I know. That sounds totally crazy.

But even when I saw the house and the empty front porch I still felt that way. I ran up the steps and I tried the door and knocked with the knocker. And when Aunt Judith unlocked the door I burst inside and just stood in the hallway listening, expecting to hear Mom coming down the stairs or Dad calling from the den.

Just then Aunt Judith let a suitcase crash down on the floor behind me and sighed a huge sigh and said, "We're home." And Margaret laughed. And the most horrible feeling I've ever felt in my life came over me. I've never felt so utterly and completely lost.

Home. I'm home. Why does that sound like a lie?

I was born here in Fell's Church. I've always lived in this house, always. This is my same old bedroom, with the scorch mark on the floorboards where Caroline and I tried to sneak cigarettes in

5th grade and nearly choked ourselves. I can look out the window and see the big quince tree Matt and the guys climbed up to crash my birthday slumber party two years ago. This is my bed, my chair, my dresser.

But right now everything looks strange to me, as if I don't belong here. It's me that's out of place. And the worst thing is that I feel there's somewhere I do belong, but I just can't find it.

I was too tired yesterday to go to Orientation. Meredith picked up my schedule for me, but I didn't feel like talking to her on the phone. Aunt Judith told everyone who called that I had jet lag and was sleeping, but she watched me at dinner with a funny look on her face.

I've got to see the crowd today, though. We're supposed to meet in the parking lot before school. Is that why I'm scared? Am I frightened of them?

Elena Gilbert stopped writing. She stared at the last line she had written and then shook her head, pen hovering over the small book with the blue velvet cover. Then, with a sudden gesture, she lifted her head and threw pen and book at the big bay window, where they bounced off harmlessly and landed on the upholstered window seat.

It was all so completely ridiculous.

Since when had she, Elena Gilbert, been scared of meeting people? Since when had she been scared of *anything*? She stood up and angrily thrust her arms into a red silk kimono. She didn't even glance at the elaborate Victorian mirror above the cherrywood dresser; she knew what she'd see. Elena Gilbert, cool and blond and slender, the fashion trendsetter, the high school senior, the girl every boy wanted and every girl wanted to be. Who just now had an unaccustomed scowl on her face and a pinch to her mouth.

A hot bath and some coffee and I'll calm down, she thought. The morning ritual of washing and dressing was soothing, and she dawdled over it, sorting through her new outfits from Paris. She finally chose a pale rose top and white linen shorts combo that made her look like a raspberry sundae. Good enough to eat, she thought, and the mirror showed a girl with a secret smile. Her earlier fears had melted away, forgotten.

"Elena! Where are you? You're going to be late for school!" The voice drifted faintly up from below.

Elena ran the brush one more time through silky hair and pulled it back with a deep rose ribbon. Then she grabbed her backpack and went down the stairs.

In the kitchen, four-year-old Margaret was eating cereal at the kitchen table, and Aunt Judith was burning something on the stove. Aunt Judith was the sort of woman who always looked vaguely flustered; she had a thin, mild face and light flyaway hair pushed back untidily. Elena landed a peck on her cheek.

"Good morning, everybody. Sorry I don't have time for breakfast."

"But, Elena, you can't just go off without eating. You need your protein—"

"I'll get a doughnut before school," said Elena briskly. She dropped a kiss on Margaret's tow head and turned to go.

"But, Elena—"

"And I'll probably go home with Bonnie or Meredith after school, so don't wait dinner. Bye!"

"Elena—"

Elena was already at the front door. She closed it behind her, cutting off Aunt Judith's distant protests, and stepped out onto the front porch.

And stopped.

All the bad feelings of the morning rushed over her again. The anxiety, the fear. And the certainty that something terrible was about to happen.

Maple Street was deserted. The tall Victorian houses looked strange and silent, as if they might all be empty inside, like the houses on an abandoned movie set. They looked as if they were empty of *people*, but full of strange watching things.

That was it; something was watching her. The sky overhead was not blue but milky and opaque, like a giant bowl turned upside down. The air was stifling, and Elena felt sure that there were eyes on her.

She caught sight of something dark in the branches of the old quince tree in front of the house.

It was a crow, sitting as still as the yellow-tinged leaves around it. And it was the thing watching her.

She tried to tell herself that this was ridiculous, but somehow she *knew*. It was the biggest crow she had ever seen, plump and sleek, with rainbows shining in its black feathers. She could see every detail of it clearly: the greedy dark claws, the sharp beak, the single glittering black eye.

It was so motionless that it might have been a wax model of a bird sitting there. But as she stared at it, Elena felt herself flush slowly, heat coming in waves up her throat and cheeks. Because it was . . . looking at her. Looking the way boys looked at her when she wore a bathing suit or a sheer blouse. As if it were undressing her with its eyes.

Before she realized what she was doing, she had dropped her backpack and picked up a stone from beside the driveway. "Get out of here," she said, and heard the shaking anger in her own voice. "Go on! Get *away*!" With the last word, she threw the stone.

There was an explosion of leaves, but the crow soared up unharmed. Its wings were huge, and they made enough racket for a whole flock of crows. Elena crouched, suddenly panicked as it flapped directly over her head, the wind of its wings ruffling her blond hair.

But it swooped up again and circled, a black silhouette against the paper-white sky. Then, with one harsh croak, it wheeled away toward the woods.

Elena straightened up slowly, then glanced around, self-conscious. She couldn't believe what she had just done. But now that the bird was gone, the sky felt ordinary again. A little wind made the leaves flutter, and Elena took a deep breath. Down the street a door opened and several children poured out, laughing.

She smiled at them, and took another breath, relief sweeping through her like sunlight. How could she have been so silly? This was a beautiful day, full of promise, and nothing bad was going to happen.

Nothing bad was going to happen—except that she was going to be late getting to school. The whole crowd would be waiting for her in the parking lot.

You could always tell everyone you stopped to throw stones at a Peeping Tom, she thought, and almost giggled. Now, *that* would give them something to think about.

Without a backward glance at the quince tree, she began to walk as quickly as she could down the street.

The crow crashed through the top of the massive oak, and Stefan's head jerked up reflexively. When he saw it was only a bird, he relaxed.

His eyes dropped to the limp white form in his hands, and he felt his face twist in regret. He hadn't meant to kill it. He would have hunted something larger than a rabbit if he'd known how hungry he was. But, of course, that was the very thing that frightened him: never knowing how strong the hunger would be, or what he might have to do to satisfy it. He was lucky that this time he'd killed only a rabbit.

He stood beneath the ancient oak trees, sunlight filtering down onto his curly hair. In jeans and a T-shirt, Stefan Salvatore looked exactly like a normal high school student.

He wasn't.

Deep in the woods, where no one would see him, he'd come to feed. Now he licked at his gums and lips painstakingly, to make sure there was no stain on them. He didn't want to take any chances. This masquerade was going to be hard enough to pull off as it was.

For a moment he wondered, again, if he should just give it all up. Perhaps he should go back to Italy, back to his hiding place. What made him think that he could rejoin the world of daylight?

But he was tired of living in shadows. He was tired of the darkness, and of the things that lived in it. Most of all, he was tired of being alone.

He wasn't sure why he'd chosen Fell's Church, Virginia. It was a young town, by his standards; the oldest buildings had been put up only a century and a half ago. But memories and ghosts of the Civil War still lived here, as real as the supermarkets and fast-food joints.

Stefan appreciated respect for the past. He thought he might come to like the people of Fell's Church. And per-haps—just perhaps—he might find a place among them.

He'd never be accepted completely, of course. A bitter smile curved his lips at the idea. He knew better than to hope for *that*. There would never be a place where he could belong completely, where he could truly be himself.

Unless he chose to belong to the shadows . . .

He slapped the thought away. He'd renounced the darkness; he'd left the shadows behind him. He was blot-ting all those long years out and starting afresh, today.

Stefan realized he was still holding the rabbit. Gently, he laid it down on the bed of brown oak leaves. Far away, too far for human ears to pick up, he recognized the noises of a fox.

Come along, brother hunter, he thought sadly. Your breakfast is waiting.

As he slung his jacket over his shoulder, he noticed the crow that had disturbed him earlier. It was still perched in the oak tree, and it seemed to be watching him. There was a wrongness about it.

He started to send a probing thought toward it, to examine the bird, and stopped himself. Remember your promise, he thought. You don't use the Powers unless it is absolutely necessary. Not unless there is no other choice.

Moving almost silently among the dead leaves and dry twigs, he made his way toward the edge of the woods. His car was parked there. He glanced back, once, and saw that the crow had left the branches and dropped down on the rabbit.

There was something sinister in the way it spread its wings over the limp white body, something sinister and triumphant. Stefan's throat tightened, and he almost strode back to chase the bird away. Still, it had as much right to eat as the fox did, he told himself.

As much right as he did.

If he encountered the bird again, he'd look into its mind, he decided. Just now, he tore his eyes from the sight of it and hurried on through the woods, jaw set. He didn't want to be late arriving at Robert E. Lee High School.

Elena was surrounded the instant she stepped into the high school parking lot. Everyone was there, the whole crowd she hadn't seen since late June, plus four or five hangers-on who hoped to gain popularity by association. One by one she accepted the welcoming hugs of her own group.

Caroline had grown at least an inch and was slinkier and more like a *Vogue* model than ever. She greeted Elena coolly and stepped back again with her green eyes narrowed like a cat's.

Bonnie hadn't grown at all, and her curly red head barely came up to Elena's chin as she flung her arms around Elena. Wait a minute—*curls?* thought Elena. She pushed the smaller girl back.

"Bonnie! What did you do to your hair?"

"Do you like it? I think it makes me look taller." Bonnie fluffed up the already fluffy bangs and smiled, her brown eyes sparkling with excitement, her little heart-shaped face alight.

Elena moved on. "Meredith. You haven't changed at all."

This hug was equally warm on both sides. She had missed Meredith more than anyone, Elena thought, looking at the tall girl. Meredith never wore any makeup; but then, with perfect olive skin and heavy black lashes, she didn't need any. Right now she had one elegant eyebrow raised as she studied Elena.

"Well, your hair is two shades lighter from the sun. . . . But where's your tan? I thought you were living it up on the French Riviera."

"You know I never tan." Elena held up her hands for her own inspection. The skin was flawless, like porcelain, but almost as fair and translucent as Bonnie's.

"Just a minute; that reminds me," Bonnie interjected, snatching one of Elena's hands. "Guess what I learned from my cousin this summer?" Before anyone could speak, she informed them triumphantly: "Palm reading!"

There were groans, and some laughter.

"Laugh while you can," said Bonnie, not at all disturbed. "My cousin told me I'm psychic. Now, let me see . . . " She peered into Elena's palm.

"Hurry up or we're going to be late," said Elena a bit impatiently.

"All right, all right. Now, this is your life line—or is it your heart line?" In the crowd, someone snickered. "Quiet; I'm reaching into the void. I see . . . I see . . . "All at once, Bonnie's face went blank, as if she were startled. Her brown eyes widened, but she no longer seemed to be staring at Elena's hand. It was as if she were looking *through* it—at something frightening.

"You will meet a tall, dark stranger," Meredith murmured from behind her. There was a flurry of giggles.

"Dark, yes, and a stranger . . . but not tall." Bonnie's voice was hushed and faraway.

"Although," she continued after a moment, looking puzzled, "he *was* tall, once." Her wide brown eyes lifted to Elena's in bewilderment. "But that's impossible . . . isn't it?" She dropped Elena's hand, almost flinging it away. "I don't want to see any more."

"Okay, show's over. Let's go," Elena told the others, vaguely irritated. She'd always felt psychic tricks were just that—tricks. So why was she annoyed? Just because that morning she'd almost freaked out herself. . . .

The girls started toward the school building, but the roar of a finely tuned motor stopped them all in their tracks.

"Well, now," Caroline said, staring. "Quite a car."

"Quite a Porsche," Meredith corrected dryly.

The sleek black 911 Turbo purred through the parking lot, searching for a space, moving as lazily as a panther stalking prey.

When the car came to a stop, the door opened, and they glimpsed the driver.

"Oh, my God," Caroline whispered.

"You can say that again," breathed Bonnie.

From where she stood, Elena could see he had a lean, flat-muscled body. Faded jeans he probably had to peel off at night, tight T-shirt, and a leather jacket of unusual cut. His hair was wavy—and dark.

He wasn't tall, though. Just average height.

Elena let out her breath.

"Who *is* that masked man?" said Meredith. And the remark was apt—dark sunglasses completely covered the boy's eyes, shielding his face like a mask.

"That masked *stranger*," someone else said, and a babble of voices rose up.

"Do you see that jacket? That's Italian, as in Roma."

"How would you know? You've never been farther than Rome, New York, in your life!"

"Uh-oh. Elena's got that look again. The hunting look."

"Short-Dark-and-Handsome had better be careful."

"He isn't short; he's perfect!"

Through the chatter, Caroline's voice suddenly rang out. "Oh, come on, Elena. You've already got Matt. What more do you want? What can you do with two that you can't do with one?"

"The same thing—only longer," drawled Meredith, and the group dissolved into laughter.

The boy had locked his car and was walking toward school. Casually, Elena started after him, the other girls right behind her in a close-knit pack. For an instant, annoyance bubbled up inside her. Couldn't she go *anywhere* without a parade on her heels? But Meredith caught her eye, and she smiled in spite of herself.

"*Noblesse oblige*," Meredith said softly.

"What?"

"If you're going to be queen of the school, you have to put up with the consequences."

Elena frowned at this as they entered the building. A long corridor stretched before them, and a figure in jeans and leather jacket was disappearing through the office doorway up ahead. Elena slowed her pace as she walked up to the office, finally stopping to glance thoughtfully at the messages on the cork bulletin board by the door. There was a large window here, through which the entire office was visible.

The other girls were openly gazing through the window, and giggling. "Nice rear view." "That is *definitely* an

Armani jacket." "You think he's from out of state?"

Elena was straining her ears for the boy's name. There seemed to be some kind of trouble in there: Mrs. Clarke, the admissions secretary, was looking at a list and shaking her head. The boy said something, and Mrs. Clarke lifted her hands in a "What can I say?" gesture. She ran a finger down the list and shook her head again, conclusively. The boy started to turn away, then turned back. And when Mrs. Clarke looked up at him, her expression changed.

The boy's sunglasses were now in his hand. Mrs. Clarke seemed startled by something; Elena could see her blink several times. Her lips opened and closed as if she were trying to speak.

Elena wished she could see more than the back of the boy's head. Mrs. Clarke was fumbling through piles of paper now, looking dazed. At last she found a form of some kind and wrote on it, then turned it around and pushed it toward the boy.

The boy wrote briefly on the form—signing it, proba-bly—and returned it. Mrs. Clarke stared at it a second, then fumbled through a new pile of papers, finally hand-ing what looked like a class schedule to him. Her eyes never left the boy as he took it, inclined his head in thanks, and turned to the door.

Elena was wild with curiosity by now. What had just happened in there? And what did this stranger's face look like? But as he emerged from the office, he was settling his sunglasses in place again. Disappointment coursed through her.

Still, she could see the rest of his face as he paused in the doorway. The dark curly hair framed features so fine that they might have been taken from an old Roman coin or medallion. High cheekbones, classical straight nose . . . and a mouth to keep you awake at night, Elena thought. The upper lip was beautifully sculpted, a little sensitive, a whole lot sensual. The chatter of the girls in the hallway had stopped as if someone had thrown a switch.

Most of them were turning away from the boy now, looking anywhere but at him. Elena held her place by the window and gave a little toss to her head, pulling the ribbon out of her hair so that it fell loose around her shoulders.

Without looking to either side, the boy moved on down the hallway. A chorus of sighs and whispers flared up the moment he was out of earshot.

Elena didn't hear any of it.

He'd walked right by her, she thought, dazed. Right by without a glance.

Dimly, she realized the bell was ringing. Meredith was tugging her arm.

"What?"

"I said here's your schedule. We've got trig on the

second floor right now. Come on!"

Elena allowed Meredith to propel her down the corridor, up a flight of stairs, and into a classroom. She slid into an empty seat automatically and fixed her eyes on the teacher at the front without really seeing her. The shock still hadn't worn off.

He'd walked right by. Without a glance. She couldn't remember how long it had been since a boy had done that. They all looked, at least. Some whistled. Some stopped to talk. Some just stared.

And that had always been fine with Elena.

After all, what was more important than boys? They were the mark of how popular you were, of how beautiful you were. And they could be useful for all sorts of things. Sometimes they were exciting, but usually that didn't last long. Sometimes they were creeps from the beginning.

Most boys, Elena reflected, were like puppies. Adorable in their place, but expendable. A very few could be more than that, could become real friends. Like Matt.

Oh, Matt. Last year she'd hoped that he was the one she was looking for, the boy who could make her feel . . . well, something more. More than the rush of triumph at making a conquest, the pride in showing your new acquisition off to the other girls. And she *had* come to feel a strong affection for Matt. But over the summer, when she'd had time to think, she'd realized it was the affection of a cousin or sister.

Ms. Halpern was passing out trigonometry books. Elena took hers mechanically and wrote her name inside, still wrapped in thought.

She liked Matt more than any other boy she'd known. And that was why she was going to have to tell him it was over.

She hadn't known how to tell him in a letter. She didn't know how to tell him now. It wasn't that she was afraid he'd kick up a fuss; he just wouldn't understand. She didn't really understand herself.

It was as if she were always reaching for . . . something. Only, when she thought she'd got it, it wasn't there. Not with Matt, not with any of the boys she'd had.

And then she had to start all over again. Fortunately, there was always fresh material. No boy had ever resisted her successfully, and no boy had ever ignored her. Until now.

Until now. Remembering that moment in the hall, Elena found that her fingers were clenched on the pen she held. She still couldn't believe he'd brushed by her that way.

The bell rang and everyone flooded out of the classroom, but Elena paused in the doorway. She bit her lip, scanning the river of students flowing through the hall. Then she spotted one of the hangers-on from the parking lot.

"Frances! Come here."

Frances came eagerly, her plain face brightening.

"Listen, Frances, you remember that boy this morning?"

"With the Porsche and the—er—assets? How could I forget?"

"Well, I want his class schedule. Get it from the office if you can, or copy it from him if you have to. But do it!"

Frances looked surprised for a moment, then grinned and nodded. "Okay, Elena. I'll try. I'll meet you at lunch if I can get it."

"Thanks." Elena watched the girl go.

"You know, you really are crazy," Meredith's voice said in her ear.

"What's the use of being queen of the school if you can't pull a little rank sometimes?" returned Elena calmly. "Where do I go now?"

"General Business. Here, take it yourself." Meredith thrust a schedule at her. "I've got to run for chemistry. Later!"

General Business and the rest of the morning passed in a blur. Elena had hoped to catch another glimpse of the new student, but he was in none of her classes. Matt *was* in one, and she felt a pang as his blue eyes met hers with a smile.

At the lunch bell, she nodded greetings right and left

as she walked to the cafeteria. Caroline was outside, posed casually against a wall with chin up, shoulders back, hips forward. The two boys she was talking to fell silent and nudged each other as Elena approached.

"Hi," Elena said briefly to the boys; and to Caroline: "Ready to go in and eat?"

Caroline's green eyes barely flickered toward Elena, and she pushed glossy auburn hair out of her face. "What, at the *royal table*?" she said.

Elena was taken aback. She and Caroline had been friends since kindergarten, and they had always competed with each other good-naturedly. But lately something had happened to Caroline. She'd begun to take the rivalry more and more seriously. And now Elena was surprised at the bitterness in the other girl's voice.

"Well, it's hardly as if you were a commoner," she said lightly.

"Oh, you're so right about that," said Caroline, turning to face Elena fully. Those green cat-eyes were slitted and smoky, and Elena was shocked by the hostility she saw there. The two boys smiled uneasily and edged away.

Caroline didn't seem to notice. "A lot of things changed while you were gone this summer, Elena," she continued. "And just maybe your time on the throne is running out."

Elena had flushed; she could feel it. She struggled to

keep her voice steady. "Maybe," she said. "But I wouldn't buy a scepter just yet if I were you, Caroline." She turned and went into the lunchroom.

It was a relief to see Meredith and Bonnie, and Frances beside them. Elena felt her cheeks cool as she selected her lunch and went to join them. She wouldn't let Caroline upset her; she wouldn't think of Caroline at all.

"I got it," said Frances, waving a piece of paper as Elena sat down.

"And I have some good stuff," said Bonnie importantly. "Elena, listen to this. He's in my biology class, and I sit right across from him. And his name is Stefan, Stefan Salvatore, and he's from Italy, and he's boarding with old Mrs. Flowers on the edge of town." She sighed. "He is *so* romantic. Caroline dropped her books, and he picked them up for her."

Elena made a wry face. "How clumsy of Caroline. What else happened?"

"Well, that's all. He didn't really talk to her. He's ver-r-ry mysterious, you see. Mrs. Endicott, my biology teacher, tried to get him to take off his glasses, but he wouldn't. He has a medical condition."

"What kind of medical condition?"

"*I* don't know. Maybe it's terminal and his days are numbered. Wouldn't that be romantic?"

"Oh, very," said Meredith.

Elena was looking over Frances's sheet of paper, biting her lip. "He's in my seventh period, European History. Anybody else have that class?"

"I do," said Bonnie. "And I think Caroline does, too. Oh, and maybe Matt; he said something yesterday about how it was just his luck, getting Mr. Tanner."

Marvelous, Elena thought, picking up a fork and stabbing at her mashed potatoes. It looked as if seventh period was going to be *extremely* interesting.

Stefan was glad the school day was almost over. He wanted to get out of these crowded rooms and corridors, just for a few minutes.

So many minds. The pressure of so many thought patterns, so many mental voices surrounding him, was making him dizzy. It had been years since he had been in a swarm of people like this.

One mind in particular stood out from the others. She had been among those watching him in the main corridor of the school building. He didn't know what she looked like, but her personality was powerful. He felt sure he'd recognize it again.

So far, at least, he'd survived the first day of the masquerade. He'd used the Powers only twice, and then sparingly. But he was tired, and, he admitted ruefully, hungry. The rabbit hadn't been enough.

Worry about that later. He found his last classroom and sat down. And immediately he felt the presence of that mind again.

It glowed at the edge of his consciousness, a golden light, soft and yet vibrant. And, for the first time, he could locate the girl it was coming from. She was seated right in front of him.

Even as he thought it, she turned around and he saw her face. It was all he could do not to gasp in shock.

Katherine! But of course it couldn't be. Katherine was dead; no one knew that better than he did.

Still, the resemblance was uncanny. That pale golden hair, so fair it almost seemed to shimmer. That creamy skin, which had always made him think of swans, or alabaster, flushing faintly pink over the cheekbones. And the eyes . . . Katherine's eyes had been a color he had never seen before; darker than sky blue, as rich as the lapis lazuli in her jeweled headband. This girl had those same eyes.

And they were fixed directly on his as she smiled.

He looked down from the smile quickly. Of all things, he did not want to think about Katherine. He didn't want to look at this girl who reminded him of her, and he didn't want to feel her presence any longer. He kept his eyes on the desk, blocking his mind as strongly as he knew how. And at last, slowly, she turned around again.

She was hurt. Even through the blocks, he could feel that. He didn't care. In fact, he was glad of it, and he hoped it would keep her away from him. Other than that, he had no feelings about her at all.

He kept telling himself this as he sat, the droning voice of the teacher pouring over him unheard. But he could smell a subtle hint of some perfume—violets, he thought. And her slender white neck was bowed over her book, the fair hair falling on either side of it.

In anger and frustration he recognized the seductive feeling in his teeth—more a tickling or a tingling than an ache. It was hunger, a specific hunger. And not one he was about to indulge.

The teacher was pacing about the room like a ferret, asking questions, and Stefan deliberately fixed his attention on the man. At first he was puzzled, for although none of the students knew the answers, the questions kept coming. Then he realized that that was the man's purpose. To shame the students with what they didn't know.

Just now he'd found another victim, a small girl with clusters of red curls and a heart-shaped face. Stefan watched in distaste as the teacher badgered her with questions. She looked wretched as he turned away from her to address the entire class.

"You see what I mean? You think you're pretty hot

stuff; you're seniors now, ready to graduate. Well, let me tell you, some of you aren't ready to graduate kindergarten. Like this!" He gestured toward the red-haired girl. "No idea about the French Revolution. Thinks Marie Antoinette was a silent film star."

Students all around Stefan were shifting uncomfortably. He could feel the resentment in their minds, and the humiliation. And the fear. They were all afraid of this thin little man with eyes like a weasel, even the husky boys who were taller than he was.

"All right, let's try another era." The teacher swung back to the same girl he'd been questioning. "During the Renaissance—" He broke off. "You *do* know what the Renaissance is, don't you? The period between the thirteenth and seventeenth centuries, in which Europe rediscovered the great ideas of ancient Greece and Rome? The period that produced so many of Europe's greatest artists and thinkers?" When the girl nodded confusedly, he continued. "During the Renaissance, what would students your age be doing at school? Well? Any idea at all? Any guesses?"

The girl swallowed hard. With a weak smile she said, "Playing football?"

At the ensuing laughter, the teacher's face darkened. "Hardly!" he snapped, and the classroom quieted. "You think this is a joke? Well, in those days, students your age would already be proficient in several languages. They would also have mastered logic, mathematics, astronomy, philosophy, and grammar. They would be ready to go on to a university, in which every course was taught in Latin. Football would be absolutely the last thing on—"

"Excuse me."

The quiet voice stopped the teacher in midharangue. Everyone turned to stare at Stefan.

"What? What did you say?"

"I said, excuse me," Stefan repeated, removing his glasses and standing up. "But you're wrong. Students in the Renaissance were encouraged to participate in games. They were taught that a healthy body goes with a healthy mind. And they certainly played team sports, like cricket, tennis—and even football." He turned to the red-haired girl and smiled, and she smiled back gratefully. To the teacher, he added, "But the most important things they learned were good manners and courtesy. I'm sure your book will tell you that."

Students were grinning. The teacher's face was red with blood, and he was sputtering. But Stefan continued to hold his eyes, and after another minute it was the teacher who looked away.

The bell rang.

Stefan put his glasses on quickly and gathered his books. He'd already drawn more attention to himself than he should, and he didn't want to have to look at the blond girl again. Besides, he needed to get out of here quickly; there was a familiar burning sensation in his veins.

As he reached the door, someone shouted, "Hey! Did they really play football back then?"

He couldn't help throwing a grin over his shoulder. "Oh, yes. Sometimes with the severed heads of prisoners of war."

Elena watched him as he went. He'd deliberately turned away from her. He'd snubbed her on purpose, and in front of Caroline, who'd been watching like a hawk. Tears burned in her eyes, but at that moment only one thought burned in her mind.

She'd have him, even if it killed her. If it killed both of them, she'd have him.

3

The first light of dawn was streaking the night sky with pink and palest green. Stefan watched it from the window of his room in the boarding house. He had rented this room specifically because of the trapdoor in the ceiling, a trapdoor that opened onto the widow's walk on the roof above. Just now that door was open, and a cool damp wind blew down the ladder below it. Stefan was fully dressed, but not because he was up early. He had never been to sleep.

He'd just returned from the woods, and a few scraps of wet leaf clung to the side of his boot. He brushed them off fastidiously. The comments of the students yesterday had not escaped him, and he knew they had been staring at his clothes. He had always dressed in the best, not merely out of vanity, but because it was the

right thing to do. His tutor had often said it: *An aristocrat should dress as befits his position. If he does not, he is
showing contempt for others.* Everyone had a place in the
world, and his place had once been among the nobility.
Once.

Why was he dwelling on these things? Of course, he
should have realized that playing the role of a student was
likely to bring his own student days back. Now the memories came thick and fast, as if he were skimming through
the pages of a journal, his eyes catching an entry here and
there. One flashed before him vividly now: his father's
face when Damon had announced he was quitting the
University. He would never forget that. He had never
seen his father so angry. . . .

"What do you mean, you are not going back?"
Giuseppe was usually a fair man, but he had a temper, and
his elder son brought out the violence in him.

Just now that son was dabbing at his lips with a saffron-
colored silk handkerchief. "I would have thought even
you could understand such a simple sentence, Father.
Shall I repeat it in Latin for you?"

"Damon—" Stefan began tightly, appalled at this dis-
respect. But his father interrupted.

"You are telling me that I, Giuseppe, Conte di
Salvatore, will have to face my friends knowing that my

son is a *scioparto*? A ne'er-do-well? An idler who makes no useful contribution to Florence?" Servants were edging away as Giuseppe worked himself into a rage.

Damon did not even blink. "Apparently. If you can call those who fawn on you in the hopes that you will lend them money your friends."

"*Sporco parassito!*" cried Giuseppe, rising from his chair. "Is it not bad enough that when you are at school you waste your time and my money? Oh, yes, I know all about the gambling, the jousting, the women. And I know that if it were not for your secretary and your tutors you would be failing every course. But now you mean to disgrace me utterly. And why? Why?" His large hand whipped up to grasp Damon's chin. "So that you may return to your hunting and hawking?"

Stefan had to give his brother credit; Damon did not wince. He stood, almost lounging in his father's grip, every inch the aristocrat, from the elegantly plain cap on his dark head to his ermine-trimmed cloak to his soft leather shoes. His upper lip was curved in a line of pure arrogance.

You've gone too far this time, thought Stefan, watching the two men whose eyes were locked together. Even you won't be able to charm your way out this time.

But just then there was a light step in the study doorway. Turning, Stefan had been dazzled by eyes the color of lapis lazuli, framed with long golden lashes. It was Katherine. Her father, Baron von Swartzschild, had brought her from the cold lands of the German princes to the Italian countryside, hoping it would help her recover from a prolonged illness. And since the day she had arrived, everything had changed for Stefan.

"I beg your pardon. I did not mean to intrude." Her voice was soft and clear. She made a slight motion as if to leave.

"No, don't go. Stay," Stefan said quickly. He wanted to say more, to catch her hand—but he didn't dare. Not with his father here. All he could do was gaze into those jewel-like blue eyes that were raised to his.

"Yes, stay," Giuseppe said, and Stefan saw that his father's thunderous expression had lightened and that he had released Damon. He stepped forward, straightening the heavy folds of his long fur-trimmed gown. "Your father should be returning from his business in the city today, and he will be delighted to see you. But your cheeks are pale, little Katherine. You are not ill again, I hope?"

"You know I am always pale, sir. I do not use rouge like your bold Italian girls."

"You don't need it," said Stefan before he could stop himself, and Katherine smiled at him. She was so beautiful. An ache began in his chest.

His father continued, "And I see all too little of you during the day. You seldom give us the pleasure of your company until twilight."

"I have my studies and devotions in my own rooms, sir," said Katherine quietly, her lashes dropping. Stefan knew this was not true, but he said nothing; he would never betray Katherine's secret. She looked up at his father again. "But I am here now, sir."

"Yes, yes, that is true. And I must see that tonight we have a very special meal for your father's return. Damon . . . we will speak later." As Giuseppe motioned to a servant and strode out, Stefan turned to Katherine in delight. It was seldom they could speak to each other without the presence of his father or of Gudren, her stolid German maid.

But what Stefan saw then was like a blow to his stomach. Katherine was smiling—the little secret smile that she had often shared with him. But she was not looking at him. She was looking at Damon.

Stefan hated his brother at that moment, hated Damon's dark beauty and grace and the sensuality that drew women to him like moths to a flame. He wanted, in that instant, to strike Damon, to smash that beauty to pieces. Instead he had to stand and watch as Katherine moved slowly toward his brother, step by step, her golden brocade gown whispering on the tiled floor.

And even as he watched, Damon held out a hand to Katherine, and smiled the cruel smile of triumph. . . .

Stefan turned away from the window sharply.

Why was he reopening old wounds? But, even as he thought it, he drew out the slender gold chain he wore under his shirt. His thumb and forefinger caressed the ring that hung from it, then he held it up to the light.

The little circlet was exquisitely worked in gold, and five centuries had not dimmed its luster. It was set with one stone, a lapis the size of his little fingernail. Stefan looked at it, then at the heavy silver ring, also set with lapis, on his own hand. In his chest was a familiar tightness.

He could not forget the past, and he didn't really wish to. Despite everything that had happened, he cherished Katherine's memory. But there was one memory he must truly not disturb, one page of the journal he must not turn. If he had to relive that horror, that . . . abomination, he would go mad. As he had been mad that day, that final day, when he had looked upon his own damnation . . .

Stefan leaned against the window, his forehead pressed to its coolness. His tutor had had another saying: *Evil will never find peace. It may triumph, but it will never find peace.*

Why had he even come to Fell's Church?

He had hoped to find peace here, but that was impossible. He would never be accepted, he would never rest. Because he was evil. He could not change what he was.

Elena was up even earlier than usual that morning. She could hear Aunt Judith pottering about in her room, getting ready for her shower. Margaret was still fast asleep, curled up like a little mouse in her bed. Elena passed her younger sister's half-open door noiselessly and continued down the hallway to let herself out of the house.

The air was fresh and clear this morning; the quince tree was inhabited only by the usual jays and sparrows. Elena, who had gone to bed with a throbbing headache, lifted her face to the clean blue sky and breathed deeply.

She felt much better than she had yesterday. She'd promised to meet Matt before school, and though she wasn't looking forward to it she was sure it was going to be all right.

Matt lived only two streets away from the high school. It was a simple frame house, like all the others on that street, except that maybe the swing on the porch was a little shabbier, the paint a little more peeled. Matt was already standing outside, and for a moment her heart picked up at the sight of him as it used to.

He *was* good-looking. There was no doubt about that. Not in the stunning, almost disturbing way that—that some people were, but in a healthy American way. Matt

Honeycutt was all-American. His blond hair was cropped short for the football season, and his skin was sunburnt from working outdoors on his grandparents' farm. His blue eyes were honest and straightforward. And just today, as he held out his arms to hug her gently, they were a little sad.

"You want to come inside?"

"No. Let's just walk," Elena said. They went side by side without touching. Maples and black walnut trees lined this street, and the air still had a morning hush. Elena watched her feet on the wet sidewalk, feeling suddenly uncertain. She didn't know how to start after all.

"So you still haven't told me about France," he said.

"Oh, it was great," said Elena. She glanced sideways at him. He was looking at the sidewalk, too. "Everything about it was great," she continued, trying to put some enthusiasm in her voice. "The people, the food, everything. It was really . . . " Her voice trailed off, and she laughed nervously.

"Yeah, I know. Great," he finished for her. He stopped and stood looking down at his scuffed tennis shoes. Elena recognized them from last year. Matt's family barely got by; maybe he hadn't been able to afford new shoes. She looked up to find those steady blue eyes on her face.

"You know, *you* look pretty great right now," he said.

Elena opened her mouth in dismay, but he was speaking again.

"And I guess you have something to tell me." She stared at him, and he smiled, a crooked, rueful smile. Then he held out his arms again.

"Oh, *Matt*," she said, hugging him hard. She stepped back to look into his face. "Matt, you are the nicest guy I've ever met. I don't deserve you."

"Oh, so that's why you're dumping me," said Matt as they started walking again. "Because I'm too good for you. I should have realized that before."

She punched him in the arm. "No, that isn't why, and I am not dumping you. We're going to be friends, right?"

"Oh, sure. Oh, absolutely."

"Because that's what I've realized we are." She stopped, looking up at him again. "Good friends. Be honest, now, Matt, isn't that how you really feel about me?"

He looked at her, then rolled his eyes heavenward. "Can I take the Fifth on that?" he said. As Elena's face fell, he added, "It doesn't have anything to do with that new guy, does it?"

"No," Elena said after a hesitation, and then added quickly, "I haven't even met him yet. I don't know him."

"But you want to. No, don't say it." He put an arm around her and gently turned her. "Come on, let's head toward school. If we have time, I'll even buy you a doughnut."

As they walked, something thrashed in the walnut tree

above them. Matt whistled and pointed. "Look at that! Biggest crow I've ever seen."

Elena looked, but it was already gone.

School that day was merely a convenient place for Elena to review her plan.

She had woken up this morning knowing what to do. And today she gathered as much information as she could on the subject of Stefan Salvatore. Which wasn't hard, because everyone at Robert E. Lee was talking about him.

It was common knowledge that he'd some sort of run-in with the admissions secretary yesterday. And today he'd been called to the principal's office. Something about his papers. But the principal had sent him back to class (after, it was rumored, a long-distance call to Rome—or was it Washington?), and everything seemed to be settled now. Officially, at least.

When Elena arrived for Euro History class that afternoon, she was greeted by a low whistle in the hall. Dick Carter and Tyler Smallwood were loitering there. A couple of prize jerks, she thought, ignoring the whistle and their staring. They thought being tackle and safety on the varsity football team made them hot stuff. She kept an eye on them as she loitered in the corridor herself, refreshing her lipstick and fiddling with her compact.

She'd given Bonnie her special instructions, and the plan was ready to be put into effect as soon as Stefan showed up. The compact mirror gave her a wonderful view of the hall behind her.

Still, she missed him coming somehow. He was beside her suddenly, and she snapped the compact shut as he passed. She meant to stop him, but something happened before she could. Stefan tensed—or, at least, there was something about him that seemed wary all at once. Just then Dick and Tyler stepped in front of the door to the history classroom. Blocking the way.

World-class jerks, thought Elena. Fuming, she glared at them over Stefan's shoulder.

They were enjoying the game, slouching in the doorway, pretending they were completely blind to Stefan standing there.

"Excuse me." It was the same tone he'd used with the history teacher. Quiet, detached.

Dick and Tyler looked at each other, then all around, as if hearing spirit voices.

"Scoozi?" Tyler said in a falsetto. "Scoozi me? Me scoozi? Jacuzzi?" They both laughed.

Elena watched muscles tighten under the T-shirt in front of her. This was completely unfair; they were both taller than Stefan, and Tyler was about twice as broad.

"Is there a problem here?" Elena was as startled as the

boys were at the new voice behind her. She turned to see Matt. His blue eyes were hard.

Elena bit her lips on a smile as Tyler and Dick moved slowly, resentfully out of the way. Good old Matt, she thought. But now good old Matt was walking into class beside Stefan, and she was left following them, staring at the backs of two T-shirts. When they sat down, she slid into the desk behind Stefan, where she could watch him without being watched herself. Her plan would have to wait until after class.

Matt was rattling change in his pocket, which meant he wanted to say something.

"Uh, hey," he began at last, uncomfortably. "Those guys, you know . . . "

Stefan laughed. It was a bitter sound. "Who am I to judge?" There was more emotion in his voice than Elena had heard before, even when he had spoken to Mr. Tanner. And that emotion was raw unhappiness. "Anyway, why should I be welcome here?" he finished, almost to himself.

"Why shouldn't you be?" Matt had been staring at Stefan; now his jaw squared with decision. "Listen," he said. "You were talking about football yesterday. Well, our star wide receiver tore a ligament yesterday afternoon, and we need a replacement. Tryouts are this afternoon. What do you think?"

"Me?" Stefan sounded caught off guard. "Ah . . . I don't know if I could."

"Can you run?"

"Can—?" Stefan half turned toward Matt, and Elena could see a faint hint of a smile curve his lips. "Yes."

"Can you catch?"

"Yes."

"That's all a wide receiver has to do. I'm the quarterback. If you can catch what I throw and run with it, you can play."

"I see." Stefan was actually almost smiling, and though Matt's mouth was serious his blue eyes were dancing. Astonished at herself, Elena realized she was jealous. There was a warmth between the two boys that shut her out completely.

But the next instant Stefan's smile disappeared. He said distantly, "Thank you . . . but no. I have other commitments."

At that moment, Bonnie and Caroline arrived and class started.

Throughout Tanner's lecture on Europe, Elena repeated to herself, "Hello. I'm Elena Gilbert. I'm on the Senior Welcoming Committee, and I've been assigned to show you around the school. Now, you wouldn't want to get me in trouble, would you, by not letting me do my job?" That last with wide, wistful eyes—but only if he looked like he might try to get out of it. It was virtually foolproof. He was a sucker for maidens who needed to be rescued.

Halfway through class, the girl sitting to her right passed her a note. Elena opened it and recognized Bonnie's round, childish handwriting. It read: "I kept C. away for as long as I could. What happened? Did it work???"

Elena looked up to see Bonnie twisted around in her front-row seat. Elena pointed to the note and shook her head, mouthing, "After class."

It seemed a century until Tanner gave some last-minute instructions about oral reports and dismissed them. Then everybody sprang up at once. Here goes, thought Elena, and, with her heart pounding, she stepped squarely into Stefan's path, blocking the aisle so that he couldn't get around her.

Just like Dick and Tyler, she thought, feeling a hysterical urge to giggle. She looked up and found her eyes exactly on a level with his mouth.

Her mind went blank. What was it she was supposed to say? She opened her mouth, and somehow the words she'd been practicing came tumbling out. "Hi, I'm Elena Gilbert, and I'm on the Senior Welcoming Committee and I've been assigned—"

"I'm sorry; I don't have time." For a minute, she couldn't

believe he was speaking, that he wasn't even going to give her a chance to finish. Her mouth went right on with the speech.

"—to show you around the school—"

"I'm sorry; I can't. I have to—to get to football try-outs." Stefan turned to Matt, who was standing by looking amazed. "You said they were right after school, didn't you?"

"Yes," Matt said slowly. "But—"

"Then I'd better get moving. Maybe you could show me the way."

Matt looked helplessly at Elena, then shrugged. "Well . . . sure. Come on." He glanced back once as they left. Stefan didn't.

Elena found herself looking around at a circle of interested observers, including Caroline, who was openly smirking. Elena felt a numbness in her body and a fullness in her throat. She couldn't stand to be here for one more second. She turned and walked as quickly as she could from the room.

4

By the time Elena reached her locker, the numbness was wearing off and the lump in her throat was trying to dissolve into tears. But she wouldn't cry at school, she told herself, she *wouldn't*. After closing her locker, she made for the main exit.

For the second day in a row, she was coming home from school right after the last bell, and alone. Aunt Judith wouldn't be able to cope. But when Elena reached her house, Aunt Judith's car was not in the driveway; she and Margaret must have gone out to the market. The house was still and peaceful as Elena let herself in.

She was glad for that stillness; she wanted to be alone right now. But, on the other hand, she didn't exactly know what to do with herself. Now that she finally *could* cry, she found that tears wouldn't come. She let her backpack sag to the floor in the front hall and walked slowly into the living room.

It was a handsome, impressive room, the only part of the house besides Elena's bedroom that belonged to the original structure. That first house had been built before 1861, and had been almost completely burned in the Civil War. All that could be saved was this room, with its elaborate fireplace framed by scrolled molding, and the big bedroom above. Elena's father's great-grandfather had built a new house, and Gilberts had lived in it ever since.

Elena turned to look out of one of the ceiling-to-floor windows. The glass was so old that it was thick and wavery, and everything outside was distorted, looking slightly tipsy. She remembered the first time her father had showed her that wavery old glass, when she had been younger than Margaret was now.

The fullness in her throat was back, but still no tears would come. Everything inside her was contradictory. She didn't want company, and yet she was achingly lonely. She *did* want to think, but now that she was trying to, her thoughts eluded her like mice running from a white owl.

White owl . . . hunting bird . . . flesh eater . . . crow, she thought. "Biggest crow I've ever seen," Matt had said.

Her eyes stung again. Poor Matt. She'd hurt him, but he'd been so nice about it. He'd even been nice to Stefan.

Stefan. Her heart thudded once, hard, squeezing two

hot tears out of her eyes. There, she was crying at last. She was crying with anger and humiliation and frustration—and what else?

What had she really lost today? What did she really feel for this stranger, this Stefan Salvatore? He was a challenge, yes, and that made him different, interesting. Stefan was exotic . . . exciting.

Funny, that was what guys had sometimes told Elena *she* was. And later she heard from them, or from their friends or sisters, how nervous they were before going out with her, how their palms got sweaty and their stomachs were full of butterflies. Elena had always found such stories amusing. No boy she'd ever met in her life had made her nervous.

But when she'd spoken to Stefan today, her pulse had been racing, her knees weak. Her palms had been wet. And there hadn't been butterflies in her stomach—there had been bats.

She was interested in the guy because he made her feel nervous? Not a very good reason, Elena, she told herself. In fact, a very bad reason.

But there was also that mouth. That sculpted mouth that made her knees weak with something entirely different than nervousness. And that night-dark hair—her fingers itched to weave themselves into its softness. That lithe, flat-muscled body, those long legs . . . and that *voice*.

It was his voice that had decided her yesterday, making her absolutely determined to have him. His voice had been cool and disdainful when talking to Mr. Tanner, but strangely compelling for all that. She wondered if it could turn night-dark as well, and how it would sound saying her name, whispering her name. . . .

"Elena!"

Elena jumped, her reverie shattered. But it wasn't Stefan Salvatore calling her, it was Aunt Judith rattling the front door open.

"Elena? Elena!" And that was Margaret, her voice shrill and piping. "Are you home?"

Misery welled up in Elena again, and she glanced around the kitchen. She couldn't face her aunt's worried questions or Margaret's innocent cheerfulness right now. Not with her eyelashes wet and new tears threatening any minute. She made a lightning decision and quietly slipped out the back door as the front door banged shut.

Once off the back porch and into the yard, she hesitated. She didn't want to run into anyone she knew. But where could she go to be alone?

The answer came almost instantly. Of course. She'd go see Mom and Dad.

It was a fairly long walk; almost to the edge of town but over the last three years it had become familiar to Elena. She crossed over Wickery Bridge and climbed up the hill, past the ruined church, then down into the little valley below.

This part of the cemetery was well-kept; it was the old section that was allowed to run slightly wild. Here, the grass was neatly trimmed, and bouquets of flowers made splashes of bright color. Elena sat down by the big marble headstone with "Gilbert" carved into the front.

"Hi, Mom. Hi, Dad," she whispered. She leaned over to place a purple impatiens blossom she'd picked along the way in front of the marker. Then she curled her legs under her and just sat.

She'd come here often after the accident. Margaret had been only one at the time of the car crash; she didn't really remember them. But Elena did. Now she let her mind leaf back through memories, and the lump in her throat swelled, and the tears came easier. She missed them so much, still. Mother, so young and beautiful, and Father, with a smile that crinkled up his eyes.

She was lucky to have Aunt Judith, of course. It wasn't every aunt who would quit her job and move back into a little town to take care of two orphaned nieces. And Robert, Aunt Judith's fiancé, was more like a stepfather to Margaret than an uncle-to-be by marriage.

But Elena remembered her parents. Sometimes, right after the funeral, she had come out here to rage at them, angry with them for being so stupid as to get themselves killed. That was when she hadn't known Aunt Judith very well, and had felt there was nowhere on earth she belonged anymore.

Where did she belong now? she wondered. The easy answer was, here, in Fell's Church, where she'd lived all her life. But lately the easy answer seemed wrong. Lately she felt there must be something else out there for her, some place she would recognize at once and call home.

A shadow fell over her, and she looked up, startled. For an instant, the two figures standing over her were alien, unfamiliar, vaguely menacing. She stared, frozen.

"Elena," said the smaller figure fussily, hands on hips, "sometimes I *worry* about you, I really do."

Elena blinked and then laughed shortly. It was Bonnie and Meredith. "What does a person have to do to get a little privacy around here?" she said as they sat down.

"Tell us to go away," suggested Meredith, but Elena just shrugged. Meredith and Bonnie had often come out here to find her in the months after the accident. Suddenly, she felt glad about that, and grateful to them both. If nowhere else, she belonged with the friends who cared about her. She didn't mind if they knew she had been crying, and she accepted the crumpled tissue Bonnie offered her and wiped her eyes. The three of them sat together in silence for a little while, watching the wind ruffle the stand of oak trees at the edge of the cemetery.

"I'm sorry about what happened," Bonnie said at last, in a soft voice. "That was really terrible."

"And your middle name is 'Tact,'" said Meredith. "It couldn't have been that bad, Elena."

"You weren't there." Elena felt herself go hot all over again at the memory. "It *was* terrible. But I don't care anymore," she added flatly, defiantly. "I'm finished with him. I don't want him anyway."

"Elena!"

"I don't, Bonnie. He obviously thinks he's too good for—for Americans. So he can just take those designer sunglasses and . . . "

There were snorts of laughter from the other girls. Elena wiped her nose and shook her head. "So," she said to Bonnie, determinedly changing the subject, "at least Tanner seemed in a better mood today."

Bonnie looked martyred. "Do you know that he made me sign up to be the very first one to give my oral report? I don't care, though; I'm going to do mine on the druids, and—"

"On the what?"

"*Droo*-ids. The weird old guys who built Stonehenge and did magic and stuff in ancient England. I'm descended from them, and that's why I'm psychic."

Meredith snorted, but Elena frowned at the blade of

grass she was twirling between her fingers. "Bonnie, did you really see something yesterday in my palm?" she asked abruptly.

Bonnie hesitated. "I don't know," she said at last. "I— I *thought* I did then. But sometimes my imagination runs away with me."

"She knew you were here," said Meredith unexpectedly. "I thought of looking at the coffee shop, but Bonnie said, 'She's at the cemetery.'"

"Did I?" Bonnie looked faintly surprised but impressed. "Well, there you see. My grandmother in Edinburgh has the second sight and so do I. It always skips a generation.

"And you're descended from the druids," Meredith said solemnly.

"We'll, it's true! In Scotland they keep up the old traditions. You wouldn't *believe* some of the things my grandmother does. She has a way to find out who you're going to marry and when you're going to die. She told me I'm going to die early."

"Bonnie!"

"She did. I'm going to be young and beautiful in my coffin. Don't you think that's romantic?"

"No, I don't. I think it's disgusting," said Elena. The shadows were getting longer, and the wind had a chill to it now.

"So who are you going to marry, Bonnie?" Meredith put in deftly.

"I don't know. My grandmother told me the ritual for finding out, but I never tried it. Of course"—Bonnie struck a sophisticated pose—"he has to be outrageously rich and totally gorgeous. Like our mysterious dark stranger, for example. Particularly if nobody else wants him." She cast a wicked glance at Elena.

Elena refused the bait. "What about Tyler Smallwood?" she murmured innocently. "His father's certainly rich enough."

"And he's not bad-looking," agreed Meredith solemnly. "That is, of course, if you're an animal lover. All those big white teeth."

The girls looked at each other and then simultaneously burst into laughter. Bonnie threw a handful of grass at Meredith, who brushed it off and threw a dandelion back at her. Somewhere in the middle of it, Elena realized that she was going to be all right. She was herself again, not lost, not a stranger, but Elena Gilbert, the queen of Robert E. Lee. She pulled the apricot ribbon out of her hair and shook the hair free about her face.

"I've decided what to do *my* oral report on," she said, watching with narrow eyes as Bonnie finger-combed grass out of her curls.

"What?" said Meredith.

Elena tilted her chin up to gaze at the red and purple sky above the hill. She took a thoughtful breath and let the suspense build for a moment. Then she said coolly, "The Italian Renaissance."

Bonnie and Meredith stared at her, then looked at each other and burst into whoops of laughter again.

"Aha," said Meredith when they recovered. "So the tiger returneth."

Elena gave her a feral grin. Her shaken confidence had returned to her. And though she didn't understand it herself, she knew one thing: she wasn't going to let Stefan Salvatore get away alive.

"All right," she said briskly. "Now, listen, you two. Nobody else can know about this, or I'll be the laughing-stock of the school. And Caroline would just love any excuse to make me look ridiculous. But I *do* still want him, and I'm going to have him. I don't know how yet, but I am. Until I come up with a plan, though, we're going to give him the cold shoulder."

"Oh, *we* are?"

"Yes, *we* are. You can't have him, Bonnie; he's mine. And I have to be able to trust you completely."

"Wait a minute," said Meredith, a glint in her eye. She unclasped the cloisonné pin from her blouse, then, holding up her thumb, made a quick jab. "Bonnie, give me your hand."

"Why?" said Bonnie, eyeing the pin suspiciously.

"Because I want to marry you. Why do you think, idiot?"

"But—but— Oh, all *right*. Ow!"

"Now you, Elena." Meredith pricked Elena's thumb efficiently, and then squeezed it to get a drop of blood. "Now," she continued, looking at the other two with sparkling dark eyes, "we all press our thumbs together and swear. Especially you, Bonnie. Swear to keep this secret and to do whatever Elena asks in relation to Stefan."

"Look, swearing with blood is dangerous," Bonnie protested seriously. "It means you have to stick to your oath no matter what happens, no matter *what*, Meredith."

"I know," said Meredith grimly. "That's why I'm telling you to do it. I remember what happened with Michael Martin."

Bonnie made a face. "That was years ago, and we broke up right away anyway and— Oh, all right. I'll swear." Closing her eyes, she said, "I swear to keep this a secret and to do anything Elena asks about Stefan."

Meredith repeated the oath. And Elena, staring at the pale shadows of their thumbs joined together in the gathering dusk, took a long breath and said softly, "And I swear not to rest until he belongs to me."

A gust of cold wind blew through the cemetery, fanning

the girls' hair out and sending dry leaves fluttering on the ground. Bonnie gasped and pulled back, and they all looked around, then giggled nervously.

"It's dark," said Elena, surprised.

"We'd better get started home," Meredith said, refastening her pin as she stood up. Bonnie stood, too, putting the tip of her thumb into her mouth.

"Good-bye," said Elena softly, facing the headstone. The purple blossom was a blur on the ground. She picked up the apricot ribbon that lay next to it, turned, and nodded to Bonnie and Meredith. "Let's go."

Silently, they headed up the hill toward the ruined church. The oath sworn in blood had given them all a solemn feeling, and as they passed the ruined church Bonnie shivered. With the sun down, the temperature had dropped abruptly, and the wind was rising. Each gust sent whispers through the grass and made the ancient oak trees rattle their dangling leaves.

"I'm freezing," Elena said, pausing for a moment by the black hole that had once been the church door and looking down at the landscape below.

The moon had not yet risen, and she could just make out the old graveyard and Wickery Bridge beyond it. The old graveyard dated from Civil War days, and many of the headstones bore the names of soldiers. It had a wild look to it; brambles and tall weeds grew on the graves, and ivy vines swarmed over crumbling granite. Elena had never liked it.

"It looks different, doesn't it? In the dark, I mean," she said unsteadily. She didn't know how to say what she really meant, that it was not a place for the living.

"We could go the long way," said Meredith. "But that would mean another twenty minutes of walking."

"I don't mind going this way," said Bonnie, swallowing hard. "I always said I wanted to be buried down there in the old one."

"Will you stop talking about being buried!" Elena snapped, and she started down the hill. But the farther down the narrow path she got, the more uncomfortable she felt. She slowed until Bonnie and Meredith caught up with her. As they neared the first headstone, her heart began beating fast. She tried to ignore it, but her whole skin was tingling with awareness and the fine hairs on her arms were standing up. Between the gusts of wind, every sound seemed horribly magnified; the crunching of their feet on the leaf-strewn path was deafening.

The ruined church was a black silhouette behind them now. The narrow path led between the lichen-encrusted headstones, many of which stood taller than Meredith. Big enough for something to hide behind, thought Elena uneasily. Some of the tombstones themselves were unnerving, like the one with the cherub that looked like a real baby, except that its head had fallen off and had been carefully placed by its body. The wide granite eyes of the head were blank. Elena couldn't look away from it, and her heart began to pound.

"Why are we stopping?" said Meredith.

"I just . . . I'm sorry," Elena murmured, but when she forced herself to turn she immediately stiffened. "Bonnie?" she said. "Bonnie, what's wrong?"

Bonnie was staring straight out into the graveyard, her lips parted, her eyes as wide and blank as the stone cherub's. Fear washed through Elena's stomach. "Bonnie, stop it. Stop it! It's not funny."

Bonnie made no reply.

"Bonnie!" said Meredith. She and Elena looked at each other, and suddenly Elena knew she had to get away. She whirled to start down the path, but a strange voice spoke behind her, and she jerked around.

"Elena," the voice said. It wasn't Bonnie's voice, but it came from Bonnie's mouth. Pale in the darkness, Bonnie was still staring out into the graveyard. There was no expression on her face at all.

"Elena," the voice said again, and added, as Bonnie's head turned toward her, "there's someone waiting out there for you."

Elena never quite knew what happened in the next few minutes. Something seemed to move out among the dark humped shapes of the headstones, shifting and rising between them. Elena screamed and Meredith cried out, and then they were both running, and Bonnie was running with them, screaming, too.

Elena pounded down the narrow path, stumbling on rocks and clumps of grass root. Bonnie was sobbing for breath behind her, and Meredith, calm and cynical Meredith, was panting wildly. There was a sudden thrashing and a shriek in an oak tree above them, and Elena found that she could run faster.

"There's something behind us," cried Bonnie shrilly. "Oh, God, what's happening?"

"Get to the bridge," gasped Elena through the fire in her lungs. She didn't know why, but she felt they had to make it there. "Don't stop, Bonnie! Don't look behind you!" She grabbed the other girl's sleeve and pulled her around.

"I can't make it," Bonnie sobbed, clutching her side, her pace faltering.

"Yes, you can," snarled Elena, grabbing Bonnie's sleeve again and forcing her to keep moving. "Come on. *Come on!*"

She saw the silver gleam of water before them. And there was the clearing between the oak trees, and the bridge just beyond. Elena's legs were wobbling and her breath was whistling in her throat, but she wouldn't let herself lag behind. Now she could see the wooden planks of the footbridge. The bridge was twenty feet away from them, ten feet away, five.

"We made it," panted Meredith, feet thundering on the wood.

"Don't stop! Get to the other side!"

The bridge creaked as they ran staggering across it, their steps echoing across the water. When she jumped onto packed dirt on the far shore, Elena let go of Bonnie's sleeve at last, and allowed her legs to stumble to a halt.

Meredith was bent over, hands on thighs, deep-breathing. Bonnie was crying.

"What was it? Oh, what was it?" she said. "Is it still coming?"

"I thought you were the expert," Meredith said unsteadily. "For God's sake, Elena, let's get out of here."

"No, it's all right now," Elena whispered. There were tears in her own eyes and she was shaking all over, but the hot breath at the back of her neck had gone. The river stretched between her and it, the waters a dark tumult. "It can't follow us here," she said.

Meredith stared at her, then at the other shore with its clustered oak trees, then at Bonnie. She wet her lips and laughed shortly. "Sure. It can't follow us. But let's go home anyway, all right? Unless you feel like spending the night out here."

Some unnameable feeling shuddered through Elena. "Not tonight, thanks," she said. She put an arm around Bonnie, who was still sniffling. "It's okay, Bonnie. We're safe now. Come on."

Meredith was looking across the river again. "You know, I don't see a thing back there," she said, her voice calmer. "Maybe there wasn't anything behind us at all; maybe we just panicked and scared ourselves. With a little help from the druid priestess here."

Elena said nothing as they started walking, keeping very close together on the dirt path. But she wondered. She wondered very much.

5

The full moon was directly overhead when Stefan came back to the boarding house. He was giddy, almost reeling, both from fatigue and from the glut of blood he'd taken. It had been a long time since he'd let himself feed so heavily. But the burst of wild Power by the graveyard had caught him up in its frenzy, shattering his already weakened control. He still wasn't sure where the Power had come from. He had been watching the human girls from his place in the shadows when it had exploded from behind him, sending the girls fleeing. He had been caught between the fear that they would run into the river and the desire to probe this Power and find its source. In the end, he had followed *her*, unable to chance her getting hurt.

Something black had winged toward the woods as the

humans reached the sanctuary of the bridge, but even
Stefan's night senses could not make out what it was. He
had watched while *she* and the other two started in the
direction of town. Then he had turned back to the graveyard.

It was empty now, purged of whatever had been there.
On the ground lay a thin strip of silk that to ordinary eyes
would have been gray in the dark. But he saw its true
color, and as he crushed it between his fingers, bringing it
slowly up to touch his lips, he could smell the scent of her
hair.

Memory engulfed him. It was bad enough when she
was out of sight, when the cool glow of her mind only
teased at the edges of his consciousness. But to be in the
same room with her at the school, to feel her presence
behind him, to smell the heady fragrance of her skin all
around him, was almost more than he could bear.

He had heard every soft breath she took, felt her
warmth radiating against his back, sensed each throb of
her sweet pulse. And eventually, to his horror, he had found
himself giving in to it. His tongue had brushed back and
forth over his canine teeth, enjoying the pleasure-pain
that was building there, encouraging it. He'd breathed
her smell into his nostrils deliberately, and let the visions
come to him, imagining it all. How soft her neck would
be, and how his lips would meet it with equal softness at

first, planting tiny kisses here, and here, until he reached the yielding hollow of her throat. How he would nuzzle there, in the place where her heart beat so strongly against the delicate skin. And how at last his lips would part, would draw back from aching teeth now sharp as little daggers, and—

No. He'd brought himself out of the trance with a jerk, his own pulse beating raggedly, his body shaking. The class had been dismissed, movement was all around him, and he could only hope no one had been observing him too closely.

When she had spoken to him, he had been unable to believe that he had to face her while his veins burned and his whole upper jaw ached. He'd been afraid for a moment that his control would break, that he would seize her shoulders and take her in front of all of them. He had no idea how he'd gotten away, only that some time later he was channeling his energy into hard exercise, dimly aware that he must not use the Powers. It didn't matter; even without them he was in every way superior to the mortal boys who competed with him on the football field. His sight was sharper, his reflexes faster, his muscles stronger. Presently a hand had clapped him on the back and Matt's voice had rung in his ears:

"Congratulations! Welcome to the team!"

Looking into that honest, smiling face, Stefan had

been overcome with shame. If you knew what I was, you wouldn't smile at me, he'd thought grimly. I've won this competition of yours by deception. And the girl you love—you do love her, don't you?—is in my thoughts right now.

And she had remained in his thoughts despite all his efforts to banish her that afternoon. He had wandered to the graveyard blindly, pulled from the woods by a force he did not understand. Once there he had watched her, fighting himself, fighting the need, until the surge of Power had sent her and her friends running. And then he'd come home—but only after feeding. After losing control of himself.

He couldn't remember exactly how it had happened, how he'd let it happen. That flare of Power had started it, awakening things inside him best left sleeping. The hunting need. The craving for the chase, for the smell of fear and the savage triumph of the kill. It had been years—centuries—since he'd felt the need with such force. His veins had begun burning like fire. And all his thoughts had turned red: he could think of nothing else but the hot coppery taste, the primal vibrancy, of blood.

With that excitement still raging through him, he'd taken a step or two after the girls. What *might* have happened if he hadn't scented the old man was better not thought about. But as he reached the end of the bridge, his nostrils had flared at the sharp, distinctive odor of human flesh.

Human *blood*. The ultimate elixir, the forbidden wine. More intoxicating than any liquor, the steaming essence of life itself. And he was so tired of fighting the need.

There had been a movement on the bank under the bridge, as a pile of old rags stirred. And the next instant, Stefan had landed gracefully, catlike, beside it. His hand shot out and pulled the rags away, exposing a wizened, blinking face atop a scrawny neck. His lips drew back.

And then there was no sound but the feeding.

Now, as he stumbled up the main staircase of the boarding house, he tried not to think about it, and not to think about her—about the girl who tempted him with her warmth, her life. *She* had been the one he truly desired, but he must put a stop to that, he must kill any such thoughts before they were started from now on. For his sake, and for her own. He was her worst nightmare come true, and she didn't even know it.

"Who's there? Is that you, boy?" a cracked voice called sharply. One of the second-story doors opened, and a gray head poked out.

"Yes, *signora*— Mrs. Flowers. I'm sorry if I disturbed you."

"Ah, it takes more than a creaky floorboard to disturb me. You locked the door behind you?"

"Yes, *signora*. You're . . . safe."

"That's right. We need to be safe here. You never know what might be out there in those woods, do you?" He looked quickly at the smiling little face surrounded by wisps of gray hair, the bright darting eyes. Was there a secret hidden in them?

"Good night, *signora*."

"Good night, boy." She shut the door.

In his own room he fell onto the bed and lay staring up at the low, slanting ceiling.

Usually he rested uneasily at night; it was not his natural sleeping time. But tonight he was tired. It took so much energy to face the sunlight, and the heavy meal only contributed to his lethargy. Soon, although his eyes did not close, he no longer saw the whitewashed ceiling above him.

Random scraps of memory floated through his mind. Katherine, so lovely that evening by the fountain, moonlight silvering her pale golden hair. How proud he had been to sit with her, to be the one to share her secret. . . .

"But can you never go out in sunlight?"

"I *can*, yes, as long as I wear this." She held up a small white hand, and the moonlight shone on the lapis ring there. "But the sun tires me so much. I have never been very strong."

Stefan looked at her, at the delicacy of her features and the slightness of her body. She was almost as insubstantial as spun glass. No, she would never have been strong.

"I was often ill as a child," she said softly, her eyes on the play of water in the fountain. "The last time, the surgeon finally said I would die. I remember Papa crying, and I remember lying in my big bed, too weak to move. Even breathing was too much effort. I was so sad to leave the world and so cold, so very cold." She shivered, and then smiled.

"But what happened?"

"I woke in the middle of the night to see Gudren, my maid, standing over my bed. And then she stepped aside, and I saw the man she had brought. I was frightened. His name was Klaus, and I'd heard the people in the village say he was evil. I cried out to Gudren to save me, but she just stood there, watching. When he put his mouth to my neck, I thought he was going to kill me."

She paused. Stefan was staring at her in horror and pity, and she smiled comfortingly at him. "It was not so terrible after all. There was a little pain at first, but that quickly went away. And then the feeling was actually pleasant. When he gave me of his own blood to drink, I felt stronger than I had for months. And then we waited out the hours together until dawn. When the surgeon came, he couldn't believe I was able to sit up and speak.

Papa said it was a miracle, and he cried again from happiness." Her face clouded. "I will have to leave my papa sometime soon. One day he will realize that since that illness I have not grown an hour older."

"And you never will?"

"No. That is the wonder of it, Stefan!" She gazed up at him with childlike joy. "I will be young forever, and I will never die! Can you imagine?"

He could not imagine her as anything other than what she was now: lovely, innocent, perfect. "But—you did not find it frightening at first?"

"At first, a little. But Gudren showed me what to do. It was she who told me to have this ring made, with a gem that would protect me from sunlight. While I lay in bed, she brought me rich warm possets to drink. Later, she brought small animals her son trapped."

"Not . . . people?"

Her laughter rang out. "Of course not. I can get all I need in a night from a dove. Gudren says that if I wish to be powerful I should take human blood, for the life essence of humans is strongest. And Klaus used to urge me, too; he wanted to exchange blood again. But I tell Gudren I do not want power. And as for Klaus . . . " She stopped and dropped her eyes, so that heavy lashes lay on her cheek. Her voice was very soft as she continued. "I do not think it is a thing to be done lightly. I will take human blood only when I have found my companion, the one who will be by my side for all eternity." She looked up at him gravely.

Stefan smiled at her, feeling light-headed and bursting with pride. He could scarcely contain the happiness he felt at that moment.

But that was before his brother Damon had returned from the University. Before Damon had come back and seen Katherine's jewel-blue eyes.

On his bed in the low-roofed room, Stefan moaned. Then the darkness drew him in deeper and new images began to flicker through his mind.

They were scattered glimpses of the past that did not form a connected sequence. He saw them like scenes briefly illuminated by flashes of lightning. His brother's face, twisted into a mask of inhuman anger. Katherine's blue eyes sparkling and dancing as she pirouetted in her new white gown. The glimmer of white behind a lemon tree. The feel of a sword in his hand; Giuseppe's voice shouting from far away. The lemon tree. He must not go behind the lemon tree. He saw Damon's face again, but this time his brother was laughing wildly. Laughing on and on, a sound like the grate of broken glass. And the lemon tree was closer now. . . .

"Damon—Katherine—*no*!"

He was sitting bolt upright on his bed.

He ran shaking hands through his hair and steadied his breath.

A terrible dream. It had been a long time since he had been tortured by dreams like that; long, indeed, since he'd dreamed at all. The last few seconds played over and over again in his mind, and he saw again the lemon tree and heard again his brother's laughter.

It echoed in his mind almost *too* clearly. Suddenly, without being aware of a conscious decision to move, Stefan found himself at the open window. The night air was cool on his cheeks, as he looked into the silvery dark.

"Damon?" He sent the thought out on a surge of Power, questing. Then he fell into absolute stillness, listening with all his senses.

He could feel nothing, no ripple of response. Nearby, a pair of night birds rose in flight. In the town, many minds were sleeping; in the woods, nocturnal animals went about their secret business.

He sighed and turned back into the room. Perhaps he'd been wrong about the laughter; perhaps he'd even been wrong about the menace in the graveyard. Fell's Church was still, and peaceful, and he should try to emulate it. He needed sleep.

September 5 (actually early September 6—about 1:00 a.m.)
Dear Diary,

I should go back to bed soon. Just a few minutes ago I woke up thinking someone was shouting, but now the house is quiet. So many strange things have happened tonight that my nerves are shot, I guess.

At least I woke up knowing exactly what I'm going to do about Stefan. The whole thing just sort of sprang into my mind. Plan B, Phase One, begins tomorrow.

Frances's eyes were blazing, and her cheeks were flushed with color as she approached the three girls at the table.

"Oh, Elena, you've got to hear this!"

Elena smiled at her, polite but not too intimate. Frances ducked her brown head. "I mean . . . can I join you? I've just heard the wildest thing about Stefan Salvatore."

"Have a seat," said Elena graciously. "But," she added, buttering a roll, "we're not really interested in the news."

"You—?" Frances stared. She looked at Meredith, then at Bonnie. "You guys are joking, right?"

"Not at all." Meredith speared a green bean and eyed it thoughtfully. "We have other things on our minds today."

"Exactly," said Bonnie after a sudden start. "Stefan's

old news, you know. Passé." She bent down and rubbed her ankle.

Frances looked at Elena appealingly. "But I thought you wanted to know all about him."

"Curiosity," Elena said. "After all, he is a visitor, and I wanted to welcome him to Fell's Church. But of course I have to be loyal to Jean-Claude."

"Jean-Claude?"

"Jean-Claude," said Meredith, raising her eyebrows and sighing.

"Jean-Claude," echoed Bonnie gamely.

Delicately, with thumb and forefinger, Elena drew a photo out of her backpack. "Here he is standing in front of the cottage where we stayed. Right afterward he picked me a flower and said . . . well"—she smiled mysteriously—"I shouldn't repeat it."

Frances was gazing at the photo. It showed a bronzed young man, shirtless, standing in front of a hibiscus bush and smiling shyly. "He's older, isn't he?" she said with respect.

"Twenty-one. Of course"—Elena glanced over her shoulder—"my aunt would never approve, so we're keeping it from her until I graduate. We have to write to each other secretly."

"How romantic," Frances breathed. "I'll never tell a soul, I promise. But about Stefan . . . "

Elena gave her a superior smile. "If," she said, "I am going to eat Continental, I prefer French to Italian every time." She turned to Meredith. "Right?"

"Mm-*hmm. Every* time." Meredith and Elena smiled knowingly at each other, then turned to Frances. "Don't you agree?"

"Oh, yes," said Frances hastily. "Me, too. Every time." She smiled knowingly herself and nodded several times as she got up and left.

When she was gone, Bonnie said piteously, "This is going to kill me. Elena, I am going to die if I don't hear the gossip."

"Oh, that? I can tell you," Elena replied calmly. "She was going to say there's a rumor going around that Stefan Salvatore is a narc."

"A *what*!" Bonnie stared, and then burst into laughter. "But that's ridiculous. What narc in the world would dress like that and wear dark glasses? I mean, he's done everything he can to draw attention to himself. . . . " Her voice trailed off, and her brown eyes widened. "But then, that may be *why* he does it. Who would ever suspect anybody so obvious? And he does live alone, and he's awfully secretive. . . . Elena! What if it's true?"

"It isn't," said Meredith.

"How do you know?"

"Because I'm the one who started it." At Bonnie's

expression, she grinned and added: "Elena told me to."

"Ohhhh." Bonnie looked admiringly at Elena. "You're wicked. Can I tell people he's got a terminal disease?"

"No, you cannot. I don't want any Florence Nightingale types lining up to hold his hand. But you can tell people whatever you want about Jean-Claude."

Bonnie picked up the photograph. "Who was he really?"

"The gardener. He was crazy about those hibiscus bushes. He was also married, with two kids."

"Pity," said Bonnie seriously. "And you told Frances not to tell anyone about him. . . ."

"Right." Elena checked her watch. "Which means that by, oh, say two o'clock, it ought to be all over the school."

After school, the girls went to Bonnie's house. They were greeted at the front door by a shrill yapping, and when Bonnie opened the door, a very old, very fat Pekingese tried to escape. His name was Yangtze, and he was so spoiled that no one except Bonnie's mother could stand him. He nipped at Elena's ankle as she went by.

The living room was dim and crowded, with lots of rather fussy furniture and heavy curtains at the windows. Bonnie's sister Mary was there, unpinning a cap from her wavy red hair. She was just two years older than Bonnie, and she worked at the Fell's Church clinic.

"Oh, Bonnie," she said, "I'm glad you're back. Hello, Elena, Meredith."

Elena and Meredith said "hello." "What's the matter? You look tired," said Bonnie.

Mary dropped her cap on the coffee table. Instead of answering, she asked a question in return. "Last night when you came home so upset, where did you say you girls had been?"

"Down in the— Just down by Wickery Bridge."

"That's what I thought." Mary took a deep breath. "Now, you listen to me, Bonnie McCullough. Don't you *ever* go out there again, and especially not alone and at night. Do you understand?"

"But why not?" Bonnie asked, bewildered.

"Because last night somebody was attacked out there, that's why not. And do you know where they found him? *Right on the bank under Wickery Bridge.*"

Elena and Meredith stared at her in disbelief, and Bonnie clutched at Elena's arm. "Somebody was attacked under the bridge? But who was it? What happened?"

"I don't know. This morning one of the cemetery workers spotted him lying there. He was some homeless person, I guess, and he'd probably been sleeping under the bridge when he was attacked. But he was half dead when they brought him in, and he hasn't regained consciousness yet. He may die."

Elena swallowed. "What do you mean, attacked?"

"I mean," said Mary distinctly, "that his throat was nearly ripped out. He lost an incredible amount of blood. They thought it might have been an animal at first, but now Dr. Lowen says it was a person. And the police think whoever did it may be hiding in the cemetery." Mary looked at each of them in turn, her mouth a straight line. "So if you *were* there by the bridge—or in the cemetery, Elena Gilbert—then this person may have been there with you. Get it?"

"You don't have to scare us anymore," said Bonnie faintly. "We get the point, Mary."

"All right. Good." Mary's shoulders slumped, and she rubbed at the back of her neck wearily. "I've got to lie down for a while. I didn't mean to be crabby." She walked out of the living room.

Alone, the three girls looked at one another.

"It could have been one of us," said Meredith quietly. "Especially you, Elena; you went there alone."

Elena's skin was prickling, that same painfully alert feeling she'd had in the old graveyard. She could feel the chill of the wind and see the rows of tall tombstones all around her. Sunshine and Robert E. Lee had never seemed so far away.

"Bonnie," she said slowly, "did you see somebody out

there? Is that what you meant when you said someone was waiting for me?"

In the dim room, Bonnie looked at her blankly. "What are you talking about? I didn't say that."

"Yes, you did."

"No, I didn't. I never said that."

"Bonnie," said Meredith, "we both heard you. You stared out at the old gravestones, and then you told Elena—"

"I don't know what you're talking about, and I didn't say *anything*." Bonnie's face was pinched with anger but there were tears in her eyes. "I don't want to talk about it anymore."

Elena and Meredith looked at one another helplessly. Outside, the sun went behind a cloud.

6

September 26

Dear Diary,
　　I'm sorry it's been so long, and I can't really explain why I haven't written—except that there are so many things I feel frightened to talk about, even to you.

　　First, the most terrible thing happened. The day that Bonnie and Meredith and I were at the cemetery, an old man was attacked there, and almost killed. The police still haven't found the person who did it. People think the old man was crazy, because when he woke up he started raving about "eyes in the dark" and oak trees and things. But I remember what happened to us that night, and

I wonder. It scares me.

Everyone was scared for a while, and all the kids had to stay inside after dark or go out in groups. But it's been about three weeks now, and no more attacks, so the excitement is dying down. Aunt Judith says it must have been another vagrant that did it. Tyler Smallwood's father even suggested that the old man might have done it to himself—though I would like to see somebody bite himself in the throat.

But mostly what I've been busy with is Plan B. As far as it goes, it's been going well. I've gotten several letters and a bouquet of red roses from "Jean-Claude" (Meredith's uncle is a florist), and everybody seems to have forgotten that I was ever interested in Stefan. So my social position's secure. Even Caroline hasn't been making any trouble.

In fact, I don't know what Caroline is doing these days, and I don't care. I never see her at lunch or after school anymore; she seems to have drawn away from her old crowd completely.

There's only one thing I do care about right now. Stefan.

Even Bonnie and Meredith don't realize how important he is to me. I'm afraid to tell them; I'm afraid they'll think I'm crazy. At school I wear a mask of calm and control, but on the inside—well, every day it just gets worse.

Aunt Judith has started to worry about me. She says I don't eat enough these days, and she's right. I can't seem to concentrate on my classes, or even on anything fun like the Haunted House fundraiser. I can't concentrate on anything but him. And I don't even understand why.

He hasn't spoken to me since that horrible afternoon. But I'll tell you something strange. Last week in history class, I glanced up and caught him looking at me. We were sitting a few seats apart, and he was turned completely sideways in his desk, just looking. For a moment I felt almost frightened, and my heart started pounding, and we just stared at each other—and then he looked away. But since then it's happened twice more, and each time I felt his eyes on me before I saw them. This is the literal truth. I know it's not my imagination.

He isn't like any boy I've ever known.

He seems so isolated, so lonely. Even though it's his own choice. He's made quite a hit on the football team, but he doesn't hang around with any of the guys, except maybe Matt. Matt's the only one he talks to. He doesn't hang around with any girls, either, that I can see, so maybe the narc rumor is doing some good. But it's more like he's avoiding other people than they're avoiding him. He disappears in between classes and after football practice, and I've never once seen him in the cafeteria. He's never invited anybody to his room at the boarding house. He never visits the coffee shop after school.

So how can I ever get him someplace where he can't run from me? This is the real problem with Plan B. Bonnie says, "Why not get stuck in a thunderstorm with him, so you have to huddle together to conserve body warmth?" And Meredith suggested that my car could break down in front of the boarding house. But neither of those ideas is practical, *and I'm going insane trying to come up with something better.*

Every day it's getting worse for me. I feel as if I were a clock or something, winding up tighter and tighter. If I don't find something to do soon, I'll—

I was going to say "die."

The solution came to her quite suddenly and simply.

She felt sorry about Matt; she knew he'd been hurt by the Jean-Claude rumor. He'd hardly spoken to her since the story had broken, usually passing her with a quick nod. And when she ran into him one day in an empty hall outside of Creative Writing, he wouldn't meet her eyes.

"Matt—" she began. She wanted to tell him that it wasn't true, that she would never have started seeing another boy without telling him first. She wanted to tell him that she'd never meant to hurt him, and that she felt terrible now. But she didn't know how to begin. Finally, she just blurted out, "I'm sorry!" and turned to go into class.

"Elena," he said, and she turned back. He was looking at her now, at least, his eyes lingering on her lips, her hair. Then he shook his head as if to say the joke was on him. "Is this French guy for real?" he finally demanded.

"No," said Elena immediately and without hesitation. "I made him up," she added simply, "to show everybody I wasn't upset about—" She broke off.

"About Stefan. I get it." Matt nodded, looking both grimmer and somewhat more understanding. "Look, Elena, that *was* pretty lousy of him. But I don't think he meant it personally. He's that way with everybody—"

"Except you."

"No. He talks to me, sometimes, but not about anything personal. He never says anything about his family or what he does outside of school. It's like—like there's a wall around him that I can't get through. I don't think he'll ever let anybody get through that wall. Which is a damn shame, because I think that behind it he's miserable."

Elena pondered this, fascinated by a view of Stefan she'd never considered before. He always seemed so controlled, so calm and undisturbed. But then, she knew she seemed that way herself to other people. Was it possible that underneath he was as confused and unhappy as she was?

It was then that the idea came, and it was ridiculously simple. No complicated schemes, no thunderstorms or cars breaking down.

"Matt," she said slowly, "don't you think it would be a good thing if somebody did get behind that wall? A good thing for Stefan, I mean? Don't you think that would be the best thing that could happen to him?" She looked up at him intensely, willing him to understand.

He stared at her a moment, then shut his eyes briefly and shook his head in disbelief. "Elena," he said, "you are incredible. You twist people around your little finger, and I don't think you even know you're doing it. And now you're going to ask me to do something to help you ambush Stefan, and I'm such a dumb sucker I might even agree to do it."

"You're not dumb, you're a gentleman. And I do want to ask you a favor, but only if you think it's right. I don't want to hurt Stefan, and I don't want to hurt you."

"Don't you?"

"*No.* I know how that must sound, but it's true. I only

want—" She broke off again. How could she explain what she wanted when she didn't even understand it herself?

"You only want everybody and everything revolving around Elena Gilbert," he said bitterly. "You only want everything you don't have."

Shocked, she stepped back and looked at him. Her throat swelled, and warmth gathered in her eyes.

"Don't," he said. "Elena, don't look like that. I'm sorry." He sighed. "All right, what is it I'm supposed to do? Hog-tie him and dump him on your doorstep?"

"No," said Elena, still trying to make the tears go back where they belonged. "I only wanted you to get him to come to the Homecoming Dance next week."

Matt's expression was odd. "You just want him to be at the dance."

Elena nodded.

"All right. I'm pretty sure he'll be there. And, Elena . . . there really isn't anybody but you I want to take."

"All right," said Elena after a moment. "And, well, thank you."

Matt's expression was still peculiar. "Don't thank me, Elena. It's nothing . . . really." She was puzzling over that when he turned away and walked down the hall.

"Hold still," said Meredith, giving Elena's hair a reproving twitch.

"I still think," said Bonnie from the window seat, "that they were both wonderful."

"Who?" Elena murmured absently.

"As if you didn't know," said Bonnie. "Those two guys of yours who pulled off the last-minute miracle at the game yesterday. When Stefan caught that last pass, I thought I was going to faint. Or throw up."

"Oh, *please*," said Meredith.

"And Matt—that boy is simply poetry in motion. . . ."

"And neither of them is mine," Elena said flatly. Under Meredith's expert fingers, her hair was becoming a work of art, a soft mass of twisted gold. And the dress was all right; the iced-violet color brought out the violet in her eyes. But even to herself she looked pale and steely, not softly flushed with excitement, but white and determined, like a very young soldier being sent to the front lines.

Standing on the football field yesterday when her name was announced as Homecoming Queen, she had had only one thought in her mind. He *couldn't* refuse to dance with her. If he came to the dance at all, he couldn't refuse the Homecoming Queen. And standing in front of the mirror now, she said it to herself again.

"Tonight anyone you want will be yours," Bonnie was saying soothingly. "And, listen, when you get rid of Matt, can I take him off and comfort him?"

Meredith snorted. "What's Raymond going to think?"

"Oh, *you* can comfort *him*. But, really, Elena, I like Matt. And once you home in on Stefan, your threesome is going to get a little crowded. So . . ."

"Oh, do whatever you want. Matt deserves some consideration." He's certainly not getting it from me, Elena thought. She still couldn't exactly believe what she was doing to him. But just now she couldn't afford to second-guess herself; she needed all her strength and concentration.

"There." Meredith put the last pin in Elena's hair. "Now look at us, the Homecoming Queen and her court—or part of it, anyway. We're beautiful."

"Is that the royal 'we'?" Elena said mockingly, but it was true. They *were* beautiful. Meredith's dress was a pure sweep of burgundy satin, gathered tight at the waist and pouring into folds from the hips. Her dark hair hung loose down her back. And Bonnie, as she stood up and joined the others in front of the mirror, was like a shimmering party favor in pink taffeta and black sequins.

As for herself . . . Elena scanned her image with an experienced eye and thought again, The dress is all right. The only other phrase that came to mind was *crystallized violets*. Her grandmother had kept a little jar of them, real flowers dipped in crystallized sugar and frozen.

They went downstairs together, as they had for every

dance since the seventh grade—except that before, Caroline had always been with them. Elena realized with faint surprise that she didn't even know who Caroline was going with tonight.

Aunt Judith and Robert—soon to be Uncle Robert—were in the living room, along with Margaret in her pajamas.

"Oh, you girls all look lovely," said Aunt Judith, as fluttery and excited as if she were going to the dance herself. She kissed Elena, and Margaret held up her arms for a hug.

"You're pretty," she said with four-year-old simplicity.

Robert was looking at Elena, too. He blinked, opened his mouth, and closed it again.

"What's the matter, Bob?"

"Oh." He looked at Aunt Judith, seeming embarrassed. "Well, actually, it just occurred to me that Elena is a form of the name Helen. And for some reason I was thinking of Helen of Troy."

"Beautiful and doomed," said Bonnie happily.

"Well, yes," said Robert, not looking happy at all. Elena said nothing.

The doorbell rang. Matt was on the step, in his familiar blue sports coat. With him were Ed Goff, Meredith's date, and Raymond Hernandez, Bonnie's. Elena looked for Stefan.

"He's probably already there," said Matt, interpreting her glance. "Listen, Elena—"

But whatever he had been about to say was cut off in the chatter from the other couples. Bonnie and Raymond went with them in Matt's car, and kept up a constant stream of witticisms all the way to the school.

Music drifted out the open doors of the auditorium. As Elena stepped out of the car, a curious certainty rushed over her. Something was going to happen, she realized, looking at the square bulk of the school building. The peaceful low gear of the last few weeks was about to slip into high.

I'm ready, she thought. And hoped it was true.

Inside, it was a kaleidoscope of color and activity. She and Matt were mobbed the instant they came in, and compliments rained down on both of them. Elena's dress . . . her hair . . . her flowers. Matt was a legend in the making: another Joe Montana, a sure bet for an athletic scholarship.

In the dizzying whirl that should have been life and breath to her, Elena kept searching for one dark head.

Tyler Smallwood was breathing heavily on her, smelling of punch and Brut and Doublemint gum. His date was looking murderous. Elena ignored him in the hopes that he would go away.

Mr. Tanner passed by with a soggy paper cup, looking

as if his collar was strangling him. Sue Carson, the other senior homecoming princess, breezed up and cooed over the violet dress. Bonnie was already out on the dance floor, shimmering under the lights. But nowhere did Elena see Stefan.

One more whiff of Doublemint and she was going to be sick. She nudged Matt and they escaped to the refreshment table, where Coach Lyman launched into a critique of the game. Couples and groups came up to them, spending a few minutes and then retreating to make room for the next in line. Just as if we really *were* royalty, thought Elena wildly. She glanced sideways to see if Matt shared her amusement, but he was looking fixedly off to his left.

She followed his gaze. And there, half concealed behind a cluster of football players, was the dark head she'd been looking for. Unmistakable, even in this dim light. A thrill went through her, more of pain than anything else.

"Now what?" said Matt, his jaw set. "The hog-tying?"

"No. I'm going to ask him to dance, that's all. I'll wait until we've danced first, if you want."

He shook his head, and she set out toward Stefan through the crowd.

Piece by piece, Elena registered information about him as she approached. His black blazer was of a subtly different cut than the other boys', more elegant, and he wore a white cashmere sweater under it. He stood quite still, not fidgeting, a little apart from the groups around him. And, although she could see him only in profile, she could see he wasn't wearing his glasses.

He took them off for football, of course, but she'd never seen him close up without them. It made her feel giddy and excited, as if this were a masquerade and the unmasking time had come. She focused on his shoulder, the line of his jaw, and then he was turning toward her.

In that instant, Elena was aware that she was beautiful. It wasn't just the dress, or the way her hair was done. She was beautiful in herself: slender, imperial, a thing made of silk and inner fire. She saw his lips part slightly, reflexively, and then she looked up into his eyes.

"Hello." Was that her own voice, so quiet and self-assured? His eyes were green. Green as oak leaves in summer. "Are you having a good time?" she said.

I am now. He didn't say it, but she knew it was what he was thinking; she could see it in the way he stared at her. She had never been so sure of her power. Except that actually he didn't look as if he were having a good time; he looked stricken, in pain, as if he couldn't take one more minute of this.

The band was starting up, a slow dance. He was still staring at her, drinking her in. Those green eyes darkening, going black with desire. She had the sudden feeling that he might jerk her to him and kiss her hard, without ever saying a word.

"Would you like to dance?" she said softly. I'm playing with fire, with something I don't understand, she thought suddenly. And in that instant she realized that she was frightened. Her heart began to pound violently. It was as if those green eyes spoke to some part of her that was buried deep beneath the surface—and that part was screaming "danger" at her. Some instinct older than civilization was telling her to run, to flee.

She never moved. The same force that was terrifying her was holding her there. This is out of control, she thought suddenly. Whatever was happening here was beyond her understanding, was nothing normal or sane. But there was no stopping it now, and even while frightened she was reveling in it. It was the most intense moment she'd ever experienced with a boy, but nothing at all was happening. He was just gazing at her, as if hypnotized, and she was gazing back, while the energy shimmered between them like heat lightning. She saw his eyes go darker, defeated, and felt the wild leap of her own heart as he slowly stretched out one hand.

And then it all shattered.

"Why, Elena, how *sweet* you look," said a voice, and Elena's vision was dazzled with gold. It was Caroline, her auburn hair rich and glossy, her skin tanned to a perfect bronze. She was wearing a dress of pure gold lamé that showed an incredibly daring amount of that perfect skin. She slipped one bare arm through Stefan's and smiled lazily up at him. They were stunning together, like a couple of international models slumming at a high school dance, far more glamorous and sophisticated than anyone else in the room.

"And that little dress is so *pretty*," continued Caroline, while Elena's mind kept on running on automatic. That casually possessive arm linked with Stefan's told her everything: where Caroline had been at lunch these past weeks, what she had been up to all this time. "I told Stefan we simply had to stop by for a moment, but we're not going to stay long. So you don't mind if I keep him to myself for the dances, do you?"

Elena was strangely calm now, her mind a humming blank. She said no, of course she didn't mind, and watched Caroline move away, a symphony in auburn and gold. Stefan went with her.

There was a circle of faces around Elena; she turned from them and came up against Matt.

"You knew he was coming with her."

"I knew she wanted him to. She's been following him around at lunchtime and after school, and kind of forcing herself on him. But . . . "

"I see." Still held in that queer, artificial calm, she scanned the crowd and saw Bonnie coming toward her, and Meredith leaving her table. They'd seen, then. Probably everyone had. Without a word to Matt, she moved toward them, heading instinctively for the girls' rest room.

It was packed with bodies, and Meredith and Bonnie kept their remarks bright and casual while looking at her with concern.

"Did you see that dress?" said Bonnie, squeezing Elena's fingers secretly. "The front must be held on with superglue. And what's she going to wear to the next dance? Cellophane?"

"Handiwrap," said Meredith. She added in a low voice, "Are you okay?"

"Yes." Elena could see in the mirror that her eyes were too bright and that there was one spot of color burning on each cheek. She smoothed her hair and turned away.

The room emptied, leaving them in privacy. Bonnie was fiddling nervously with the sequined bow at her waist now. "Maybe it isn't such a bad thing after all," she said quietly. "I mean, you haven't thought about anything else but him in weeks. Nearly a month. And so maybe it's just for the best, and you can move on to other things now, instead of . . . well, chasing him."

Et tu, Brute? thought Elena. "Thank you so much for

your support," she said aloud.

"Now, Elena, don't be like that," Meredith put in. "She isn't trying to hurt you, she just thinks—"

"And I suppose you think so, too? Well, that's fine. I'll just go out and find myself some other things to move on to. Like some other best friends." She left them both staring after her.

Outside, she threw herself into the whirl of color and music. She was brighter than she had ever been at any dance before. She danced with everyone, laughing too loudly, flirting with every boy in her path.

They were calling her to come up and be crowned. She stood on the stage, looking down on the butterfly-bright figures below. Someone gave her flowers; someone put a rhinestone tiara on her head. There was clapping. It all passed as if in a dream.

She flirted with Tyler because he was closest when she came off the stage. Then she remembered what he and Dick had done to Stefan, and she broke off one of the roses from her bouquet and gave it to him. Matt was looking on from the sidelines, his mouth tight. Tyler's forgotten date was almost in tears.

She could smell alcohol along with the mint on Tyler's breath now, and his face was red. His friends were around her, a shouting, laughing crowd, and she saw Dick pour something from a brown paper bag into his glass of punch.

She'd never been with this group before. They welcomed her, admiring her, the boys vying for her attention. Jokes flew back and forth, and Elena laughed even when they didn't make sense. Tyler's arm circled her waist, and she just laughed harder. Out of the corner of her eye she saw Matt shake his head and walk away. The girls were getting shrill, the boys rowdy. Tyler was nuzzling moistly at her neck.

"I've got an idea," he announced to the group, hugging Elena more tightly to him. "Let's go someplace more fun."

Somebody shouted, "Like where, Tyler? Your dad's house?"

Tyler was grinning, a big, boozy, reckless grin. "No, I mean someplace where we can leave our mark. Like the cemetery."

The girls squealed. The boys elbowed each other and faked punches.

Tyler's date was still standing outside the circle. "Tyler, that's crazy," she said, her voice high and thin. "You know what happened to that old man. I won't go there."

"Great, then, you stay here." Tyler fished keys out of his pocket and waved them at the rest of the crowd. "Who *isn't* afraid?" he said.

"Hey, I'm up for it," said Dick, and there was a chorus of approval.

"Me, too," said Elena, clear and defiant. She smiled up at Tyler, and he practically swung her off her feet.

And then she and Tyler were leading a noisy, rough-housing group out into the parking lot, where they were all piling into cars. And then Tyler was putting the top of his convertible down and she was climbing in, with Dick and a girl named Vickie Bennett squashing into the back-seat.

"Elena!" somebody shouted, far away, from the lighted doorway at the school.

"Drive," she said to Tyler, taking off her tiara, and the engine growled to life. They burned rubber out of the parking lot, and the cool night wind blew into Elena's face.

onnie was on the dance floor, eyes shut, letting the music flow through her. When she opened her eyes for an instant, Meredith was beckoning from the sidelines. Bonnie thrust her chin out mutinously, but as the gestures became more insistent she rolled her eyes up at Raymond and obeyed. Raymond followed.

Matt and Ed were behind Meredith. Matt was scowling. Ed was looking uncomfortable.

"Elena just left," said Meredith.

"It's a free country," said Bonnie.

"She went with Tyler Smallwood," said Meredith. "Matt, are you sure you didn't hear where they were going?"

Matt shook his head. "I'd say she deserves whatever

happens—but it's my fault, too, in a way," he said bleakly. "I guess we ought to go after her."

"Leave the *dance*?" Bonnie said. She looked at Meredith, who mouthed the words *you promised*. "I don't believe this," she muttered savagely.

"I don't know how we'll find her," said Meredith, "but we've got to try." Then she added, in a strangely hesitant voice, "Bonnie, *you* don't happen to know where she is, do you?"

"What? No, of course not; I've been dancing. You've heard of that, haven't you: what you go to a dance for?"

"You and Ray stay here," Matt said to Ed. "If she comes back, tell her we're out looking."

"And if we're going, we'd better go now," Bonnie put in ungraciously. She turned and promptly ran into a dark blazer.

"Well, excuse *me*," she snapped, looking up and seeing Stefan Salvatore. He said nothing as she and Meredith and Matt headed for the door, leaving an unhappy-looking Raymond and Ed behind.

The stars were distant and ice-bright in the cloudless sky. Elena felt just like them. Part of her was laughing and shouting with Dick and Vickie and Tyler over the roar of the wind, but part of her was watching from far away.

Tyler parked halfway up the hill to the ruined church,

leaving his headlights on as they all got out. Although there had been several cars behind them when they left the school, they appeared to be the only ones who'd made it all the way to the cemetery.

Tyler opened the trunk and pulled out a six-pack. "All the more for us." He offered a beer to Elena, who shook her head, trying to ignore the sick feeling in the pit of her stomach. She felt all wrong being here—but there was no way she was going to admit that now.

They climbed the flagstone path, the girls staggering in their high heels and leaning on the boys. When they reached the top, Elena gasped and Vickie gave a little scream.

Something huge and red was hovering just above the horizon. It took Elena a moment to realize it was actually the moon. It was as large and unrealistic as a prop in a science-fiction movie, and its bloated mass glowed dully with an unwholesome light.

"Like a big rotten pumpkin," said Tyler, and lobbed a stone at it. Elena made herself smile brilliantly up at him.

"Why don't we go inside?" Vickie said, pointing a white hand at the empty hole of the church doorway.

Most of the roof had fallen in, although the belfry was still intact, a tower stretching up high above them. Three of the walls were standing; the fourth was only knee-high. There were piles of rubble everywhere.

A light flared by Elena's cheek, and she turned, startled, to see Tyler holding a lighter. He grinned, showing strong white teeth, and said, "Want to flick my Bic?"

Elena's laughter was the loudest, to cover her uneasiness. She took the lighter, using it to illuminate the tomb in the side of the church. It was like no other tomb in the cemetery, although her father said he'd seen similar things in England. It looked like a large stone box, big enough for two people, with two marble statues lying in repose on the lid.

"Thomas Keeping Fell and Honoria Fell," said Tyler with a grand gesture, as if introducing them. "Old Thomas allegedly founded Fell's Church. Although actually the Smallwoods were also there at the time. My great-grandfather's great-great-grandfather lived in the valley by Drowning Creek—"

"—until he got eaten by wolves," said Dick, and he threw back his head in a wolf imitation. Then he belched. Vickie giggled. Annoyance crossed Tyler's handsome features, but he forced a smile.

"Thomas and Honoria are looking kind of pale," said Vickie, still giggling. "I think what they need is a little color." She produced a lipstick from her purse and began to coat the white marble mouth of the woman's statue with waxy scarlet. Elena felt another sick twinge. As a child, she'd always been awed by the pale lady and the grave man who lay with their eyes closed, hands folded on their breasts. And, after her parents died, she'd thought of them as lying side by side like this down in the cemetery. But she held the lighter while the other girl put a lipstick mustache and clown's nose on Thomas Fell.

Tyler was watching them. "Hey, they're all dressed up with no place to go." He put his hands on the edge of the stone lid and leaned on it, trying to shift it sideways. "What do you say, Dick—want to give them a night out on the town? Like maybe right in the center of town?"

No, thought Elena, appalled, as Dick guffawed and Vickie shrieked with laughter. But Dick was already beside Tyler, getting braced and ready, the heels of his hands on the stone lid.

"On three," said Tyler, and counted, "One, two, *three.*"

Elena's eyes were fixed on the horrible clownlike face of Thomas Fell as the boys strained forward and grunted, muscles bunching under cloth. They couldn't budge the lid an inch.

"Damn thing must be attached somehow," said Tyler angrily, turning away.

Elena felt weak with relief. Trying to seem casual, she leaned against the stone lid of the tomb for support—and that was when it happened.

She heard the grinding of stone and felt the lid shift under her left hand all at once. It was moving away from her, making her lose her balance. The lighter went flying, and she screamed and screamed again, trying to keep her feet. She was falling into the open tomb, and an icy wind roared all around her. Screams rang in her ears.

And then she was outside and the moonlight was bright enough that she could see the others. Tyler had hold of her. She stared around her wildly.

"Are you crazy? What happened?" Tyler was shaking her.

"It moved! The lid moved! It slid open and—I don't know—I almost fell in. It was cold . . . "

The boys were laughing. "Poor baby's got the jitters," Tyler said. "C'mon, Dicky-boy, we'll check it out."

"Tyler, no—"

But they went inside anyway. Vickie hung in the doorway, watching, while Elena shivered. Presently, Tyler beckoned her from the door.

"Look," he said when she reluctantly stepped back inside. He'd retrieved the lighter, and he held it above Thomas Fell's marble chest. "It still fits, snug as a bug in a rug. See?"

Elena stared down at the perfect alignment of lid and tomb. "It did move. I nearly fell into it. . . . "

"Sure, whatever you say, baby." Tyler wound his arms around her, clasping her to him backwards. She looked over to see Dick and Vickie in much the same position, except that Vickie, eyes shut, was looking as if she enjoyed it. Tyler rubbed a strong chin over her hair.

"I'd like to go back to the dance now," she said flatly.

There was a pause in the rubbing. Then Tyler sighed and said, "Sure, baby." He looked at Dick and Vickie. "What about you two?"

Dick grinned. "We'll just stay here awhile." Vickie giggled, her eyes still shut.

"Okay." Elena wondered how they were going to get back, but she allowed Tyler to lead her out. Once outside, however, he paused.

"I can't let you go without one look at my grandfather's headstone," he said. "Aw, c'mon, Elena," he said as she started to protest, "don't hurt my feelings. You've got to see it; it's the family pride and joy."

Elena made herself smile, although her stomach felt like ice. Maybe if she humored him, he would get her out of here. "All right," she said, and started toward the cemetery.

"Not that way. This way." And the next moment, he was leading her down toward the old graveyard. "It's okay, honest, it's not far off the path. Look, there, you see?" He pointed to something that shone in the moonlight.

Elena gasped, muscles tightening around her heart. It looked like a person standing there, a giant with a round hairless head. And she didn't like being here at all, among the worn and leaning granite, stones of centuries past. The bright moonlight cast strange shadows, and there were pools of impenetrable darkness everywhere.

"It's just the ball on top. Nothing to be scared of," said Tyler, pulling her with him off the path and up to the shining headstone. It was made of red marble, and the huge ball that surmounted it reminded her of the bloated moon on the horizon. Now that same moon shone down on them, as white as Thomas Fell's white hands. Elena couldn't contain her shivering.

"Poor baby, she's cold. Got to get her warmed up," said Tyler. Elena tried to push him away, but he was too strong, wrapping her in his arms, pulling her against him.

"Tyler, I want to go; I want to go right *now*. . . . "

"Sure, baby, we'll go," he said. "But we've got to get you warm first. Gosh, you're cold."

"Tyler, stop," she said. His arms around her had merely been annoying, restricting, but now with a sense of shock she felt his hands on her body, groping for bare skin.

Never in her life had Elena been in a situation like this, far away from any help. She aimed a spiked heel for his patent-leather instep, but he evaded her. "Tyler, *take your hands off me.*"

"C'mon, Elena, don't be like that, I just want to warm you up all over. . . . "

"Tyler, let go," she choked out. She tried to wrench

herself away from him. Tyler stumbled, and then his full weight was on her, crushing her into the tangle of ivy and weeds on the ground. Elena spoke desperately. "I'll kill you, Tyler. I mean it. Get *off me.*"

Tyler tried to roll off, giggling suddenly, his limbs heavy and uncoordinated, almost useless. "Aw, c'mon, Elena, don' be mad. I was jus' warmin' you up. Elena the Ice Princess, warmin' up . . . You're gettin' warm now, aren' you?"

Then Elena felt his mouth hot and wet on her face. She was still pinned beneath him, and his sloppy kisses were moving down her throat. She heard cloth tear.

"Oops," Tyler mumbled. "Sorry 'bout that."

Elena twisted her head, and her mouth met Tyler's hand, clumsily caressing her cheek. She bit it, sinking her teeth into the fleshy palm. She bit *hard*, tasting blood, hearing Tyler's agonized yowl. The hand jerked away.

"Hey! I said I was sorry!" Tyler looked aggrievedly at his maimed hand. Then his face darkened, as, still staring at it, he clenched the hand into a fist.

This is it, Elena thought with nightmare calmness. He's either going to knock me out or kill me. She braced herself for the blow.

Stefan had resisted coming into the cemetery; everything within him had cried out against it. The last time he'd been here had been the night of the old man.

Horror shifted through his gut again at the memory. He would have sworn that he had not drained the man under the bridge, that he had not taken enough blood to do harm. But everything that night after the surge of Power was muddled, confused. If there *had* been a surge of Power at all. Perhaps that had been his own imagination, or even his own doing. Strange things could happen when the need got out of control.

He shut his eyes. When he'd heard that the old man was hospitalized, near death, his shock had been beyond words. How *could* he have let himself get so far out of hand? To kill, almost, when he had not killed since . . .

He wouldn't let himself think about that.

Now, standing in front of the cemetery gate in the midnight darkness, he wanted nothing so much as to turn around and go away. Go back to the dance where he'd left Caroline, that supple, sun-bronzed creature who was absolutely safe because she meant absolutely nothing to him.

But he couldn't go back, because Elena was in the cemetery. He could sense her, and sense her rising distress. Elena was in the cemetery and in trouble, and he had to find her.

He was halfway up the hill when the dizziness hit. It sent him reeling, struggling on toward the church because it was the only thing he could keep in focus. Gray waves of fog swept through his brain, and he fought to keep moving. Weak, he felt so weak. And helpless against the sheer power of this vertigo.

He needed . . . to go to Elena. But he was weak. He couldn't be . . . weak . . . if he were to help Elena. He needed . . . to . . .

The church door yawned before him.

Elena saw the moon over Tyler's left shoulder. It was strangely fitting that it would be the last thing she ever saw, she thought. The scream had caught in her throat, choked off by fear.

And then something picked Tyler up and threw him against his grandfather's headstone.

That was what it looked like to Elena. She rolled to the side, gasping, one hand clutching her torn dress, the other groping for a weapon.

She didn't need one. Something moved in the darkness, and she saw the person who had plucked Tyler off her. Stefan Salvatore. But it was a Stefan she had never seen before: that fine-featured face was white and cold with fury, and there was a killing light in those green eyes. Without even moving, Stefan emanated such anger and menace that Elena found herself more frightened of him than she had been of Tyler.

"When I first met you, I knew you'd never learned any manners," said Stefan. His voice was soft and cold and light, and somehow it made Elena dizzy. She couldn't take her eyes off him as he moved toward Tyler, who was shaking his head dazedly and starting to get up. Stefan moved like a dancer, every movement easy and precisely controlled. "But I had no idea that your character was quite so underdeveloped."

He hit Tyler. The larger boy had been reaching out one beefy hand, and Stefan hit him almost negligently on the side of the face, before the hand made contact.

Tyler flew against another headstone. He scrambled up and stood panting, his eyes showing white. Elena saw a trickle of blood from his nose. Then he charged.

"A *gentleman* doesn't force his company on anyone," said Stefan, and knocked him aside. Tyler went sprawling again, facedown in the weeds and briars. This time he was slower in getting up, and blood flowed from both nostrils and from his mouth. He was blowing like a frightened horse as he threw himself at Stefan.

Stefan grabbed the front of Tyler's jacket, whirling them both around and absorbing the impact of the murderous rush. He shook Tyler twice, hard, while those big beefy fists windmilled around him, unable to connect. Then he let Tyler drop.

"He doesn't insult a woman," he said. Tyler's face was

contorted, his eyes rolling, but he grabbed for Stefan's leg. Stefan jerked him to his feet and shook him again, and Tyler went limp as a rag doll, his eyes rolling up. Stefan went on speaking, holding the heavy body upright and punctuating every word with a bone-wrenching shake. "And, above all, he does not hurt her. . . . "

"Stefan!" Elena cried. Tyler's head was snapping back and forth with every shake. She was frightened of what she was seeing; frightened of what Stefan might do. And frightened above all else of Stefan's voice, that cold voice that was like a rapier dancing, beautiful and deadly and utterly merciless. "Stefan, *stop.*"

His head jerked toward her, startled, as if he had forgotten her presence. For a moment he looked at her without recognition, his eyes black in the moonlight, and she thought of some predator, some great bird or sleek carnivore incapable of human emotion. Then understanding came to his face and some of the darkness faded from his gaze.

He looked down at Tyler's lolling head, then set him gently against the red marble tombstone. Tyler's knees buckled and he slid down the face of it, but to Elena's relief his eyes opened—or at least the left one did. The right was swelling to a slit.

"He'll be all right," said Stefan emptily.

As her fear ebbed, Elena felt empty herself. Shock, she

thought. I'm in shock. I'll probably start screaming hysterically any minute now.

"Is there someone to take you home?" said Stefan, still in that chillingly deadened voice.

Elena thought of Dick and Vickie, doing God knew what beside Thomas Fell's statue. "No," she said. Her mind was beginning to work again, to take notice of things around her. The violet dress was ripped all the way down the front; it was ruined. Mechanically, she pulled it together over her slip.

"I'll drive you," said Stefan.

Even through the numbness, Elena felt a quick thrill of fear. She looked at him, a strangely elegant figure among the tombstones, his face pale in the moonlight. He had never looked so . . . so *beautiful* to her before, but that beauty was almost alien. Not just foreign, but inhuman, because no human could project that aura of power, or of distance.

"Thank you. That would be very kind," she said slowly. There was nothing else to do.

They left Tyler painfully getting to his feet by his ancestor's headstone. Elena felt another chill as they reached the path and Stefan turned toward Wickery Bridge.

"I left my car at the boarding house," he said. "This is the fastest way for us to get back."

"Is this the way you came?"

"No. I didn't cross the bridge. But it'll be safe."

Elena believed him. Pale and silent, he walked beside her without touching, except when he took off his blazer to put it around her bare shoulders. She felt oddly sure he would kill anything that tried to get at her.

Wickery Bridge was white in the moonlight, and under it the icy waters swirled over ancient rocks. The whole world was still and beautiful and cold as they walked through the oak trees to the narrow country road.

They passed fenced pastures and dark fields until they reached a long winding drive. The boarding house was a vast building of rust-red brick made from the native clay, and it was flanked with age-old cedars and maples. All but one of the windows were dark.

Stefan unlocked one of the double doors and they stepped into a small hallway, with a flight of stairs directly in front of them. The banister, like the doors, was natural light oak so polished that it seemed to glow.

They went up the stairs to a second-story landing that was poorly lit. To Elena's surprise, Stefan led her into one of the bedrooms and opened what looked like a closet door. Through it she could see a very steep, very narrow stairway.

What a strange place, she thought. This hidden stairway buried deep in the heart of the house, where no sound from outside could penetrate. She reached the top of the stairs and stepped out into a large room that made up the whole third story of the house.

It was almost as dimly lit as the stairway, but Elena could see the stained wood floor and the exposed beams in the slanting ceiling. There were tall windows on all sides, and many trunks scattered among a few pieces of massive furniture.

She realized he was watching her. "Is there a bathroom where I—?"

He nodded toward a door. She took off the blazer, held it toward him without looking at him, and went inside.

8

Elena had gone into the bathroom dazed and numbly grateful. She came out angry.

She wasn't quite sure how the transformation had taken place. But sometime while she was washing the scratches on her face and arms, annoyed at the lack of a mirror and at the fact she'd left her purse in Tyler's convertible, she started *feeling* again. And what she felt was anger.

Damn Stefan Salvatore. So cold and controlled even while saving her life. Damn him for his politeness, and for his gallantry, and for the walls around him that seemed thicker and higher than ever.

She pulled the remaining bobby pins out of her hair and used them to fasten the front of her dress together. Then she ran through her loosened hair quickly with an engraved bone comb she found by the sink. She came out of the bathroom with her chin held high and her eyes narrowed.

He hadn't put his coat back on. He was standing by the window in his white sweater with bowed head, tense, waiting. Without lifting his head, he gestured to a length of dark velvet laid over the back of a chair.

"You might want to put that on over your dress."

It was a full-length cloak, very rich and soft, with a hood. Elena pulled the heavy material around her shoulders. But she was not mollified by the gift; she noticed that Stefan hadn't come any closer to her, or even looked at her while speaking.

Deliberately, she invaded his territorial space, pulling the cloak more tightly about her and feeling, even at that moment, a sensual appreciation of the way the folds fell about her, trailing behind her on the floor. She walked up to him and made an examination of the heavy mahogany dresser by the window.

On it lay a wicked-looking dagger with an ivory hilt and a beautiful agate cup mounted in silver. There were also a golden sphere with some sort of dial set into it and several loose gold coins.

She picked up one of the coins, partly because it was interesting and partly because she knew it would upset him to see her handling his things. "What's this?"

It was a moment before he answered. Then he said:

"A gold florin. A Florentine coin."

"And what's this?"

"A German pendant watch. Late fifteenth century," he said distractedly. He added, "Elena—"

She reached for a small iron coffer with a hinged lid. "What about this? Does it open?"

"*No.*" He had the reflexes of a cat; his hand slapped over the coffer, holding the lid down. "That's private," he said, the strain obvious in his voice.

She noticed that his hand made contact only with the curving iron lid and not with her flesh. She lifted her fingers, and he drew back at once.

Suddenly, her anger was too great to hold in any longer. "Careful," she said savagely. "Don't touch me, or you might get a disease."

He turned away toward the window.

And yet even as she moved away herself, walking back to the center of the room, she could sense his watching her reflection And she knew, suddenly, what she must look like to him, pale hair spilling over the blackness of the cape, one white hand holding the velvet closed at her throat. A ravaged princess pacing in her tower.

She tilted her head far back to look at the trapdoor in the ceiling, and heard a soft, distinct intake of breath. When she turned, his gaze was fixed on her exposed throat; the look in his eyes confused her. But the next moment his face hardened, closing her out.

"I think," he said, "that I had better get you home."

In that instant, she wanted to hurt him, to make him feel as bad as he'd made her feel. But she also wanted the truth. She was tired of this game, tired of scheming and plotting and trying to read Stefan Salvatore's mind. It was terrifying and yet a wonderful relief to hear her own voice saying the words she'd been thinking so long.

"Why do you hate me?"

He stared at her. For a moment he couldn't seem to find words. Then he said, "I don't hate you."

"You do," said Elena. "I know it's not . . . not good manners to say it, but I don't care. I know I should be grateful to you for saving me tonight, but I don't care about that, either. I didn't ask you to save me. I don't know why you were even in the graveyard in the first place. And I certainly don't understand why you did it, considering the way you feel about me."

He was shaking his head, but his voice was soft. "I don't hate you."

"From the very beginning, you've avoided me as if I were . . . were some kind of leper. I tried to be friendly to you, and you threw it back in my face. Is that what a *gentleman* does when someone tries to welcome him?"

He was trying to say something now, but she swept on,

heedless. "You've snubbed me in public time after time; you've humiliated me at school. You wouldn't be speaking to me now if it hadn't been a matter of life or death. Is that what it takes to get a word out of you? Does someone have to nearly be murdered?

"And even now," she continued bitterly, "you don't want me to get anywhere near you. What's the matter with you, Stefan Salvatore, that you have to live this way? That you have to build walls against other people to keep them out? That you can't trust anyone? *What's wrong with you?*"

He was silent now, his face averted. She took a deep breath and then straightened her shoulders, holding her head up even though her eyes were sore and burning. "And what's wrong with *me*," she added, more quietly, "that you can't even look at me, but you can let Caroline Forbes fall all over you? I have a right to know that, at least. I won't ever bother you again, I won't even talk to you at school, but I want to know the truth before I go. Why do you hate me so much, Stefan?"

Slowly, he turned and raised his head. His eyes were bleak, sightless, and something twisted in Elena at the pain she saw on his face.

His voice was still controlled—but barely. She could hear the effort it cost him to keep it steady.

"Yes," he said, "I think you do have a right to know.

Elena." He looked at her then, meeting her eyes directly, and she thought, That bad? What could be as bad as that? "I don't hate you," he continued, pronouncing each word carefully, distinctly. "I've never hated you. But you . . . remind me of someone."

Elena was taken aback. Whatever she'd expected, it wasn't this. "I remind you of someone else you know?"

"Of someone I knew," he said quietly. "But," he added slowly, as if puzzling something out for himself, "you're not like her, really. She looked like you, but she was fragile, delicate. Vulnerable. Inside as well as out."

"And I'm not."

He made a sound that would have been a laugh if there had been any humor in it. "No. You're a fighter. You are . . . yourself."

Elena was silent for a moment. She could not keep hold of her anger, seeing the pain on his face. "You were very close to her?"

"Yes."

"What happened?"

There was a long pause, so long that Elena thought he wasn't going to answer her. But at last he said, "She died."

Elena let out a tremulous breath. The last of her anger folded up and disappeared from under her. "That must have hurt terribly," she said softly, thinking of the white Gilbert headstone among the rye grass. "I'm so sorry."

He said nothing. His face had closed again, and he seemed to be looking far away at something, something terrible and heartbreaking that only he could see. But there was not just grief in his expression. Through the walls, through all his trembling control, she could see the tortured look of unbearable guilt and loneliness. A look so lost and haunted that she had moved to his side before she knew what she was doing.

"Stefan," she whispered. He didn't seem to hear her; he seemed to be adrift in his own world of misery.

She could not stop herself from laying a hand on his arm. "Stefan, I know how it can hurt—"

"You *can't* know," he exploded, all his quietness erupting into white rage. He looked down at her hand as if just realizing it was there, as if infuriated at her effrontery in touching him. His green eyes were dilated and dark as he shook her hand off, flinging a hand up to bar her from touching him again—

—and somehow, instead, he was holding her hand, his fingers tightly interlocked with hers, hanging on for dear life. He looked down at their locked hands in bewilderment. Then, slowly, his gaze moved from their clasping fingers to her face.

"Elena . . . " he whispered.

And then she saw it, the anguish shattering his gaze, as if he simply couldn't fight any longer. The defeat as the walls finally crumbled and she saw what was underneath.

And then, helplessly, he bent his head down to her lips.

"Wait—stop here," said Bonnie. "I thought I saw something."

Matt's battered Ford slowed, edging toward the side of the road, where brambles and bushes grew thickly. Something white glimmered there, coming toward them.

"Oh, my God," said Meredith. "It's Vickie Bennett."

The girl stumbled into the path of the headlights and stood there, wavering, as Matt hit the brakes. Her light-brown hair was tangled and in disarray, and her eyes stared glassily out of a face that was smudged and grimy with dirt. She was wearing only a thin white slip.

"Get her in the car," said Matt. Meredith was already opening the car door. She jumped out and ran up to the dazed girl.

"Vickie, are you all right? What happened to you?"

Vickie moaned, still looking straight ahead. Then she suddenly seemed to see Meredith, and she clutched at her, digging her nails into Meredith's arms.

"Get out of here" she said, her eyes filled with desperate intensity, her voice strange and thick, as if she had something in her mouth. "All of you—get out of here! It's coming."

"What's coming? Vickie, where is Elena?"

"Get out *now*. . . . "

Meredith looked down the road, then led the shaking girl back to the car. "We'll take you away," she said, "but you have to tell us what's happened. Bonnie, give me your wrap. She's freezing."

"She's been hurt," said Matt grimly. "And she's in shock or something. The question is, where are the others? Vickie, was Elena with you?"

Vickie sobbed, putting her hands over her face as Meredith settled Bonnie's iridescent pink wrap around her shoulders. "No . . . Dick," she said indistinctly. It seemed to hurt her to speak. "We were in the church . . . it was horrible. It came . . . like mist all around. Dark mist. And eyes. I saw its eyes in the dark there, burning. They burnt me. . . . "

"She's delirious," said Bonnie. "Or hysterical, or whatever you call it."

Matt spoke slowly and clearly. "Vickie, please, just tell us one thing. Where is Elena? What happened to her?"

"I don't *know*." Vickie lifted a tear-stained face to the sky. "Dick and I—we were alone. We were . . . and then suddenly it was all around us. I couldn't run. Elena said the tomb had opened. Maybe that was where it came from. It was horrible. . . . "

"They were in the cemetery, in the ruined church," Meredith interpreted. "And Elena was with them. And look at this." In the overhead light, they could all see the deep fresh scratches running down Vickie's neck to the lace bodice of her slip.

"They look like animal marks," said Bonnie. "Like the marks of cat's claws, maybe."

"No cat got that old man under the bridge," said Matt. His face was pale, and muscles stood out in his jaw. Meredith followed his gaze down the road and then shook her head.

"Matt, we have to take her back first. We *have* to," she said. "Listen to me, I'm as worried about Elena as you are. But Vickie needs a doctor, and we need to call the police. We don't have any choice. We have to go back."

Matt stared down the road for another long moment, then let out his breath in a hiss. Slamming the door shut, he put the car into gear and turned it around, each motion violent.

All the way back to town, Vickie moaned about the eyes.

Elena felt Stefan's lips meet hers.

And . . . it was as simple as that. All questions answered, all fears put to rest, all doubts removed. What she felt was not merely passion, but a bruising tenderness and a love so strong it made her shake inside. It would have been frightening in its intensity, except that while she was with him, she could not be afraid of anything.

She had come home.

This was where she belonged, and she had found it at last. With Stefan, she was home.

He pulled back slightly, and she could feel that he was trembling.

"Oh, Elena," he whispered against her lips. "We can't—"

"We already have," she whispered, and drew him back down again.

It was almost as If she could hear his thoughts, could feel his feelings. Pleasure and desire raced between them, connecting them, drawing them closer. And Elena sensed, too, a wellspring of deeper emotions within him. He wanted to hold her forever, to protect her from all harm. He wanted to defend her from any evil that threatened her. He wanted to join his life with hers.

She felt the tender pressure of his lips on hers, and she could hardly bear the sweetness of it. *Yes*, she thought. Sensation rippled through her like waves on a still, clear pond. She was drowning in it, both the joy she sensed in Stefan and the delicious answering surge in herself. Stefan's love bathed her, shone through her, lighting every dark place in her soul like the sun. She trembled with pleasure, with love, and with longing.

He drew back slowly, as if he could not bear to part

from her, and they looked into each other's eyes with wondering joy.

They did not speak. There was no need for words. He stroked her hair, with a touch so light that she could scarcely feel it, as if he was afraid she might break in his hands. She knew, then, that it had not been hatred that had made him avoid her for so long. No, it had not been hatred at all.

Elena had no idea how much later it was that they quietly went down the stairs of the boarding house. At any other time, she would have been thrilled to get into Stefan's sleek black car, but tonight she scarcely noticed it. He held her hand as they drove through the deserted streets.

The first thing Elena saw as they approached her house was the lights.

"It's the police," she said, finding her voice with some difficulty. It was odd to talk after being silent so long. "And that's Robert's car in the driveway, and there's Matt's," she said. She looked at Stefan, and the peace that had filled her suddenly seemed fragile. "I wonder what happened. You don't suppose Tyler's already told them . . . ?"

"Even Tyler wouldn't be that stupid," said Stefan.

He pulled up behind one of the police cars, and reluctantly Elena unclasped her hand from his. She wished with all her heart that she and Stefan could just be alone together, that they would never need to face the world.

But there was no help for it. They walked up the pathway to the door, which was open. Inside, the house was a blaze of lights.

Entering, Elena saw what seemed like dozens of faces turned toward her. She had a sudden vision of what she must look like, standing there in the doorway in the sweeping black velvet cloak, with Stefan Salvatore at her side. And then Aunt Judith gave a cry and was holding her in her arms, shaking her and hugging her all at once.

"Elena! Oh, thank God you're safe. But where have you been? And why didn't you call? Do you realize what you've put everyone through?"

Elena stared around the room in bewilderment. She didn't understand a thing.

"We're just glad to see you back," said Robert.

"I've been at the boarding house, with Stefan," she said slowly. "Aunt Judith, this is Stefan Salvatore; he rents a room there. He brought me back."

"Thank you," said Aunt Judith to Stefan over Elena's head. Then, pulling back to look at Elena, she said, "But your dress, your hair—what happened?"

"You don't know? Then Tyler didn't tell you. But then why are the police here?" Elena edged toward Stefan instinctively, and she felt him move closer to her in protection.

"They're here because Vickie Bennett was attacked in the cemetery tonight," said Matt. He and Bonnie and Meredith were standing behind Aunt Judith and Robert, looking relieved and a little awkward and more than a little tired. "We found her maybe two, three hours ago, and we've been looking for you ever since."

"*Attacked?*" said Elena, stunned. "Attacked by what?"

"Nobody knows," said Meredith.

"Well, now, it may be nothing to worry about," said Robert comfortingly. "The doctor said she'd had a bad scare, and that she'd been drinking. The whole thing may have been in her imagination."

"Those scratches weren't imaginary," said Matt, polite but stubborn.

"What scratches? What are you talking about?" Elena demanded, looking from one face to another.

"I'll tell you," said Meredith, and she explained, succinctly, how she and the others had found Vickie. "She kept saying she didn't know where you were, that she was alone with Dick when it happened. And when we got her back here, the doctor said he couldn't find anything conclusive. She wasn't really hurt except for the scratches, and they could have been from a cat."

"There were no other marks on her?" said Stefan sharply. It was the first time he'd spoken since entering the house, and Elena looked at him, surprised by his tone.

"No," said Meredith. "Of course, a cat didn't tear her clothes off—but Dick might have. Oh, and her tongue was bitten."

"*What?*" said Elena.

"Badly bitten, I mean. It must have bled a lot, and it hurts her to talk now."

Beside Elena, Stefan had gone very still. "Did she have any explanation for what happened?"

"She was hysterical," Matt said. "Really hysterical; she wasn't making any sense. She kept babbling about eyes and dark mist and not being able to run—which is why the doctor thinks maybe it was some sort of hallucination. But as far as anyone can make out, the facts are that she and Dick Carter were in the ruined church by the cemetery at about midnight, and that something came in and attacked her there."

Bonnie added, "It didn't attack Dick, which at least shows it had some taste. The police found him passed out on the church floor, and he doesn't remember a thing."

But Elena scarcely heard the last words. Something had gone terribly wrong with Stefan. She couldn't tell how she knew it, but she knew. He had stiffened as Matt finished speaking, and now, though he hadn't moved, she felt as if a great distance was separating them, as if she and he were on opposite sides of a rifting, cracking floe of ice.

He said, in the terribly controlled voice she had heard

before in his room, "In the church, Matt?"

"Yes, in the ruined church," Matt said.

"And you're sure she said it was midnight?"

"She couldn't be positive but it must have been some-time around then. We found her not long after. Why?"

Stefan said nothing. Elena could feel the gulf between them widening. "Stefan," she whispered. Then, aloud, she said desperately, "Stefan, what is it?"

He shook his head. Don't shut me out, she thought, but he wouldn't even look at her. "Will she live?" he asked abruptly.

"The doctor said there was nothing much wrong with her," Matt said. "Nobody's even suggested she might die."

Stefan's nod was abrupt; then he turned to Elena. "I've got to go," he said. "You're safe now."

She caught his hand as he turned away. "Of course I'm safe," she said. "Because of you."

"Yes," he said. But there was no response in his eyes. They were shielded, dull.

"Call me tomorrow." She squeezed his hand, trying to convey what she felt under the scrutiny of all those watching eyes. She willed him to understand.

He looked down at their hands with no expression at all, then, slowly, back up at her. And then, at last, he returned the pressure of her fingers. "Yes, Elena," he whispered, his eyes clinging to hers. The next minute he was gone.

She took a deep breath and turned back to the crowded room. Aunt Judith was still hovering, her gaze fixed on what could be seen of Elena's torn dress underneath the cloak.

"Elena," she said, "what *happened?*" And her eyes went to the door through which Stefan had just left.

A sort of hysterical laughter surged up in Elena's throat, and she choked it back. "Stefan didn't do it," she said. "Stefan saved me." She felt her face harden, and she looked at the police officer behind Aunt Judith. "It was Tyler, Tyler Smallwood. . . . "

9

She was not the reincarnation of Katherine.

Driving back to the boarding house in the faint lavender hush before dawn, Stefan thought about that.

He'd said as much to her, and it was true, but he was only now realizing how long he'd been working toward that conclusion. He'd been aware of Elena's every breath and move for weeks, and he'd catalogued every difference.

Her hair was a shade or two paler than Katherine's, and her eyebrows and lashes were darker. Katherine's had been almost silvery. And she was taller than Katherine by a good handspan. She moved with greater freedom, too; the girls of this age were more comfortable with their bodies.

Even her eyes, those eyes that had transfixed him with

the shock of recognition that first day, were not really the same. Katherine's eyes had usually been wide with child-like wonder, or else cast down as was proper for a young girl of the late fifteenth century. But Elena's eyes met you straight on, looked at you steadily and without flinching. And sometimes they narrowed with determination or challenge in a way Katherine's never had.

In grace and beauty and sheer fascination, they were alike. But where Katherine had been a white kitten, Elena was a snow-white tigress.

As he drove past the silhouettes of maple trees, Stefan cringed from the memory that sprang up suddenly. He would not think about that, he would not let himself . . . but the images were already unreeling before him. It was as if the journal had fallen open and he could do no more than stare helplessly at the page while the story played itself out in his mind.

White, Katherine had been wearing white that day. A new white gown of Venetian silk with slashed sleeves to show the fine linen chemise underneath. She had a neck-lace of gold and pearls about her neck and tiny pearl drop earrings in her ears.

She had been so delighted with the new dress her father had commissioned especially for her.

She had pirouetted in front of Stefan, lifting the full,

floor-length skirt in one small hand to show the yellow brocaded underskirt beneath. . . .

"You see, it is even embroidered with my initials. Papa had that done. *Mein lieber Papa* . . . " Her voice trailed off, and she stopped twirling, one hand slowly settling to her side. "But what is wrong, Stefan? You are not smiling."

He could not even try. The sight of her there, white and gold like some ethereal vision, was a physical pain to him. If he lost her, he did not know how he could live.

His fingers closed convulsively around the cool engraved metal. "Katherine, how can I smile, how can I be happy when . . . "

"When?"

"When I see how you look at Damon." There, it was said. He continued, painfully. "Before he came home, you and I were together every day. My father and yours were pleased, and spoke of marriage plans. But now the days grow shorter, summer is almost gone—and you spend as much time with Damon as you do with me. The only reason Father allows him to stay here is that you asked it. But *why* did you ask it, Katherine? I thought you cared for me."

Her blue eyes were dismayed. "I do care for you, Stefan. Oh, you know I do!"

"Then why intercede for Damon with my father? If not for you, he'd have thrown Damon out into the street. . . . "

"Which I'm sure would have pleased *you*, little brother." The voice at the door was smooth and arrogant, but when Stefan turned he saw that Damon's eyes were smoldering.

"Oh, no, that isn't true," said Katherine. "Stefan would never wish to see you hurt."

Damon's lip quirked, and he threw Stefan a wry glance as he moved to Katherine's side. "Perhaps not," he said to her, his voice softening slightly. "But my brother is right about one thing at least. The days grow shorter, and soon your father will be leaving Florence. And he will take you with him—unless you have a reason to stay."

Unless you have a husband to stay with. The words were unspoken, but they all heard them. The baron was too fond of his daughter to force her to marry against her will. In the end it would have to be Katherine's decision. Katherine's choice.

Now that the subject was broached, Stefan could not keep silent. "Katherine knows she must leave her father sometime soon—" he began, flaunting his secret knowledge, but his brother interrupted.

"Ah, yes, before the old man grows suspicious," Damon said casually. "Even the most doting of fathers must start to wonder when his daughter comes forth only at night."

Anger and hurt swept through Stefan. It was true, then;

Damon knew. Katherine had shared her secret with his brother.

"Why did you tell him, Katherine? Why? What can you see in him: a man who cares for nothing but his own pleasure? How can he make you happy when he thinks only of himself?"

"And how can this *boy* make you happy when he knows nothing of the world?" Damon interposed, his voice razor-sharp with contempt. "How will he protect you when he has never faced reality? He has spent his life among books and paintings; let him stay there."

Katherine was shaking her head in distress, her jewel-blue eyes misted with tears.

"Neither of you understand," she said. "You are thinking that I can marry and settle here like any other lady of Florence. But I cannot be like other ladies. How could I keep a household of servants who will watch my every move? How could I live in one place where the people will see that the years do not touch me? There will never be a normal life for me."

She drew a deep breath and looked at them each in turn. "Who chooses to be my husband must give up the life of sunlight," she whispered. "He must choose to live under the moon and in the hours of darkness."

"Then *you* must choose someone who is not afraid of shadows," Damon said, and Stefan was surprised by the intensity of his voice. He had never heard Damon speak so earnestly or with so little affectation. "Katherine, look at my brother: will he be able to renounce the sunlight? He is too attached to ordinary things: his friends, his family, his duty to Florence. The darkness would destroy him."

"Liar!" cried Stefan. He was seething now. "I am as strong as you are, *brother*, and I fear nothing in the shadows or the sunlight either. And I love Katherine more than friends or family—"

" or your duty? Do you love her enough to give that up as well?"

"Yes," Stefan said defiantly. "Enough to give up everything."

Damon gave one of his sudden, disturbing smiles. Then he turned back to Katherine. "It would seem," he said, "that the choice is yours alone. You have two suitors for your hand; will you take one of us or neither?"

Katherine slowly bowed her golden head. Then she lifted wet blue eyes to both of them.

"Give me until Sunday to think. And in the meantime, do not press me with questions."

Stefan nodded reluctantly. Damon said, "And on Sunday?"

"Sunday evening at twilight I will make my choice."

* * *

Twilight . . . the violet deep darkness of twilight . . .

The velvet hues faded around Stefan, and he came to himself. It was not dusk, but dawn, that stained the sky around him. Lost in his thoughts, he had driven up to the edge of the woods.

To the northwest he could see Wickery Bridge and the graveyard. New memory set his pulse pounding.

He had told Damon he was willing to give up everything for Katherine. And that was just what he had done. He had renounced all claim to the sunlight, and had become a creature of darkness for her. A hunter doomed to be forever hunted himself, a thief who had to steal life to fill his own veins.

And perhaps a murderer.

No, they had said the girl Vickie would not die. But his next victim might. The worst thing about this last attack was that he remembered nothing of it. He remembered the weakness, the overpowering need, and he remembered staggering through the church door, but nothing after. He'd come to his senses outside with Elena's scream echoing in his ears—and he had raced to her without stopping to think about what might have happened.

Elena . . . For a moment he felt a rush of pure joy and awe, forgetting everything else. Elena, warm as sunlight, soft as morning, but with a core of steel that could not be broken. She was like fire burning in ice, like the keen edge of a silver dagger.

But did he have the right to love her? His very feeling for her put her in danger. What if the next time the need took him Elena was the nearest living human, the nearest vessel filled with warm renewing blood?

I will die before touching her, he thought, making a vow of it. Before I broach her veins, I will die of thirst. And I swear she will never know my secret. She will never have to give up the sunlight because of me.

Behind him, the sky was lightening. But before he left, he sent out one probing thought, with all the force of his pain behind it, seeking for some other Power that might be near. Searching for some other solution to what had happened in the church.

But there was nothing, no hint of an answer. The graveyard mocked him with silence.

Elena woke with the sun shining in her window. She felt, at once, as if she'd just recovered from a long bout of the flu, and as if it were Christmas morning. Her thoughts jumbled together as she sat up.

Oh. She hurt all over. But she and Stefan—that made everything right. That drunken slob Tyler . . . But Tyler didn't matter anymore. Nothing mattered except that Stefan loved her.

She went downstairs in her nightgown, realizing from the

light slanting in the windows that she must have slept in very late. Aunt Judith and Margaret were in the living room.

"Good morning, Aunt Judith." She gave her surprised aunt a long, hard hug. "And good morning, pumpkin." She swept Margaret off her feet and waltzed around the room with her. "And—oh! Good morning, Robert." A little embarrassed at her exuberance and her state of undress, she put Margaret down and hurried into the kitchen.

Aunt Judith came in. Though there were dark circles under her eyes, she was smiling. "You seem in good spirits this morning."

"Oh, I am." Elena gave her another hug, to apologize for the dark circles.

"You know we have to go back to the sheriff's to talk to them about Tyler."

"Yes." Elena got juice out of the refrigerator and poured herself a glass. "But can I go over to Vickie Bennett's house first? I know she must be upset, especially since it sounds like not everybody believes her."

"Do you believe her, Elena?"

"Yes," she said slowly, "I do believe her. And, Aunt Judith," she added, coming to a decision, "something happened to me in the church, too. I thought—"

"Elena! Bonnie and Meredith are here to see you." Robert's voice sounded from the hallway.

The mood of confidence was broken. "Oh . . . send them in," Elena called, and took a sip of orange juice. "I'll tell you about it later," she promised Aunt Judith, as footsteps approached the kitchen.

Bonnie and Meredith stopped in the doorway, standing with unaccustomed formality. Elena herself felt awkward, and waited until her aunt left the room again to speak.

Then she cleared her throat, her eyes fixed on a worn tile in the linoleum. She sneaked a quick glance up and saw that both Bonnie and Meredith were staring at that same tile.

She burst into laughter, and at the sound they both looked up.

"I'm too happy to even be defensive," Elena said, holding out her arms to them. "And I know I ought to be sorry about what I said, and I *am* sorry, but I just can't be all pathetic about it. I was terrible and I deserve to be executed, and now can we just pretend it never happened?"

"You *ought* to be sorry, running off on us like that," Bonnie scolded as the three of them joined in a tangled embrace.

"And with Tyler Smallwood, of all people," said Meredith.

"Well, I learned my lesson on that score," Elena said, and for a moment her mood darkened. Then Bonnie trilled laughter.

"And you scored the big one yourself—Stefan Salvatore! Talk about dramatic entrances. When you came in the door with him, I thought I was hallucinating. How did you *do* it?"

"I didn't. He just showed up, like the cavalry in one of those old movies."

"Defending your honor," said Bonnie. "What could be more thrilling?"

"I can think of one or two things," said Meredith. "But then, maybe Elena's got those covered, too."

"I'll tell you all about it," Elena said, releasing them and stepping back. "But first will you come over to Vickie's house with me? I want to talk to her."

"You can talk to *us* while you're dressing, and while we're walking, and while you're brushing your teeth for that matter," said Bonnie firmly. "And if you leave out one tiny detail, you're going to be facing the Spanish Inquisition."

"You see," said Meredith archly, "all Mr. Tanner's work has paid off. Bonnie now knows the Spanish Inquisition is not a rock group."

Elena was laughing with sheer ebullience as they went up the stairs.

Mrs. Bennett looked pale and tired, but invited them in. "Vickie's been resting; the doctor said to keep her in bed," she explained, with a smile that trembled slightly. Elena, Bonnie, and Meredith crowded into the narrow hallway.

Mrs. Bennett tapped lightly at Vickie's door. "Vickie, sweetheart, some girls from school to see you. Don't keep her long," she added to Elena, opening the door.

"We won't," Elena promised. She stepped into a pretty blue-and-white bedroom, the others right behind her. Vickie was lying in bed propped up on pillows, with a powder-blue comforter drawn up to her chin. Her face was paper-white against it, and her heavy-lidded eyes stared straight ahead.

"That's how she looked last night," Bonnie whispered.

Elena moved to the side of the bed. "Vickie," she said softly. Vickie went on staring, but Elena thought her breathing changed slightly. "Vickie, can you hear me? It's Elena Gilbert." She glanced uncertainly at Bonnie and Meredith.

"Looks like they gave her tranquilizers," said Meredith.

But Mrs. Bennett hadn't said they'd given her any drugs. Frowning, Elena turned back to the unresponsive girl.

"Vickie, it's me, Elena. I just wanted to talk to you about last night. I want you to know that I believe you about what happened." Elena ignored the sharp glance

Meredith gave her and continued. "And I wanted to ask you—"

"No!" It was a shriek, raw and piercing, torn from Vickie's throat. The body that had been as still as a wax figure exploded into violent action. Vickie's light-brown hair whipped across her cheeks as she tossed her head back and forth and her hands flailed at the empty air. "No! No!" she screamed.

"Do something!" Bonnie gasped. "Mrs. Bennett! Mrs. Bennett!"

Elena and Meredith were trying to hold Vickie on the bed, and she was fighting them. The shrieking went on and on. Then suddenly Vickie's mother was beside them, helping to hold her, pushing the others away.

"What did you do to her?" she cried.

Vickie clutched at her mother, calming down, but then the heavy-lidded eyes glimpsed Elena over Mrs. Bennett's shoulder.

"You're part of it! You're evil!" she screamed hysterically at Elena. "Keep away from me!"

Elena was dumbfounded. "Vickie! I only came to ask—"

"I think you'd better leave now. Leave us alone," said Mrs. Bennett, clasping her daughter protectively. "Can't you see what you're doing to her?"

In stunned silence, Elena left the room. Bonnie and

Meredith followed.

"It must be drugs," said Bonnie once they were out of the house. "She just went completely nonlinear."

"Did you notice her hands?" Meredith said to Elena. "When we were trying to restrain her, I got hold of one of her hands. And it was cold as ice."

Elena shook her head in bewilderment. None of it made sense, but she *wouldn't* let it spoil her day. She wouldn't. Desperately, she searched her mind for something that would offset the experience, that would allow her to hold on to her happiness.

"*I* know," she said. "The boarding house."

"What?"

"I told Stefan to call me today, but why don't we walk over to the boarding house instead? It's not far from here."

"Only a twenty-minute walk," said Bonnie. She brightened. "At least we can finally see that room of his."

"Actually," said Elena, "I was thinking you two could wait downstairs. Well, I'll only get to see him for a few minutes," she added, defensively, as they looked at her. It was odd, perhaps, but she didn't want to share Stefan with her friends just yet. He was so new to her that he felt almost like a secret.

Their knock on the shining oak door was answered by Mrs. Flowers. She was a wrinkled little gnome of a woman with surprisingly bright black eyes.

"You must be Elena," she said. "I saw you and Stefan go out last night, and he told me your name when he came back."

"You saw us?" said Elena, startled. "I didn't see you."

"No, no you didn't," said Mrs. Flowers, and chuckled. "What a pretty girl you are, my dear," she added. "A very pretty girl." She patted Elena's cheek.

"Uh, thank you," said Elena uneasily. She didn't like the way those birdlike eyes were fixed on her. She looked past Mrs. Flowers to the stairs. "Is Stefan home?"

"He must be, unless he's flown off the roof!" said Mrs. Flowers, and chuckled again. Elena laughed politely.

"We'll stay down here with Mrs. Flowers," said Meredith to Elena, while Bonnie rolled her eyes in martyrdom. Hiding a grin, Elena nodded and mounted the stairs.

Such a strange old house, she thought again as she located the second stairway in the bedroom. The voices below were very faint from here, and as she went up the steps they faded entirely. She was wrapped in silence, and as she reached the dimly lit door at the top, she had the feeling she had entered some other world.

Her knocking sounded very timid. "Stefan?"

She could hear nothing from inside, but suddenly the door swung open. Everyone must look pale and tired today, thought Elena, and then she was in his arms.

Those arms tightened about her convulsively. "Elena. Oh, Elena . . . "

Then he drew back. It was just the way it had been last night; Elena could feel the chasm opening between them. She saw the cold, correct look gather in his eyes.

"No," she said, hardly aware that she spoke aloud. "I won't let you." And she pulled his mouth down to hers.

For a moment there was no response, and then he shuddered, and the kiss became searing. His fingers tangled in her hair, and the universe shrank around Elena. Nothing else existed but Stefan, and the feel of his arms around her, and the fire of his lips on hers.

A few minutes or a few centuries later they separated, both shaking. But their gaze remained connected, and Elena saw that Stefan's eyes were too dilated for even this dim light, there was only a thin band of green around the dark pupils. He looked dazed, and his mouth—that mouth!—was swollen.

"I think," he said, and she could hear the control in his voice, "that we had better be careful when we do that."

Elena nodded, dazed herself. Not in public, she was thinking. And not when Bonnie and Meredith were waiting downstairs. And not when they were absolutely alone, unless . . .

"But you can just hold me," she said.

How odd, that after that passion she could feel so safe,

so peaceful, in his arms. "I love you," she whispered into the rough wool of his sweater.

She felt a quiver go through him. "Elena," he said again, and it was a sound almost of despair.

She raised her head. "What's wrong with that? What could possibly be wrong with that, Stefan? Don't you love me?"

"I . . . " He looked at her, helplessly—and they heard Mrs. Flowers's voice calling faintly from the bottom of the stairs.

"Boy! Boy! Stefan!" It sounded as if she were pounding on the banister with her shoe.

Stefan sighed. "I'd better go see what she wants." He slipped away from her, his face unreadable.

Left alone, Elena folded her arms across her chest and shivered. It was so cold here. He ought to have a fire, she thought, eyes moving idly around the room to rest finally on the mahogany dresser she'd examined last night.

The coffer.

She glanced at the closed door. If he came back in and caught her . . . She really shouldn't—but she was already moving toward the dresser.

Think of Bluebeard's wife, she told herself. Curiosity killed *her*. But her fingers were on the iron lid. Her heart beating rapidly, she eased the lid open.

In the dim light, the coffer appeared at first to be

empty, and Elena gave a nervous laugh. What had she expected? Love letters from Caroline? A bloody dagger?

Then she saw the thin strip of silk, folded over and over on itself neatly in one corner. She drew it out and ran it between her fingers. It was the apricot ribbon she'd lost the second day of school.

Oh, Stefan. Tears stung her eyes, and in her chest love welled up helplessly, overflowing. That long ago? You cared about me that long ago? Oh, Stefan, I love you. . . .

And it doesn't matter if you can't say it to me, she thought. There was a sound outside the door, and she folded the ribbon quickly and replaced it in the coffer. Then she turned toward the door, blinking tears from her eyes.

It doesn't matter if you can't say it right now. I'll say it for both of us. And someday you'll learn.

10

October 7, about 8:00 a.m.

*D*ear Diary,
        *I'm writing this during trig class,
        and I just hope Ms. Halpern doesn't*
see me.

I didn't have time to write last night, even
though I wanted to. Yesterday was a crazy, mixed-
up day, just like the night of the Homecoming
Dance. Sitting here in school this morning I almost
feel like everything that happened this weekend was
a dream. The bad things were so bad, but the good
things were so very, very good.

I'm not going to press criminal charges against
Tyler. He's suspended from school, though, and off

the football team. So's Dick, for being drunk at the dance. Nobody is saying so, but I think a lot of people think he was responsible for what happened to Vickie. Bonnie's sister saw Tyler at the clinic yesterday, and she said he had two black eyes and his whole face was purple. I can't help worrying about what's going to happen when he and Dick get back to school. They have more reason than ever to hate Stefan now.

Which brings me to Stefan. When I woke up this morning I panicked, thinking "What if it all isn't true? What if it never happened, or if he's changed his mind?" And Aunt Judith was worried at breakfast because I couldn't eat again. But then when I got to school I saw him in the corridor by the office, and we just looked at each other. And I knew. Just before he turned away, he smiled, sort of wryly. And I understood that, too, and he was right, it was better not to go up to each other in a public hallway, not unless we want to give the secretaries a thrill.

We are very definitely together. Now I just have to find a way to explain all this to Jean-Claude. Ha-ha.

What I don't understand is why Stefan isn't as happy about it as I am. When we're with each other I can feel how he feels, and I know how much he wants me, how much he cares. There's an almost desperate hunger inside him when he kisses me, as if he wants to pull the soul out of my body. Like a black hole that

Still October 7, now about 2:00 p.m.

Well, a little break there because Miss Halpern caught me. *She even started to read what I'd written out loud, but then I think the subject matter steamed her glasses up and she stopped. She was Not Amused. I'm too happy to care about minor things like flunking trigonometry.*

Stefan and I had lunch together, or at least we went off into a corner of the field and sat down with my lunch. He didn't even bother to bring anything, and of course as it turned out I couldn't eat either. We didn't touch each other much—we didn't—but we talked and looked at each other a lot. I want to touch him. More than any boy I've ever known. And I know he wants it, too, but he's holding back on me.

That's *what I can't understand, why he's fighting this, why he's holding back. Yesterday in his room I found proof positive that he's been watching me from the beginning. You remember how I told you that on the second day of school Bonnie and Meredith and I were in the cemetery? Well, yesterday in Stefan's room I found the apricot ribbon I was wearing that day. I remember it falling out of my hand while I was running, and he must have picked it up and kept it. I haven't told him I know, because he obviously wants to keep it a secret, but that* shows, *doesn't it, that he cares about me?*

I'll tell you someone else who is Not Amused. Caroline. Apparently she's been dragging him off into the photography room for lunch every day, and when he didn't show up today she went searching until she found us. Poor Stefan, he'd forgotten about her completely, and he was shocked at himself. Once she left—a nasty unhealthy shade of green, I might add—he told me how she'd attached herself to him the first week of school. She said she'd noticed he didn't really eat at lunch and she didn't either since she was on a diet, and why didn't they go someplace quiet and relax? He wouldn't really say anything bad about her (which I think is his idea of manners again, a gentleman doesn't do that), but he did say there was nothing at all between them. And for Caroline I think being forgotten was worse than if he'd thrown rocks at her.

I wonder why Stefan hasn't been eating lunch, though. It's strange in a football player.

Uh-oh. Mr. Tanner just walked by and I slammed my note pad over this diary just in time. Bonnie is snickering behind her history book, I can see her shoulders shaking. And Stefan, who's in front of me, looks as tense as if he's going to leap out of his chair any minute. Matt is giving me "you nut" looks and Caroline is glaring. I am being very, very innocent, writing with my eyes fixed on Tanner up front. So if this is a bit wobbly and messy, you'll understand why.

For the last month, I haven't really been myself. I haven't been able to think clearly or concentrate on anything but Stefan. There is so much I've left undone that I'm almost scared. I'm supposed to be in charge of decorations for the Haunted House and I haven't done one thing *about it yet. Now I've got exactly three and a half weeks to get it organized—and I want to be with* Stefan.

I could quit the committee. But that would leave Bonnie and Meredith holding the bag. And I keep remembering what Matt said when I asked him to get Stefan to come to the dance: "You want everybody and everything revolving around Elena Gilbert."

That isn't true. Or at least, if it has been in the past, I'm not going to let it be true anymore. I want—oh, this is going to sound completely stupid, but I want to be worthy of Stefan. I know he wouldn't let the guys on the team down just to suit his own convenience. I want him to be proud of me.

I want him to love me as much as I love him.

"Hurry up!" called Bonnie from the doorway of the gym. Beside her the high school janitor, Mr. Shelby, stood waiting.

Elena cast one last glance at the distant figures on the football field, then reluctantly crossed the blacktop to join Bonnie.

"I just wanted to tell Stefan where I was going," she said. After a week of being with Stefan, she still felt a thrill of excitement just saying his name. Every night this week he'd come to her house, appearing at the door around sunset, hands in pockets, wearing his jacket with the collar turned up. They usually took a walk in the dusk, or sat on the porch, talking. Although nothing was said about it, Elena knew it was Stefan's way of making sure they weren't alone together in private. Since the night of the dance, he'd made sure of that. Protecting her honor, Elena thought wryly, and with a pang, because she knew in her heart that there was more to it than that.

"He can live without you for one evening," said Bonnie callously. "If you get talking to him you'll never get away, and I'd *like* to get home in time for some kind of dinner."

"Hello, Mr. Shelby," said Elena to the janitor, who was still patiently waiting. To her surprise, he closed one eye in a solemn wink at her. "Where's Meredith?" she added.

"Here," said a voice behind her, and Meredith appeared with a cardboard box of file folders and note pads in her arms. "I've got the stuff from your locker."

"Is that all of you?" said Mr. Shelby. "All right, now, you gals leave the door shut and locked, you hear? That way nobody can get in."

Bonnie, about to enter, pulled up short. "You're sure there's nobody *already* in?" she said warily.

Elena gave her a push between the shoulder blades. "Hurry up," she mimicked unkindly. "I want to get home in time for dinner."

"There's nobody inside," said Mr. Shelby, mouth twitching under his mustache. "But you gals yell if you want anything. I'll be around."

The door slammed shut behind them with a curiously final sound.

"Work," said Meredith resignedly, and put the box on the floor.

Elena nodded, looking up and down the big empty

room. Every year the Student Council held a Haunted House as a fund-raiser. Elena had been on the decorating committee for the last two years, along with Bonnie and Meredith, but it was different being chairman. She had to make decisions that would affect everyone, and she couldn't even rely on what had been done in years past.

The Haunted House was usually set up in a lumber-yard warehouse, but with the growing uneasiness about town it had been decided that the school gym was safer. For Elena, it meant rethinking the whole interior design, and with less than three weeks now until Halloween.

"It's actually pretty spooky here," said Meredith quietly. And there *was* something disturbing about being in the big closed room, Elena thought. She found herself lowering her voice.

"Let's measure it first," she said. They moved down the room, their footsteps echoing hollowly.

"All right," said Elena when they had finished. "Let's get to work." She tried to shake off her feeling of uneasiness, telling herself that it was ridiculous to feel unsettled in the school gym, with Bonnie and Meredith beside her and an entire football team practicing not two hundred yards away.

The three of them sat on the bleachers with pens and notebooks in hand. Elena and Meredith consulted the design sketches for previous years while Bonnie bit her pen and gazed around thoughtfully.

"Well, here's the gym," said Meredith, making a quick sketch in her notebook. "And here's where the people are going to have to come in. Now we could have the Bloody Corpse at the very end. . . . By the way, who's going to be the Bloody Corpse this year?"

"Coach Lyman, I think. He did a good job last year, and he helps keep the football guys in line." Elena pointed to their sketch. "Okay, we'll partition this off and make it the Medieval Torture Chamber. They'll go straight out of that and into the Room of the Living Dead. . . . "

"I think we should have druids," said Bonnie abruptly.

"Have what?" said Elena, and then, as Bonnie started to yell "*droo*-ids," she waved a quelling hand. "All right, all right, I remember. But why?"

"Because they're the ones who invented Halloween. Really. It started out as one of their holy days, when they would build fires and put out turnips with faces carved in them to keep evil spirits away. They believed it was the day when the line between the living and the dead was thinnest. And they were scary, Elena. They performed human sacrifices. We could sacrifice Coach Lyman."

"Actually, that's not a bad idea," said Meredith. "The Bloody Corpse could be a sacrifice. You know, on a stone altar, with a knife and pools of blood all around. And then when you get really close, he suddenly sits up."

"And gives you heart failure," said Elena, but she had to admit it *was* a good idea, definitely scary. It made her feel a little sick just thinking about it. All that blood . . . but it was only Karo syrup, really.

The other girls had gone quiet, too. From the boys' locker next door, they could hear the sound of water running and lockers banging, and over that indistinct voices shouting.

"Practice is over," murmured Bonnie. "It must be dark outside."

"Yes, and Our Hero is getting all washed up," said Meredith, cocking an eyebrow at Elena. "Want to peek?"

"I wish," said Elena, only half jokingly. Somehow, indefinably, the atmosphere in the room had darkened. Just at the moment she *did* wish she could see Stefan, could be with him.

"Have you heard anything more about Vickie Bennett?" she asked suddenly.

"Well," said Bonnie after a moment, "I did hear that her parents were getting her a psychiatrist."

"A shrink? Why?"

"Well . . . I guess they think that those things she told us were hallucinations of something. And I heard her nightmares are pretty bad."

"Oh," said Elena. The sounds from the boys' locker room were fading, and they heard an outside door slam.

Hallucinations, she thought, hallucinations and nightmares. For some reason, she suddenly remembered that night in the graveyard, that night when Bonnie had sent them all running from something none of them could see.

"We'd better get back to business," said Meredith. Elena shook herself out of her reverie and nodded.

"We . . . we could have a graveyard," Bonnie said tentatively, as if she'd been reading Elena's thoughts. "In the Haunted House, I mean."

"*No*," said Elena sharply. "No, we'll just stick with what we have," she added in a calmer voice, and bent over her pad again.

Once again there was no sound but the soft scratching of pens and the rustle of paper.

"Good," said Elena at last. "Now we only need to measure for the different partitions. Somebody's going to have to get in behind the bleachers. . . . What now?"

The lights in the gym had flickered and gone down to half power.

"Oh, *no*," said Meredith, exasperated. The lights flickered again, went out, and returned dimly once more.

"I can't read a thing," said Elena, staring at what now seemed to be a featureless piece of white paper. She looked up at Bonnie and Meredith and saw two white blobs of faces.

"Something must be wrong with the emergency generator," said Meredith. "I'll get Mr. Shelby."

"Can't we just finish tomorrow?" Bonnie said plaintively.

"Tomorrow's Saturday," said Elena. "And we were supposed to have this done last week."

"I'll get Shelby," said Meredith again. "Come on Bonnie, you're going with me."

Elena began, "We could all go—" but Meredith interrupted.

"If we all go and we can't find him, then we can't get back in. Come on, Bonnie, it's only inside the school."

"But it's *dark* there."

"It's dark everywhere; it's nighttime. Come *on*; with two of us it'll be safe." She dragged an unwilling Bonnie to the door. "Elena, don't let anybody else in."

"As if you had to tell me," said Elena, letting them out and then watching them go a few paces down the hall. At the point at which they began to merge with the dimness, she stepped back inside and shut the door.

Well, this was a fine mess, as her mother used to say. Elena moved over to the cardboard box Meredith had brought and began stacking filing folders and notebooks back inside it. In this light she could see them only as vague shapes. There was no sound at all but her own breathing and the sounds she made. She was alone in the huge, dim room—

Someone was watching her.

She didn't know how she knew, but she was sure. Someone was behind her in the dark gymnasium, watching. *Eyes in the dark*, the old man had said. Vickie had said it, too. And now there were eyes on her.

She whirled quickly to face the room, straining her own eyes to see into the shadows, trying not even to breathe. She was terrified that if she made a sound the thing out there would get her. But she could see nothing, hear nothing.

The bleachers were dim, menacing shapes stretching out into nothingness. And the far end of the room was simply a featureless gray fog. Dark mist, she thought, and she could feel every muscle agonizingly tense as she listened desperately. Oh God, what was that soft whispering sound? It must be her imagination. . . . Please let it be her imagination.

Suddenly, her mind was clear. She had to get out of this place, *now*. There was real danger here, not just fantasy. Something was out there, something evil, something that wanted her. And she was all alone.

Something moved in the shadows.

Her scream froze in her throat. Her muscles were frozen, too, held motionless by her terror—and by some nameless force. Helplessly, she watched as the shape in the darkness moved out of the shadows and toward her. It seemed almost as if the darkness itself had come to life and was coalescing as she watched, taking on form—human form, the form of a young man.

"I'm sorry if I frightened you."

The voice was pleasant, with a slight accent she couldn't place. It didn't sound sorry at all.

Relief was so sudden and complete that it was painful. She slumped and heard her own breath sigh out.

It was only a guy, some former student or an assistant of Mr. Shelby's. An ordinary guy, who was smiling faintly, as if it had amused him to see her almost pass out.

Well . . . perhaps not quite ordinary. He was remarkably good-looking. His face was pale in the artificial twilight, but she could see that his features were cleanly defined and nearly perfect under a shock of dark hair. Those cheekbones were a sculptor's dream. And he'd been almost invisible because he was wearing black: soft black boots, black jeans, black sweater, and leather jacket.

He was still smiling faintly. Elena's relief turned to anger.

"How did you get in?" she demanded. "And what are you doing here? Nobody else is supposed to be in the gym."

"I came in the door," he said. His voice was soft, cultured, but she could still hear the amusement and she found it disconcerting.

"All the doors are locked," she said flatly, accusingly.

He raised his eyebrows and smiled. "Are they?"

Elena felt another quiver of fear, hairs lifting on the back of her neck. "They were supposed to be," she said in the coldest voice she could manage.

"You're angry," he said gravely. "I said I was sorry to frighten you."

"I wasn't frightened!" she snapped. She felt foolish in front of him somehow, like a child being humored by someone much older and more knowledgeable. It made her even angrier. "I was just startled," she continued. "Which is hardly surprising, what with you lurking in the dark like that."

"Interesting things happen in the dark . . . sometimes." He was still laughing at her; she could tell by his eyes. He had taken a step closer, and she could see that those eyes were unusual, almost black, but with odd lights in them. As if you could look deeper and deeper until you fell into them, and went on falling forever.

She realized she was staring. Why didn't the lights come on? She wanted to get out of here. She moved away, putting the end of a bleacher between them, and stacked the last folders into the box. Forget the rest of the work for tonight. All she wanted to do now was leave.

But the continuing silence made her uneasy. He was just standing there, unmoving, watching her. Why didn't he say something?

"Did you come looking for somebody?" She was annoyed with herself for being the one to speak.

He was still gazing at her, those dark eyes fixed on her in a way that made her more and more uncomfortable. She swallowed.

With his eyes on her lips, he murmured, "Oh, yes."

"What?" She'd forgotten what she'd asked. Her cheeks and throat were flushing, burning with blood. She felt so light-headed. If only he'd stop *looking* at her . . .

"Yes, I came here looking for someone," he repeated, no louder than before Then, in one step, he moved toward her so that they were separated only by the corner of one bleacher seat.

Elena couldn't breathe. He was standing so close. Close enough to touch. She could smell a faint hint of cologne and the leather of his jacket. And his eyes still held hers—she could not look away from them. They were like no eyes she had ever seen, black as midnight, the pupils dilated like a cat's. They filled her vision as he leaned toward her, bending his head down to hers. She felt her own eyes half close, losing focus. She felt her head tilt back, her lips part.

No! Just in time she whipped her head to the side. She felt as if she'd just pulled herself back from the edge of a precipice. What am I doing? she thought in shock. I was about to let him kiss me. A total stranger, someone I met only a few minutes ago.

But that wasn't the worst thing. For those few minutes, something unbelievable had happened. For those few minutes, she had forgotten Stefan.

But now his image filled her mind, and the longing for him was like a physical pain in her body. She wanted Stefan, wanted his arms around her, wanted to be safe with him.

She swallowed. Her nostrils flared as she breathed hard. She tried to keep her voice steady and dignified.

"I'm going to leave now," she said. "If you're looking for somebody, I think you'd better look somewhere else."

He was looking at her oddly, with an expression she couldn't understand. It was a mixture of annoyance, and grudging respect—and something else. Something hot and fierce that frightened her in a different way.

He waited until her hand was on the doorknob to answer, and his voice was soft but serious, with no trace of amusement. "Perhaps I've already found her . . . Elena."

When she turned, she could see nothing in the darkness.

lena stumbled down the dim corridor, trying to visualize what was around her. Then the world suddenly flickered to brightness and she found herself surrounded by familiar rows of lockers. Her relief was so great that she almost cried out. She'd never have thought she would be so glad just to *see*. She stood for a minute looking around gratefully.

"Elena! What are you doing out here?"

It was Meredith and Bonnie, hurrying down the hall toward her.

"Where have you been?" she said fiercely.

Meredith grimaced. "We couldn't find Shelby. And when we finally did find him, he was asleep. I'm serious," she added at Elena's incredulous look. "Asleep. And then we couldn't get him to wake up. It wasn't until the lights went back on that he opened his eyes. Then we started back to you. But what are you doing *here*?"

Elena hesitated "I got tired of waiting," she said as lightly as she could. "I think we've done enough work for one day, anyway."

"Now you tell us," said Bonnie.

Meredith said nothing, but she gave Elena a keen, searching look. Elena had the uncomfortable feeling that those dark eyes saw beneath the surface.

All that weekend and throughout the following week, Elena worked on plans for the Haunted House. There was never enough time to be with Stefan, and that was frustrating, but even more frustrating was Stefan himself. She could sense his passion for her, but she could also sense that he was fighting it, still refusing to be completely alone with her. And in many ways he was just as much a mystery to her as he had been when she first saw him.

He never spoke about his family or his life before coming to Fell's Church, and if she asked any questions he turned them aside. Once she had asked him if he missed Italy, if he was sorry he'd come here. And for an instant his eyes had lightened, the green sparkling like oak leaves reflected in a running stream. "How could I be sorry, when *you* are here?" he said, and kissed her in a way that put all inquiries out of her mind. In that moment, Elena had known what it was like to be completely happy. She'd felt his joy, too, and when he pulled back she had seen that his face was alight, as if the sun shone through it.

"Oh, Elena," he'd whispered.

The good times were like that. But he had kissed her less and less frequently of late, and she felt the distance between them widening.

That Friday, she and Bonnie and Meredith decided to sleep over at the McCulloughs'. The sky was gray and threatening to drizzle as she and Meredith walked to Bonnie's house. It was unusually chilly for mid-October, and the trees lining the quiet street had already felt the nip of cold winds. The maples were a blaze of scarlet, while the ginkgoes were radiant yellow.

Bonnie greeted them at the door with: "Everybody's gone! We'll have the whole house to ourselves until tomorrow afternoon, when my family gets back from Leesburg." She beckoned them inside, grabbing for the overfed Pekingese that was trying to get out. "No, Yangtze, stay in. Yangtze, no, don't! No!"

But it was too late. Yangtze had escaped and was dashing through the front yard up to the single birch tree, where he yapped shrilly up into the branches, rolls of fat on his back jiggling.

"Oh, what's he after *now*?" said Bonnie, putting her hands over her ears.

"It looks like a crow," said Meredith.

Elena stiffened. She took a few steps toward the tree, looking up into the golden leaves. And there it was. The same crow she had seen twice before. Perhaps three times before, she thought, remembering the dark shape winging up from the oak trees in the cemetery.

As she looked at it she felt her stomach clench in fear and her hands grow cold. It was staring at her again with its bright black eye, an almost human stare. That eye . . . where had she seen an eye like that before?

Suddenly all three girls jumped back as the crow gave a harsh croak and thrashed its wings, bursting out of the tree toward them. At the last moment it swooped down instead on the little dog, which was now barking hysterically. It came within inches of canine teeth and then soared back up again, flying over the house to disappear into the black walnut trees beyond.

The three girls stood frozen in astonishment. Then Bonnie and Meredith looked at each other, and the tension shattered in nervous laughter.

"For a moment I thought he was coming for us," said Bonnie, going over to the outraged Pekingese and dragging him, still barking, back into the house.

"So did I," said Elena quietly. And as she followed her friends inside, she did not join in the laughter.

Once she and Meredith had put their things away,

however, the evening fell into a familiar pattern. It was hard to keep hold of her uneasiness sitting in Bonnie's cluttered living room beside a roaring fire, with a cup of hot chocolate in her hand. Soon the three of them were discussing the final plans for the Haunted House, and she relaxed.

"We're in pretty good shape," said Meredith at last. "Of course, we've spent so much time figuring out everyone else's costumes that we haven't even thought about our own."

"Mine's easy," said Bonnie. "I'm going to be a druid priestess, and I only need a garland of oak leaves in my hair and some white robes. Mary and I can sew it in one night."

"I think I'll be a witch," said Meredith thoughtfully. "All that takes is a long black dress. What about you, Elena?"

Elena smiled. "Well, it was supposed to be a secret, but . . . Aunt Judith let me go to a dressmaker. I found a picture of a Renaissance gown in one of the books I used for my oral report, and we're having it copied. It's Venetian silk, ice blue, and it's absolutely beautiful."

"It sounds beautiful," Bonnie said. "And expensive."

"I'm using my own money from my parents' trust. I just hope Stefan likes it. It's a surprise for him, and . . . well, I just hope he likes it."

"What's Stefan going to be? Is he helping with the

Haunted House?" said Bonnie curiously.

"I don't know," Elena said after a moment. "He doesn't seem too thrilled with the whole Halloween thing."

"It's hard to see him all wrapped up in torn sheets and covered with fake blood like the other guys," agreed Meredith. "He seems . . . well, too dignified for that."

"I know!" said Bonnie. "I know exactly what he can be, and he'll hardly have to dress up at all. Look, he's foreign, he's sort of pale, he has that wonderful brooding look. . . . Put him in tails and you've got a perfect Count Dracula!"

Elena smiled in spite of herself. "Well, I'll ask him," she said.

"Speaking of Stefan," said Meredith, her dark eyes on Elena's, "how are things going?"

Elena sighed, looking away into the fire. "I'm . . . not sure," she said at last, slowly. "There are times when everything is wonderful, and then there are other times when . . . "

Meredith and Bonnie exchanged a glance, and then Meredith spoke gently. "Other times when what?"

Elena hesitated, debating. Then she came to a decision. "Just a sec," she said, and got up and hurried up the stairs. She came back down with a small blue velvet book in her hands.

"I wrote some of it down last night when I couldn't

sleep," she said. "This says it better than I could now."
She found the page, took a deep breath, and began:

> *"October 17*
> *"Dear Diary,*
>   *"I feel awful tonight. And I have to share it*
> *with someone.*
>   *"Something is going wrong with Stefan and me.*
> *There is this terrible sadness inside him that I can't*
> *reach, and it's driving us apart. I don't know*
> *what to do.*
>   *"I can't bear the thought of losing him. But he's*
> *so very unhappy about something, and if he won't*
> *tell me what it is, if he won't trust me that much, I*
> *don't see any hope for us.*
>   *"Yesterday when he was holding me I felt some-*
> *thing smooth and round underneath his shirt, some-*
> *thing on a chain. I asked him, teasingly, if it was a*
> *gift from Caroline. And he just froze and wouldn't*
> *talk anymore. It was as if he were suddenly a thou-*
> *sand miles away, and his eyes . . . there was so much*
> *pain in his eyes that I could hardly stand it."*

Elena stopped reading and traced the last lines written
in the journal silently with her eyes. *I feel as if someone has*
hurt him terribly in the past and he's never got over it. But I also

think there's something he's afraid of, some secret he's afraid I'll find out. If I only knew what that was, I could prove to him that he can trust me. That he can trust me no matter what happens, to the end.

"If only I knew," she whispered.

"If only you knew what?" said Meredith, and Elena looked up, startled.

"Oh—if only I knew what was going to happen," she said quickly, closing the diary. "I mean, if I knew we were going to break up eventually, I suppose I'd just want to get it over with. And if I knew it was going to turn out all right in the end, I wouldn't mind anything that happens now. But just going day after day without being sure is awful."

Bonnie bit her lip, then sat up, eyes sparkling. "I can show you a way to find out, Elena," she said. "My grandmother told me the way to find out who you're going to marry. It's called a dumb supper."

"Let me guess, an old druid trick," said Meredith.

"I don't know how old it is," said Bonnie. "My grandmother says there have always been dumb suppers. Anyway, it works. My mother saw my father's image when she tried it, and a month later they were married. It's easy, Elena; and what have you got to lose?"

Elena looked from Bonnie to Meredith. "I don't know," she said. "But, look, you don't really believe . . . "

Bonnie drew herself up with affronted dignity. "Are

you calling my mother a liar? Oh, come on, Elena, there's no harm in trying. Why not?"

"What would I have to do?" said Elena doubtfully. She felt strangely intrigued, but at the same time rather frightened.

"It's simple. We have to get everything ready before the stroke of midnight. . . . "

Five minutes before midnight Elena stood in the McCulloughs' dining room, feeling more foolish than anything else. From the backyard, she could hear Yangtze's frantic barking, but inside the house there was no sound except the unhurried tick of the grandfather clock. Following Bonnie's instructions, she had set the big black walnut table with one plate, one glass, and one set of silverware, all the time not saying a word. Then she had lit a single candle in a candleholder in the center of the table, and positioned herself behind the chair with the place setting.

According to Bonnie, on the stroke of midnight she was supposed to pull the chair back and invite her future husband in. At that point, the candle would blow out and she would see a ghostly figure in the chair.

Earlier, she'd been a little uneasy about this, uncertain that she wanted to see *any* ghostly figures, even of her husband-to-be. But just now the whole thing seemed silly and harmless. As the clock began to chime, she straightened up and got a better grip on the chair back. Bonnie had told her not to let go until the ceremony was over.

Oh, this *was* silly. Maybe she wouldn't say the words . . . but when the clock started to toll out the hour, she heard herself speaking.

"Come in," she said self-consciously to the empty room, drawing out the chair. "Come in, come in . . . "

The candle went out.

Elena started in the sudden darkness. She'd felt the wind, a cold gust that had blown out the candle. It came from the French doors behind her, and she turned quickly, one hand still on the chair. She would have sworn those doors were shut.

Something moved in the darkness.

Terror washed through Elena, sweeping away her self-consciousness and any trace of amusement. Oh, God, what had she done, what had she brought on herself? Her heart contracted and she felt as if she had been plunged, without warning, into her most dreadful nightmare. It was not only dark but utterly silent; there was nothing to see and nothing to hear, and she was falling . . .

"Allow me," said a voice, and a bright flame sputtered in the darkness.

For a terrible, sickening instant she thought it was Tyler, remembering his lighter in the ruined church on the hill. But as the candle on the table sprang to life, she saw the pale, long-fingered hand that held it. Not Tyler's beefy red first. She thought for an instant it was Stefan's, and then her eyes lifted to the face.

"You!" she said, astounded. "What do you think you're *doing* here?" She looked from him to the French doors, which were indeed open, showing the side lawn. "Do you always just walk into other people's houses uninvited?"

"But you asked me to come in." His voice was as she remembered it, quiet, ironical, and amused. She remembered the smile, too. "Thank you," he added, and gracefully sat down in the chair she had drawn out.

She snatched her hand off the back. "I wasn't inviting *you*," she said helplessly, caught between indignation and embarrassment. "What were you doing hanging around outside Bonnie's house?"

He smiled. In the candlelight, his black hair shone almost like liquid, too soft and fine for human hair. His face was very pale, but at the same time utterly compelling. And his eyes caught her own and held them.

"'Helen, thy beauty is to me/Like those Nicean barks of yore/That gently, over a perfumed sea . . . '"

"I think you'd better leave now." She didn't want him to talk anymore. His voice did strange things to her, made her feel oddly weak, started a melting in her stomach. "You shouldn't be here. Please." She reached for the candle, meaning to take it and leave him, fighting off the dizziness that threatened to overcome her.

But before she could grasp it, he did something extraordinary. He caught her reaching hand, not roughly but gently, and held it in his cool slender fingers. Then he turned her hand over, bent his dark head, and kissed her palm.

"Don't . . . " whispered Elena, stunned.

"Come with me," he said, and looked up into her eyes.

"Please don't . . . " she whispered again, the world swimming around her. He was mad; what was he talking about? Come with him where? But she felt so dizzy, so faint.

He was standing, supporting her. She leaned against him, felt those cool fingers on the first button of the shirt at her throat. "Please, no . . . "

"It's all right. You'll see." He pulled the shirt away from her neck, his other hand behind her head.

"*No.*" Suddenly, strength returned to her, and she jerked away from him, stumbling against the chair. "I told you to leave, and I meant it. Get out—now!"

For an instant, pure fury surged in his eyes, a dark wave of menace. Then they went calm and cold and he smiled, a swift, brilliant smile that he turned off again instantly.

"I'll leave," he said. "For the moment."

She shook her head and watched him go out the French doors without speaking. When they had shut behind him, she stood in the silence, trying to get her breath.

The silence . . . but it shouldn't be silent. She turned

toward the grandfather clock in bewilderment and saw that it had stopped. But before she could examine it closely, she heard Meredith's and Bonnie's raised voices.

She hurried out into the hall, feeling the unaccustomed weakness in her legs, pulling her shirt back up and buttoning it. The back door was open, and she could see two figures outside, stooping over something on the lawn.

"Bonnie? Meredith? What's wrong?"

Bonnie looked up as Elena reached them. Her eyes were filled with tears. "Oh, Elena, he's dead."

With a chill of horror, Elena stared down at the little bundle at Bonnie's feet. It was the Pekingese, lying very stiffly on his side, eyes open. "Oh, *Bonnie*," she said.

"He was old," said Bonnie, "but I never expected him to go this quickly. Just a little while ago, he was barking."

"I think we'd better go inside," said Meredith, and Elena looked up at her and nodded. Tonight was not a night to be out in the dark. It was not a night to invite things inside, either. She knew that now, although she still didn't understand what had happened.

It was when they got back in the living room that she found her diary was missing.

Stefan lifted his head from the velvet-soft neck of the doe. The woods were filled with night noises, and he couldn't be sure which had disturbed him.

With the Power of his mind distracted, the deer roused from its trance. He felt muscles quiver as she tried to get her feet under her.

Go, then, he thought, sitting back and releasing her entirely. With a twist and a heave, she was up and running.

He'd had enough. Fastidious, he licked at the corners of his mouth, feeling his canine teeth retract and blunt, oversensitive as always after a prolonged feed. It was hard to know what enough was anymore. There had been no spells of dizziness since the one beside the church, but he lived in fear of their return.

He lived in one specific fear: that he would come to his senses one day, his mind reeling with confusion, to find Elena's graceful body limp in his arms, her slim throat marked with two red wounds, her heart stilled forever.

That was what he had to look forward to.

The blood lust, with all its myriad terrors and pleasures, was a mystery to him even now. Although he had lived with it every day for centuries, he still did not understand it. As a living human, he would no doubt have been disgusted, sickened, by the thought of drinking the rich warm stuff directly from a breathing body. That is, if someone had proposed such a thing to him in so many words.

But no words had been used that night, the night

Katherine had changed him.

Even after all these years, the memory was clear. He had been asleep when she appeared in his chamber, moving as softly as a vision or a ghost. He had been asleep, alone. . . .

She was wearing a fine linen shift when she came to him.

It was the night before the day she had named, the day when she would announce her choice. And she came to him.

A white hand parted the curtains around his bed, and Stefan woke from sleep, sitting up in alarm. When he saw her, pale golden hair gleaming about her shoulders, blue eyes lost in shadow, he was struck silent with amazement.

And with love. He had never seen anything more beautiful in his life. He trembled and tried to speak, but she put two cool fingers over his lips.

"Hush," she whispered, and the bed sank under new weight as she got in.

His face flamed, his heart was thundering with embarrassment and with excitement. There had never been a woman in his bed before. And this was Katherine, Katherine whose beauty seemed to come from heaven, Katherine whom he loved more than his own soul.

And because he loved her, he made a great effort. As

she slipped under the sheets, drawing so near to him that he could feel the cool freshness of night air in her thin shift, he managed to speak.

"Katherine," he whispered. "We—I can wait. Until we are married in the church. I will have my father arrange it next week. It—it will not be long. . . . "

"Hush," she whispered again, and he felt that coolness on his skin. He couldn't help himself; he put his arms around her, holding her to him. "What we do now has nothing to do with that," she said, and reached out her slim fingers to stroke his throat.

He understood. And felt a flash of fear, which disappeared as her fingers went on stroking. He wanted this, wanted anything that would let him be with Katherine.

"Lie back, my love," she whispered.

My love. The words sang through him as he lay back on the pillow, tilting his chin back so that his throat was exposed. His fear was gone, replaced by a happiness so great that he thought it would shatter him.

He felt the soft brush of her hair on his chest, and tried to calm his breathing. He felt her breath on his throat, and then her lips. And then her teeth.

There was a stinging pain, but he held himself still and made no sound, thinking only of Katherine, of how he wished to give to her. And almost at once the pain eased, and he felt the blood being drawn from his body. It was not terrible, as he had feared. It was a feeling of giving, of nurturing.

Then it was as if their minds were merging, becoming one. He could feel Katherine's joy in drinking from him, her delight in taking the warm blood that gave her life. And he knew she could feel his delight in giving. But reality was receding, the boundaries between dreams and waking becoming blurred. He could not think clearly; he could not think at all. He could only *feel*, and his feelings were spiraling up and up, carrying him higher and higher, breaking his last ties with earth.

Sometime later, without knowing how he had gotten there, he found himself in her arms. She was cradling him like a mother holding an infant child, guiding his mouth to rest on the bare flesh just above the low neck of her night shift. There was a tiny wound there, a cut showing dark against the pale skin. He felt no fear or hesitation, and when she stroked his hair encouragingly, he began to suck.

Cold and precise, Stefan brushed dirt off his knees. The human world was asleep, lost in stupor, but his own senses were knife-keen. He should have been sated, but he was hungry again; the memory had wakened his appetite. Nostrils flaring wide to catch the musky scent of fox, he began to hunt.

12

Elena revolved slowly before the full-length mirror in Aunt Judith's bedroom. Margaret sat at the foot of the big four-poster bed, her blue eyes large and solemn with admiration.

"I wish I had a dress like that for trick-or-treat," she said.

"I like you best as a little white cat," said Elena, dropping a kiss between the white velvet ears attached to Margaret's headband. Then she turned to her aunt, who stood by the door with needle and thread ready. "It's perfect," she said warmly. "We don't have to change a thing."

The girl in the mirror could have stepped out of one of Elena's books on the Italian Renaissance. Her throat and shoulders were bare, and the tight bodice of the ice-blue dress showed off her tiny waist. The long, full sleeves were slashed so that the white silk of the chemise underneath showed through, and the wide, sweeping skirt just brushed the floor all around her. It was a beautiful dress, and the pale clear blue seemed to heighten the darker blue of Elena's eyes.

As she turned away, Elena's gaze fell on the old-fashioned pendulum clock above the dresser. "Oh, no—it's almost seven. Stefan will be here any minute."

"That's his car now," said Aunt Judith, glancing out the window. "I'll go down and let him in."

"That's all right," said Elena briefly. "I'll meet him myself. Good-bye, have a good time trick-or-treating!" She hurried down the stairs.

Here goes, she thought. As she reached for the door-knob, she was reminded of that day, nearly two months ago now, when she'd stepped directly into Stefan's path in European History class. She'd had this same feeling of anticipation, of excitement and tension.

I just hope this turns out better than that plan did, she thought. For the last week and a half, she'd pinned her hopes to this moment, to this night. If she and Stefan didn't come together tonight, they never would.

The door swung open, and she stepped back with her eyes down, feeling almost shy, afraid to see Stefan's face. But when she heard his sharp indrawn breath, she looked up quickly—and felt her heart go cold.

He was staring at her in wonder, yes. But it was not the wondering joy she'd seen in his eyes that first night in his room. This was something closer to shock.

"You don't like it," she whispered, horrified at the stinging in her eyes.

He recovered swiftly, as always, blinking and shaking his head. "No, no, it's beautiful. You're beautiful."

Then why are you standing there looking as if you'd seen a ghost? she thought. Why don't you hold me, kiss me—something!

"You look wonderful," she said quietly. And it was true; he was sleek and handsome in the tux and cape he'd donned for his part. She was surprised he'd agreed to it, but when she'd made the suggestion he'd seemed more amused than anything else. Just now, he looked elegant and comfortable, as if such clothes were as natural as his jeans.

"We'd better go," he said, equally quiet and serious.

Elena nodded and went with him to the car, but her heart was no longer merely cold; it was ice. He was further away from her than ever, and she had no idea how to get him back.

Thunder growled overhead as they drove to the high school, and Elena glanced out of the car window with dull dismay. The cloud cover was thick and dark, although it hadn't actually begun to rain yet. The air had a charged, electric feel, and the sullen purple thunderheads gave the sky a nightmarish look. It was a perfect atmosphere for Halloween, menacing and otherworldly, but it woke only dread in Elena. Since that night at Bonnie's, she'd lost her appreciation for the eerie and uncanny.

Her diary had never turned up, although they'd searched Bonnie's house top to bottom. She still couldn't believe that it was really gone, and the idea of a stranger reading her most private thoughts made her feel wild inside. Because, of course, it had been stolen; what other explanation was there? More than one door had been open that night at the McCullough house; someone could have just walked in. She wanted to *kill* whoever had done it.

A vision of dark eyes rose before her. That boy, the boy she'd almost given in to at Bonnie's house, the boy who'd made her forget Stefan. Was he the one?

She roused herself as they pulled up to the school and forced herself to smile as they made their way through the halls. The gym was barely organized chaos. In the hour since Elena had left, everything had changed. Then, the place had been full of seniors: Student Council members, football players, the Key Club, all putting the finishing touches on props and scenery. Now it was full of strangers, most of them not even human.

Several zombies turned as Elena came in, their

grinning skulls visible through the rotting flesh of their faces. A grotesquely deformed hunchback limped toward her, along with a corpse with livid white skin and hollow eyes. From another direction came a werewolf, its snarling muzzle covered with blood, and a dark and dramatic witch.

Elena realized, with a jolt, that she couldn't recognize half these people in their costumes. Then they were around her, admiring the ice-blue gown, announcing problems that had developed already. Elena waved them quiet and turned toward the witch, whose long dark hair flowed down the back of a tight-fitting black dress.

"What is it, Meredith?" she said.

"Coach Lyman's sick," Meredith replied grimly, "so somebody got Tanner to substitute."

"Mr. *Tanner*?" Elena was horrified.

"Yes, and he's making trouble already. Poor Bonnie's just about had it. You'd better get over there."

Elena sighed and nodded, then made her way along the twisting route of the Haunted House tour. As she passed through the grisly Torture Chamber and the ghastly Mad Slasher Room, she thought they had almost built *too* well. This place was unnerving even in the light.

The Druid Room was near the exit. There, a cardboard Stonehenge had been constructed. But the pretty little druid priestess who stood among the rather realistic-looking monoliths wearing white robes and an oak-leaf garland looked ready to burst into tears.

"But you've *got* to wear the blood," she was saying pleadingly. "It's part of the scene; you're a sacrifice."

"Wearing these ridiculous robes is bad enough," replied Tanner shortly. "No one informed me I was going to have to smear syrup all over myself."

"It doesn't really get on *you*," said Bonnie. "It's just on the robes and on the altar. You're a sacrifice," she repeated, as if somehow this would convince him.

"As for that," said Mr. Tanner in disgust, "the accuracy of this whole setup is highly suspect. Contrary to popular belief, the druids did not build Stonehenge; it was built by a Bronze Age culture that—"

Elena stepped forward. "Mr. Tanner, that isn't really the point."

"No, it wouldn't be, to you," he said. "Which is why you and your neurotic friend here are both failing history."

"That's uncalled for," said a voice, and Elena looked quickly over her shoulder at Stefan.

"Mister Salvatore," said Tanner, pronouncing the words as if they meant *Now my day is complete.* "I suppose you have some new words of wisdom to offer. Or are you going to give *me* a black eye?" His gaze traveled over Stefan, who stood there, unconsciously elegant in his perfectly tailored tux, and Elena felt a sudden shock of insight.

Tanner isn't really that much older than we are, she thought. He looks old because of that receding hairline, but I'll bet he's in his twenties. Then, for some reason, she remembered how Tanner had looked at Homecoming, in his cheap and shiny suit that didn't fit well.

I'll bet he never even made it to his own Homecoming, she thought. And, for the first time, she felt something like sympathy for him.

Perhaps Stefan felt it, too, for although he stepped right up to the little man, standing face-to-face with him, his voice was quiet. "No, I'm not. I think this whole thing is getting blown out of proportion. Why don't . . . " Elena couldn't hear the rest, but he was speaking in low, calming tones, and Mr. Tanner actually seemed to be listening. She glanced back at the crowd that had gathered behind her: four or five ghouls, the werewolf, a gorilla, and a hunchback.

"All right, everything's under control," she said, and they dispersed. Stefan was taking care of things, although she was not sure how, since she could see only the back of his head.

The back of his head . . . For an instant, an image flashed before her of the first day of school. Of how Stefan had stood in the office talking to Mrs. Clarke, the secretary, and of how oddly Mrs. Clarke had acted. Sure enough, when Elena looked at Mr. Tanner now, he wore the same slightly dazed expression. Elena felt a slow ripple of disquiet.

"Come on," she said to Bonnie. "Let's go up front."

They cut straight through the Alien Landing Room and the Living Dead Room, slipping between the partitions, coming out in the first room where visitors would enter and be greeted by a werewolf. The werewolf had taken his head off and was talking to a couple of mummies and an Egyptian princess.

Elena had to admit that Caroline looked good as Cleopatra, the lines of that bronzed body frankly visible through the sheer linen sheath she wore. Matt, the werewolf, could hardly be blamed if his eyes kept straying downward from Caroline's face.

"How's it going here?" said Elena with forced lightness.

Matt started slightly, then turned toward her and Bonnie. Elena had scarcely seen him since the night of Homecoming, and she knew that he and Stefan had drawn apart, too. Because of her. And though Matt could hardly be blamed for *that*, either, she could tell how much it hurt Stefan.

"Everything's fine," said Matt, looking uncomfortable.

"When Stefan finishes with Tanner, I think I'll send him up here," Elena said. "He can help bring people in."

Matt lifted one shoulder indifferently. Then he said,

"Finishes what with Tanner?"

Elena looked at him in surprise. She could have sworn he'd been in the Druid Room a minute ago to see it. She explained.

Outside, thunder rumbled again, and through the open door Elena saw a flash light the night sky. There was another, louder clap of thunder a few seconds later.

"I hope it doesn't rain," Bonnie said.

"Yes," said Caroline, who had been standing silent while Elena spoke to Matt. "It would be such a *pity* if nobody came."

Elena glanced at her sharply and saw open hatred in Caroline's narrow, catlike eyes.

"Caroline," she said impulsively, "look. Can't you and I call it quits? Can't we forget what's happened and start over?"

Under the cobra on her forehead, Caroline's eyes widened and then slitted again. Her mouth twisted, and she stepped closer to Elena.

"I will *never* forget," she said, and then she turned and left.

There was a silence, Bonnie and Matt looking at the floor. Elena stepped over to the doorway to feel cool air on her cheeks. Outside she could see the field and the tossing branches of the oak trees beyond, and once again she was overcome with that strange feeling of foreboding.

Tonight's the night, she thought wretchedly. Tonight's the night when it all happens. But what "it" was, she had no idea.

A voice sounded through the transformed gym. "All right, they're about to let the line in from the parking lot. Cut the lights, Ed!" Suddenly, gloom descended and the air was filled with groans and maniacal laughter, like an orchestra tuning up. Elena signed and turned.

"Better get ready to start herding them through," she told Bonnie quietly. Bonnie nodded and disappeared into the darkness. Matt had donned his werewolf head, and was turning on a tape deck that added eerie music to the cacophony.

Stefan came around the corner, his hair and clothing melting into the darkness. Only his white shirtfront showed up clearly. "Everything worked out with Tanner," he said. "Is there anything else I can do?"

"Well, you could work here, with Matt, bringing people in. . . . " Elena's voice trailed off. Matt was bent over the tape deck, minutely adjusting the volume, not looking up. Elena looked at Stefan and saw his face was tight and blank. "Or you could go into the boys' locker room and be in charge of coffee and things for the workers," she finished tiredly.

"I'll go to the locker room," he said. As he turned away, she noticed a slight faltering in his step.

"Stefan? Are you all right?"

"Fine," he said, recovering his balance. "A little tired, that's all." She watched him go, her chest feeling heavier every minute.

She turned to Matt, meaning to say something to him, but at that moment the line of visitors reached the door.

"Show's on," he said, and crouched in the shadows.

Elena moved from room to room, troubleshooting. In years before, she had enjoyed this part of the night the most, watching the gruesome scenes being acted out and the delicious terror of the visitors, but tonight there was a feeling of dread and tension underlying all her thoughts. Tonight's the night, she thought again, and the ice in her chest seemed to thicken.

A Grim Reaper—or at least that was what she supposed the hooded figure in black robes was—passed by her, and she found herself absent-mindedly trying to remember if she had seen it at any of the Halloween parties. There was something familiar about the way the figure moved.

Bonnie exchanged a harassed smile with the tall, slender witch who was directing traffic into the Spider Room. Several junior high boys were slapping at the dangling rubber spiders and shouting and generally making a nuisance of themselves. Bonnie hustled them on into the Druid Room.

Here the strobe lights gave the scene a dreamlike quality. Bonnie felt a grim triumph to see Mr. Tanner stretched out on the stone altar, his white robes heavily stained with blood, his eyes glaring at the ceiling.

"Cool!" shouted one of the boys, racing up to the altar. Bonnie stood back and grinned, waiting for the bloody sacrifice to rear up and scare the wits out of the kid.

But Mr. Tanner didn't move, even when the boy plunged a hand into the pool of blood by the sacrifice's head.

That's strange, Bonnie thought, hurrying up to prevent the kid from grabbing the sacrificial knife.

"Don't do that," she snapped, so he held up his gory hand instead, and it showed red in every sharp flash of the strobe. Bonnie felt a sudden irrational fear that Mr. Tanner was going to wait until she bent over him and then make her jump. But he just kept staring at the ceiling.

"Mr. Tanner, are you okay? Mr. Tanner? Mr. Tanner!"

Not a movement, not a sound. Not a flicker of those wide white eyes. Don't touch him, something in Bonnie's mind told her suddenly and urgently. Don't touch him don't touch him don't touch . . .

Under the strobe lights she saw her own hand move forward, saw it grasp Mr. Tanner's shoulder and shake it, saw his head flop bonelessly toward her. Then she saw his throat.

Then she began to scream.

Elena heard the screams. They were shrill and sustained and unlike any other sounds in the Haunted House, and she knew at once that they were no joke.

Everything after that was a nightmare.

Reaching the Druid Room at a run, she saw a tableau, but not the one prepared for visitors. Bonnie was screaming, Meredith holding her shoulders. Three young boys were trying to get out of the curtained exit, and two bouncers were looking in, blocking their way. Mr. Tanner was lying on the stone altar, sprawled out, and his face . . .

"He's dead," Bonnie was sobbing, the screams turning into words. "Oh, God, the blood's real, and he's dead. I *touched* him, Elena, and he's dead, he's really dead. . . . "

People were coming into the room. Someone else began screaming and it spread, and then everyone was trying to get out, pushing each other in panic, knocking into the partitions.

"Get the lights on!" Elena shouted, and heard the shout taken up by others. "Meredith, quick, get to a phone, in the gym and call an ambulance, call the police. . . . Get those lights *on*!"

When the lights snapped on, Elena looked around, but she could see no adults, no one entitled to take charge of the situation. Part of her was ice-cold, her mind racing as it tried to think what to do next. Part of her was simply numb with horror. Mr. Tanner . . . She had never liked him, but somehow that only made it worse.

"Get all the kids out of here. Everybody but staff out," she said.

"No! Shut the doors! Don't let *anybody* out until the police get here," shouted a werewolf beside her, taking off his mask. Elena turned in astonishment at the voice and saw that it was not Matt, it was Tyler Smallwood.

He'd been allowed back in school only this week, and his face was still discolored from the beating he had taken at Stefan's hands. But his voice had the ring of authority, and Elena saw the bouncers close the exit door. She heard another door close across the gym.

Of the dozen or so people crowded into the Stonehenge area, Elena recognized only one as a worker. The rest were people she knew from school, but none she knew well. One of them, a boy dressed as a pirate, spoke to Tyler.

"You mean . . . you think somebody in here did it?"

"Somebody in here did it, all right," said Tyler. There was a queer, excited sound to his voice, as if he were almost enjoying this. He gestured to the pool of blood on the rock. "That's still liquid; it can't have happened too long ago. And look at the way his throat's cut. The killer must have done it with that." He pointed to the sacrificial knife.

"Then the killer might be here right now," whispered a girl in a kimono.

"And it's not hard to guess who it is," said Tyler. "Somebody who hated Tanner, who was always getting in arguments with him. Somebody who was arguing with him earlier tonight. I saw it."

So *you* were the werewolf in this room, thought Elena dazedly. But what were you doing here in the first place? You're not on staff.

"Somebody who has a history of violence," Tyler was continuing, his lips drawing back from his teeth. "Somebody who, for all we know, is a psychopath who came to Fell's Church just to kill."

"Tyler, what are you talking about?" Elena's dazed feeling had burst like a bubble. Furious, she stepped toward the tall, husky boy. "You're crazy!"

He gestured at her without looking at her. "So says his girlfriend—but maybe she's a little prejudiced."

"And maybe *you're* a little prejudiced, Tyler," said a voice from behind the crowd, and Elena saw a second werewolf pushing his way into the room. Matt.

"Oh, yeah? Well, why don't you tell us what you know about Salvatore? Where does he come from? Where's his family? Where did he get all that money?" Tyler turned to address the rest of the crowd. "Who knows *anything* about him?"

People were shaking their heads. Elena could see, in face after face, distrust blossoming. The distrust of anything unknown, anything different. And Stefan was different. He was the stranger in their midst, and just now they needed a scapegoat.

The girl in the kimono began, "I heard a rumor—"

"That's all anybody's heard, rumors!" Tyler said. "No one really *knows* a thing about him. But there's one thing I *do* know. The attacks in Fell's Church started the first week of school—*which was the week Stefan Salvatore came.*"

There was a swelling murmur at this, and Elena herself felt a shock of realization. Of course, it was all ridiculous, it was just a coincidence. But what Tyler was saying was true. The attacks had started when Stefan arrived.

"I'll tell you something else," shouted Tyler, gesturing at them to be quiet. "Listen to me! I'll tell you something else!" He waited until everyone was looking at him and then said slowly, impressively, "He was *in* the cemetery the night Vickie Bennett was attacked."

"Sure he was in the cemetery—rearranging your face," said Matt, but his voice lacked its usual strength. Tyler grabbed the comment and ran with it.

"Yes, and he almost killed me. And tonight somebody *did* kill Tanner. I don't know what *you* think, but *I* think he did it. I think he's the one!"

"But where is he?" shouted someone from the crowd.

Tyler looked around. "If he did it, he must still be here," he shouted. "Let's find him."

"Stefan hasn't done anything! Tyler—" cried Elena, but the noise from the crowd overrode her. Tyler's words were being taken up and repeated. *Find him . . . find him . . . find him.* Elena heard it pass from person to person. And the faces in the Druid Room were filled with more than distrust now; Elena could see anger and a thirst for vengeance in them too. The crowd had turned into something ugly, something beyond controlling.

"Where is he, Elena?" said Tyler, and she saw the blazing triumph in his eyes. He *was* enjoying this.

"I don't know," she said fiercely, wanting to hit him.

"He must still be here! Find him!" someone shouted, and then it seemed everyone was moving, pointing, pushing, at once. Partitions were being knocked down and shoved aside.

Elena's heart was pounding. This was no longer a crowd; it was a mob. She was terrified of what they would do to Stefan if they did find him. But if she tried to go warn him, she would lead Tyler right to him.

She looked around desperately. Bonnie was still staring into Mr. Tanner's dead face. No help there. She turned to scan the crowd again, and her eyes met Matt's.

He was looking confused and angry, his blond hair ruffled up, cheeks flushed and sweaty. Elena put all her strength of will into a look of pleading.

Please, Matt, she thought. You can't believe all this. You know it isn't true.

But his eyes showed that he *didn't* know. There was a tumult of bewilderment and agitation in them.

Please, thought Elena, gazing into those blue eyes, willing him to understand. Oh, please, Matt, only you can save him. Even if you don't believe, please try to trust . . . please ɩ ɩ ɩ

She saw the change come over his face, the confusion lifting as grim determination appeared. He stared at her another moment, eyes boring into hers, and nodded once. Then he turned and slipped into the milling, hunting crowd.

Matt knifed through the crowd cleanly until he got to the other side of the gym. There were some freshmen standing near the door to the boys' locker room; he brusquely ordered them to start moving fallen partitions, and when their attention was distracted he jerked the door open and ducked inside.

He looked around quickly, unwilling to shout. For that matter, he thought, Stefan must have heard all the racket going on in the gym. He'd probably already cut out. But then Matt saw the black-clad figure on the white tile floor.

"Stefan! What happened?" For a terrible instant, Matt thought he was looking down on a second dead body. But as he knelt by Stefan's side, he saw movement.

"Hey, you're okay, just sit up slowly . . . easy. Are you all right, Stefan?"

"Yes," said Stefan. He didn't look okay, Matt thought. His face was dead white and his pupils were dilated hugely. He looked disoriented and sick. "Thank you," he said.

"You may not thank me in a minute. Stefan, you've got to get out of here. Can't you hear them? They're after you."

Stefan turned toward the gym, as if listening. But there was no comprehension on his face. "Who's after me? Why?"

"Everybody. It doesn't matter. What matters is that you've got to get out before they come in here." As Stefan continued simply to stare blankly, he added, "There's been another attack, this time on Tanner, Mr. Tanner. He's dead, Stefan, and they think you did it."

Now, at last, he saw understanding come to Stefan's eyes. Understanding and horror and a kind of resigned defeat that was more frightening than anything Matt had seen tonight. He gripped Stefan's shoulder hard.

"I *know* you didn't," he said, and at that moment it was

true. "They'll realize that, too, when they can think again.
But meanwhile, you'd better get out."

"Get out . . . yes," said Stefan. The look of disorienta-
tion was gone, and there was a searing bitterness in the
way he pronounced the words. "I will . . . get out."

"Stefan . . . "

"Matt." The green eyes were dark and burning, and
Matt found he could not look away from them. "Is Elena
safe? Good. Then, take care of her. Please."

"Stefan, what are you talking about? You're innocent;
this will all blow over. . . .

"Just take care of her, Matt."

Matt stepped back, still looking into those compelling
green eyes. Then, slowly, he nodded.

"I will," he said quietly. And watched Stefan go.

lena stood within the circle of adults and police, waiting for a chance to escape. She knew that Matt had warned Stefan in time—his face told her that—but he hadn't been able to get close enough to speak with her.

At last, with all attention turned toward the body, she detached herself from the group and edged toward Matt.

"Stefan got out all right," he said, his eyes on the group of adults. "But he told me to take care of you, and I want you to stay here."

"To take *care* of me?" Alarm and suspicion flashed through Elena. Then, almost in a whisper, she said, "I see." She thought a moment and then spoke carefully. "Matt, I need to go wash my hands. Bonnie got blood on me. Wait here; I'll be back."

He started to say something in protest, but she was already moving away. She held up her stained hands in explanation as she reached the door of the girls' locker room, and the teacher who was now standing there let her through. Once in the locker room, however, she kept on going, right out the far door and into the darkened school. And from there, into the night.

Zuccone! Stefan thought, grabbing a bookcase and flinging it over, sending its contents flying. Fool! Blind, hateful fool. How could he have been so stupid?

Find a place with them here? Be accepted as one of them? He must have been mad to have thought it was possible.

He picked up one of the great heavy trunks and threw it across the room, where it crashed against the far wall, splintering a window. Stupid, *stupid*.

Who was after him? Everybody. Matt had said it. *"There's been another attack. . . . They think you did it."*

Well, for once it looked as if the *barbari*, the petty living humans with their fear of anything unknown, were right. How else did you explain what had happened? He had felt the weakness, the spinning, swirling confusion; and then darkness had taken him. When he'd awakened it was to hear Matt saying that another human had been pillaged, assaulted. Robbed this time not only of his blood, but of his life. How did you explain *that* unless he, Stefan, were the killer?

A killer was what he was. Evil. A creature born in the dark, destined to live and hunt and hide there forever. Well, why not kill, then? Why not fulfill his nature? Since he could not change it, he might as well revel in it. He would unleash his darkness upon this town that hated him, that hunted him even now.

But first . . . he was thirsty. His veins burned like a network of dry, hot wires. He needed to feed . . . soon . . . now.

The boarding house was dark. Elena knocked at the door but received no answer. Thunder cracked overhead. There was still no rain.

After the third barrage of knocking, she tried the door, and it opened. Inside, the house was silent and pitch black. She made her way to the staircase by feel and went up it.

The second landing was just as dark, and she stumbled, trying to find the bedroom with the stairway to the third floor. A faint light showed at the top of the stairs, and she climbed toward it, feeling oppressed by the walls, which seemed to close in on her from either side.

The light came from beneath the closed door. Elena tapped on it lightly and quickly. "Stefan," she whispered, and then she called more loudly, "Stefan, it's me."

No answer. She grasped the knob and pushed the door open, peering around the side. "Stefan—"

She was speaking to an empty room.

And a room filled with chaos. It looked as if some great wind had torn through, leaving destruction in its path. The trunks that had stood in corners so sedately were lying at grotesque angles, their lids gaping open, their contents strewn about the floor. One window was shattered. All Stefan's possessions, all the things he had kept so carefully and seemed to prize, were scattered like rubbioh.

Terror swept through Elena. The fury, the violence in this scene of devastation were painfully clear, and they made her feel almost giddy. Somebody who has a history of violence, Tyler had said.

I don't care, she thought, anger surging up to push back the fear. I don't care about anything, Stefan; I still want to see you. But where are you?

The trapdoor in the ceiling was open, and cold air was blowing down. Oh, thought Elena, and she had a sudden chill of fear. That roof was so high. . . .

She'd never climbed the ladder to the widow's walk before, and her long skirt made it difficult. She emerged through the trapdoor slowly, kneeling on the roof and then standing up. She saw a dark figure in the corner, and she moved toward it quickly.

"Stefan, I had to come—" she began, and broke off short, because a flash of lightning lit the sky just as the figure in the corner whirled around. And then it was as if every foreboding and fear and nightmare she'd ever had were coming true all at once. It was beyond screaming at; it was beyond anything.

Oh, God . . . no. Her mind refused to make sense of what her eyes were seeing. No. No. She wouldn't look at this, she wouldn't believe it. . . .

But she could not help seeing. Even if she could have shut her eyes, every detail of the scene was etched upon her memory. As if the flash of lightning had seared it onto her brain forever.

Stefan. Stefan, so sleek and elegant in his ordinary clothes, in his black leather jacket with the collar turned up. Stefan, with his dark hair like one of the roiling storm clouds behind him. Stefan had been caught in that flash of light, half turned toward her, his body twisted into a bestial crouch, with a snarl of animal fury on his face.

And blood. That arrogant, sensitive, sensual mouth was smeared with blood. It showed ghastly red against the pallor of his skin, against the sharp whiteness of his bared teeth. In his hands was the limp body of a mourning dove, white as those teeth, wings outspread. Another lay on the ground at his feet, like a crumpled and discarded hand-kerchief.

"Oh, God, no," Elena whispered. She went on whispering it, backing away, scarcely aware that she was doing either. Her mind simply could not cope with this horror; her thoughts were running wildly in panic, like mice trying to escape a cage. She wouldn't believe this, she wouldn't *believe*. Her body was filled with unbearable tension, her heart was bursting, her head reeling.

"Oh, God, *no*—"

"Elena!" More terrible than anything else was this, to see *Stefan* looking at her out of that animal face, to see the snarl changing into a look of shock and desperation. "Elena, please. Please, don't . . . "

"Oh, God, *no*!" The screams were trying to rip their way out of her throat. She backed farther away, stumbling, as he took a step toward her. "No!"

"Elena, please—be careful—" That terrible thing, the thing with Stefan's face, was coming after her, green eyes burning. She flung herself backward as he took another step, his hand outstretched. That long, slender-fingered hand that had stroked her hair so gently—

"Don't *touch* me!" she cried. And then she did scream, as her motion brought her back against the iron railing of the widow's walk. It was iron that had been there for nearly a century and a half, and in places it was nearly rusted through. Elena's panicked weight against it was too much, and she felt it give way. She heard the tearing sound of overstressed metal and wood mingling with her own shriek. And then there was nothing behind her, nothing to grab on to, and she was falling.

In that instant, she saw the seething purple clouds, the dark bulk of the house beside her. It seemed that she had enough time to see them clearly, and to feel an infinity of terror as she screamed and fell, and fell.

But the terrible, shattering impact never came. Suddenly there were arms around her, supporting her in the void. There was a dull thud and the arms tightened, weight giving against her, absorbing the crash. Then all was still.

She held herself motionless within the circle of those arms, trying to get her bearings. Trying to believe yet another unbelievable thing. She had fallen from a three-story roof, and yet she was alive. She was standing in the garden behind the boarding house, in the utter silence between claps of thunder, with fallen leaves on the ground where her broken body should be.

Slowly, she brought her gaze upward to the face of the one who held her. Stefan.

There had been too much fear, too many blows tonight. She could react no longer. She could only stare up at him with a kind of wonder.

There was such sadness in his eyes. Those eyes that had burned like green ice were now dark and empty, hopeless. The same look that she'd seen that first night in his room, only now it was worse. For now there was self-hatred mixed with the sorrow, and bitter condemnation. She couldn't bear it.

"Stefan," she whispered, feeling that sadness enter her own soul. She could still see the tinge of red on his lips, but now it awakened a thrill of pity along with the instinctive horror. To be so alone, so alien and so alone . . .

"Oh, Stefan," she whispered.

There was no answer in those bleak, lost eyes. "Come," he said quietly, and led her back toward the house.

Stefan felt a rush of shame as they reached the third story and the destruction that was his room. That Elena, of all people, should see this was insupportable. But then, perhaps it was also fitting that she should see what he truly was, what he could do.

She moved slowly, dazedly to the bed and sat. Then she looked up at him, her shadowed eyes meeting his. "Tell me," was all she said.

He laughed shortly, without humor, and saw her flinch. It made him hate himself more. "What do you need to know?" he said. He put a foot on the lid of an overturned trunk and faced her almost defiantly, indicating the room with a gesture. "Who did this? I did."

"You're strong," she said, her eyes on a capsized trunk. Her gaze lifted upward, as if she were remembering what had happened on the roof. "And quick."

"Stronger than a human," he said, with deliberate emphasis on the last word. Why didn't she cringe from him now, why didn't she look at him with the loathing he had seen before? He didn't care what she thought any longer. "My reflexes are faster, and I'm more resilient. I have to be. I'm a hunter," he said harshly.

Something in her look made him remember how she had interrupted him. He wiped his mouth with the back of his hand, then went quickly to pick up a glass of water that stood unharmed on the nightstand. He could feel her eyes on him as he drank it and wiped his mouth again. Oh, he still cared what she thought, all right.

"You can eat and drink . . . other things," she said.

"I don't need to," he said quietly, feeling weary and subdued. "I don't need anything else." He whipped around suddenly and felt passionate intensity rise in him again. "You said I was quick—but that's just what I'm not. Have you ever heard the saying 'the quick and the dead,' Elena? Quick means living; it means those who have life. I'm the other half."

He could see that she was trembling. But her voice was calm, and her eyes never left his. "Tell me," she said again. "Stefan, I have a right to know."

He recognized those words. And they were as true as when she had first said them. "Yes, I suppose you do," he said, and his voice was tired and hard. He stared at the broken window for a few heartbeats and then looked back at her and spoke flatly. "I was born in the late fifteenth century. Do you believe that?"

She looked at the objects that lay where he'd scattered them from the bureau with one furious sweep of his arm. The florins, the agate cup, his dagger. "Yes," she said softly. "Yes, I believe it."

"And you want to know more? How I came to be what I am?" When she nodded, he turned to the window again. How could he tell her? He, who had avoided questions for so long, who had become such an expert at hiding and deceiving.

There was only one way, and that was to tell the absolute truth, concealing nothing. To lay it all before her, what he had never offered to any other soul.

And he wanted to do it. Even though he knew it would make her turn away from him in the end, he needed to show Elena what he was.

And so, staring into the darkness outside the window, where flashes of blue brilliance occasionally lit the sky, he began.

He spoke dispassionately, without emotion, carefully choosing his words. He told her of his father, that solid Renaissance man, and of his world in Florence and at their country estate. He told her of his studies and his ambitions. Of his brother, who was so different than he, and of the ill feeling between them.

"I don't know when Damon started hating me," he said. "It was always that way, as long as I can remember. Maybe it was because my mother never really recovered from my birth. She died a few years later. Damon loved her very much, and I always had the feeling that he blamed me." He paused and swallowed. "And then, later, there was a girl."

"The one I remind you of?" Elena said softly. He nodded. "The one," she said, more hesitantly, "who gave you the ring?"

He glanced down at the silver ring on his finger, then met her eyes. Then, slowly, he drew out the ring he wore on the chain beneath his shirt and looked at it.

"Yes. This was her ring," he said. "Without such a talisman, we die in sunlight as if in a fire."

"Then she was . . . like you?"

"She made me what I am." Haltingly, he told her about Katherine. About Katherine's beauty and sweetness, and about his love for her. And about Damon's.

"She was too gentle, filled with too much affection," he said at last, painfully. "She gave it to everyone, including my brother. But finally, we told her she had to choose between us. And then . . . she came to me."

The memory of that night, of that sweet, terrible night came sweeping back. She had come to him. And he had been so happy, so full of awe and joy. He tried to tell Elena about that, to find the words. All that night he had been so happy, and even the next morning, when he had awakened and she was gone, he had been throned on highest bliss. . . .

It might almost have been a dream, but the two little wounds on his neck were real. He was surprised to find that they did not hurt and that they seemed to be partially healed already. They were hidden by the high neck of his shirt.

Her blood burned in his veins now, he thought, and the very words made his heart race. She had given her strength to him; she had chosen him.

He even had a smile for Damon when they met at the designated place that evening. Damon had been absent from the house all day, but he showed up in the meticulously landscaped garden precisely on time, and stood lounging against a tree, adjusting his cuff. Katherine was late.

"Perhaps she is tired," Stefan suggested, watching the melon-colored sky fade into deep midnight blue. He tried to keep the shy smugness from his voice. "Perhaps she needs more rest than usual."

Damon glanced at him sharply, his dark eyes piercing under the shock of black hair. "Perhaps," he said on a rising note, as if he would have said more.

But then they heard a light step on the path, and Katherine appeared between the box hedges. She was wearing her white gown, and she was as beautiful as an angel.

She had a smile for both of them. Stefan returned the smile politely, speaking their secret only with his eyes. Then he waited.

"You asked me to make my choice," she said, looking first at him and then at his brother. "And now you have come at the hour I appointed, and I will tell you what I have chosen."

She held up her small hand, the one with the ring on it, and Stefan looked at the stone, realizing it was the same deep blue as the evening sky. It was as if Katherine carried a piece of the night with her, always.

"You have both seen this ring," she said quietly. "And you know that without it I would die. It is not easy to have such talismans made, but fortunately my woman Gudren is clever. And there are many silversmiths in Florence."

Stefan was listening without comprehension, but when she turned to him he smiled again, encouragingly.

"And so," she said, gazing into his eyes. "I have had a present made for you." She took his hand and pressed something into it. When he looked he saw that it was a ring in the same fashion as her own, but larger and heavier, and wrought in silver instead of gold.

"You do not need it yet to face the sun," she said softly, smiling. "But very soon you will."

Pride and rapture made him mute. He reached for her hand to kiss it, wanting to take her into his arms right then, even, in front of Damon. But Katherine was turning away.

"And for you," she said, and Stefan thought his ears must be betraying him, for surely the warmth, the fondness in Katherine's voice could not be for his brother, "for you, also. You will need it very soon as well."

Stefan's eyes must be traitors, too. They were showing him what was impossible, what could not be. Into Damon's hand Katherine was putting a ring just like his own.

The silence that followed was absolute, like the silence after the world's ending.

"Katherine—" Stefan could barely force out the words. "How can you give that to *him*? After what we shared—"

"What *you* shared?" Damon's voice was like the crack of a whip, and he turned on Stefan angrily. "Last night she came to *me*. The choice is already made." And Damon jerked down his high collar to show two tiny wounds in his throat. Stefan stared at them, fighting down the bright sickness. They were identical to his own wounds.

He shook his head in utter bewilderment. "But, Katherine . . . it was not a dream. You came to *me*. . . . "

"I came to both of you." Katherine's voice was tranquil,

even pleased, and her eyes were serene. She smiled at Damon and then at Stefan in turn. "It has weakened me, but I am so glad I did. Don't you see?" she continued as they stared at her, too stunned to speak. "This is my choice! I love you both, and I will not give either of you up. Now we all three will be together, and be happy."

"Happy—" Stefan choked out.

"Yes, happy! The three of us will be companions, joyous companions, forever." Her voice rose with elation, and the light of a radiant child shone in her eyes. "We will be together always, never feeling sickness, never growing old, until the end of time! That is my choice."

"Happy . . . with *him*?" Damon's voice was shaking with fury, and Stefan saw that his normally self-contained brother was white with rage. "With this *boy* standing between us, this prating, mouthing paragon of virtue? I can barely stand the sight of him now. I wish to God that I should never see him again, never hear his voice again!"

"And I wish the same of *you*, brother," snarled Stefan, his heart tearing in his breast. This was Damon's fault; Damon had poisoned Katherine's mind so that she no longer knew what she was doing. "And I have half a mind to make sure of it," he added savagely.

Damon did not mistake his meaning. "Then get your sword, if you can find it," he hissed back, his eyes black with menace.

"Damon, Stefan, please! Please, no!" Katherine cried, putting herself between them, catching Stefan's arm. She looked from one to the other, her blue eyes wide with shock and bright with unshed tears. "Think of what you are saying. You are brothers."

"By no fault of mine," Damon grated, making the words a curse.

"But can you not make peace? For me, Damon . . . Stefan? *Please.*"

Part of Stefan wanted to melt at Katherine's desperate look, at her tears. But wounded pride and jealousy were too strong, and he knew his face was as hard, as unyielding, as Damon's.

"No," he said. "We cannot. It must be one or the other, Katherine. I will never share you with *him.*"

Katherine's hand fell away from his arm, and the tears fell from her eyes, great droplets that splashed onto the white gown. She caught her breath in a wrenching sob. Then, still weeping, she picked up her skirts and ran.

"And then Damon took the ring she had given him and put it on," Stefan said, his voice hoarse with use and emotion. "And he said to me, 'I'll have her yet, *brother.*' And then he walked away." He turned, blinking as if he'd come into a bright light from the dark, and looked at Elena.

She was sitting quite still on the bed, watching him

with those eyes that were so much like Katherine's. Especially now, when they were filled with sorrow and dread. But Elena did not run. She spoke to him.

"And . . . what happened then?"

Stefan's hands clenched violently, reflexively, and he jerked away from the window. Not that memory. He could not endure that memory himself, much less try to *speak* it. How could he do that? How could he take Elena down into that darkness and show her the terrible things lurking there?

"*No,*" he said. "I can't. I *can't.*"

"You have to tell me," she said softly. "Stefan, it's the end of the story, isn't it? That's what's behind all your walls, that's what you're afraid to let me see. But you must let me see it. Oh, Stefan, you can't stop now."

He could feel the horror reaching for him, the yawning pit he had seen so clearly, felt so clearly that day long ago. The day when it had all ended—when it had all begun.

He felt his hand taken, and when he looked he saw Elena's fingers closed about it, giving him warmth, giving him strength. Her eyes were on his. "Tell me."

"You want to know what happened next, what became of Katherine?" he whispered. She nodded, her eyes nearly blind but still steady. "I'll tell you, then. She died the next day. My brother Damon and I, we killed her."

14

Elena felt her flesh creep at the words.

"You don't mean that," she said shakily. She remembered what she had seen on the roof, the blood smeared on Stefan's lips, and she forced herself not to recoil from him. "Stefan, I know you. You couldn't have done that. . . . "

He ignored her protestations, just went on staring with eyes that burned like the green ice at the bottom of a glacier. He was looking through her, into some incomprehensible distance. "As I lay in bed that night, I hoped against hope that she would come. Already I was noticing some of the changes in myself. I could see better in the dark; it seemed I could hear better. I felt stronger than ever before, full of some elemental energy. And I was hungry.

"It was a hunger I had never imagined. At dinner I found that ordinary food and drink did nothing to satisfy it. I couldn't understand that. And then I saw the white neck of one of the serving girls, and I knew why." He drew a long breath, his eyes dark and tortured. "That night, I resisted the need, though it took all my will. I was thinking of Katherine, and praying she would come to me. Praying!" He gave a short laugh. "If a creature like me can pray."

Elena's fingers were numb within his grasp, but she tried to tighten them, to send him reassurance. "Go on, Stefan."

He had no trouble speaking now. He seemed almost to have forgotten her presence, as if he were telling this story to himself.

"The next morning the need was stronger. It was as if my own veins were dry and cracked, desperate for moisture. I knew that I couldn't stand it for long.

"I went to Katherine's chambers. I meant to ask her, to plead with her—" His voice cracked. He paused and then went on. "But Damon was there already, waiting outside her rooms. I could see that *he* hadn't resisted the need. The glow of his skin, the spring in his step, told me that. He looked as smug as the cat who's had the cream.

"But he hadn't had Katherine. 'Knock all you like,' he said to me, 'but the female dragon inside won't let you past. I've tried already. Shall we overpower her, you and I?'

"I wouldn't answer him. The look on his face, that sly, self-satisfied look, repelled me. I pounded on that door to wake . . . " He faltered, and then gave another humorless laugh. "I was going to say, 'to wake the dead.' But the dead aren't so hard to wake after all, are they?" After a moment, he went on.

"The maid, Gudren, opened the door. She had a face like a flat white plate, and eyes like black glass. I asked her if I could see her mistress. I expected to be told that Katherine was asleep, but instead Gudren just looked at me, then at Damon over my shoulder.

"'I would not tell *him*,' she said at last, 'but I will tell you. My lady Katerina is not within. She went out early this morning, to walk in the gardens. She said she had much need of thought.'

"I was surprised. 'Early this morning?' I said.

"'Yes,' she replied. She looked at both Damon and me without liking. 'My mistress was very unhappy last night,' she said meaningfully. 'All night long, she wept.'

"When she said that, a strange feeling came over me. It wasn't just shame and grief that Katherine should be so unhappy. It was fear. I forgot my hunger and weakness. I even forgot my enmity for Damon. I was filled with haste and a great driving urgency. I turned to Damon and told him that we had to find Katherine, and to my surprise he just nodded.

"We began to search the gardens, calling Katherine's name. I remember just what everything looked like that day. The sun was shining on the high cypress trees and the pines in the garden. Damon and I hurried between them, moving more and more quickly, and calling. We kept calling her . . . "

Elena could feel the tremors in Stefan's body, communicated to her through his tightly gripping fingers. He was breathing rapidly but shallowly.

"We had almost reached the end of the gardens when I remembered a place that Katherine had loved. It was a little way out onto the grounds, a low wall beside a lemon tree. I started there, shouting for her. But as I got closer, I stopped shouting. I felt . . . a fear—a terrible premonition. And I knew I mustn't—mustn't go—"

"Stefan!" said Elena. He was hurting her, his fingers biting into her own, crushing them. The tremors racing through his body were growing, becoming shudders. "Stefan, please!"

But he gave no sign that he heard her. "It was like—a nightmare—everything happening so slowly. I couldn't move—and yet I had to. I had to keep walking. With each step, the fear grew stronger. I could smell it. A smell like burned fat. I mustn't go there—I don't want to see it—"

His voice had become high, and urgent, his breath coming in gasps. His eyes were wide and dilated, like a terrified child's. Elena gripped his viselike fingers with her other hand, enfolding them completely. "Stefan it's all right. You're not there. You're here with me."

"I don't want to see it—but I can't help it. There's something white. Something white under the tree. Don't make me look at it!"

"Stefan, Stefan, look at me!"

He was beyond hearing. His words came in heaving spasms, as if he could not control them, could not get them out fast enough. "I can't go any closer—but I do. I see the tree, the wall. And that white. Behind the tree. White with gold underneath. And then I know, I know, and I'm moving toward it because it's her dress. Katherine's white dress. And I get around the tree and I see it on the ground and it's true. It's Katherine's dress"— his voice rose and broke in unimaginable horror—"but Katherine isn't in it."

Elena felt a chill, as if her body had been plunged into ice water. Her skin rose in goose-flesh, and she tried to speak to him but couldn't. He was rattling on as if he could keep the terror away if he kept on talking.

"Katherine isn't there, so maybe it's all a joke, but her dress is on the ground and it's full of ashes. Like the ashes in the hearth, just like that, only these smell of burned flesh. They stink. The smell is making me sick and faint. Beside the sleeve of the dress is a piece of parchment.

And on a rock, on a rock a little way away is a ring. A ring with a blue stone, Katherine's ring. Katherine's ring . . . " Suddenly, he called out in a terrible voice, "Katherine, what have you *done*?" Then he fell to his knees, releasing Elena's fingers at last, to bury his face in his hands.

Elena held him as he was gripped by wracking sobs. She held his shoulders, pulling him to her lap. "Katherine took the ring off," she whispered. It was not a question. "She exposed herself to the sun."

His harsh sobs went on and on, as she held him to the full skirts of the blue gown, stroking his quivering shoulders. She murmured nonsense meant to soothe him, pushing away her own horror. And, presently, he quieted and lifted his head. He spoke thickly, but he seemed to have returned to the present, to have come back.

"The parchment was a note, for me and for Damon. It said she had been selfish, wanting to have both of us. It said—she couldn't bear to be the cause of strife between us. She hoped that once she was gone we would no longer hate each other. She did it to bring us together."

"Oh, Stefan," whispered Elena. She felt burning tears fill her own eyes in sympathy. "Oh, Stefan, I'm so sorry. But don't you see, after all this time, that what Katherine did was wrong? It was selfish, even, and it was *her* choice. In a way, it had nothing to do with you, or with Damon."

Stefan shook his head as if to shake off the truth of the

words. "She gave her life . . . for that. We killed her." He was sitting up now. But his eyes were still dilated, great disks of black, and he had the look of a small bewildered boy.

"Damon came up behind me. He took the note and read it. And then—I think he went mad. We were both mad. I had picked up Katherine's ring, and he tried to take it. He shouldn't have. We struggled. We said terrible things to each other. We each blamed the other for what had happened. I don't remember how we got back to the house; but suddenly I had my sword. We were fighting. I wanted to destroy that arrogant face forever, to kill him. I remember my father shouting from the house. We fought harder, to finish it before he reached us.

"And we were well matched. But Damon had always been stronger, and that day he seemed faster, too, as if he had changed more than I had. And so while my father was still shouting from the window I felt Damon's blade get past my guard. Then I felt it enter my heart."

Elena stared, aghast, but he went on without pause. "I felt the pain of the steel, I felt it stab through me, deep, deep inside. All the way through, a hard thrust. And then the strength poured out of me and I fell. I lay there on the paved ground."

He looked up at Elena and finished simply, "And that is how . . . I died."

Elena sat frozen, as if the ice she'd felt in her chest earlier tonight had flooded out and trapped her.

"Damon came and stood over me and bent down. I could hear my father's cries from far away, and screams from the household, but all I could see was Damon's face. Those black eyes that were like a moonless night. I wanted to hurt him for what he had done to me. For everything he had done to me, and to Katherine." Stefan was quiet a moment, and then he said, almost dreamily, "And so I lifted my sword and I killed him. With the last of my strength, I stabbed my brother through the heart."

The storm had moved on, and through the broken window Elena could hear soft night noises, the chirp of crickets, the wind sifting through trees. In Stefan's room, it was very still.

"I knew nothing more until I woke up in my tomb," said Stefan. He leaned back, away from her, and shut his eyes. His face was pinched and weary, but that awful childlike dreaminess was gone.

"Both Damon and I had had just enough of Katherine's blood to keep us from truly dying. Instead we changed. We woke together in our tomb, dressed in our best clothing, laid on slabs side by side. We were too weak to hurt each other anymore; the blood had been just barely enough. And we were confused. I called to Damon, but he ran outside into the night.

"Fortunately, we had been buried with the rings Katherine had given us. And I found her ring in my pocket." As if unconsciously, Stefan reached up to stroke the golden circlet. "I suppose they thought she had given it to me.

"I tried to go home. That was stupid. The servants screamed at the sight of me and ran to fetch a priest. I ran, too. Into the only place where I was safe, into the dark.

"And that is where I've stayed ever since. It's where I belong, Elena. I killed Katherine with my pride and my jealousy, and I killed Damon with my hatred. But I did worse than kill my brother. I damned him.

"If he hadn't died then, with Katherine's blood so strong in his veins, he would have had a chance. In time the blood would have grown weaker, and then passed away. He would have become a normal human again. By killing him then, I condemned him to live in the night. I took away his only chance of salvation."

Stefan laughed bitterly. "Do you know what the name Salvatore means in Italian, Elena? It means salvation, savior. I'm named that, and for St. Stephen, the first Christian martyr. And I damned my brother to hell."

"No," said Elena. And then, in a stronger voice, she said, "No, Stefan. He damned himself. He killed *you*. But what happened to him after that?"

"For a while he joined one of the Free Companies, ruthless mercenaries whose business was to rob and plunder. He wandered across the country with them, fighting and drinking the blood of his victims.

"I was living beyond the city gates by then, half starved, preying on animals, an animal myself. For a long time, I heard nothing about Damon. Then one day I heard his voice in my mind.

"He was stronger than I, because he was drinking human blood. And killing. Humans have the strongest life essence, and their blood gives power. And when they're killed, somehow the life essence they give is strongest of all. It's as if in those last moments of terror and struggle the soul is the most vibrant. Because Damon killed humans, he was able to draw on the Powers more than I was."

"What . . . powers?" said Elena. A thought was growing in her mind.

"Strength, as you said, and quickness. A sharpening of all the senses, especially at night. Those are the basics. We can also . . . feel minds. We can sense their presence, and sometimes the nature of their thoughts. We can cast confusion about weaker minds, either to overwhelm them or to bend them to our will. There are others. With enough human blood we can change our shapes, become animals. And the more you kill, the stronger all the Powers become.

"Damon's voice in my mind was very strong. He said he was now the *condottieri* of his own company and he was coming back to Florence. He said that if I was there when he arrived he would kill me. I believed him, and I left. I've seen him once or twice since then. The threat is always the same, and he's always more powerful. Damon's made the most of his nature, and he seems to glory in its darkest side.

"But it's my nature, too. The same darkness is inside me. I thought that I could conquer it, but I was wrong. That's why I came here, to Fell's Church. I thought if I settled in some small town, far away from the old memories, I might escape the darkness. And instead, tonight, I killed a man."

"*No,*" said Elena forcefully. "I don't believe that, Stefan." His story had filled her with horror and pity . . . and fear, too. She admitted that. But her disgust had vanished, and there was one thing she was sure about. Stefan wasn't a murderer. "What happened tonight, Stefan? Did you argue with Tanner?"

"I . . . don't remember," he said bleakly. "I used the Power to persuade him to do what you wanted. Then I left. But later I felt the dizziness and the weakness come over me. As it has before." He looked up at her directly. "The last time it happened was in the cemetery, right by the church, the night Vickie Bennett was attacked."

"But you didn't do that. You *couldn't* have done that. . . . Stefan?"

"I don't know," he said harshly. "What other explanation is there? And I did take blood from the old man under the bridge, that night you girls ran away from the graveyard. I would have sworn I didn't take enough to harm him, but he almost died. And I was there when both Vickie and Tanner were attacked."

"But you don't remember attacking them," said Elena, relieved. The idea that had been growing in her mind was now almost a certainty.

"What difference does it make? Who else could have done it, if not me?"

"Damon," said Elena.

He flinched, and she saw his shoulders tighten again. "It's a nice thought. I hoped at first that there might be some explanation like that. That it might be someone else, someone like my brother. But I've searched with my mind and found nothing, no other presence. The simplest explanation is that I'm the killer."

"No," said Elena, "you don't understand. I don't just mean that someone like Damon might do the things we've seen. I mean Damon is here, in Fell's Church. I've seen him."

Stefan just stared at her.

"It must be him," Elena said, taking a deep breath.

"I've seen him twice now, maybe three times. Stefan, you just told me a long story, and now I've got one to tell you."

As quickly and simply as she could, she told him about what had happened in the gym, and at Bonnie's house. His lips tightened into a white line as she told him how Damon had tried to kiss her. Her cheeks grew hot as she remembered her own response, how she had almost given in to him. But she told Stefan everything.

About the crow, too, and all the other strange things that had happened since she had come home from France.

"And, Stefan, I think Damon was at the Haunted House tonight," she finished. "Just after you felt dizzy in the front room, someone passed me. He was dressed up like—like Death, in black robes and a hood, and I couldn't see his face. But something about the way he moved was familiar. It was him, Stefan. Damon was there."

"But that still wouldn't explain the other times. Vickie and the old man. I *did* take blood from the old man." Stefan's face was taut, as if he were almost afraid to hope.

"But you said yourself you didn't take enough to harm him. Stefan, who knows what happened to that man after you left? Wouldn't it be the easiest thing in the world for Damon to attack him then? Especially if Damon's been spying on you all along, maybe in some other form . . . "

"Like a crow," murmured Stefan.

"Like a crow. And as for Vickie . . . Stefan, you said that you can cast confusion over weaker minds, overpower them. Couldn't that be what Damon was doing to you? Overpowering your mind as you can overpower a human's?"

"Yes, and shielding his presence from me." There was mounting excitement in Stefan's voice. "That's why he hasn't answered my calls. He wanted—"

"He wanted just what's happened to happen. He wanted you to doubt yourself, to think you were a killer. *But it isn't true, Stefan.* Oh, Stefan, you know that now, and you don't have to be afraid anymore." She stood up, feeling joy and relief course through her. Out of this hideous night, something wonderful had come.

"That's why you've been so distant with me, isn't it?" she said, holding out her hands to him. "Because you're afraid of what you might do. But there's no need for that any longer."

"*Isn't there?*" He was breathing quickly again, and he eyed her outstretched hands as if they were two snakes. "You think there's no reason to be afraid? Damon may have attacked those people, but he doesn't control my thoughts. And you don't know what I've thought about you."

Elena kept her voice level. "You don't want to hurt me," she said positively.

"No? There have been times, watching you in public, when I could scarcely bear not to touch you. When I was so tempted by your white throat, your little white throat with the faint blue veins beneath the skin . . . " His eyes were fixed on her neck in a way that reminded her of Damon's eyes, and she felt her heartbeat step up. "Times when I thought I would grab you and force you right there in the school."

"There's no need to force me," said Elena. She could feel her pulse everywhere now; in her wrists and the inside of her elbows—and in her throat. "I've made my decision, Stefan," she said softly, holding his eyes. "I want to."

He swallowed thickly. "You don't know what you're asking for."

"I think I do. You told me how it was with Katherine, Stefan. I want it to be like that with us. I don't mean I want you to change me. But we can share a little without that happening, can't we? I know," she added, even more softly, "how much you loved Katherine. But she's gone now, and I'm here. And I love you, Stefan. I want to be with you."

"You don't know what you're talking about!" He was standing rigid, his face furious, his eyes anguished. "If I once let go, what's to *keep* me from changing you, or killing you? The passion is stronger than you can imagine.

Don't you understand yet what I am, what I can do?"

She stood there and looked at him quietly, her chin raised slightly. It seemed to enrage him.

"Haven't you seen enough yet? Or do I have to show you more? Can't you picture what I might do to you?" He strode over to the cold fireplace and snatched out a long piece of wood, thicker than both Elena's wrists together. With one motion, he snapped it in two like a match stick. "*Your* fragile bones," he said.

Across the room was a pillow from the bed; he caught it up and with a slash of his nails left the silk cover in ribbons. "*Your* soft skin." Then he moved toward Elena with preternatural quickness; he was there and had hold of her shoulders before she knew what was happening. He stared into her face a moment, then, with a savage hiss that raised the hairs at the nape of her neck, drew his lips back.

It was the same snarl she'd seen on the roof, those white teeth bared, the canines grown to unbelievable length and sharpness. They were the fangs of a predator, a hunter. "*Your* white neck," he said in a distorted voice.

Elena stood paralyzed another instant, gazing as if compelled into that chilling visage, and then something deep in her unconscious took over. She reached up within the restraining circle of his arms and caught his face between her two hands. His cheeks were cool against her palms. She held him that way, softly, so softly, as if to reprove his hard grip on her bare shoulders. And she saw the confusion slowly come to his face, as he realized she was not doing it to fight him or to shove him away.

Elena waited until that confusion reached his eyes, shattering his gaze, becoming almost a look of pleading. She knew that her own face was fearless, soft yet intense, her lips slightly parted. They were both breathing quickly now, together, in rhythm. Elena could feel it when he started to shake, trembling as he had when the memories of Katherine had become too much to bear. Then, very gently and deliberately, she drew that snarling mouth down to her own.

He tried to oppose her. But her gentleness was stronger than all his inhuman strength. She shut her eyes and thought only of Stefan, not of the dreadful things she had learned tonight but of Stefan, who had stroked her hair as lightly as if she might break in his hands. She thought of that, and she kissed the predatory mouth that had threatened her a few minutes ago.

She felt the change, the transformation in his mouth as he yielded, responding helplessly to her, meeting her soft kisses with equal softness. She felt the shudder go through Stefan's body as the hard grip on her shoulders softened, too, becoming an embrace. And she knew she'd won.

"You will never hurt me," she whispered.

It was as if they were kissing away all the fear and desolation and loneliness inside them. Elena felt passion surge through her like summer lightning, and she could sense the answering passion in Stefan. But infusing everything else was a gentleness almost frightening in its intensity. There was no need for haste or roughness, Elena thought as Stefan gently guided her to sit down.

Gradually, the kisses grew more urgent, and Elena felt the summer lightning flicker all through her body, charging it, making her heart pound and her breath catch. It made her feel strangely soft and dizzy, made her shut her eyes and let her head fall back in abandon.

It's time, Stefan, she thought. And, very gently, she drew his mouth down again, this time to her throat. She felt his lips graze her skin, felt his breath warm and cool at once. Then she felt the sharp sting.

But the pain faded almost instantly. It was replaced by a feeling of pleasure that made her tremble. A great rushing sweetness filled her, flowing through her to Stefan.

At last she found herself gazing into his face, into a face that at last had no barriers against her, no walls. And the look she saw there made her feel weak.

"Do you trust me?" he whispered. And when she simply nodded, he held her eyes and reached for something beside the bed. It was the dagger. She regarded it without fear, and then fixed her eyes again on his face.

He never looked away from her as he unsheathed it and made a small cut at the base of his throat. Elena looked at it wide-eyed, at the blood as bright as holly berries, but when he urged her forward she did not try to resist him.

Afterward he just held her a long time, while the crickets outside made their music. Finally, he stirred.

"I wish you could stay here," he whispered. "I wish you could stay forever. But you can't."

"I know," she said, equally quiet. Their eyes met again in silent communion. There was so much to say, so many reasons to be together. "Tomorrow," she said. Then, leaning against his shoulder, she whispered, "Whatever happens, Stefan, I'll be with you. Tell me you believe that."

His voice was hushed, muffled in her hair. "Oh, Elena, I believe it. Whatever happens, we'll be together."

15

As soon as he left Elena at her house, Stefan went to the woods.

He took Old Creek Road, driving under the sullen clouds through which no patch of sky could be seen, to the place where he had parked on the first day of school.

Leaving the car, he tried to retrace his steps exactly to the clearing where he had seen the crow. His hunter's instincts helped him, recalling the shape of this bush and that knotted root, until he stood in the open place ringed with ancient oak trees.

Here. Under this blanket of dingy-brown leaves, some of the rabbit's bones might even remain.

Taking a long breath to still himself, to gather his Powers, he cast out a probing, demanding thought.

And for the first time since he'd come to Fell's Church, he felt the flicker of a reply. But it seemed faint and wavering, and he could not locate it in space.

He sighed and turned around—and stopped dead.

Damon stood before him, arms crossed over his chest, lounging against the largest oak tree. He looked as if he might have been there for hours.

"So," said Stefan heavily, "it is true. It's been a long time, brother."

"Not as long as you think, *brother*." Stefan remembered that voice, that velvety, ironical voice. "I've kept track of you over the years," Damon said calmly. He flicked a bit of bark from the sleeve of his leather jacket as casually as he had once arranged his brocade cuffs. "But then, you wouldn't know that, would you? Ah, no, your Powers are as weak as ever."

"Be careful, Damon," Stefan said softly, dangerously. "Be very careful tonight. I'm not in a tolerant mood."

"St. Stefan in a pique? Imagine. You're distressed, I suppose, because of my little excursions into your territory. I only did it because I wanted to be close to you. Brothers should be close."

"You *killed* tonight. And you tried to make me think I'd done it."

"Are you quite sure you didn't? Perhaps we did it together. Careful!" he said as Stefan stepped toward him.

"My mood is not the most tolerant tonight, either. I only had a wizened little history teacher; you had a pretty girl."

The fury inside Stefan coalesced, seeming to focus in one bright burning spot, like a sun inside him. "Keep away from Elena," he whispered with such menace that Damon actually tilted his head back slightly. "Keep away from her, Damon. I know you've been spying on her, watching her. But no more. Go near her again and you'll regret it."

"You always *were* selfish. Your one fault. Not willing to share anything, are you?" Suddenly, Damon's lips curved in a singularly beautiful smile. "But fortunately the lovely Elena is more generous. Didn't she tell you about our little liaisons? Why, the first time we met she almost gave herself to me on the spot."

"That's a lie!"

"Oh, no, dear brother. I never lie about anything important. Or do I mean unimportant? Anyway, your beauteous damsel nearly swooned into my arms. I think she likes men in black." As Stefan stared at him, trying to control his breathing, Damon added, almost gently, "You're wrong about her, you know. You think she's sweet and docile, like Katherine. She isn't. She's not your type at all, my saintly brother. She has a spirit and a fire in her that you wouldn't know what to do with."

"And you would, I suppose."

Damon uncrossed his arms and slowly smiled again. "Oh, yes."

Stefan wanted to leap for him, to smash that beautiful, arrogant smile, to tear Damon's throat out. He said, in a barely controlled voice, "You're right about one thing. She's strong. Strong enough to fight you off. And now that she knows what you really are, she will. All she feels for you now is disgust."

Damon's eyebrows lifted. "Does she, now? We'll see about that. Perhaps she'll find that real darkness is more to her taste than feeble twilight. I, at least, can admit the truth about my nature. But I worry about you, little brother. You're looking weak and ill-fed. She's a tease, is she?"

Kill him, something in Stefan's mind demanded. Kill him, snap his neck, rip his throat to bloody shreds. But he knew Damon had fed very well tonight. His brother's dark aura was swollen, pulsing, almost shining with the life essence he had taken.

"Yes, I drank deeply," Damon said pleasantly, as if he knew what was in Stefan's mind. He sighed and ran his tongue over his lips in satisfied remembrance. "He was small, but there was a surprising amount of juice in him. Not pretty like Elena, and he certainly didn't smell as good. But it's always exhilarating to feel the new blood singing inside you." Damon breathed expansively, stepping away from the tree and looking around. Stefan remembered those graceful movements, too, each gesture controlled and precise. The centuries had only refined Damon's natural poise.

"It makes me feel like doing this," said Damon, moving to a sapling a few yards away. It was half again as tall as he was, and when he grasped it his fingers did not meet around the trunk. But Stefan saw the quick breath and the ripple of muscles under Damon's thin black shirt, and then the tree tore loose from the ground, its roots dangling. Stefan could smell the pungent dampness of disturbed earth.

"I didn't like it there anyway," said Damon, and heaved it as far away as the still-entangled roots would allow. Then he smiled engagingly. "It also makes me feel like doing *this*."

There was a shimmer of motion, and then Damon was gone. Stefan looked around but could see no sign of him.

"Up here, brother." The voice came from overhead, and when Stefan looked up he saw Damon perching among the spreading branches of the oak tree. There was a rustle of tawny brown leaves, and he disappeared again.

"Back here, brother." Stefan spun at the tap on his shoulder, only to see nothing behind him. "Right here, brother." He spun again. "No, try here." Furious, Stefan whipped the other way, trying to catch hold of Damon. But his fingers grasped only air.

Here, Stefan. This time the voice was in his mind, and the Power of it shook him to the core. It took enormous strength to project thoughts that clearly. Slowly, he turned around once more, to see Damon back in his original position, leaning against the big oak tree.

But this time the humor in those dark eyes had faded. They were black and fathomless, and Damon's lips were set in a straight line.

What more proof do you need, Stefan? I'm as much stronger than you as you are stronger than these pitiful humans. I'm faster than you, too, and I have other Powers you've scarcely heard of. The Old Powers, Stefan. And I'm not afraid to use them. If you fight me, I'll use them against you.

"Is that what you came here for? To torture me?"

I've been merciful with you, brother. Many times you've been mine for the killing, but I've always spared your life. But this time is different. Damon stepped away from the tree again and spoke aloud. "I am warning you, Stefan, don't oppose me. It doesn't matter what I came here for. What I want now is Elena. And if you try to stop me from taking her, I will kill you."

"You can try," said Stefan. The hot pinpoint of fury inside him burned brighter than ever, pouring forth its brilliance like a whole galaxy of stars. He knew, somehow, that it threatened Damon's darkness.

"You think I can't do it? You never learn, do you, little

brother?" Stefan had just enough time to note Damon's weary shake of the head when there was another blur of motion and he felt strong hands seize him. He was fighting instantly, violently, trying with all his strength to throw them off. But they were like hands of steel.

He lashed out savagely, trying to strike at the vulnerable area under Damon's jaw. It did no good; his arms were pinioned behind him, his body immobilized. He was as helpless as a bird under the claws of a lean and expert cat.

He went limp for an instant, making himself a deadweight, and then he suddenly surged with all his muscles, trying to break free, trying to get a blow in. The cruel hands only tightened on him, making his struggles useless. Pathetic.

You always were stubborn. Perhaps this will convince you. Stefan looked into his brother's face, pale as the frosted-glass windows at the boarding house, and at those black bottomless eyes. Then he felt fingers grasp his hair, jerk his head back, exposing his throat.

His struggles redoubled, became frantic. *Don't bother,* came the voice in his head, and then he felt the sharp rending pain of teeth. He felt the humiliation and helplessness of the hunter's victim, of the hunted, of the prey. And then the pain of blood being drawn out against his will.

He refused to give in to it, and the pain grew worse, a

feeling as if his soul was tearing loose like the sapling. It stabbed through him like spears of fire, concentrating on the punctures in his flesh where Damon's teeth had sunk in. Agony flamed up his jaw and cheek and down his chest and shoulder. He felt a wave of vertigo and realized he was losing consciousness.

Then, abruptly, the hands released him and he fell to the ground, onto a bed of damp and moldering oak leaves. Gasping for breath, he painfully got to his hands and knees.

"You see, little brother, I'm stronger than you. Strong enough to take you, take your blood and your life if I wish it. Leave Elena to me, or I will."

Stefan looked up. Damon was standing with head thrown back, legs slightly apart, like a conqueror putting his foot on the neck of the conquered. Those night-black eyes were hot with triumph, and Stefan's blood was on his lips.

Hatred filled Stefan, such hatred as he had never known before. It was as if all his earlier hatred of Damon had been a drop of water to this crashing, foaming ocean. Many times in the last long centuries he had regretted what he had done to his brother, when he'd wished with all his soul to change it. Now he only wanted to do it again.

"Elena is not yours," he ground out, getting to his feet,

trying not to show what an effort it cost him. "And she never will be." Concentrating on each step, putting one foot in front of the other, he began walking away. His entire body hurt, and the shame he felt was even greater than the physical ache. There were bits of wet leaves and crumbs of earth adhering to his clothes, but he did not brush them off. He fought to keep moving, to hold out against the weakness that lapped at his limbs.

You never learn, brother.

Stefan did not look back or try to reply. He gritted his teeth and kept his legs moving. Another step. And another step. And another step.

If he could just sit down for a moment, rest . . .

Another step, and another step. The car couldn't be far now. Leaves crackled under his feet, and then he heard leaves crackle behind him.

He tried to turn quickly, but his reflexes were almost gone. And the sharp motion was too much for him. Darkness, filled him, filled his body and his mind, and he was falling. He fell forever into the black of absolute night. And then, mercifully, he knew no more.

lena hurried toward Robert E. Lee, feeling as if she'd been away from it for years. Last night seemed like something from her distant childhood, barely remembered. But she knew that today there would be its consequences to face.

Last night she'd had to face Aunt Judith. Her aunt had been terribly upset when neighbors had told her about the murder, and even more upset that no one seemed to know where Elena was. By the time Elena had arrived home at nearly two in the morning, she had been frantic with worry.

Elena hadn't been able to explain. She could only say that she'd been with Stefan, and that she knew he had been accused, and that she knew he was innocent. All the rest, everything else that had happened, she had had to keep to herself. Even if Aunt Judith had believed it, she would never have understood.

And this morning Elena had slept in, and now she was late. The streets were deserted except for her, as she hurried on toward the school. Overhead, the sky was gray and a wind was rising. She desperately wanted to see Stefan. All night, while she'd been sleeping so heavily, she'd had nightmares about him.

One dream had been especially real. In it she saw Stefan's pale face and his angry, accusing eyes. He held up a book to her and said, "How could you, Elena? How could you?" Then he dropped the book at her feet and walked away. She called after him, pleading, but he went on walking until he disappeared in darkness. When she looked down at the book, she saw it was bound in dark blue velvet. Her diary.

A quiver of anger went through her as she thought again of how her diary had been stolen. But what did the dream mean? What was in her diary to make Stefan look like that?

She didn't know. All she knew was that she needed to see him, to hear his voice, to feel his arms around her. Being away from him was like being separated from her own flesh.

She ran up the steps of the high school into the nearly empty corridors. She headed toward the foreign-language wing, because she knew that Stefan's first class was Latin. If she could just see him for a moment, she would be all right.

But he wasn't in class. Through the little window in the door, she saw his empty seat. Matt was there, and the expression on his face made her feel more frightened than ever. He kept glancing at Stefan's desk with a look of sick apprehension.

Elena turned away from the door mechanically. Like an automaton, she climbed the stairs and walked to her trigonometry classroom. As she opened the door, she saw every face turn toward her, and she slipped hastily into the empty desk beside Meredith.

Ms. Halpern stopped the lesson for a moment and looked at her, then continued. When the teacher had turned back to the blackboard, Elena looked at Meredith.

Meredith reached over to take her hand. "Are you all right?" she whispered.

"I don't know," said Elena stupidly. She felt as if the very air around her was smothering her, as if there were a crushing weight all around her. Meredith's fingers felt dry and hot. "Meredith, do you know what's happened to Stefan?"

"You mean *you* don't know?" Meredith's dark eyes widened, and Elena felt the weight grow even more crushing. It was like being deep, deep under water without a pressure suit.

"They haven't . . . arrested him, have they?" she said, forcing the words out.

"Elena, it's worse than that. He's disappeared. The

police went to the boarding house early this morning and he wasn't there. They came to school, too, but he never showed up today. They said they'd found his car abandoned out by Old Creek Road. Elena, they think he's left, skipped town, because he's guilty."

"That's not true," said Elena through her teeth. She saw people turn around and look at her, but she was beyond caring. "He's innocent!"

"I know you think so, Elena, but why else would he leave?"

"He wouldn't. He didn't." Something was burning inside Elena, a fire of anger that pushed back at the crushing fear. She was breathing raggedly. "He would never have left of his own free will."

"You mean someone forced him? But who? Tyler wouldn't dare—"

"Forced him, or worse," Elena interrupted. The entire class was staring at them now, and Ms. Halpern was opening her mouth. Elena stood up suddenly, looking at them without seeing. "God help him if he's hurt Stefan," she said. "God *help* him." Then she whirled and made for the door.

"Elena, come back! Elena!" She could hear shouts behind her, Meredith's and Ms. Halpern's. She walked on, faster and faster, seeing only what was straight ahead of her, her mind fixed on one thing.

They thought she was going after Tyler Smallwood. Good. They could waste their time running in the wrong direction. She knew what she had to do.

She left the school, plunging into the cold autumn air. She moved quickly, legs eating up the distance between the school and the Old Creek Road. From there she turned toward Wickery Bridge and the graveyard.

An icy wind whipped her hair back and stung her face. Oak leaves were flying around her, swirling in the air. But the conflagration in her heart was searing hot and burned away the cold. She knew now what a towering rage meant. She strode past the purple beeches and the weeping willows into the center of the old graveyard and looked around her with feverish eyes.

Above, the clouds were flowing along like a lead-gray river. The limbs of the oaks and beeches lashed together wildly. A gust threw handfuls of leaves into her face. It was as if the graveyard were trying to drive her out, as if it were showing her its power, gathering itself to do something awful to her.

Elena ignored all of it. She spun around, her burning gaze searching between the headstones. Then she turned and shouted directly into the fury of the wind. Just one word, but the one she knew would bring him.

"Damon!"

"**D**amon!"

Icy wind whipped Elena's hair around her face, tearing at her light sweater. Oak leaves swirled among the rows of granite headstones, and the trees lashed their branches together in frenzy. Elena's hands were cold, her lips and cheeks were numb, but she stood facing the screaming wind directly, shouting into it.

"*Damon!*"

This weather was a show of his Power, meant to frighten her away. It wouldn't work. The thought of that same Power being turned against Stefan woke a hot fury inside her that burned against the wind. If Damon had done anything to Stefan, if Damon had hurt him . . .

"Damn you, answer me!" she shouted at the oak trees that bordered the graveyard.

A dead oak leaf like a withered brown hand skittered up to her foot, but there was no answer. Above, the sky was gray as glass, gray as the tombstones that surrounded her. Elena felt rage and frustration sting her throat and she sagged. She'd been wrong. Damon wasn't here after all; she was alone with the screaming wind.

She turned—and gasped.

He was just behind her, so close that her clothes brushed his as she turned. At that distance, she should have sensed another human being standing there, should have felt his body warmth or heard him. But Damon, of course, wasn't human.

She reeled back a couple of steps before she could stop herself. Every instinct that had lain quiet while she shouted into the violence of the wind was now begging her to run.

She clenched her fists. "Where's Stefan?"

A line appeared between Damon's dark eyebrows. "Stefan who?"

Elena stepped forward and slapped him.

She had no thought of doing it before she did it, and afterward she could scarcely believe what she had done. But it was a good hard slap, with the full force of her body behind it, and it snapped Damon's head to one side. Her hand stung. She stood, trying to calm her breath, and watched him.

He was dressed as she had first seen him, in black. Soft black boots, black jeans, black sweater, and leather jacket. And he looked like Stefan. She didn't know how she could have missed that before. He had the same dark hair, the same pale skin, the same disturbing good looks. But his hair was straight, not wavy, and his eyes were black as midnight, and his mouth was cruel.

He turned his head slowly back to look at her, and she saw blood rising in the cheek she'd slapped.

"Don't lie to me," she said, her voice shaking. "I know who you are. I know *what* you are. You killed Mr. Tanner last night. And now Stefan's disappeared."

"Has he?"

"You know he has!"

Damon smiled and then turned it off instantly.

"I'm warning you; if you've hurt him—"

"Then, what?" he said. "What will you do, Elena? What *can* you do, against me?"

Elena fell silent. For the first time, she realized that the wind had died away. The day had gone deadly quiet around them, as if they stood motionless at the center of some great circle of power. It seemed as if everything, the leaden sky, the oaks and purple beeches, the ground itself, was connected to him, as if he drew Power from all of it. He stood with his head tilted back slightly, his eyes fathomless and full of strange lights.

"I don't know," she whispered, "but I'll find something. Believe me."

He laughed suddenly, and Elena's heart jerked and began pounding hard. God, he was beautiful. Handsome was too weak and colorless a word. As usual, the laughter lasted only a moment, but even when his lips had sobered it left traces in his eyes.

"I do believe you," he said, relaxing, looking around the graveyard. Then he turned back and held out a hand to her. "You're too good for my brother," he said casually.

Elena thought of slapping the hand away, but she didn't want to touch him again. "Tell me where he is."

"Later, possibly—for a price." He withdrew his hand, just as Elena realized that on it he wore a ring like Stefan's: silver and lapis lazuli. Remember that, she thought fiercely. It's important.

"My brother," he went on, "is a fool. He thinks that because you look like Katherine you're weak and easily led like her. But he's wrong. I could feel your anger from the other side of town. I can feel it now, a white light like the desert sun. You have strength, Elena, even as you are. But you could be so much stronger. . . ."

She stared at him, not understanding, not liking the change of subject. "I don't know what you're talking about. And what has it got to do with Stefan?"

"I'm talking about Power, Elena." Suddenly, he

stepped close to her, his eyes fixed on hers, his voice soft and urgent. "You've tried everything else, and nothing has satisfied you. You're the girl who has everything, but there's always been something just out of your reach, something you need desperately and can't have. That's what I'm offering you. Power. Eternal life. And feelings you've never felt before."

She *did* understand then, and bile rose in her throat. She choked on horror and repudiation. "No."

"Why not?" he whispered. "Why not try it, Elena? Be honest. Isn't there a part of you that wants to?" His dark eyes were full of a heat and intensity that held her transfixed, unable to look away. "I can waken things inside you that have been sleeping all your life. You're strong enough to live in the dark, to glory in it. You can become a queen of the shadows. Why not take that Power, Elena? Let me help you take it."

"*No,*" she said, wrenching her eyes away from his. She wouldn't look at him, wouldn't let him do this to her. She wouldn't let him make her forget . . . make her forget . . .

"It's the ultimate secret, Elena," he said. His voice was as caressing as the fingertips that touched her throat. "You'll be happy as never before."

There was something terribly important she must remember. He was using Power to make her forget it, but she wouldn't let him make her forget. . . .

"And we'll be together, you and I." The cool fingertips stroked the side of her neck, slipping under the collar of her sweater. "Just the two of us, forever."

There was a sudden twinge of pain as his fingers brushed two tiny wounds in the flesh of her neck, and her mind cleared.

Make her forget . . . *Stefan*.

That was what he wanted to drive out of her mind. The memory of Stefan, of his green eyes and his smile that always had sadness lurking behind it. But nothing could force Stefan out of her thoughts now, not after what they had shared. She pulled away from Damon, knocking those cool fingertips aside. She looked straight at him.

"I've already found what I want," she said brutally. "And who I want to be with forever."

Blackness welled up in his eyes, a cold rage that swept through the air between them. Looking into those eyes, Elena thought of a cobra about to strike.

"Don't you be as stupid as my brother is," he said. "Or I might have to treat you the same way."

She was frightened now. She couldn't help it, not with cold pouring into her, chilling her bones. The wind was picking up again, the branches tossing. "Tell me where he is, Damon."

"At this moment? I don't know. Can't you stop thinking about him for an instant?"

"No!" She shuddered, hair lashing about her face again.

"And that's your final answer, today? Be very sure you want to play this game with me, Elena. The consequences are nothing to laugh about."

"I *am* sure." She had to stop him before he got to her again. "And you can't intimidate me, Damon, or haven't you noticed? The moment Stefan told me what you were, what you'd done, you lost any power you might have had over me. I *hate* you. You disgust me. And there's nothing you can do to me, not anymore."

His face altered, the sensuousness twisting and freezing, becoming cruel and bitterly hard. He laughed, but this laugh went on and on. "Nothing?" he said. "I can do *anything* to you, and to the ones you love. You have no idea, Elena, of what I can do. But you'll learn."

He stepped back, and the wind cut through Elena like a knife. Her vision seemed to be blurring; it was as if flecks of brightness filled the air in front of her eyes.

"Winter is coming, Elena," he said, and his voice was clear and chilling even over the howl of the wind. "An unforgiving season. Before it comes, you'll have learned what I can and can't do. Before winter is here, you'll have joined me. You'll be mine."

The swirling whiteness was blinding her, and she could no longer see the dark bulk of his figure. Now even his voice was fading. She hugged herself with her arms, head bent down, her whole body shaking. She whispered, "Stefan—"

"Oh, and one more thing," Damon's voice came back. "You asked earlier about my brother. Don't bother looking for him, Elena. I killed him last night."

Her head jerked up, but there was nothing to see, only the dizzying whiteness, which burned her nose and cheeks and clogged her eyelashes. It was only then, as the fine grains settled on her skin, that she realized what they were: snowflakes.

It was snowing on the first of November. Overhead, the sun was gone.

An unnatural twilight hung over the abandoned graveyard. Snow blurred Elena's eyes, and the wind numbed her body as if she'd stepped into a current of ice water. Nevertheless, stubbornly, she did not turn around toward the modern cemetery and the road beyond it. As best she could judge, Wickery Bridge was straight in front of her. She headed for that.

The police had found Stefan's abandoned car by Old Creek Road. That meant he'd left it somewhere between Drowning Creek and the woods. Elena stumbled on the overgrown path through the graveyard, but she kept moving, head down, arms hugging her light sweater to her. She had known this graveyard all her life, and she could find her way through it blind.

By the time she crossed the bridge, her shivering had

become painful. It wasn't snowing as hard now, but the wind was even worse. It cut through her clothes as if they were made of tissue paper, and took her breath away.

Stefan, she thought, and turned onto Old Creek Road, trudging northward. She didn't believe what Damon had said. If Stefan were dead she would *know*. He was alive, somewhere, and she had to find him. He could be any-where out in this swirling whiteness; he could be hurt, freezing. Dimly, Elena sensed that she was no longer rational. All her thoughts had narrowed down to one sin-gle idea. Stefan. Find Stefan.

It was getting harder to keep to the road. On her right were oak trees, on her left, the swift waters of Drowning Creek. She staggered and slowed. The wind didn't seem quite so bad anymore, but she did feel very tired. She needed to sit down and rest, just for a minute.

As she sank down beside the road, she suddenly real-ized how silly she had been to go out searching for Stefan. Stefan would come to her. All she needed to do was sit here and wait. He was probably coming right now.

Elena shut her eyes and leaned her head against her drawn-up knees. She felt much warmer now. Her mind drifted and she saw Stefan, saw him smile at her. His arms around her were strong and secure, and she relaxed against him, glad to let go of fear and tension. She was home. She was where she belonged. Stefan would never let anything hurt her.

But then, instead of holding her, Stefan was shaking her. He was ruining the beautiful tranquility of her rest. She saw his face, pale and urgent, his green eyes dark with pain. She tried to tell him to be still, but he wouldn't listen. *Elena, get up*, he said, and she felt the compelling force of those green eyes willing her to do it. *Elena, get up now—*

"Elena, get up!" The voice was high and thin and frightened. "Come on, Elena! Get up! We can't carry you!"

Blinking, Elena brought a face into focus. It was small and heart-shaped, with fair, almost translucent skin, framed by masses of soft red curls. Wide brown eyes, with snowflakes caught in the lashes, stared worriedly into hers.

"Bonnie," she said slowly. "What are you doing here?"

"Helping me look for you," said a second, lower voice on Elena's other side. She turned slightly to see elegantly arched eyebrows and an olive complexion. Meredith's dark eyes, usually so ironic, were worried now, too. "Stand up, Elena, unless you want to become an ice princess for real."

There was snow all over her, like a white fur coat. Stiffly, Elena stood, leaning heavily on the two other girls. They walked her back to Meredith's car.

It should have been warmer inside the car, but Elena's nerve endings were coming back to life, making her shake, telling her how cold she really was. Winter is an unforgiving season, she thought as Meredith drove.

"What's going on, Elena?" said Bonnie from the backseat. "What did you think you were doing, running away from school like that? And how could you come out *here*?"

Elena hesitated, then shook her head. She wanted nothing more than to tell Bonnie and Meredith everything. To tell them the whole terrifying story about Stefan and Damon and what had really happened last night to Mr. Tanner—and about after. But she couldn't. Even if they would believe her, it wasn't her secret to tell.

"Everyone's out looking for you," Meredith said. "The whole school's upset, and your aunt was nearly frantic."

"Sorry," said Elena dully, trying to stop her violent shivering. They turned onto Maple Street and pulled up to her house.

Aunt Judith was waiting inside with heated blankets. "I knew if they found you, you'd be half-frozen," she said in a determinedly cheerful voice as she reached for Elena. "Snow on the day after Halloween! I can hardly believe it. Where did you girls find her?"

"On Old Creek Road, past the bridge," said Meredith.

Aunt Judith's thin face lost color. "Near the graveyard?

Where the attacks were? Elena, how *could* you? . . . " Her voice trailed off as she looked at Elena. "We won't say anything more about it right now," she said, trying to regain her cheerful manner. "Let's get you out of those wet clothes."

"I have to go back once I'm dry," said Elena. Her brain was working again, and one thing was clear: she hadn't really seen Stefan out there; it had been a dream. Stefan was still missing.

"You have to do nothing of the kind," said Robert, Aunt Judith's fiancé. Elena had scarcely noticed him standing off to one side until then. But his tone brooked no argument. "The police are looking for Stefan; you leave them to their job," he said.

"The police think he killed Mr. Tanner. But he didn't. You know that, don't you?" As Aunt Judith pulled her sodden outer sweater off, Elena looked from one face to another for help, but they were all the same. "You *know* he didn't do it," she repeated, almost desperately.

There was a silence. "Elena," Meredith said at last, "no one wants to think he did. But—well, it looks bad, his running away like this."

"He didn't run away. He didn't! He *didn't*—"

"Elena, hush," said Aunt Judith. "Don't get yourself worked up. I think you must be getting sick. It was so cold out there, and you got only a few hours of sleep last night. . . ." She laid a hand on Elena's cheek.

Suddenly it was all too much for Elena. Nobody believed her, not even her friends and family. At that moment, she felt surrounded by enemies.

"I'm not sick," she cried, pulling away. "And I'm not crazy, either—whatever you think. Stefan didn't run away and he didn't kill Mr. Tanner, and I don't care if none of you believes me. . . ." She stopped, choking. Aunt Judith was fussing around her, hurrying her upstairs, and she let herself be hurried. But she wouldn't go to bed when Aunt Judith suggested she must be tired. Instead, once she had warmed up, she sat on the living room couch by the fireplace, with blankets heaped around her. The phone rang all afternoon, and she heard Aunt Judith talking to friends, neighbors, the school. She assured all of them that Elena was fine. The . . . the tragedy last night had unsettled her a bit, that was all, and she seemed a little feverish. But she'd be good as new after a rest.

Meredith and Bonnie sat beside her. "Do you want to talk?" Meredith said in a low voice. Elena shook her head, staring into the fire. They were all against her. And Aunt Judith was wrong; she wasn't fine. She wouldn't be fine until Stefan was found.

Matt stopped by, snow dusting his blond hair and his dark blue parka. As he entered the room, Elena looked up at him hopefully. Yesterday Matt had helped save Stefan, when the rest of the school had wanted to lynch him. But today he returned her hopeful look with one of sober regret, and the concern in his blue eyes was only for her.

The disappointment was unbearable. "What are you doing here?" Elena demanded. "Keeping your promise to 'take care of me'?"

There was a flicker of hurt in his eyes. But Matt's voice was level. "That's part of it, maybe. But I'd try to take care of you anyway, no matter what I promised. I've been worried about you. Listen, Elena—"

She was in no mood to listen to anyone. "Well, I'm just fine, thank you. Ask anybody here. So you can stop worrying. Besides, I don't see why you should keep a promise to a *murderer*."

Startled, Matt looked at Meredith and Bonnie. Then he shook his head helplessly. "You're not being fair."

Elena was in no mood to be fair either. "I told you, you can stop worrying about me, and about my business. I'm fine, thanks."

The implication was obvious. Matt turned to the door just as Aunt Judith appeared with sandwiches.

"Sorry, I've got to go," he muttered, hurrying to the door. He left without looking back.

Meredith and Bonnie and Aunt Judith and Robert tried to make conversation while they ate an early supper by the fire. Elena couldn't eat and wouldn't talk. The only one who wasn't miserable was Elena's little sister, Margaret. With four-year-old optimism, she cuddled up to Elena and offered her some of her Halloween candy.

Elena hugged her sister hard, her face pressed into Margaret's white-blond hair for a moment. If Stefan could have called her or gotten a message to her, he would have done it by now. Nothing in the world would have stopped him, unless he were badly hurt, or trapped somewhere, or . . .

She wouldn't let herself think about that last "or." Stefan was alive; he had to be alive. Damon was a liar.

But Stefan was in trouble, and she had to find him somehow. She worried about it all through the evening, desperately trying to come up with a plan. One thing was clear; she was on her own. She couldn't trust anyone.

It grew dark. Elena shifted on the couch and forced a yawn.

"I'm tired," she said quietly. "Maybe I am sick after all. I think I'll go to bed."

Meredith was looking at her keenly. "I was just thinking, Miss Gilbert," she said, turning to Aunt Judith, "that maybe Bonnie and I should stay the night. To keep Elena company."

"What a good idea," said Aunt Judith, pleased. "As long as your parents don't mind, I'd be glad to have you."

"It's a long drive back to Herron. I think I'll stay, too,"

Robert said. "I can just stretch out on the couch here." Aunt Judith protested that there were plenty of guest bedrooms upstairs, but Robert was adamant. The couch would do just fine for him, he said.

After looking once from the couch to the hall where the front door stood plainly in view, Elena sat stonily. They'd planned this between them, or at least they were all in on it now. They were making sure she didn't leave the house.

When she emerged from the bathroom a little while later, wrapped in her red silk kimono, she found Meredith and Bonnie sitting on her bed.

"Well, hello, Rosencrantz and Guildenstern," she said bitterly.

Bonnie, who had been looking depressed, now looked alarmed. She glanced at Meredith doubtfully.

"She knows who we are. She means she thinks we're spies for her aunt," Meredith interpreted. "Elena, you should realize that isn't so. Can't you trust us at all?"

"I don't know. Can I?"

"Yes, because we're your *friends*." Before Elena could move, Meredith jumped off the bed and shut the door. Then she turned to face Elena. "Now, for once in your life, listen to me, you little idiot. It's true we don't know what to think about Stefan. But, don't you see, that's your own fault. Ever since you and he got together, you've been shutting us out. Things have been happening that you haven't told us about. At least you haven't told us the whole story. But in spite of that, in spite of everything, we still trust you. We still care about you. We're still behind you, Elena, and we want to help. And if you can't see that, then you *are* an idiot."

Slowly, Elena looked from Meredith's dark, intense face to Bonnie's pale one. Bonnie nodded.

"It's true," she said, blinking hard as if to keep back tears. "Even if you don't like us, we still like *you*."

Elena felt her own eyes fill and her stern expression crumple. Then Bonnie was off the bed, and they were all hugging, and Elena found she couldn't help the tears that slid down her face.

"I'm sorry if I haven't been talking to you," she said. "I know you don't understand, and I can't even explain why I can't tell you everything. I just *can't*. But there's one thing I can tell you." She stepped back, wiping her cheeks, and looked at them earnestly. "No matter how bad the evidence against Stefan looks, *he didn't kill Mr. Tanner.* I know he didn't, because I know who did. And it's the same person who attacked Vickie, and the old man under the bridge. And"—she stopped and thought a moment—"and, oh, Bonnie, I think he killed Yangtze, too."

"*Yangtze?*" Bonnie's eyes widened. "But why would he want to kill a dog?"

"I don't know, but he was there that night, in your house. And he was . . . angry. I'm sorry, Bonnie."

Bonnie shook her head dazedly. Meredith said, "Why don't you tell the police?"

Elena's laugh was slightly hysterical. "I can't. It's not something they can deal with. And that's another thing I can't explain. You said you still trusted me; well, you'll just have to trust me about that."

Bonnie and Meredith looked at each other, then at the bedspread, where Elena's nervous fingers were picking a thread out of the embroidery. Finally Meredith said, "All right. What can we do to help?"

"I don't know. Nothing, unless . . . " Elena stopped and looked at Bonnie. "Unless," she said, in a changed voice, "you can help me find Stefan."

Bonnie's brown eyes were genuinely bewildered. "Me? But what can I do?" Then, at Meredith's indrawn breath, she said, "Oh. *Oh.*"

"You knew where I was that day I went to the cemetery," said Elena. "And you even predicted Stefan's coming to school."

"I thought you didn't believe in all that psychic stuff," said Bonnie weakly.

"I've learned a thing or two since then. Anyway, I'm willing to believe *anything* if it'll help find Stefan. If there's any chance at all it will help."

Bonnie was hunching up, as if trying to make her already tiny form as small as possible. "Elena, you don't understand," she said wretchedly. "I'm not trained; it's not something I can control. And—and it's not a game, not anymore. The more you use those powers, the more they use *you*. Eventually they can end up using you all the time, whether you want it or not. It's *dangerous*."

Elena got up and walked to the cherry wood dresser, looking down at it without seeing it. At last she turned.

"You're right; it's not a game. And I believe you about how dangerous it can be. But it's not a game for Stefan, either. Bonnie, I think he's out there, somewhere, terribly hurt. And there's nobody to help him; nobody's even looking for him, except his enemies. He may be dying right now. He—he may even be . . . " Her throat closed. She bowed her head over the dresser and made herself take a deep breath, trying to steady herself. When she looked up, she saw Meredith was looking at Bonnie.

Bonnie straightened her shoulders, sitting up as tall as she could. Her chin lifted and her mouth set. And in her normally soft brown eyes, a grim light shone as they met Elena's.

"We need a candle," was all she said.

The match rasped and threw sparks in the darkness, and then the candle flame burned strong and bright. It lent a golden glow to Bonnie's pale face as she bent over it.

"I'm going to need both of you to help me focus," she said. "Look into the flame, and think about Stefan. Picture him in your mind. No matter what happens, keep on looking at the flame. And whatever you do, don't say anything."

Elena nodded, and then the only sound in the room was soft breathing. The flame flickered and danced, throwing patterns of light over the three girls sitting cross-legged around it. Bonnie, eyes closed, was breathing deeply and slowly, like someone drifting into sleep.

Stefan, thought Elena, gazing into the flame, trying to pour all her will into the thought. She created him in her mind, using all her senses, conjuring him to her. The roughness of his woolen sweater under her cheek, the smell of his leather jacket, the strength of his arms around her. Oh, Stefan . . .

Bonnie's lashes fluttered and her breathing quickened, like a sleeper having a bad dream. Elena resolutely kept her eyes on the flame, but when Bonnie broke the silence a chill went up her spine.

At first it was just a moan, the sound of someone in pain. Then, as Bonnie tossed her head, breath coming in short bursts, it became words.

"Alone . . . " she said, and stopped. Elena's nails bit into her hand. "Alone . . . in the dark," said Bonnie. Her voice was distant and tortured.

There was another silence, and then Bonnie began to speak quickly.

"It's dark and cold. And I'm alone. There's something behind me . . . jagged and hard. Rocks. They used to hurt—but not now. I'm numb now, from the cold. So cold . . ." Bonnie twisted, as if trying to get away from something, and then she laughed, a dreadful laugh almost like a sob. "That's . . . funny. I never thought I'd want to see the sun so much. But it's always dark here. And cold. Water up to my neck, like ice. That's funny, too. Water everywhere—and me dying of thirst. So thirsty . . . hurts . . ."

Elena felt something tighten around her heart. Bonnie was inside Stefan's thoughts, and who knew what she might discover there? Stefan, tell us where you are, she thought desperately. Look around; tell me what you see.

"Thirsty. I need . . . life?" Bonnie's voice was doubtful, as if not sure how to translate some concept. "I'm weak. He said I'll always be the weak one. He's strong . . . a killer. But that's what I am, too. I killed Katherine; maybe I deserve to die. Why not just let go? . . ."

"No!" said Elena before she could stop herself. In that instant, she forgot everything but Stefan's pain. "Stefan—"

"Elena!" Meredith cried sharply at the same time. But Bonnie's head fell forward, the flow of words cut off.

Horrified, Elena realized what she had done.

"Bonnie, are you all right? Can you find him again? I didn't mean to . . . "

Bonnie's head lifted. Her eyes were open now, but they looked at neither the candle nor Elena. They stared straight ahead, expressionless. When she spoke, her voice was distorted, and Elena's heart stopped. It wasn't Bonnie's voice, but it was a voice Elena recognized. She'd heard it coming from Bonnie's lips once before, in the graveyard.

"Elena," the voice said, "don't go to the bridge. It's Death, Elena. Your death is waiting there." Then Bonnie slumped forward.

Elena grabbed her shoulders and shook. "Bonnie!" she almost screamed. "Bonnie!"

"What . . . oh, don't. Let go." Bonnie's voice was weak and shaken, but it was her own. Still bent over, she put a hand to her forehead.

"Bonnie, are you all right?"

"I think so . . . yes. But it was so strange." Her tone sharpened and she looked up, blinking. "What was that, Elena, about being a killer?"

"You remember that?"

"I remember everything. I can't describe it; it was awful. But what did that *mean*?"

"Nothing," said Elena. "He's hallucinating, that's all."

Meredith broke in. "He? Then you really think she tuned in to Stefan?"

Elena nodded, her eyes sore and burning as she looked away. "Yes. I think that was Stefan. It had to be. And I think she even told us where he is. Under Wickery Bridge, in the water."

3

Bonnie stared. "I don't remember anything about the bridge. It didn't feel like
a bridge."

"But you said it yourself, at the end. I thought
you remembered . . . " Elena's voice died away. "You
don't remember that part," she said flatly. It was not a
question.

"I remember being alone, somewhere cold and dark,
and feeling weak . . . and thirsty. Or was it hungry? I don't
know, but I needed . . . something. And I almost wanted
to die. And then you woke me up."

Elena and Meredith exchanged a glance. "And after
that," Elena said to Bonnie, "you said one more thing, in
a strange voice. You said not to go near the bridge."

"She told *you* not to go near the bridge," Meredith

corrected. "You in particular, Elena. She said Death was waiting."

"I don't care what's waiting," said Elena. "If that's where Stefan is, that's where I'm going."

"Then that's where we're all going," said Meredith.

Elena hesitated. "I can't ask you to do that," she said slowly. "There might be danger—of a kind you don't know about. It might be best for me to go alone."

"Are you kidding?" Bonnie said, sticking her chin out. "We *love* danger. I want to be young and beautiful in my grave, remember?"

"Don't," said Elena quickly. "You were the one who said it wasn't a game."

"And not for Stefan, either," Meredith reminded them. "We're not doing him much good standing around here."

Elena was already shrugging out of her kimono, moving toward the closet. "We'd better all bundle up. Borrow anything you want to keep warm," she said.

When they were more or less dressed for the weather, Elena turned to the door. Then she stopped.

"Robert," she said. "There's no way we can get past him to the front door, even if he's asleep."

Simultaneously, the three of them turned to look at the window.

"Oh, wonderful," said Bonnie.

As they climbed out into the quince tree, Elena realized that it had stopped snowing. But the bite of the air on her cheek made her remember Damon's words. Winter is an unforgiving season, she thought, and shivered.

All the lights in the house were out, including those in the living room. Robert must have gone to sleep already. Even so, Elena held her breath as they crept past the darkened windows. Meredith's car was a little way down the street. At the last minute, Elena decided to get some rope, and she soundlessly opened the back door to the garage. There was a swift current in Drowning Creek, and wading would be dangerous.

The drive to the end of town was tense. As they passed the outskirts of the woods, Elena remembered the way the leaves had blown at her in the cemetery. Particularly oak leaves.

"Bonnie, do oak trees have any special significance? Did your grandmother ever say anything about them?"

"Well, they were sacred to the druids. All trees were, but oak trees were the most sacred. They thought the spirit of the trees brought them power."

Elena digested that in silence. When they reached the bridge and got out of the car, she gave the oak trees on the right side of the road an uneasy glance. But the night was clear and strangely calm, and no breeze stirred the dry brown leaves left on the branches.

"Keep your eyes out for a crow," she said to Bonnie and Meredith.

"A crow?" Meredith said sharply. "Like the crow outside Bonnie's house the night Yangtze died?"

"The night Yangtze was killed. Yes." Elena approached the dark waters of Drowning Creek with a rapidly beating heart. Despite its name, it was not a creek, but a swiftly flowing river with banks of native clay. Above it stood Wickery Bridge, a wooden structure built nearly a century ago. Once, it had been strong enough to support wagons; now it was just a footbridge that nobody used because it was so out of the way. It was a barren, lonely, unfriendly place, Elena thought. Here and there patches of snow lay on the ground.

Despite her brave words earlier, Bonnie was hanging back. "Remember the last time we went over this bridge?" she said.

Too well, Elena thought. The last time they had crossed it, they were being chased by . . . something . . . from the graveyard. Or someone, she thought.

"We're not going over it yet," she said. "First we've got to look under it on this side."

"Where the old man was found with his throat torn open," Meredith muttered, but she followed.

The car headlights illuminated only a small portion of the bank under the bridge. As Elena stepped out of the narrow wedge of light, she felt a sick thrill of foreboding. Death was waiting, the voice had said. Was Death down here?

Her feet slipped on the damp, scummy stones. All she could hear was the rushing of the water, and its hollow echo from the bridge above her head. And, though she strained her eyes, all she could see in the darkness was the raw riverbank and the wooden trestles of the bridge.

"Stefan?" she whispered, and she was almost glad that the noise of the water drowned her out. She felt like a person calling "who's there?" to an empty house, yet afraid of what might answer.

"This isn't right," said Bonnie from behind her.

"What do you mean?"

Bonnie was looking around, shaking her head slightly, her body taut with concentration. "It just feels wrong. I don't—well, for one thing I didn't hear the river before. I couldn't hear anything at all, just dead silence."

Elena's heart dropped with dismay. Part of her knew that Bonnie was right, that Stefan wasn't in this wild and lonely place. But part of her was too scared to listen.

"We've got to make sure," she said through the constriction in her chest, and she moved farther into the darkness, feeling her way along because she couldn't see. But at last she had to admit that there was no sign that any person had recently been here. No sign of a dark head in the water, either. She wiped cold muddy hands on her jeans.

"We can check the other side of the bridge," said Meredith, and Elena nodded mechanically. But she didn't need to see Bonnie's expression to know what they'd find. This was the wrong place.

"Let's just get out of here," she said, climbing through vegetation toward the wedge of light beyond the bridge. Just as she reached it, Elena froze.

Bonnie gasped. "Oh, God—"

"Get back," hissed Meredith. "Up against the bank."

Clearly silhouetted against the car headlights above was a black figure. Elena, staring with a wildly beating heart, could tell nothing about it except that it was male. The face was in darkness, but she had a terrible feeling.

It was moving toward them.

Ducking out of sight, Elena cowered back against the muddy riverbank under the bridge, pressing herself as flat as possible. She could feel Bonnie shaking behind her, and Meredith's fingers sank into her arm.

They could see nothing from here, but suddenly there was a heavy footfall on the bridge. Scarcely daring to breathe, they clung to one another, faces turned up. The heavy footsteps rang across the wooden planks, moving away from them.

Please let him keep going, thought Elena. Oh, please...

She sank her teeth into her lip, and then Bonnie whim-

pered softly, her icy hand clutching Elena's. The footsteps were coming back.

I should go out there, Elena thought. It's me he wants,
not them. He said as much. I should go out there and face
him, and maybe he'll let Bonnie and Meredith leave. But
the fiery rage that had sustained her that morning was in
ashes now. With all her strength of will, she could not
make her hand let go of Bonnie's, could not tear herself
away.

The footsteps sounded right above them. Then there
was silence, followed by a slithering sound on the bank.

No, thought Elena, her body charged with fear. He was
coming down. Bonnie moaned and buried her head
against Elena's shoulder, and Elena felt every muscle
tense as she saw movement—feet, legs—appear out of
the darkness. *No . . .*

"What are you *doing* down there?"

Elena's mind refused to process this information at
first. It was still panicking, and she almost screamed as
Matt took another step down the bank, peering under the
bridge.

"Elena? What are you *doing*?" he said again.

Bonnie's head flew up. Meredith's breath exploded in
relief. Elena herself felt as if her knees might give way.

"*Matt*," she said. It was all she could manage.

Bonnie was more vocal. "What do you think *you're*

doing?" she said in rising tones. "Trying to give us a heart attack? What are you out here for at this time of night?"

Matt thrust a hand into his pocket, rattling change. As they emerged from under the bridge, he stared out over the river. "I followed you."

"You *what*?" said Elena.

Reluctantly, he swung to face her. "I followed you," he repeated, shoulders tense. "I figured you'd find a way to get around your aunt and go out again. So I sat in my car across the street and watched your house. Sure enough, you three came climbing out the window. So I followed you here."

Elena didn't know what to say. She was angry, and of course, he had probably done it only to keep his promise to Stefan. But the thought of Matt sitting out there in his battered old Ford, probably freezing to death and without any supper . . . it gave her a strange pang she didn't want to dwell on.

He was looking out at the river again. She stepped closer to him and spoke quietly.

"I'm sorry, Matt," she said. "About the way I acted back at the house, and—and about—" She fumbled for a minute and then gave up. About everything, she thought hopelessly.

"Well, I'm sorry for scaring you just now." He turned back briskly to face her, as if that settled the matter.

"Now could you please tell me what you think you're doing?"

"Bonnie thought Stefan might be here."

"Bonnie did *not*," said Bonnie. "Bonnie said right away that it was the wrong place. We're looking for somewhere quiet, no noises, and closed in. I felt . . . surrounded," she explained to Matt.

Matt looked back at her warily, as if she might bite. "Sure you did," he said.

"There were rocks around me, but not like these river rocks."

"Uh, no, of course they weren't." He looked sideways at Meredith, who took pity on him.

"Bonnie had a vision," she said.

Matt backed up a little, and Elena could see his profile in the headlights. From his expression, she could tell he didn't know whether to walk away or to round them all up and cart them to the nearest insane asylum.

"It's no joke," she said. "Bonnie's psychic, Matt. I know I've always said I didn't believe in that sort of thing, but I've been wrong. You don't know how wrong. Tonight, she—she tuned in to Stefan somehow and got a glimpse of where he is."

Matt drew a long breath. "I see. Okay . . . "

"Don't patronize me! I'm not stupid, Matt, and I'm telling you this is for real. She was there, with Stefan; she knew things only he would know. And she saw the place he's trapped in."

"Trapped," said Bonnie. "That's it. It was definitely nothing open like a river. But there was water, water up to my neck. *His* neck. And rock walls around, covered with thick moss. The water was ice cold and still, and it smelled bad."

"But what did you *see*?" Elena said.

"Nothing. It was like being blind. Somehow I knew that if there was even the faintest ray of light I would be able to see, but I couldn't. It was black as a tomb."

"As a tomb . . . " Thin chills went through Elena. She thought about the ruined church on the hill above the graveyard. There was a tomb there, a tomb she thought had opened once.

"But a tomb wouldn't be that wet," Meredith was saying.

"No . . . but I don't get any sense of where it *could* be then," Bonnie said. "Stefan wasn't really in his right mind; he was so weak and hurt. And so thirsty—"

Elena opened her mouth to stop Bonnie from going on, but just then Matt broke in.

"I'll tell you what it sounds like to me," he said.

The three girls looked at him, standing slightly apart from their group like an eavesdropper. They had almost forgotten about him.

"Well?" said Elena.

"Exactly," he said. "I mean, it sounds like a well."

Elena blinked, excitement stirring in her. "Bonnie?"

"It *could* be," said Bonnie slowly. "The size and the walls and everything would be right. But a well is open; I should have been able to see the stars."

"Not if it were covered," said Matt. "A lot of the old farmhouses around here have wells that are no longer in use, and some farmers cover them to make sure little kids don't fall in. My grandparents do."

Elena couldn't contain her excitement any longer. "That could be it. That *must* be it. Bonnie, remember, you said it was *always* dark there."

"Yes, and it did have a sort of underground feeling." Bonnie was excited, too, but Meredith interrupted with a dry question.

"How many wells do you think there are in Fell's Church, Matt?"

"Dozens, probably," he said. "But covered? Not as many. And if you're suggesting somebody dumped Stefan in this one, then it can't be any place where people would see it. Probably somewhere abandoned . . . "

"And his car was found on this road," said Elena.

"The old Francher place," said Matt.

They all looked at one another. The Francher farmhouse had been ruined and deserted for as long as anybody could remember. It stood in the middle of the woods, and the woods had taken it over nearly a century ago.

"Let's go," added Matt simply.

Elena put a hand on his arm. "You believe—?"

He looked away a moment. "I don't know what to believe," he said at last. "But I'm coming."

They split up and took both cars, Matt with Bonnie in the lead, and Meredith following with Elena. Matt took a disused little cart track into the woods until it petered out.

"From here we walk," he said.

Elena was glad she'd thought of bringing rope; they'd need it if Stefan were really in the Francher well. And if he wasn't . . .

She wouldn't let herself think about that.

It was hard going through the woods, especially in the dark. The underbrush was thick, and dead branches reached out to snatch at them. Moths fluttered around them, brushing Elena's cheek with unseen wings.

Eventually they came to a clearing. The foundations of the old house could be seen, building stones tied to the ground now by weeds and brambles. For the most part, the chimney was still intact, with hollow places where concrete had once held it together, like a crumbling monument.

"The well would be somewhere out back," Matt said.

It was Meredith who found it and called the others. They gathered around and looked at the flat, square block of stone almost level with the ground.

Matt stooped and examined the dirt and weeds around it. "It's been moved recently," he said.

That was when Elena's heart began pounding in earnest. She could feel it reverberating in her throat and her fingertips. "Let's get it off," she said in a voice barely above a whisper.

The stone slab was so heavy that Matt couldn't even shift it. Finally all four of them pushed, bracing themselves against the ground behind it, until, with a groan, the block moved a fraction of an inch. Once there was a tiny gap between stone and well, Matt used a dead branch to lever the opening wider. Then they all pushed again.

When there was an aperture large enough for her head and shoulders, Elena bent down, looking in. She was almost afraid to hope.

"Stefan?"

The seconds afterward, hovering over that black opening, looking down into darkness, hearing only the echoes of pebbles disturbed by her movement, were agonizing. Then, incredibly, there was another sound.

"Who—? Elena?"

"Oh, Stefan!" Relief made her wild. "Yes! I'm here, we're here, and we're going to get you out. Are you all right? Are you hurt?" The only thing that stopped her from tumbling in herself was Matt grabbing her from behind. "Stefan, hang on, we've got a rope. Tell me you're all right."

There was a faint, almost unrecognizable sound, but Elena knew what it was. A laugh. Stefan's voice was thready but intelligible. "I've—been better," he said. "But I'm—alive. Who's with you?"

"It's me. Matt," said Matt, releasing Elena. He bent over the hole himself. Elena, nearly delirious with elation, noted that he wore a slightly dazed look. "And Meredith and Bonnie, who's going to bend some spoons for us next. I'm going to throw you down a rope . . . that is, unless Bonnie can levitate you out." Still on his knees, he turned to look at Bonnie.

She slapped the top of his head. "Don't joke about it! Get him up!"

"Yes, ma'am," said Matt, a little giddily. "Here, Stefan. You're going to have to tie this around you."

"Yes," said Stefan. He didn't argue about fingers numb with cold or whether or not they could haul his weight up. There was no other way.

The next fifteen minutes were awful for Elena. It took all four of them to pull Stefan out, although Bonnie's main contribution was saying, "come on, come *on*," whenever they paused for breath. But at last Stefan's hands gripped the edge of the dark hole, and Matt reached forward to grab him under the shoulders.

Then Elena was holding him, her arms locked around his chest. She could tell just how wrong things were by his unnatural stillness, by the limpness of his body. He'd used the last of his strength helping to pull himself out; his hands were cut and bloody. But what worried Elena most was the fact that those hands did not return her desperate embrace.

When she released him enough to look at him, she saw that his skin was waxen, and there were black shadows under his eyes. His skin was so cold that it frightened her.

She looked up at the others anxiously

Matt's brow was furrowed with concern. "We'd better get him to the clinic fast. He needs a doctor."

"No!" The voice was weak and hoarse, and it came from the limp figure Elena cradled. She felt Stefan gather himself, felt him slowly raise his head. His green eyes fixed on hers, and she saw the urgency in them.

"No . . . doctors." Those eyes burned into hers. "Promise . . . Elena."

Elena's own eyes stung and her vision blurred. "I promise," she whispered. Then she felt whatever had been holding him up, the current of sheer willpower and determination, collapse. He slumped in her arms, unconscious.

4

"But he's got to have a doctor. He looks like he's dying!" said Bonnie.

"He can't. I can't explain right now. Let's just get him home, all right? He's wet and freezing out here. Then we can discuss it."

The job of getting Stefan through the woods was enough to occupy everyone's mind for a while. He remained unconscious, and when they finally laid him out in the backseat of Matt's car they were all bruised and exhausted, in addition to being wet from the contact with his soaking clothes. Elena held his head in her lap as they drove to the boarding house. Meredith and Bonnie followed.

"I see lights on," Matt said, pulling in front of the large

rust-red building. "She must be awake. But the door's probably locked."

Elena gently eased Stefan's head down and slipped out of the car, and saw one of the windows in the house brighten as a curtain was pushed aside. Then she saw a head and shoulders appear at the window, looking down.

"Mrs. Flowers!" she called, waving. "It's Elena Gilbert, Mrs. Flowers. We've found Stefan, and we need to get in!"

The figure at the window did not move or otherwise acknowledge her words. Yet from its posture, Elena could tell it was still looking down on them.

"Mrs. Flowers, we have Stefan," she called again, gesturing to the lighted interior of the car. "Please!"

"Elena! It's unlocked already!" Bonnie's voice floated to her from the front porch, distracting Elena from the figure at the window. When she looked back up, she saw the curtains falling into place, and then the light in that upstairs room snapped off.

It was strange, but she had no time to puzzle over it. She and Meredith helped Matt lift Stefan and carry him up the front steps.

Inside, the house was dark and still. Elena directed the others up the staircase that stood opposite the door, and onto the second-floor landing. From there they went into a bedroom, and Elena had Bonnie open the door of what looked like a closet. It revealed another stairway, very dim and narrow.

"Who would leave their—front door unlocked—after all that's happened recently?" Matt grunted as they hauled their lifeless burden. "She must be crazy."

"She *is* crazy," Bonnie said from above, pushing the door at the top of the staircase open. "Last time we were here she talked about the weirdest—" Her voice broke off in a gasp.

"What is it?" said Elena. But as they reached the threshold of Stefan's room, she saw for herself.

She'd forgotten the condition the room had been in the last time she'd seen it. Trunks filled with clothing were upended or lying on their sides, as if they'd been thrown by some giant hand from wall to wall. Their contents were strewn about the floor, along with articles from the dresser and tables. Furniture was overturned, and a window was broken, allowing a cold wind to blow in. There was only one lamp on, in a corner, and grotesque shadows loomed against the ceiling.

"*What happened?*" said Matt.

Elena didn't answer until they had stretched Stefan out on the bed. "I don't know for certain," she said, and this was true, if just barely. "But it was already this way last night. Matt, will you help me? He needs to get dry."

"I'll find another lamp," said Meredith, but Elena spoke quickly.

"No, we can see all right. Why don't you try to get a fire going?"

Spilling from one of the gaping trunks was a terry cloth robe of some dark color. Elena took it, and she and Matt began to strip off Stefan's wet and clinging clothes. She worked on getting his sweater off, but one glimpse of his neck was enough to freeze her in place.

"Matt, could you—could you hand me that towel?"

As soon as he turned, she tugged the sweater over Stefan's head and quickly wrapped the robe around him. When Matt turned back and handed her the towel, she wound it around Stefan's throat like a scarf. Her pulse was racing, her mind working furiously.

No wonder he was so weak, so lifeless. Oh, God. She had to examine him, to see how bad it was. But how could she, with Matt and the others here?

"I'm going to get a doctor," Matt said in a tight voice, his eyes on Stefan's face. "He needs help, Elena."

Elena panicked. "Matt, no . . . please. He—he's afraid of doctors. I don't know what would happen if you brought one here." Again, it was the truth, if not the whole truth. She had an idea of what might help Stefan, but she couldn't do it with the others there. She bent over Stefan, rubbing his hands between her own, trying to think.

What could she do? Protect Stefan's secret at the cost of his life? Or betray him in order to save him? *Would* it save him to tell Matt and Bonnie and Meredith? She looked at her friends, trying to picture their response if they were to learn the truth about Stefan Salvatore.

It was no good. She couldn't risk it. The shock and horror of the discovery had nearly sent Elena herself reeling into madness. If she, who loved Stefan, had been ready to run from him screaming, what would these three do? And then there was Mr. Tanner's murder. If they knew what Stefan was, would they ever be able to believe him innocent? Or, in their heart of hearts, would they always suspect him?

Elena shut her eyes. It was just too dangerous. Meredith and Bonnie and Matt were her friends, but this was one thing she couldn't share with them. In all the world, there was no one she could trust with this secret. She would have to keep it alone.

She straightened up and looked at Matt. "He's afraid of doctors but a nurse might be all right." She turned to where Bonnie and Meredith were kneeling before the fireplace. "Bonnie, what about your sister?"

"Mary?" Bonnie glanced at her watch. "She has the late shift at the clinic this week, but she's probably home by now. Only—"

"Then that's it. Matt, you go with Bonnie and ask Mary

to come here and look at Stefan. If she thinks he needs a doctor, I won't argue anymore."

Matt hesitated, then exhaled sharply. "All right. I still think you're wrong, but—let's go, Bonnie. We're going to break some traffic laws."

As they went to the door, Meredith remained standing by the fireplace, watching Elena with steady dark eyes.

Elena made herself meet them. "Meredith . . . I think you should all go."

"Do you?" Those dark eyes remained on hers unwaveringly, as if trying to pierce through and read her mind. But Meredith did not ask any other questions. After a moment she nodded, and followed Matt and Bonnie without a word.

When Elena heard the door at the bottom of the staircase close, she hastily righted a lamp that lay overturned by the bedside and plugged it in. Now, at last, she could take stock of Stefan's injuries.

His color seemed worse than before; he was literally almost as white as the sheets below him. His lips were white, too, and Elena suddenly thought of Thomas Fell, the founder of Fell's Church. Or, rather, of Thomas Fell's statue, lying beside his wife's on the stone lid of their tomb. Stefan was the color of that marble.

The cuts and gashes on his hands showed livid purple, but they were no longer bleeding. She gently turned his head to look at his neck.

And there it was. She touched the side of her own neck automatically, as if to verify the resemblance. But Stefan's marks were not small punctures. They were deep, savage tears in the flesh. He looked as if he had been mauled by some animal that had tried to rip out his throat.

White-hot anger blazed through Elena again. And with it, hatred. She realized that despite her disgust and fury, she had not really hated Damon before. Not really. But now . . . now, she *hated*. She loathed him with an intensity of emotion that she had never felt for anyone else in her life. She wanted to hurt him to make him pay. If she'd had a wooden stake at that moment, she would have hammered it through Damon's heart without regret.

But just now she had to think of Stefan. He was so terrifyingly still. That was the hardest thing to bear, the lack of purpose or resistance in his body, the emptiness. That was it. It was as if he had vacated this form and left her with an empty vessel.

"Stefan!" Shaking him did nothing. With one hand on the center of his cold chest, she tried to detect a heartbeat. If there was one, it was too faint to feel.

Keep calm, Elena, she told herself, pushing back the part of her mind that wanted to panic. The part that was saying, "What if he's dead? What if he's really dead, and nothing you can do will save him?"

Glancing about the room, she saw the broken window. Shards of glass lay on the floor beneath it. She went over and picked one up, noting how it sparkled in the firelight. A pretty thing, with an edge like a razor, she thought. Then, deliberately, setting her teeth, she cut her finger with it.

The pain made her gasp. After an instant, blood began welling out of the cut, dripping down her finger like wax down a candlestick. Quickly, she knelt by Stefan and put her finger to his lips.

With her other hand, she clasped his unresponsive one, feeling the hardness of the silver ring he wore. Motionless as a statue herself, she knelt there and waited.

She almost missed the first tiny flicker of response. Her eyes were fixed on his face, and she caught the minute lifting of his chest only in her peripheral vision. But then the lips beneath her finger quivered and parted slightly, and he swallowed reflexively.

"That's it," Elena whispered. "Come on, Stefan."

His eyelashes fluttered, and with dawning joy she felt his fingers return the pressure of hers. He swallowed again.

"Yes." She waited until his eyes blinked and slowly opened before sitting back. Then she fumbled one-handed with the high neck of her sweater, folding it out of the way.

Those green eyes were dazed and heavy, but as stubborn as she had ever seen them. "No," Stefan said, his voice a cracked whisper.

"You have to, Stefan. The others are coming back and bringing a nurse with them. I had to agree to that. And if you're not well enough to convince her you don't need a hospital . . . " She left the sentence unfinished. She herself didn't know what a doctor or lab technician would find examining Stefan. But she knew he knew, and that it made him afraid.

But Stefan only looked more obstinate, turning his face away from her. "Can't," he whispered. "It's too dangerous. Already took . . . too much . . . last night."

Could it have been only last night? It seemed a year ago. "Will it kill me?" she asked. "Stefan, answer me! Will it kill me?"

"No . . . " His voice was sullen. "But—"

"Then we have to do it. Don't argue with me!" Bending over him, holding his hand in hers, Elena could feel his overpowering need. She was amazed that he was even trying to resist. It was like a starving man standing before a banquet, unable to take his eyes from the steaming dishes, but refusing to eat.

"No," Stefan said again, and Elena felt frustration surge through her. He was the only person she'd ever met who was as stubborn as she was.

"Yes. And if you won't cooperate I'll cut something else, like my wrist." She had been pressing her finger into the sheet to staunch the blood; now she held it up to him.

His pupils dilated, his lips parted. "Too much . . . already," he murmured, but his gaze remained on her finger, on the bright drop of blood at the tip. "And I can't . . . control . . . "

"It's all right," she whispered. She drew the finger across his lips again, feeling them open to take it in; then, she leaned over him and shut her eyes.

His mouth was cool and dry as it touched her throat. His hand cupped the back of her neck as his lips sought the two little punctures already there. Elena willed herself not to recoil at the brief sting of pain. Then she smiled.

Before, she had felt his agonizing need, his driving hunger. Now, through the bond they shared, she felt only fierce joy and satisfaction. Deep satisfaction as the hunger was gradually assuaged.

Her own pleasure came from giving, from knowing that she was sustaining Stefan with her own life. She could sense the strength flowing into him.

In time, she felt the intensity of the need lessen. Still, it was by no means gone, and she could not understand when Stefan tried to push her away.

"That's enough," he grated, forcing her shoulders up.

Elena opened her eyes, her dreamy pleasure broken. His own eyes were green as mandrake leaves, and in his face she saw the fierce hunger of the predator.

"It isn't enough. You're still weak—"

"It's enough for *you*." He pushed at her again, and she saw something like desperation spark in those green eyes. "Elena, if I take much more, you will begin to change. And if you don't move away, if you don't move away from me *right now* . . ."

Elena withdrew to the foot of the bed. She watched him sit up and adjust the dark robe. In the lamplight, she saw that his skin had regained some color, a slight flush glazing its pallor. His hair was drying into a tumbled sea of dark waves.

"I missed you," she said softly. Relief throbbed within her suddenly, an ache that was almost as bad as the fear and tension had been. Stefan was alive; he was talking to her. Everything was going to be all right after all.

"Elena . . ." Their eyes met and she was held by green fire. Unconsciously, she moved toward him, and then stopped as he laughed aloud.

"I've never seen you look like this before," he said, and she looked down at herself. Her shoes and jeans were caked with red mud, which was also liberally smeared over the rest of her. Her jacket was torn and leaking its down stuffing. She had no doubt that her face was smudged and dirty, and she *knew* her hair was tangled and straggly. Elena Gilbert, immaculate fashion plate of Robert E. Lee, was a mess.

"I like it," Stefan said, and this time she laughed with him.

They were still laughing as the door opened. Elena stiffened alertly, twitching at her turtleneck, glancing around the room for evidence that might betray them. Stefan sat up straighter and licked his lips.

"He's better!" Bonnie caroled out as she stepped into the room and saw Stefan. Matt and Meredith were right behind her, and their faces lit with surprise and pleasure. The fourth person who came in was only a little older than Bonnie, but she had an air of brisk authority that belied her youth. Mary McCullough went straight over to her patient and reached for his pulse.

"So you're the one afraid of doctors," she said.

Stefan looked disconcerted for a moment; then, he recovered. "It's sort of a childhood phobia," he said, sounding embarrassed. He glanced sideways at Elena, who smiled nervously and gave a tiny nod. "Anyway, I don't need one now, as you can see."

"Why don't you let me be the judge of that? Your pulse is all right. In fact, it's surprisingly slow, even for an athlete. I don't think you're hypothermic, but you're still chilled. Let's get a temperature."

"No, I really don't think that's necessary." Stefan's voice was low, calming. Elena had heard him use that voice before, and she knew what he was trying to do. But Mary took not the slightest notice.

"Open up, please."

"Here, I'll do it," said Elena quickly, reaching to take the thermometer from Mary. Somehow, as she did so, the little glass tube slipped out of her hand. It fell to the hardwood floor and smashed into several pieces. "Oh, I'm sorry!"

"It doesn't matter," Stefan said. "I'm feeling much better than I was, and I'm getting warmer all the time."

Mary regarded the mess on the floor, then looked around the room, taking in its ransacked state. "All right," she demanded, turning around with hands on hips. "What's been going on here?"

Stefan didn't even blink. "Nothing much. Mrs. Flowers is just a terrible housekeeper," he said, looking her straight in the eye.

Elena wanted to laugh, and she saw that Mary did, too. The older girl grimaced and crossed her arms over her chest instead. "I suppose it's useless to hope for a straight answer," she said. "And it's clear you're not dangerously ill. I can't *make* you go to the clinic. But I'd strongly suggest you get a checkup tomorrow."

"Thank you," said Stefan, which, Elena noticed, was

not the same as agreeing.

"Elena, *you* look as if you could use a doctor," said Bonnie. "You're white as a ghost."

"I'm just tired," Elena said. "It's been a long day."

"My advice is to go home and go to bed—and stay there," Mary said. "You're not anemic, are you?"

Elena resisted the impulse to put a hand to her cheek. Was she so pale? "No, I'm just tired," she repeated. "We can go home now, if Stefan's all right."

He nodded reassuringly, the message in his eyes for her alone. "Give us a minute, will you?" he said to Mary and the others, and they stepped back to the staircase.

"Good-bye. Take care of yourself," Elena said aloud as she hugged him. She whispered, "Why didn't you use your Powers on Mary?"

"I did," he said grimly in her ear. "Or at least I tried. I must still be weak. Don't worry; it'll pass."

"Of course, it will," said Elena, but her stomach lurched. "Are you sure you should be alone, though? What if—"

"I'll be fine. You're the one who shouldn't be alone." Stefan's voice was soft but urgent. "Elena, I didn't get a chance to warn you. You were right about Damon being in Fell's Church."

"I know. *He* did this to you, didn't he?" Elena didn't mention that she'd gone searching for him.

"I—don't remember. But he's dangerous. Keep Bonnie and Meredith with you tonight, Elena. I don't want you alone. And make sure no one invites a stranger into your house."

"We're going straight to bed," Elena promised, smiling at him. "We won't be inviting anybody in."

"Make sure of it." There was no flippancy in his tone at all, and she nodded slowly.

"I understand, Stefan. We'll be careful."

"Good." They kissed, a mere brushing of lips, but their joined hands separated only reluctantly. "Tell the others 'thank you,'" he said.

"I will."

The five of them regrouped outside the boarding house, Matt offering to drive Mary home so Bonnie and Meredith could go back with Elena. Mary was still clearly suspicious about the night's goings-on, and Elena couldn't blame her. She also couldn't think. She was too tired.

"He said to say 'thanks' to all of you," she remembered after Matt had left.

"He's . . . welcome," Bonnie said, splitting the words with an enormous yawn as Meredith opened the car door for her.

Meredith said nothing. She had been very quiet since leaving Elena alone with Stefan.

Bonnie laughed suddenly. "One thing we all forgot

about," she said. "The prophecy."

"What prophecy?" said Elena.

"About the bridge. The one you say I said. Well, you went to the bridge and Death wasn't waiting there after all. Maybe you misunderstood the words."

"No," said Meredith. "We heard the words correctly all right."

"Well, then, maybe it's another bridge. Or . . . mmm . . ." Bonnie snuggled down in her coat, shutting her eyes, and didn't bother to finish.

But Elena's mind completed the sentence for her. *Or another time.*

An owl hooted outside as Meredith started the car.

5

November 2, Saturday

ear Diary,

This morning I woke up and felt so strange. I don't know how to describe it. On the one hand, I was so weak that when I tried to stand up my muscles wouldn't support me. But on the other hand I felt . . . pleasant. So comfortable, so relaxed. As if I were floating on a bed of golden light. I didn't care if I never moved again.

Then I remembered Stefan, and I tried to get up, but Aunt Judith put me back to bed. She said Bonnie and Meredith had left hours ago, and that I'd been so fast asleep they couldn't wake me. She said what I needed was rest.

So here I am. Aunt Judith brought the TV in, but I don't care about watching it. I'd rather lie here and write, or just lie here.

I'm expecting Stefan to call. He told me he would. Or maybe he didn't. I can't remember. When he does call I have to

November 3, Sunday, 10:30 p.m.

I've just read over yesterday's entry and I'm shocked. What was wrong with me? I broke off in the middle of a sentence, and now I don't even know what I was going to say. And I didn't explain about my new diary or anything. I must have been completely spaced out.

Anyway, this is the official start of my new diary. I bought this blank book at the drugstore. It's not as beautiful as the other one, but it will have to do. I've given up hope of ever seeing my old one again. Whoever stole it isn't going to bring it back. But when I think of them reading it, all my inner thoughts and my feelings about Stefan, I want to kill them. While simultaneously dying of humiliation myself.

I'm not ashamed of the way I feel about Stefan. But it's private. And there are things in there, about the way it is when we kiss, when he holds me, *that I know he wouldn't want anybody else to read.*

Of course, it hasn't got anything about his secret in it. I hadn't found that out yet. It wasn't until I did that I really understood him, and we got together, really together, at last. Now we're part of each other. I feel as if I've been waiting for him all my life.

Maybe you think I'm terrible for loving him, considering what he is. He can be violent, and I know there are some things in his past that he's ashamed of. But he could never be violent toward me, and the past is over. He has so much guilt and he hurts so much inside. I want to heal him.

I don't know what will happen now; I'm just so glad that he's safe. I went to the boarding house today and found out that the police had been there yesterday. Stefan was still weak and couldn't use his Powers to get rid of them, but they didn't accuse him of anything. They just asked questions. Stefan says they acted friendly, which makes me suspicious. What all the questions really boil down to is: where were you on the night the old man was attacked under the bridge, and the night Vickie Bennett was attacked in the ruined church, and the night Mr. Tanner was killed at school?

They don't have any evidence against him. So the crimes started right after he came to Fell's Church, so what? That's not proof of anything. So he argued with Mr. Tanner that night. Again, so what? Everybody argued with Mr. Tanner. So he disappeared after Mr. Tanner's body was found. He's back now and it's pretty clear that he was attacked himself, by the same person who committed the other crimes. Mary told the police about the condition he was in. And if they ever ask us, Matt and Bonnie and Meredith and I can all testify how we found him. There's no case against him at all.

Stefan and I talked about that, and about other things. It was so good to be with him again, even if he did look white and tired. He still doesn't remember how Thursday night ended, but most of it is just as I suspected. Stefan went to find Damon Thursday night after he took me home. They argued. Stefan ended up half-dead in a well. It doesn't take a genius to figure out what happened in between.

I still haven't told him that I went looking for Damon in the graveyard Friday morning. I suppose I'd better do it tomorrow. I know he's going to be upset, especially when he hears what Damon said to me.

> *Well, that's all. I'm tired. This diary is going to be well-hidden, for obvious reasons.*

Elena paused and looked at the last line on the page. Then she added:

P.S. I wonder who our new European History teacher will be?

She tucked the diary under her mattress and turned out the light.

Elena walked down the hallway in a curious vacuum. At school she was usually peppered with greetings from all sides; it was "hi, Elena," after "hi, Elena," wherever she went. But today eyes slid away furtively as she approached, or people suddenly became very busy doing something that required them to keep their backs to her. It had been happening all day long.

She paused in the doorway of the European History classroom. There were several students already sitting down, and at the chalkboard was a stranger.

He looked almost like a student himself. He had sandy hair, worn a little long, and the build of an athlete. Across the board he had written "Alaric K. Saltzman." As he turned around, Elena saw that he also had a boyish smile.

He went on smiling as Elena sat down and other students filed in. Stefan was among them, and his eyes met Elena's as he took his seat beside her, but they didn't speak. No one was talking. The room was dead silent.

Bonnie sat down on Elena's other side. Matt was only a few desks away, but he was looking straight ahead.

The last two people to come in were Caroline Forbes and Tyler Smallwood. They walked in together, and Elena didn't like the look on Caroline's face. She knew that catlike smile and those narrowed green eyes all too well. Tyler's handsome, rather fleshy features were shining with satisfaction. The discoloration under his eyes caused by Stefan's fist was almost gone.

"Okay, to start off, why don't we put all these desks in a circle?"

Elena's attention snapped back to the stranger at the front of the room. He was still smiling.

"Come on, let's do it. That way we can all see each other's faces when we talk," he said.

Silently, the students obeyed. The stranger didn't sit at Mr. Tanner's desk; instead, he pulled a chair to the circle and straddled it backward.

"Now," he said, "I know you all must be curious about me. My name's on the board: Alaric K. Saltzman. But I want you to call me Alaric. I'll tell you a little more about me later, but first I want to give you a chance to talk.

"Today's probably a difficult day for most of you. Someone you cared about is gone, and that must hurt. I want to give you a chance to open up and share those feelings with me and with your classmates. I want you to try to get in touch with the pain. Then we can start to build our own relationship on trust. Now who would like to go first?"

They stared at him. No one so much as moved an eyelash.

"Well, let's see . . . what about you?" Still smiling, he gestured encouragingly to a pretty, fair-haired girl. "Tell us your name and how you feel about what's happened."

Flustered, the girl stood. "My name's Sue Carson, and, uh . . ." She took a deep breath and went doggedly on. "And I feel scared. Because whoever this maniac is, he's still loose. And next time it could be me." She sat down.

"Thank you, Sue. I'm sure a lot of your classmates share your concern. Now, do I understand that some of you were actually there when this tragedy occurred?"

Desks creaked as students shifted uneasily. But Tyler Smallwood stood up, his lips drawing back from strong white teeth in a smile.

"*Most* of us were there," he said, and his eyes flickered toward Stefan. Elena could see other people following his gaze. "I got there right after Bonnie discovered the body. And what I feel is concern for the community. There's a dangerous killer on the streets, and so far nobody's done anything to stop him. And—" He broke off. Elena wasn't sure how, but she felt Caroline had signaled him to do it.

Caroline tossed back gleaming auburn hair and recrossed her long legs as Tyler took his seat again.

"Okay, thank you. So most of you were there. That makes it doubly hard. Can we hear from the person who actually found the body? Is Bonnie here?" He looked around.

Bonnie raised her hand slowly, then stood. "I *guess* I discovered the body," she said. "I mean, I was the first person who knew that he was really dead, and not just faking."

Alaric Saltzman looked slightly startled. "Not just faking? Did he often fake being dead?" There were titters, and he flashed that boyish smile again. Elena turned and glanced at Stefan, who was frowning.

"No—no," said Bonnie. "You see, he was a sacrifice. At the Haunted House. So he was covered with blood anyway, only it was fake blood. And that was partly my fault, because he didn't want to put it on, and I told him he had to do it. He was supposed to be a Bloody Corpse. But he kept saying it was too messy, and it wasn't until Stefan came and argued with him—" She stopped. "I mean, we talked to him and he finally agreed to do it, and then the Haunted House started. And a little while later I noticed that he wasn't sitting up and scaring the kids like he was supposed to, and I went over and asked him what was wrong. And he didn't answer. He just—he just kept staring at the ceiling. And then I touched him and he—it was terrible. His head just sort of *flopped*." Bonnie's voice wavered and gave out. She gulped.

Elena was standing up, and so were Stefan and Matt and a few other people. Elena reached over to Bonnie.

"Bonnie, it's okay. Bonnie, don't; it's okay."

"And blood got all over my hands. There was blood everywhere, so much blood . . ." She sniffed hysterically.

"Okay, time out," Alaric Saltzman said. "I'm sorry; I didn't mean to distress you so much. But I think you need to work through these feelings sometime in the future. It's clear that this has been a pretty devastating experience."

He stood up and paced around the center of the circle, his hands opening and shutting nervously. Bonnie was still sniffling softly.

"I know," he said, the boyish smile coming back full force. "I'd like to get our student-teacher relationship off to a good start, away from this whole atmosphere. How about if you all come around to my place this evening, and we can all talk informally? Maybe just get to know each other, maybe talk about what happened. You can even bring a friend if you want. How about it?"

There was another thirty seconds or so of staring. Then someone said, "Your place?"

"Yes . . . oh, I'm forgetting. Stupid of me. I'm staying

at the Ramsey house, on Magnolia Avenue." He wrote the address on the board. "The Ramseys are friends of mine, and they loaned me the house while they're on vacation. I come from Charlottesville, and your principal called me Friday to ask me if I could take over here. I jumped at the chance. This is my first real teaching job."

"Oh, that explains it," said Elena under her breath.

"Does it?" said Stefan.

"Anyway, what do you think? Is it a plan?" Alaric Saltzman looked around at them.

No one had the heart to refuse. There were scattered "yeses" and "sures."

"Great, then it's settled. I'll provide the refreshments, and we'll all get to know each other. Oh, by the way . . . " He opened a grade book and scanned it. "In this class, participation makes up half your final grade." He glanced up and smiled. "You can go now."

"The nerve of him," somebody muttered as Elena went out the door. Bonnie was behind her, but Alaric Saltzman's voice called her back.

"Would the students who shared with us please stay behind for a minute?"

Stefan had to leave, too. "I'd better go check about football practice," he said. "It's probably canceled, but I'd better make sure."

Elena was concerned. "If it's not canceled, do you

think you're feeling up to it?"

"I'll be fine," he said evasively. But she noticed that his face still looked drawn, and he moved as if he were in pain. "Meet you at your locker," he said.

She nodded. When she got to her locker, she saw Caroline nearby talking to two other girls. Three pairs of eyes followed Elena's every move as she put away her books, but when Elena glanced up, two of them suddenly looked away. Only Caroline remained staring at her, head slightly cocked as she whispered something to the other girls.

Elena had had enough. Slamming her locker, she walked straight toward the group. "Hello, Becky; hello, Sheila," she said. Then, with heavy emphasis: "Hello, Caroline."

Becky and Sheila mumbled "hello" and added something about having to leave. Elena didn't even turn to watch them slink away. She kept her eyes on Caroline's.

"What's going on?" she demanded.

"Going on?" Caroline was obviously enjoying this, trying to draw it out as long as possible. "Going on with who?"

"With you, Caroline. With everybody. Don't pretend you're not up to something, because I know you are. People have been avoiding me all day as if I had the plague, and you look like you just won the lottery. What have you done?"

Caroline's expression of innocent inquiry slipped, and she smiled a feline smile. "I told you when school started that things were going to be different this year, Elena," she said. "I warned you your time on the throne might be running out. But it isn't *my* doing. What's happening is simply natural selection. The law of the jungle."

"And just what *is* happening?"

"Well, let's just say that going out with a murderer can put a cramp in your social life."

Elena's chest tightened as if Caroline had hit her. For a moment, the desire to hit Caroline back was almost irresistible. Then, with the blood pounding in her ears, she said through clenched teeth, "That isn't true. Stefan hasn't done anything. The police questioned him, and he was cleared."

Caroline shrugged. Her smile now was patronizing. "Elena, I've known you since kindergarten," she said, "so I'll give you some advice for old times' sake: drop Stefan. If you do it right now you might just avoid being a complete social leper. Otherwise you might as well buy yourself a little bell to ring in the street."

Rage held Elena hostage as Caroline turned and walked away, her auburn hair moving like liquid under the lights. Then Elena found her tongue.

"Caroline." The other girl turned back. "Are you going to go to that party at the Ramsey house tonight?"

"I suppose so. Why?"

"Because I'll be there. With Stefan. See you in the jungle." This time Elena was the one to turn away.

The dignity of her exit was slightly marred when she saw a slim, shadowed figure at the far end of the hallway. Her step faltered for an instant, but as she drew closer she recognized Stefan.

She knew the smile she gave him looked forced, and he glanced back toward the lockers as they walked side by side out of the school.

"So football practice was canceled?" she said.

He nodded. "What was that all about?" he said quietly.

"Nothing. I asked Caroline if she was going to the party tonight." Elena tilted back her head to look at the gray and dismal sky.

"And that's what you were talking about?"

She remembered what he had told her in his room. He could see better than a human, and hear better, too. Well enough to catch words spoken down forty feet of corridor?

"Yes," she said defiantly, still inspecting the clouds.

"And that's what made you so angry?"

"Yes," she said again, in the same tone.

She could feel his eyes on her. "Elena, that's not true."

"Well, if you can read my mind, you don't need to ask me questions, do you?"

They were facing each other now. Stefan was tense, his

mouth set in a grim line. "You know I wouldn't do that. But I thought you were the one who was so big on honesty in relationships."

"All right. Caroline was being her usual bitchy self and shooting her mouth off about the murder. So what? Why do you care?"

"Because," said Stefan simply, brutally, "she might be right. Not about the murder but about you. About you and me. I should have realized this would happen. It's not just her, is it? I've been sensing hostility and fear all day, but I was too tired to try and analyze it. They think I'm the killer and they're taking it out on you."

"What they think doesn't matter! They're wrong, and they'll realize that eventually. Then everything will be the way it was again."

A wistful smile tugged at the corner of Stefan's mouth. "You really believe that, don't you?" He looked away, and his face hardened. "And what if they don't? What if it only gets worse?"

"What are you saying?"

"It might be better . . ." Stefan took a deep breath and continued, carefully. "It might be better if we didn't see each other for a while. If they think we're not together, they'll leave you alone."

She stared at him. "And you think you could do that? Not see me or talk to me for however long?"

"If it's necessary—yes. We could pretend we've broken up." His jaw was set.

Elena stared another moment. Then she circled him and moved in closer, so close that they were almost touching. He had to look down at her, his eyes only a few inches from her own.

"There is," she said, "only one way I'm going to announce to the rest of the school that we've broken up. And that's if you tell me that you don't love me and you don't want to see me. Tell me that, Stefan, right now. Tell me that you don't want to be with me anymore."

He'd stopped breathing. He stared down at her, those green eyes striated like a cat's in shades of emerald and malachite and holly green.

"Say it," she told him. "Tell me how you can get along without me, Stefan. Tell me—"

She never got to finish the sentence. It was cut off as his mouth descended on hers.

tefan sat in the Gilbert living room, agreeing
politely with whatever it was Aunt Judith was
saying. The older woman was uncomfortable
having him here; you didn't need to be a mind reader to
know that. But she was trying, and so Stefan was trying,
too. He wanted Elena to be happy.

Elena. Even when he wasn't looking at her, he was
aware of her more than of anything else in the room. Her
living presence beat against his skin like sunlight against
closed eyelids. When he actually let himself turn to face
her, it was a sweet shock to all his senses.

He loved her so much. He never saw her as Katherine
anymore; he had almost forgotten how much she looked
like the dead girl. In any case there were so many differences. Elena had the same pale gold hair and creamy skin,

the same delicate features as Katherine, but there the resemblance ended. Her eyes, looking violet in the firelight just now but normally a blue as dark as lapis lazuli, were neither timid nor childlike as Katherine's had been. On the contrary, they were windows to her soul, which shone like an eager flame behind them. Elena was Elena, and her image had replaced Katherine's gentle ghost in his heart.

But her very strength made their love dangerous. He hadn't been able to resist her last week when she'd offered him her blood. Granted, he might have died without it, but it had been far too soon for Elena's own safety. For the hundredth time, his eyes moved over Elena's face, searching for the telltale signs of change. Was that creamy skin a little paler? Was her expression slightly more remote?

They would have to be careful from now on. *He* would have to be more careful. Make sure to feed often, satisfy himself with animals, so he wouldn't be tempted. Never let the need get too strong. Now that he thought of it, he was hungry right now. The dry ache, the burning, was spreading along his upper jaw, whispering through his veins and capillaries. He should be out in the woods—senses alert to catch the slightest crackle of dry twigs, muscles ready for the chase—not here by a fire watching the tracery of pale blue veins in Elena's throat.

That slim throat turned as Elena looked at him.

"Do you want to go to that party tonight? We can take Aunt Judith's car," she said.

"But you ought to stay for dinner first," said Aunt Judith quickly.

"We can pick up something on the way." Elena meant they could pick up something for her, Stefan thought. He himself could chew and swallow ordinary food if he had to, though it did him no good, and he had long since lost any taste for it. No, his . . . appetites . . . were more particular now, he thought. And if they went to this party, it would mean hours more before he could feed. But he nodded agreement to Elena.

"If you want to," he said.

She did want to; she was set on it. He'd seen that from the beginning. "All right then, I'd better change."

He followed her to the base of the stairway. "Wear something with a high neck. A sweater," he told her in a voice too low to carry.

She glanced through the doorway, to the empty living room, and said, "It's all right. They're almost healed already. See?" She tugged her lacy collar down, twisting her head to one side.

Stefan stared, mesmerized, at the two round marks on the fine-grained skin. They were a very light translucent burgundy color, like much-watered wine. He set his teeth and forced his eyes away. Looking much longer at that would drive him crazy.

"That wasn't what I meant," he said brusquely.

The shining veil of her hair fell over the marks again, hiding them. "Oh."

"Come in!"

As they did, walking into the room, conversations stopped. Elena looked at the faces turned toward them, at the curious, furtive eyes and the wary expressions. Not the kind of looks she was used to getting when she made an entrance.

It was another student who'd opened the door for them; Alaric Saltzman was nowhere in sight. But Caroline was, seated on a bar stool, which showed off her legs to their best advantage. She gave Elena a mocking look and then made some remark to a boy on her right. He laughed.

Elena could feel her smile start to go painful, while a flush crept up toward her face. Then a familiar voice came to her.

"Elena, Stefan! Over here."

Gratefully, she spotted Bonnie sitting with Meredith and Ed Goff on a loveseat in the corner. She and Stefan settled on a large ottoman opposite them, and she heard conversations start to pick up again around the room.

By tacit agreement, no one mentioned the awkwardness of Elena and Stefan's arrival. Elena was determined to pretend that everything was as usual.

And Bonnie and Meredith were backing her. "You look great," said Bonnie warmly. "I just love that red sweater."

"She does look nice. Doesn't she, Ed?" said Meredith, and Ed, looking vaguely startled, agreed.

"So your class was invited to this, too," Elena said to Meredith. "I thought maybe it was just seventh period."

"I don't know if *invited* is the word," replied Meredith dryly. "Considering that participation is half our grade."

"Do you think he was serious about that? He couldn't be serious," put in Ed.

Elena shrugged. "He sounded serious to me. Where's Ray?" she asked Bonnie.

"Ray? Oh, Ray. I don't know, around somewhere, I suppose. There's a lot of people here."

That was true. The Ramsey living room was packed, and from what Elena could see the crowd flowed into the dining room, the front parlor, and probably the kitchen as well. Elbows kept brushing Elena's hair as people circulated behind her.

"What did Saltzman want with you after class?" Stefan was saying.

"Alaric," Bonnie corrected primly. "He wants us to call him Alaric. Oh, he was just being nice. He felt awful for making me relive such an agonizing experience. He didn't know exactly how Mr. Tanner died, and he hadn't realized I was so sensitive. Of course, he's incredibly sensitive himself, so he understands what it's like. He's an Aquarius."

"With a moon rising in pickup lines," said Meredith under her breath. "Bonnie, you don't believe that garbage, do you? He's a teacher; he shouldn't be trying that out on students."

"He wasn't trying anything out! He said exactly the same thing to Tyler and Sue Carson. He said we should form a support group for each other or write an essay about that night to get our feelings out. He said teenagers are all very impressionable and he didn't want the tragedy to have a lasting impact on our lives."

"Oh, brother," said Ed, and Stefan turned a laugh into a cough. He wasn't amused, though, and his question to Bonnie hadn't been just idle curiosity. Elena could tell; she could feel it radiating from him. Stefan felt about Alaric Saltzman the way that most of the people in this room felt about Stefan. Wary and mistrustful.

"It *was* strange, him acting as if the party was a sponta-neous idea in our class," she said, responding uncon-sciously to Stefan's unspoken words, "when obviously it had been planned."

"What's even stranger is the idea that the school would hire a teacher without telling him how the previous teacher died," said Stefan. "Everyone was talking about it; it must have been in the papers."

"But not all the details," said Bonnie firmly. "In fact, there are things the police still haven't let out because they think it might help them catch the killer. For instance"—she dropped her voice—"do you know what Mary said? Dr. Feinberg was talking to the guy who did the autopsy, the medical examiner. And he said that there was no blood left in the body at all. Not a drop."

Elena felt an icy wind blow through her, as if she stood once again in the graveyard. She couldn't speak. But Ed said, "Where'd it go?"

"Well, all over the floor, I suppose," said Bonnie calmly. "All over the altar and everything. That's what the police are investigating now. But it's unusual for a corpse not to have any blood left; usually there's some that settles down on the underside of the body. Postmortem lividity, it's called. It looks like big purple bruises. What's wrong?"

"Your incredible sensitivity has me ready to throw up," said Meredith in a strangled voice. "Could we possibly talk about something else?"

"*You* weren't the one with blood all over you," Bonnie began, but Stefan interrupted her.

"Have the investigators come to any conclusions from what they've learned? Are they any closer to finding the killer?"

"I don't know," said Bonnie, and then she brightened. "That's right, Elena, you said you knew—"

"Shut up, Bonnie," said Elena desperately. If there ever were a place not to discuss this, it was in a crowded room surrounded by people who hated Stefan. Bonnie's eyes widened, and then she nodded, subsiding.

Elena could not relax, though. Stefan hadn't killed Mr. Tanner, and yet the same evidence that would lead to Damon could as easily lead to him. And *would* lead to him, because no one but she and Stefan knew of Damon's existence. He was out there, somewhere, in the shadows. Waiting for his next victim. Maybe waiting for Stefan—or for her.

"I'm hot," she said abruptly. "I think I'll go see what kinds of refreshments *Alaric* has provided."

Stefan started to rise, but Elena waved him back down. He wouldn't have any use for potato chips and punch. And she wanted to be alone for a few minutes, to be moving instead of sitting, to calm herself.

Being with Meredith and Bonnie had given her a false sense of security. Leaving them, she was once again confronted by sidelong glances and suddenly turned backs. This time it made her angry. She moved through the crowd with deliberate insolence, holding any eye she accidentally caught. I'm already notorious, she thought. I might as well be brazen, too.

She was hungry. In the Ramsey dining room someone had set up an assortment of finger foods that looked surprisingly good. Elena took a paper plate and dropped a few carrot sticks on it, ignoring the people around the bleached oak table. She wasn't going to speak to them unless they spoke first. She gave her full attention to the refreshments, leaning past people to select cheese wedges and Ritz crackers, reaching in front of them to pluck grapes, ostentatiously looking up and down the whole array to see if there was anything she'd missed.

She'd succeeded in riveting everyone's attention, something she knew without raising her eyes. She bit delicately down on a bread stick, holding it between her teeth like a pencil, and turned from the table.

"Mind if I have a bite?"

Shock snapped her eyes wide open and froze her breath. Her mind jammed, refusing to acknowledge what was going on, and leaving her helpless, vulnerable, in the face of it. But though rational thought had disappeared, her senses went right on recording mercilessly: dark eyes dominating her field of vision, a whiff of some kind of cologne in her nostrils, two long fingers tilting her chin up. Damon leaned in, and, neatly and precisely, bit off the other end of the bread stick.

In that moment, their lips were only inches apart. He was leaning in for a second bite before Elena's wits revived enough to throw her backward, her hand grabbing the bit of crisp bread and tossing it away. He caught it in midair, a virtuoso display of reflex.

His eyes were still on hers. Elena got in a breath at last and opened her mouth; she wasn't sure what for. To scream, probably. To warn all these people to run out into the night. Her heart was pounding like a trip-hammer, her vision blurred.

"Easy, easy." He took the plate from her and then somehow got hold of her wrist. He was holding it lightly, the way Mary had felt for Stefan's pulse. As she continued to stare and gasp, he stroked it with his thumb, as if comforting her. "Easy. It's all right."

What are you doing here? she thought. The scene around her seemed eerily bright and unnatural. It was like one of those nightmares when everything is ordinary, just like waking life; and then suddenly something grotesque happens. He was going to kill them all.

"Elena? Are you okay?" Sue Carson was talking to her, gripping her shoulder.

"I think she choked on something," Damon said, releasing Elena's wrist. "But she's all right now. Why don't you introduce us?"

He was going to kill them all. . . .

"Elena; this is Damon, um . . .." Sue spread an apologetic hand, and Damon finished for her.

"Smith." He lifted a paper cup toward Elena. *"La vita."*

"What are you doing here?" she whispered.

"He's a college student," Sue volunteered, when it became apparent that Damon wasn't going to answer. "From—University of Virginia, was it? William and Mary?"

"Among other places," Damon said, still looking at Elena. He hadn't glanced at Sue once. "I like to travel."

The world had snapped into place again around Elena, but it was a chilling world. There were people on every side, watching this exchange with fascination, keeping her from speaking freely. But they were also keeping her safe. For whatever reason, Damon was playing a game, pretending to be one of them. And while the masquerade went on, he wouldn't do anything to her in front of a crowd . . . she hoped.

A game. But he was making up the rules. He was standing here in the Ramseys' dining room playing with her.

"He's just down for a few days," Sue was continuing helpfully. "Visiting—friends, did you say? Or relatives?"

"Yes," said Damon.

"You're lucky to be able to take off whenever you want," Elena said. She didn't know what was possessing her, to make her try and unmask him.

"Luck has very little to do with it," said Damon. "Do you like dancing?"

"What's your major?"

He smiled at her. "American folklore. Did you know, for instance, that a mole on the neck means you'll be wealthy? Do you mind if I check?"

"*I* mind." The voice came from behind Elena. It was clear and cold and quiet. Elena had heard Stefan speak in that tone only once: when he had found Tyler trying to assault her in the graveyard. Damon's fingers stilled on her throat, and, released from his spell, she stepped back.

"But do you matter?" he said.

The two of them faced each other under the faintly flickering yellow light of the brass chandelier.

Elena was aware of layers of her own thoughts, like a parfait. Everyone's staring; this must be better than the movies. . . . I didn't realize Stefan was taller. . . . There's Bonnie and Meredith wondering what's going on. . . . Stefan's angry but he's still weak, still hurting. . . . If he goes for Damon now, he'll lose. . . .

And in front of all these people. Her thoughts came to a clattering halt as everything fell into place. That was what Damon was here for, to make Stefan attack him, apparently unprovoked. No matter what happened after that, he won. If Stefan drove him away, it would just be more proof of Stefan's "tendency toward violence." More evidence for

Stefan's accusers. And if Stefan lost the fight . . .

It would mean his life, thought Elena. Oh, Stefan, he's so much stronger right now; please don't do it. Don't play into his hands. He *wants* to kill you; he's just looking for a chance.

She made her limbs move, though they were stiff and awkward as a marionette's. "Stefan," she said, taking his cold hand in hers, "let's go home."

She could feel the tension in his body, like an electric current running underneath his skin. At this moment, he was completely focused on Damon, and the light in his eyes was like fire reflecting off a dagger blade. She didn't recognize him in this mood, didn't know him. He frightened her.

"*Stefan,*" she said, calling to him as if she were lost in fog and couldn't find him. "Stefan, *please.*"

And slowly, slowly, she felt him respond. She heard him breathe and felt his body go off alert, clicking down to some lower energy level. The deadly concentration of his mind was diverted and he looked at her, and saw her.

"All right," he said softly, looking into her eyes. "Let's go."

She kept her hands on him as they turned away, one clasping his hand, the other tucked inside his arm. By sheer force of will, she managed not to look over her shoulder as they walked away, but the skin on her back tingled and crawled as if expecting the stab of a knife.

Instead, she heard Damon's low ironical voice: "And have you heard that kissing a red-haired girl cures fever blisters?" And then Bonnie's outrageous, flattered laughter.

On the way out, they finally ran into their host.

"Leaving so soon?" Alaric said. "But I haven't even had a chance to talk to you yet."

He looked both eager and reproachful, like a dog that knows perfectly well it's *not* going to be taken on a walk but wags anyway. Elena felt worry blossom in her stomach for him and everyone else in the house. She and Stefan were leaving them to Damon.

She'd just have to hope her earlier assessment was right and he wanted to continue the masquerade. Right now she had enough to do getting Stefan out of here before he changed his mind.

"I'm not feeling very well," she said as she picked up her purse where it lay by the ottoman. "Sorry." She increased the pressure on Stefan's arm. It would take very little to get him to turn back and head for the dining room right now.

"*I'm* sorry," said Alaric. "Good-bye."

They were on the threshold before she saw the little slip of violet paper stuck into the side pocket of her purse. She pulled it out and unfolded it almost by reflex, her mind on other things.

There was writing on it, plain and bold and unfamiliar. Just three lines. She read them and felt the world rock. This was too much; she couldn't deal with anything more.

"What is it?" said Stefan.

"Nothing." She thrust the bit of paper back into the side pocket, pushing it down with her fingers. "It's nothing, Stefan. Let's get outside."

They stepped out into driving needles of rain.

7

"Next time," Stefan said quietly, "I won't leave." Elena knew he meant it, and it terrified her. But just now her emotions were quietly coasting in neutral, and she didn't want to argue.

"He was there," she said. "Inside an ordinary house full of ordinary people, just as if he had every right to be. I wouldn't have thought he would dare."

"Why not?" Stefan said briefly, bitterly. "I was there in an ordinary house full of ordinary people, just as if I had every right to be."

"I didn't mean that the way it sounded. It's just that the only other time I've seen him in public was at the Haunted House when he was wearing a mask and costume, and it was dark. Before that it was always somewhere deserted,

like the gym that night I was there alone, or the graveyard. . . ."

She knew as soon as she said that last part that it was a
mistake. She still hadn't told Stefan about going to find
Damon three days ago. In the driver's seat, he stiffened.

"Or the graveyard?"

"Yes . . . I meant that day Bonnie and Meredith and I
got chased out. I'm assuming it must have been Damon
who chased us. And the place was deserted except for the
three of us."

Why was she lying to him? Because, a small voice in
her head answered grimly, otherwise he might snap.
Knowing what Damon had said to her, what he had promised was in store, might be all that was needed to send
Stefan over the edge.

I can never tell him, she realized with a sick jolt. Not
about that time or about anything Damon does in the
future. If he fights Damon, he dies.

Then he'll never know, she promised herself. No matter what I have to do, I'll keep them from fighting each
other over me. No matter what.

For a moment apprehension chilled her. Five hundred
years ago, Katherine had tried to keep them from fighting,
and had succeeded only in forcing them into a death
match. But she wouldn't make the same mistake, Elena

told herself fiercely. Katherine's methods had been stupid and childish. Who else but a stupid child would kill herself in the hope that the two rivals for her hand would become friends? It had been the worst mistake of the whole sorry affair. Because of it, the rivalry between Stefan and Damon had turned into implacable hatred. And what's more, Stefan had lived with the guilt of it ever since; he blamed himself for Katherine's stupidity and weakness.

Groping for another subject, she said, "Do you think someone invited him in?"

"Obviously, since he *was* in."

"Then it's true about—people like you. You have to be invited in. But Damon got into the gym without an invitation."

"That's because the gym isn't a dwelling place for the living. That's the one criterion. It doesn't matter if it's a house or a tent or an apartment above a store. If living humans eat and sleep there, we need to be invited inside."

"But I didn't invite you into *my* house."

"Yes, you did. That first night, when I drove you home, you pushed the door open and nodded to me." It doesn't have to be a verbal invitation. If the intent is there, that's enough. And the person inviting you doesn't have to be someone who actually lives in the house. Any human will do."

Elena was thinking. "What about a houseboat?"

"Same thing. Although running water can be a barrier in itself. For some of us, it's almost impossible to cross."

Elena had a sudden vision of herself and Meredith and Bonnie racing for Wickery Bridge. Because somehow she had known that if they got to the other side of the river they'd be safe from whatever was after them.

"So *that's* why," she whispered. It still didn't explain how she'd known, though. It was as if the knowledge had been put into her head from some outside source. Then she realized something else.

"You took me across the bridge. You can cross running water."

"That's because I'm weak." It was said flatly, with no emotion behind it. "It's ironic, but the stronger your Powers are, the more you're affected by certain limitations. The more you belong to the dark, the more the rules of the dark bind you."

"What other rules are there?" said Elena. She was beginning to see the glimmer of a plan. Or at least of the hope of a plan.

Stefan looked at her. "Yes," he said, "I think it's time you knew. The more you know about Damon, the more chance you'll have of protecting yourself."

Of protecting herself? Perhaps Stefan knew more than she thought. But as he turned the car onto a side street and parked, she just said, "Okay. Should I be stocking up on garlic?"

He laughed. "Only if you want to be unpopular. There are certain plants, though, that might help you. Like vervain. That's an herb that's supposed to protect you against bewitchment, and it can keep your mind clear even if someone is using Powers against you. People used to wear it around their necks. Bonnie would love it; it was sacred to the druids."

"Vervain," said Elena, tasting the unfamiliar word. "What else?"

"Strong light, or direct sunlight, can be very painful. You'll notice the weather's changed."

"I've noticed," said Elena after a beat. "You mean Damon's doing that?"

"He must be. It takes enormous power to control the elements, but it makes it easy for him to travel in daylight. As long as he keeps it cloudy, he doesn't even need to protect his eyes."

"And neither do you," Elena said. "What about—well, crosses and things?"

"No effect," said Stefan. "Except that if the person holding one *believes* it's a protection, it can strengthen their will to resist tremendously."

"Uh . . . silver bullets?"

Stefan laughed again shortly. "That's for werewolves.

From what I've heard they don't like silver in any form. A wooden stake through the heart is still the approved method for my kind. There are other ways that are more or less effective, though: burning, beheading, driving nails through the temples. Or, best of all—"

"Stefan!" The lonely, bitter smile on his face dismayed her. "What about changing into animals?" she said. "Before, you said that with enough Power you could do that. If Damon can be any animal he likes, how will we ever recognize him?"

"Not any animal he likes. He's limited to one animal, or at the most two. Even with his Powers I don't think he could sustain any more than that."

"So we keep looking out for a crow."

"Right. You may be able to tell if he's around, too, by looking at regular animals. They usually don't react very well to us; they sense that we're hunters."

"Yangtze kept barking at that crow. It was as if he knew there was something wrong about it," Elena remembered. "Ah . . . Stefan," she added in a changed tone as a new thought struck her, "what about mirrors? I don't remember ever seeing you in one."

For a moment, he didn't answer. Then he said, "Legend has it that mirrors reflect the soul of the person who looks into them. That's why primitive people are afraid of mirrors; they're afraid that their souls will be trapped and stolen. My kind is supposed to have no reflection—because we have no souls." Slowly, he reached up to the rearview mirror and tilted it downward, adjusting it so that Elena could look into it. In the silvered glass, she saw his eyes, lost, haunted, and infinitely sad.

There was nothing to do but hold on to him, and Elena did. "I love you," she whispered. It was the only comfort she could give him. It was all they had.

His arms tightened around her; his face was buried in her hair. "You're the mirror," he whispered back.

It was good to feel him relax, tension flowing out of his body as warmth and comfort flowed in. She was comforted, too, a sense of peace infusing her, surrounding her. It was so good that she forgot to ask him what he meant until they were at her front door, saying good-bye.

"I'm the mirror?" she said then, looking up at him.

"You've stolen my soul," he said. "Lock the door behind you, and don't open it again tonight." Then he was gone.

"Elena, thank heavens," said Aunt Judith. When Elena stared at her, she added, "Bonnie called from the party. She said you'd left unexpectedly, and when you didn't come home I was worried."

"Stefan and I went for a ride." Elena didn't like the expression on her aunt's face when she said that. "Is there a problem?"

"No, no. It's just . . . " Aunt Judith didn't seem to know how to finish her sentence. "Elena, I wonder if it might be a good idea to . . . not see quite so much of Stefan."

Elena went still. "You, too?"

"It isn't that I believe the gossip," Aunt Judith assured her. "But, for your own sake, it might be best to get a little distance from him, to—"

"To dump him? To abandon him because people are spreading rumors about him? To keep myself away from the mudslinging in case any of it sticks on me?" Anger was a welcome release, and the words crowded in Elena's throat, all trying to get out at once. "No, I *don't* think that's a good idea, Aunt Judith. And if it were Robert we were talking about, you wouldn't either. Or maybe you would!"

"Elena, I will not have you speaking to me in that tone—"

"I'm finished anyway!" Elena cried, and whirled blindly for the stairs. She managed to keep the tears back until she was in her own room with the door locked. Then she threw herself on the bed and sobbed.

She dragged herself up a while later to call Bonnie. Bonnie was excited and voluble. What on earth did Elena mean, had anything unusual happened after she and Stefan left? The unusual thing was their leaving! No, that new guy Damon hadn't said anything about Stefan afterward; he'd just hung around for a while and then disappeared. No, Bonnie hadn't seen if he left with anybody. Why? Was Elena jealous? Yes, that was meant to be a joke. But, really, he *was* gorgeous, wasn't he? Almost more gorgeous than Stefan, that is assuming you liked dark hair and eyes. Of course, if you liked lighter hair and hazel eyes . . .

Elena immediately deduced that Alaric Saltzman's eyes were hazel.

She got off the phone at last and only then remembered the note she'd found in her purse. She should have asked Bonnie if anyone had gone near her purse while she was in the dining room. But then, Bonnie and Meredith had been in the dining room part of the time themselves. Someone might have done it then.

The very sight of the violet paper made her taste tin at the back of her mouth. She could hardly bear to look at it. But now that she was alone she *had* to unfold it and read it again, all the time hoping that somehow this time the words might be different, that she might have been mistaken before.

But they weren't different. The sharp, clean block letters stood out against the pale background as if they were ten feet high.

I want to touch him. More than any boy I've ever known.

And I know he wants it, too, but he's holding back on me.

Her words. From her diary. The one that had been stolen.

The next day Meredith and Bonnie rang her doorbell.

"Stefan called me last night," said Meredith. "He said he wanted to make sure you weren't walking to school alone. He's not going to be at school today, so he asked if Bonnie and I could come over and walk with you."

"Escort you," said Bonnie, who was clearly in a good mood. "Chaperone you. I think it's terribly sweet of him to be so protective."

"He's probably an Aquarius, too," said Meredith. "Come on, Elena, before I kill her to shut her up about Alaric."

Elena walked in silence, wondering what Stefan was doing that kept him from school. She felt vulnerable and exposed today, as if her skin were on inside out. One of those days when she was ready to cry at the drop of a hat.

On the office bulletin board was tacked a piece of violet paper.

She should have known. She *had* known somewhere deep inside. The thief wasn't satisfied with letting her know her private words had been read. He was showing her they could be made public.

She ripped the note off the board and crumpled it, but

not before she glimpsed the words. In one glance they were seared onto her brain.

I feel as if someone has hurt him terribly in the past and he's never gotten over it. But I also think there's something he's afraid of, some secret he's afraid I'll find out.

"Elena, what is that? What's the matter? Elena, come back here!"

Bonnie and Meredith followed her to the nearest girls' bathroom, where she stood over the wastebasket shredding the note into microscopic pieces, breathing as if she'd just run a race. They looked at each other and then turned to survey the bathroom stalls.

"Okay," said Meredith loudly, "senior privilege. You!" She rapped on the only closed door. "Come out."

Some rustling, then a bewildered freshman emerged. "But I didn't even—"

"Out. Outside," Bonnie ordered. "And *you*," she said to the girl washing her hands, "stand out there and make sure nobody comes in."

"But why? What are you—"

"*Move*, chick. If anybody comes through that door we're holding you responsible."

When the door was closed again, they rounded on Elena.

"Okay, this is a stickup," said Meredith. "Come on, Elena, give."

Elena ripped the last tiny shred of paper, caught between laughter and tears. She wanted to tell them everything, but she couldn't. She settled for telling them about the diary.

They were as angry, as indignant, as she was.

"It had to be someone at the party," Meredith said at last, once they had each expressed their opinion of the thief's character, morals, and probable destination in the afterlife. "But anybody there could have done it. I don't remember anyone in particular going near your purse, but that room was wall-to-wall people, and it could have happened without my noticing."

"But why would anyone *want* to do this?" Bonnie put in. "Unless . . . Elena, the night we found Stefan you were hinting around at some things. You said you thought you knew who the killer was."

"I don't think I know; I *know*. But if you're wondering if this might be connected, I'm not sure. I suppose it could be. The same person might have done it."

Bonnie was horrified. "But that means the killer is a student at this school!" When Elena shook her head, she went on. "The only people at that party who weren't students were that new guy and Alaric." Her expression changed. "Alaric didn't kill Mr. Tanner! He wasn't even in Fell's Church then."

"I know. Alaric didn't do it." She'd gone too far to stop

now; Bonnie and Meredith already knew too much. "Damon did."

"That guy was the *killer*? The guy that *kissed* me?"

"Bonnie, calm down." As always, other people's hysteria made Elena feel more in control. "Yes, he's the killer, and we all three have to be on guard against him. That's why I'm telling you. Never, never ask him into your house."

Elena stopped, regarding the faces of her friends. They were staring at her, and for a moment she had the sickening feeling that they didn't believe her. That they were going to question her sanity.

But all Meredith asked, in an even, detached voice, was: "Are you sure about this?"

"Yes. I'm sure. He's the murderer and the one who put Stefan in the well, and he might be after one of us next. And I don't know if there's any way to stop him."

"Well, then," said Meredith, lifting her eyebrows. "No wonder you and Stefan were in such a hurry to leave the party."

Caroline gave Elena a vicious smirk as Elena walked into the cafeteria. But Elena was almost beyond noticing.

One thing she noticed right away, though. Vickie Bennett was there.

Vickie hadn't been to school since the night Matt and

Bonnie and Meredith had found her wandering on the road, raving about mist and eyes and something terrible in the graveyard. The doctors who checked her afterward said there was nothing much wrong with her physically, but she still hadn't returned to Robert E. Lee. People whispered about psychologists and the drug treatments they were trying.

She didn't look crazy, though, Elena thought. She looked pale and subdued and sort of crumpled into her clothing. And when Elena passed her and she looked up, her eyes were like a startled fawn's.

It was strange to sit at a half-empty table with only Bonnie and Meredith for company. Usually people were crowding to get seats around the three of them.

"We didn't finish talking this morning," Meredith said. "Get something to eat, and then we'll figure out what to do about those notes."

"I'm not hungry," said Elena flatly. "And what *can* we do? If it's Damon, there's no way we can stop him. Trust me, it's not a matter for the police. That's why I haven't told them he's the killer. There isn't any proof, and besides, they would never . . . Bonnie, you're not listening."

"Sorry," said Bonnie, who was staring past Elena's left ear. "But something weird is going on up there."

Elena turned. Vickie Bennett was standing at the front of the cafeteria, but she no longer seemed crumpled and subdued. She was looking around the room in a sly and assessing manner, smiling.

"Well, she doesn't look normal, but I wouldn't say she was being weird, exactly," Meredith said. Then she added, "Wait a minute."

Vickie was unbuttoning her cardigan. But it was the *way* she was doing it—with deliberate little flicks of her fingers, all the while looking around with that secretive smile—that was odd. When the last button was undone, she took the sweater daintily between forefinger and thumb and slid it down over first one arm and then the other. She dropped the sweater on the floor.

"Weird is the word," confirmed Meredith.

Students crossing in front of Vickie with laden trays glanced at her curiously and then looked back over their shoulders when they had passed. They didn't actually stop walking, though, until she took off her shoes.

She did it gracefully, catching the heel of one pump on the toe of the other and pushing it off. Then she kicked off the second pump.

"She can't keep going," murmured Bonnie, as Vickie's fingers moved to the simulated pearl buttons on her white silk blouse.

Heads were turning; people were poking one another and gesturing. Around Vickie a small group had gathered, standing far enough back that they didn't interfere with everyone else's view.

The white silk blouse rippled off, fluttering like a wounded ghost to the floor. Vickie was wearing a lacy off-white slip underneath.

There was no longer any sound in the cafeteria except the sibilance of whispers. No one was eating. The group around Vickie had gotten larger.

Vickie smiled demurely and began to unfasten clasps at her waist. Her pleated skirt fell to the floor. She stepped out of it and pushed it to one side with her foot.

Somebody stood up at the back of the cafeteria and chanted, "Take it *off*! Take it *off*!" Other voices joined in.

"Isn't anybody going to stop her?" fumed Bonnie.

Elena got up. The last time she'd gone near Vickie the other girl had screamed and struck out at her. But now, as she got close, Vickie gave her the smile of a conspirator. Her lips moved, but Elena couldn't make out what she was saying over the chanting.

"Come on, Vickie. Let's go," she said.

Vickie's light brown hair tossed and she plucked at the strap of her slip.

Elena stooped to pick up the cardigan and wrap it around the girl's slender shoulders. As she did, as she touched Vickie, those half-closed eyes opened wide like a startled fawn's again. Vickie stared about her wildly, as if she'd just been awakened from a dream. She looked down at herself and her expression turned to disbelief. Pulling the cardigan around her more tightly, she backed away, shivering.

The room was quiet again.

"It's okay," said Elena soothingly. "Come on."

At the sound of her voice, Vickie jumped as if touched by a live wire. She stared at Elena, and then she exploded into action.

"You're one of them! I saw you! You're evil!"

She turned and ran barefoot out of the cafeteria, leaving Elena stunned.

8

"Do you know what's strange about what Vickie did at school? I mean aside from all the obvious things," Bonnie said, licking chocolate frosting off her fingers.

"What?" said Elena dully.

"Well, the way she ended up, in her slip. She looked just like she did when we found her on the road, only then she was all scratched up, too."

"Cat scratches, we thought," said Meredith, finishing the last bite of her cake. She seemed to be in one of her quiet, thoughtful moods; right now she was watching Elena closely. "But that doesn't seem very likely."

Elena looked straight back at her. "Maybe she fell in some brambles," she said. "Now, if you guys are finished eating, do you want to see that first note?"

They left their dishes in the sink and climbed the stairs to Elena's room. Elena felt herself flush as the other girls read the note. Bonnie and Meredith were her best friends, maybe her only friends now. She'd read them passages from her diary before. But this was different. It was the most humiliating feeling she'd ever had. "Well?" she said to Meredith.

"The person who wrote this is five feet eleven inches tall, walks with a slight limp, and wears a false mustache," Meredith intoned. "Sorry," she added, seeing Elena's face. "Not funny. Actually, there's not much to go on, is there? The writing looks like a guy's, but the paper looks feminine."

"And the whole thing has sort of a feminine touch," put in Bonnie, bouncing slightly on Elena's bed. "Well, it does," she said defensively. "Quoting bits of your diary back at you is the kind of thing a woman would think of. Men don't care about diaries."

"You just don't want it to be Damon," said Meredith. "I would think you'd be more worried about him being a psycho killer than a diary thief."

"I don't know; killers are sort of romantic. Imagine your dying with his hands around your throat. He'd strangle the life out of you, and the last thing you'd see would be his face." Putting her own hands to her throat, Bonnie gasped and expired tragically, ending up draped across the bed. "He can have me anytime," she said, eyes still closed.

It was on Elena's lips to say, "Don't you understand, this is *serious*," but instead she hissed in a breath. "Oh, God," she said, and ran to the window. The day was humid and stifling, and the window had been opened. Outside on the skeletal branches of the quince tree was a crow.

Elena threw the sash down so hard that the glass rattled and tinkled. The crow gazed at her through the trembling panes with eyes like obsidian. Rainbows glimmered in its sleek black plumage.

"Why did you *say* that?" she said, turning to Bonnie.

"Hey, there's nobody out there," said Meredith gently. "Unless you count the birds."

Elena turned away from them. The tree was empty now.

"I'm sorry," said Bonnie in a small voice, after a moment. "It's just that it all doesn't seem real sometimes, even Mr. Tanner's being dead doesn't seem real. And Damon did look . . . well, exciting. But dangerous. I can believe he's dangerous."

"And besides, he wouldn't squeeze your throat; he'd cut it," Meredith said. "Or at least that was what he did to Tanner. But the old man under the bridge had his throat ripped open, as if some animal had done it." Meredith looked to Elena for clarification. "Damon doesn't have an animal, does he?"

"No. I don't know." Suddenly, Elena felt very tired. She was worried about Bonnie, about the consequences of those foolish words.

"I can do anything to you, to you and the ones you love," she remembered. What might Damon do now? She didn't understand him. He was different every time they met. In the gym he'd been taunting, laughing at her. But the next time she would swear that he'd been serious, quoting poetry to her, trying to get her to come away with him. Last week, with the icy graveyard wind lashing around him, he'd been menacing, cruel. And underneath his mocking words last night, she'd felt the same menace. She couldn't predict what he'd do next.

But, whatever happened, she had to protect Bonnie and Meredith from him. Especially since she couldn't warn them properly.

And what was Stefan up to? She needed him right now, more than anything. Where *was* he?

It started that morning.

"Let me get this straight," Matt said, leaning against the scarred body of his ancient Ford sedan when Stefan approached him before school. "You want to borrow my car."

"Yes," Stefan said.

"And the reason you want to borrow it is flowers. You want to get some flowers for Elena."

"Yes,"

"And these particular flowers, these flowers you've just got to get, don't grow around here."

"They might. But their blooming season is over this far north. And the frost would have finished them off anyway."

"So you want to go down south—how far south you don't know—to find some of these flowers that you've just got to give to Elena."

"Or at least some of the plants," Stefan said. "I'd rather have the actual flowers though."

"And since the police still have your car, you want to borrow mine, for however long it takes you to go down south and find these flowers that you've just got to give to Elena."

"I figure driving is the least conspicuous way to leave town," Stefan explained. "I don't want the police to follow me."

"Uh-huh. And that's why you want my car."

"Yes. Are you going to give it to me?"

"Am I going to give my car to the guy who stole my girlfriend and now wants to take a jaunt down south to get her some kind of special flowers she's just got to have?

Are you crazy?" Matt, who had been staring out over the roofs of the frame houses across the street, turned at last to look at Stefan. His blue eyes, usually cheerful and straightforward, were full of utter disbelief, and surmounted by twisted, puckered brows.

Stefan looked away. He should have known better. After everything Matt had already done for him, to expect more was ridiculous. Especially these days, when people flinched from the sound of his step and avoided his eyes when he came near. To expect Matt, who had the best of reasons to resent him, to do him such a favor with no explanation, on the basis of faith alone, really *was* insane.

"No, I'm not crazy," he said quietly, and turned to go.

"Neither am I," Matt had said. "And I'd have to be crazy to turn my car over to you. Hell, no. I'm going with you."

By the time Stefan had turned back around, Matt was looking at the car instead of him, lower lip thrust forward in a wary, judicious pout.

"After all," he'd said, rubbing at the flaking vinyl of the roof, "you might scratch the paint or something."

Elena put the phone back on the hook. *Somebody* was at the boarding house, because somebody kept picking up the phone when it rang, but after that there was only silence and then the click of disconnection. She suspected it was Mrs. Flowers, but that didn't tell her anything about where Stefan was. Instinctively, she wanted to go to him. But it was dark outside, and Stefan had warned her specifically not to go out in the dark, especially not anywhere near the cemetery or the woods. The boarding house was near both.

"No answer?" said Meredith as Elena came back and sat down on the bed.

"She keeps hanging up on me," Elena said, and muttered something under her breath.

"Did you say she was a witch?"

"No, but it rhymes with that," said Elena.

"Look," said Bonnie, sitting up. "If Stefan's going to call, he'll call here. There's no reason for you to come and stay the night with me."

There *was* a reason, although Elena couldn't quite explain it even to herself. After all, Damon had kissed Bonnie at Alaric Saltzman's party. It was Elena's fault that Bonnie was in danger in the first place. Somehow she felt that if she were at least on the scene, she might be able to protect Bonnie.

"My mom and dad and Mary are all home," Bonnie persisted. "And we lock all our doors and windows and everything since Mr. Tanner was murdered. This weekend Dad even put on extra locks. I don't see what *you* can do."

Elena didn't either. But she was going just the same.

She left a message for Stefan with Aunt Judith, telling him where she was. There was still a lingering constraint between her and her aunt. And there would be, Elena thought, until Aunt Judith changed her mind about Stefan.

At Bonnie's house, she was given a room that had belonged to one of Bonnie's sisters who was now in college. The first thing she did was check the window. It was closed and locked, and there was nothing outside that someone could climb, like a drainpipe or tree. As inconspicuously as possible, she also checked Bonnie's room and any others she could get into. Bonnie was right; they were all sealed up tight from the inside. Nothing from the outside could get in.

She lay in bed a long time that night, staring at the ceiling, unable to sleep. She kept remembering Vickie dreamily doing a striptease in the cafeteria. What was wrong with the girl? She would remember to ask Stefan that next time she saw him.

Thoughts of Stefan were pleasant, even with all the terrible things that had happened recently. Elena smiled in the darkness, letting her mind wander. Someday all this harassment would be over, and she and Stefan could plan a life together. Of course, he hadn't actually said anything about that, but Elena herself was sure. She was going to marry Stefan, or no one. And Stefan was going to marry no one but her. . . .

The transition into dreaming was so smooth and gradual that she scarcely noticed it. But she knew, somehow, that she was dreaming. If was as if a little part of her was standing aside and watching the dream like a play.

She was sitting in a long hallway, which was covered with mirrors on one side and windows on the other. She was waiting for something. Then she saw a flicker of movement, and Stefan was standing outside the window. His face was pale and his eyes were hurt and angry. She went over to the window, but she couldn't hear what he was saying because of the glass. In one hand, he was holding a book with a blue velvet cover, and he kept gesturing to it and asking her something. Then he dropped the book and turned away.

"Stefan, don't go! Don't leave me!" she cried. Her fingers flattened whitely on the glass. Then she noticed that there was a latch on one side of the window and she opened it, calling to him. But he had disappeared and outside she saw only swirling white mist.

Disconsolately, she turned away from the window and began walking down the hall. Her own image glimmered in mirror after mirror as she went by them. Then something about one of the reflections caught her eye. The eyes were her eyes, but there was a new look in them, a predatory, sly look. Vickie's eyes had looked that way when she was undressing. And there was something disturbing and hungry about her smile.

As she watched, standing still, the image suddenly whirled around and around, as if dancing. Horror swept over Elena. She began to run down the hall, but now all the reflections had a life of their own, dancing, beckoning to her, laughing at her. Just when she thought her heart and lungs would burst with terror, she reached the end of the corridor and flung open a door.

She was standing in a large and beautiful room. The lofty ceiling was intricately carved and inlaid with gold; the doorways were faced with white marble. Classical statues stood in niches along the walls. Elena had never seen a room of such splendor, but she knew where she was. In Renaissance Italy, when Stefan had been alive.

She looked down at herself and saw she was wearing a dress like the one she'd had made for Halloween, the ice blue Renaissance ball gown. But this dress was a deep ruby red, and around her waist she wore a thin chain set with brilliant red stones. The same stones were in her hair. When she moved, the silk shimmered like flames in the light of hundreds of torches.

At the far end of the room, two huge doors swung inward. A figure appeared between them. It walked toward her, and she saw that it was a young man dressed in Renaissance clothing, doublet and hose and fur-trimmed jerkin.

Stefan! She started toward him eagerly, feeling the weight of her dress swing from the waist. But when she got closer she stopped, drawing in a sharp breath. It was Damon.

He kept on walking toward her, confident, casual. He was smiling, a smile of challenge. Reaching her, he put one hand over his heart and bowed. Then he held out the hand to her as if daring her to take it.

"Do you like dancing?" he said. Except that his lips didn't move. The voice was in her mind.

Her fear drained away, and she laughed. What was wrong with her, to have ever been afraid of him? They understood each other very well. But instead of taking his hand, she turned away, the silk of the dress turning after her. She moved lightly toward one of the statues along the wall, not glancing back to see if he was following her. She knew he would. She pretended to be absorbed in the statue, moving away again just as he reached her, biting her lip to hold in the laughter. She felt wonderful right now, so alive, so beautiful. Dangerous? Of course, this game was dangerous. But she had always enjoyed danger.

The next time he drew near her, she glanced at him teasingly as she turned. He reached out, but caught only the jeweled chain at her waist. He let go quickly, and, looking back, she saw that the pronged setting on one of the gems had cut him.

The drop of blood on his finger was just the color of her dress. His eyes flashed at her sideways, and his lips curved in a taunting smile as he held the wounded finger up. You wouldn't dare, those eyes said.

Oh, wouldn't I? Elena told him with her own eyes. Boldly, she took his hand and held it a moment, teasing him. Then she brought the finger to her lips.

After a few moments, she released it and looked up at him. "I *do* like dancing," she said, and found that, like him, she could speak with her mind. It was a thrilling sensation. She moved to the center of the room and waited.

He followed her, graceful as a stalking beast. His fingers were warm and hard when they clasped hers.

There was music, although it faded in and out and sounded far away. Damon placed his other hand on her waist. She could feel the warmth of his fingers there, the pressure. She picked up her skirts, and they began dancing.

It was lovely, like flying, and her body knew every move to make. They danced around and around that empty room, in perfect timing, together.

He was laughing down at her, his dark eyes glittering with enjoyment. She felt so beautiful; so poised and alert and ready for anything. She couldn't remember when she'd had this much fun.

Gradually, though, his smile faded, and their dancing

slowed. At last she stood unmoving in the circle of his arms. His dark eyes were not amused any longer, but fierce and heated. She looked up at him soberly, unafraid. And then for the first time she felt as if she *were* dreaming; she felt slightly dizzy and very languid and weak.

The room around her was blurring. She could see only his eyes, and they were making her feel more and more sleepy. She allowed her own eyes to half close, her head to fall back. She sighed.

She could *feel* his gaze now, on her lips, on her throat. She smiled to herself and let her eyes close completely.

He was supporting her weight now, keeping her from falling down. She felt his lips on the skin of her neck, burning hot as if he had a fever. Then she felt the sting, like the jabs of two needles. It was over quickly, though, and she relaxed to the pleasure of having her blood drawn out.

She remembered this feeling, the feeling of floating on a bed of golden light. A delicious languor stole through all her limbs. She felt drowsy, as if it were too much trouble to move. She didn't want to move anyway; she felt too good.

Her fingers were resting on his hair, clasping his head to her. Idly, she threaded them through the soft dark strands. His hair was like silk, warm and alive under her fingers. When she opened her eyes a slit, she saw that it reflected rainbows in the candlelight. Red and blue and purple, just like—just like the feathers . . .

And then everything shattered. There was pain at her throat suddenly, as if her soul was being torn out of her. She was pushing at Damon, clawing at him, trying to force him away. Screams rang in her ears. Damon was fighting her, but it wasn't Damon; it was a crow. Huge wings beat against her, thrashing in the air.

Her eyes were open. She was awake and screaming. The ballroom was gone, and she was in a darkened bedroom. But the nightmare had followed her. Even as she reached for the light, it came at her again, wings thrashing in her face, sharp beak diving for her.

Elena struck out at it, one hand flung up to protect her eyes. She was still screaming. She couldn't get away from it, those terrible wings kept flailing frantically, with a sound like a thousand decks of cards being shuffled at once.

The door burst open, and she heard shouts. The warm, heavy body of the crow struck her and her screams went higher. Then someone was pulling her off the bed, and she was standing protected behind Bonnie's father. He had a broom and he was beating at the bird with it.

Bonnie was standing in the doorway. Elena ran into her arms. Bonnie's father was shouting, and then came the slam of a window.

"It's out," Mr. McCullough said, breathing hard.

Mary and Mrs. McCullough were just outside in the hallway, clad in bathrobes. "You're hurt," Mrs. McCullough said to Elena in amazement. "The nasty thing's pecked you."

"I'm okay," Elena said, brushing at a spot of blood on her face. She was so shaken that her knees were about to give out.

"How did it get *in*?" said Bonnie.

Mr. McCullough was inspecting the window. "You shouldn't have left this open," he said "And what did you want to take the locks off for?"

"I didn't," Elena cried.

"It was unlocked and open when I heard you screaming and came in," Bonnie's father said. "I don't know who else could have opened it but you."

Elena choked back her protests. Hesitantly, cautiously, she moved to the window. He was right; the locks had been unscrewed. And it could have been done only from the inside.

"Maybe you were sleepwalking," said Bonnie, leading Elena away from the window as Mr. McCullough began putting the locks back on. "We'd better get you cleaned up."

Sleepwalking. Suddenly the entire dream flooded back to Elena. The hall of mirrors, and the ballroom, and

Damon. Dancing with Damon. She pulled out of Bonnie's grasp.

"I'll do it myself," she said, hearing her own voice quaver on the edge of hysteria. "No—really—I want to." She escaped into the bathroom and stood with her back to the locked door, trying to breathe.

The last thing she wanted to do was look in a mirror. But at last, slowly, she approached the one over the sink, trembling as she saw the edge of her reflection, moving inch by inch until she was framed in the silvery surface.

Her image stared back, ghastly pale, with eyes that looked bruised and frightened. There were deep shadows under them and smears of blood on her face.

Slowly, she turned her head slightly and lifted up her hair. She almost cried out loud when she saw what was underneath.

Two little wounds, fresh and open on the skin of her neck.

9

"I know I'm going to be sorry I asked this," Matt said, turning red-rimmed eyes from their contemplation of I-95 to Stefan in the passenger seat beside him. "But can you tell me why we want these extra-special, not-available-locally, semi-tropical weeds for Elena?"

Stefan looked into the backseat at the results of their search through hedgerows and rough grass. The plants, with their branching green stems and their small-toothed leaves, did look more like weeds than anything else. The dried remains of blossoms at the ends of the shoots were almost invisible, and no one could pretend the shoots themselves were decorative.

"What if I said they could be used to make an all-natural eyewash?" he offered, after a moment's thought. "Or an herbal tea?"

"Why? Were you thinking of saying something like that?"

"Not really."

"Good. Because if you did I'd probably deck you."

Without actually looking at Matt, Stefan smiled. There was something new stirring inside him, something he hadn't felt for nearly five centuries, except with Elena. Acceptance. Warmth and friendship shared with a fellow being, who did not know the truth about him but who trusted him anyway. Who was willing to take him on faith. He wasn't sure he deserved it, but he couldn't deny what it meant to him. It almost made him feel . . . human again.

Elena stared at her image in the mirror. It hadn't been a dream. Not entirely. The wounds in her neck proved that. And now that she'd seen them, she noticed the feeling of light-headedness, of lethargy.

It was her own fault. She'd taken so much trouble to warn Bonnie and Meredith not to invite any strangers into their houses. And all the time she'd forgotten that she herself had invited Damon into Bonnie's house. She'd done it that night she had set up the dumb supper in Bonnie's dining room and called out into the darkness, "Come in."

And the invitation was good forever. He could return any time he liked, even now. Especially now, while she was weak and might easily be hypnotized into unlocking a window again.

Elena stumbled out of the bathroom, past Bonnie, and into the guest bedroom. She grabbed her tote bag and began stuffing things into it.

"Elena, you can't go home!"

"I can't stay here," Elena said. She looked around for her shoes, spotted them by the bed, and started forward. Then she stopped, with a strangled sound. Lying on the dainty crumpled linen of the bed there was a single black feather. It was huge, horribly huge and real and solid, with a thick, waxy-looking shaft. It looked almost obscene resting there on the white percale sheets.

Nausea swept over Elena, and she turned away. She couldn't breathe.

"Okay, okay," Bonnie said. "If you feel that way about it, I'll get Dad to take you home."

"You have to come, too." It had just dawned on Elena that Bonnie was no safer in this house than she was. *You and your loved ones*, she remembered, and turned to grasp Bonnie's arm. "You *have* to, Bonnie. I need you with me."

And at last she got her way. The McCulloughs thought she was hysterical, that she was overreacting, possibly that she was having a nervous breakdown. But finally they gave in. Mr. McCullough drove her and Bonnie to the Gilbert house, where, feeling like burglars, they unlocked the door and crept inside without waking anyone up.

Even here, Elena couldn't sleep. She lay beside Bonnie's softly breathing form, staring toward her bedroom window, watching. Outside, the quince branches squeaked against the glass, but nothing else moved until dawn.

That was when she heard the car. She'd know the wheezing sound of Matt's engine anywhere. Alarmed, she tiptoed to the window and looked out into the early-morning stillness of another gray day. Then she hurried downstairs and opened the front door.

"Stefan!" She had never been so glad to see anyone in her life. She flung herself upon him before he could even shut the car door. He swayed backward with the force of her impact, and she could feel his surprise. She wasn't usually so demonstrative in public.

"Hey," he said, returning the hug gently. "Me, too, but don't crush the flowers."

"Flowers?" She pulled back to look at what he was carrying; then, she looked at his face. Then at Matt, who was emerging from the other side of the car. Stefan's face was pale and drawn; Matt's was puffy with tiredness, with bloodshot eyes.

"You'd better come inside," she said at last, bewildered. "You both look awful."

"It's vervain," said Stefan, some time later. He and Elena were sitting at the kitchen table. Through the open doorway, Matt could be seen stretched out on the family room sofa, snoring gently. He'd flopped there after eating three bowls of cereal. Aunt Judith, Bonnie, and Margaret were still upstairs asleep, but Stefan kept his voice low just the same. "You remember what I told you about it?" he said.

"You said it helps keep your mind clear even when someone is using Power to influence it." Elena was proud of how steady her voice was.

"Right. And that's one of the things Damon might try. He can use the power of his mind even from a distance, and he can do it whether you're awake or asleep."

Tears filled Elena's eyes, and she looked down to hide them, gazing at the long slender stems with the dried remains of tiny lilac flowers at the very tips. "Asleep?" she said, afraid that this time her voice was not as steady.

"Yes. He could influence you to come out of the house, say, or to let him in. But the vervain should prevent that." Stefan sounded tired, but satisfied with himself.

Oh, Stefan, if you only knew, Elena thought. The gift had come one night too late. In spite of all her efforts, a tear fell, dripping onto the long green leaves.

"Elena!" He sounded startled. "What is it? Tell me."

He was trying to look into her face, but she bowed her head, pressing it into his shoulder. He put his arms around her, not trying to force her up again. "Tell me," he repeated softly.

This was the moment. If she was ever going to tell him, it should be now. Her throat felt burned and swollen, and she wanted to let all the words inside pour out.

But she couldn't. No matter what, I won't let them fight over me, she thought.

"It's just that—I was worried about you," she managed. "I didn't know where you'd gone, or when you were coming back."

"I should have told you. But that's all? There's nothing else upsetting you?"

"That's all." Now she would have to swear Bonnie to secrecy about the crow. Why did one lie always lead to another? "What should we do with the vervain?" she asked, sitting back.

"I'll show you tonight. Once I've extracted the oil from the seeds, you can rub it into your skin or add it to a bath. And you can make the dried leaves into a sachet and carry it with you or put it under your pillow at night."

"I'd better give them to Bonnie and Meredith, too. They'll need protection."

He nodded. "For now"—he broke off a sprig and placed it in her hand—"just take this to school with you. I'm going back to the boarding house to extract the oil." He paused a moment and then spoke. "Elena . . ."

"Yes?"

"If I thought it would do you any good, I'd leave. I wouldn't expose you to Damon. But I don't think he'd follow me if I went, not anymore. I think he might stay— because of you."

"Don't even *think* about leaving," she said fiercely, looking up at him. "Stefan, that's the one thing I couldn't stand. Promise you won't; promise me."

"I won't leave you alone with him," Stefan said, which was not quite the same thing. But there was no point in pushing him further.

Instead, she helped him wake up Matt, and saw them both off. Then, with a stem of dried vervain in her hand, she went upstairs to get ready for school.

Bonnie yawned all the way through breakfast and she didn't really wake up until they were outside, walking to school with a brisk breeze in their faces. It was going to be a cold day.

"I had a very weird dream last night," Bonnie said.

Elena's heart jumped. She'd already tucked a sprig of vervain into Bonnie's backpack, down at the bottom, where Bonnie wouldn't see it. But if Damon had gotten to Bonnie last night . . .

"What about?" she said, bracing herself.

"About you. I saw you standing under a tree and the wind was blowing. For some reason, I was afraid of you, and I didn't want to go any closer. You looked . . . different. Very pale but almost glowing. And then a crow flew down from the tree, and you reached out and grabbed it in midair. You were so fast it was unbelievable. And then you looked over at me, with this expression. You were smiling, but it made me want to run. And then you twisted the crow's neck, and it was dead."

Elena had listened to this with growing horror. Now she said, "That's a *disgusting* dream."

"It is, isn't it?" said Bonnie composedly. "I wonder what it means? Crows are birds of ill omen in the legends. They can foretell a death."

"It probably meant that you knew how upset I was, finding that crow in the room."

"Yes," Bonnie said. "Except for one thing. I had this dream *before* you woke us all up screaming."

That day at lunchtime there was another piece of violet paper on the office bulletin board. This one, though, read simply: *LOOK IN PERSONALS*.

"What personals?" said Bonnie.

Meredith, walking up at that moment with a copy of the *Wildcat Weekly*, the school newspaper, provided the answer. "Have you seen this?" she said.

It was in the personals section, completely anonymous, with neither salutation nor signature. *I can't bear the thought of losing him. But he's so very unhappy about something, and if he won't tell me what it is, if he won't trust me that much, I don't see any hope for us.*

Reading it, Elena felt a burst of new energy through her tiredness. Oh, God, she hated whoever was doing this. She imagined shooting them, stabbing them, watching them fall. And then, vividly, she imagined something else. Yanking back a fistful of the thief's hair and sinking her teeth into an unprotected throat. It was a strange, unsettling vision, but for a moment it almost seemed real.

She became aware that Bonnie and Meredith were looking at her.

"Well?" she said, feeling slightly uncomfortable.

"I could tell you weren't listening," sighed Bonnie. "I just said it still doesn't look like Da—like the killer's work to me. It doesn't seem like a murderer would be so petty."

"Much as I hate to agree with her, she's right," Meredith said. "This smells like someone sneaky. Someone who has a grudge against you personally and who really wants to make you suffer."

Saliva had collected in Elena's mouth, and she swallowed. "Also somebody who's familiar with the school. They had to fill out a form for a personals message in one of the journalism classes," she said.

"And somebody who knew you kept a diary, assuming

they stole it on purpose. Maybe they were in one of your classes that day you took it to school. Remember? When Mr. Tanner almost caught you," Bonnie added.

"Ms. Halpern *did* catch me; she even read some of it aloud, a bit about Stefan. That was right after Stefan and I got together. Wait a minute, Bonnie. That night at your house when the diary was stolen, how long were you two out of the living room?"

"Just a few minutes. Yangtze had stopped barking, and I went to the door to let him in, and . . ." Bonnie pressed her lips together and shrugged.

"So the thief had to be familiar with your house," said Meredith swiftly, "or he or she wouldn't have been able to get in, get the diary, and get out again before we saw them. All right, then, we're looking for someone sneaky and cruel, probably in one of your classes, Elena, and most likely familiar with Bonnie's house. Someone who has a personal grudge and will stoop to anything to get you . . . Oh, my God."

The three of them stared at one another.

"It has to be," whispered Bonnie. "It has to."

"We're so stupid; we should have seen it right away," said Meredith.

For Elena, it meant the sudden realization that all the anger she'd felt about this before was nothing to the anger she was capable of feeling. A candle flame to the sun.

"Caroline," she said, and clenched her teeth so hard her jaw hurt.

Caroline. Elena actually felt she could kill the green-eyed girl right now. And she might have rushed out to try if Bonnie and Meredith hadn't stopped her.

"After school," said Meredith firmly, "when we can take her somewhere private. Just wait that long, Elena."

But as they headed for the cafeteria, Elena noticed an auburn head disappearing down the art and music corridor. And she remembered something Stefan had said earlier this year, about Caroline taking him into the photography room at lunchtime. For privacy, Caroline had told him.

"You two go on; I forgot something," she said as soon as Bonnie and Meredith both had food on their cafeteria trays. Then she pretended to be deaf as she walked rapidly out and backtracked to the art wing.

All the rooms were dark, but the photography room's door was unlocked. Something made Elena turn the knob cautiously, and move quietly once she was inside, rather than marching in to start a confrontation as she'd planned. Was Caroline in here? If so, what was she doing alone in the dark?

The room appeared at first to be deserted. Then Elena heard the murmur of voices from a small alcove at the back, and she saw that the darkroom door was ajar.

Silently, stealthily, she made her way until she stood

just outside the doorway, and the murmur of sound resolved itself into words.

"But how can we be sure she'll be the one they pick?" That was Caroline.

"My father's on the school board. They'll pick her, all right." And *that* was Tyler Smallwood. His father was a lawyer, and on every board there was. "Besides, who else would it be?" he continued. "'The Spirit of Fell's Church' is supposed to be brainy as well as built."

"And *I* don't have brains, I suppose?"

"Did I say that? Look, if you want to be the one to parade in a white dress on Founders' Day, fine. But if you want to see Stefan Salvatore run out of town on the evidence of his own girlfriend's diary . . ."

"But why wait so long?"

Tyler sounded impatient. "Because this way it'll ruin the celebration, too. The Fells' celebration. Why should they get the credit for founding this town? The Smallwoods were here first."

"Oh, who cares about who founded the town? All I want is to see Elena humiliated in front of the entire school."

"And Salvatore." The pure hatred and malice in Tyler's voice made Elena's flesh crawl. "He'll be lucky if he doesn't end up hanging from a tree. You're sure the evidence is there?"

"How many times do I have to tell you? First, it says

she lost the ribbon on September second in the cemetery. Then, it says Stefan picked it up that day and kept it. Wickery Bridge is right beside the cemetery. That means Stefan was near the bridge on September second, the night the old man was attacked there. Everybody already knows he was on hand for the attacks on Vickie and Tanner. What more do you want?"

"It would never stand up in court. Maybe I should get some corroborating evidence. Like ask old Mrs. Flowers what time he got home that night."

"Oh, who *cares*? Most people think he's guilty already. The diary talks about some big secret he's hiding from everyone. People will get the idea."

"You're keeping it in a safe place?"

"No, Tyler, I'm keeping it out on the coffee table. How stupid do you think I am?"

"Stupid enough to send Elena notes tipping her off." There was a crackle, as of newspaper. "Look at this, this is unbelievable. And it's got to stop, *now*. What if she figures out who's doing it?"

"What's she going to do about it, call the police?"

"I still want you to lay off. Just wait until Founders' Day, then you'll get to watch the Ice Princess melt."

"And to say *ciao* to Stefan. Tyler . . . nobody's really going to hurt him, are they?

"Who *cares*?" Tyler mocked her earlier tone. "You leave

that to me and my friends, Caroline. You just do your part, okay?"

Caroline's voice dropped to a throaty murmur. "Convince me." After a pause Tyler chuckled.

There was movement, rustling sounds, a sigh. Elena turned and slipped out of the room as quietly as she had come in.

She got into the next hallway, and then she leaned against the lockers there, trying to think.

It was almost too much to absorb at once. Caroline, who had once been her best friend, had betrayed her and wanted to see her humiliated in front of the whole school. Tyler, who'd always seemed more an annoying jerk than a real threat, was planning to get Stefan driven out of town—or killed. And the worst thing was that they were using Elena's own diary to do it.

Now she understood the beginning of her dream last night. She'd had a dream like it the day before she had discovered that Stefan was missing. In both, Stefan had looked at her with angry, accusing eyes, and then he had thrown a book at her feet and walked away.

Not a book. Her diary. Which had in it evidence that could be deadly to Stefan. Three times people in Fell's Church had been attacked, and three times Stefan had been on the scene. What would that look like to the town, to the police?

And there was no way to tell the truth. Supposing she said, "Stefan isn't guilty. It's his brother Damon who hates him and who knows how much Stefan hates even the thought of hurting and killing. And who followed Stefan around and attacked people to make Stefan think maybe Stefan had done it, to drive him mad. And who's here in town *somewhere*—look for him in the cemetery or in the woods. But, oh, by the way, don't just search for a good-looking guy, because he might be a crow at the moment.

"Incidentally, he's a vampire."

She didn't even believe it herself. It sounded ludicrous

A twinge from the side of her neck reminded her how serious the ludicrous story really was. She felt odd today, almost as if she were sick. It was more than just tension and lack of sleep. She felt slightly dizzy, and at times the ground seemed to be spongy, giving way under her feet and then springing back. Flu symptoms, except that she was sure they weren't due to any *virus* in her bloodstream.

Damon's fault, again. Everything was Damon's fault except the diary. She had no one to blame for that but herself. If only she hadn't written about Stefan, if only she hadn't brought the diary to school. If only she hadn't left it in Bonnie's living room. If only, if only.

Right now all that mattered was that she had to get it back.

10

The bell rang. There was no time to go back to the cafeteria and tell Bonnie and Meredith. Elena set off for her next class, past the averted faces and hostile eyes that were becoming all too familiar these days.

It was hard, in history class, not to stare at Caroline, not to let Caroline know she knew. Alaric asked about Matt and Stefan being absent for the second day in a row, and Elena shrugged, feeling exposed and on display. She didn't trust this man with the boyish smile and the hazel eyes and the thirst for knowledge about Mr. Tanner's death. And Bonnie, who simply gazed at Alaric soulfully, was no help at all.

After class she caught a scrap of Sue Carson's conversation. " . . . he's on vacation from college—I forget exactly where . . . "

Elena had had enough of discreet silence. She spun around and spoke directly to Sue and the girl Sue was talking to, bursting uninvited into their discussion.

"If I were you," she said to Sue, "I would keep away from Damon. I mean that."

There was startled, embarrassed laughter. Sue was one of the few people at school who hadn't shunned Elena, and now she was looking as if she wished she had.

"You mean," said the other girl hesitantly, "because he's yours, too? Or—"

Elena's own laughter was harsh. "I mean because he's *dangerous*," she said. "And I'm not joking."

They just looked at her. Elena saved them the further embarrassment of having to reply or to get tactfully away by turning on her heel and leaving. She collected Bonnie from Alaric's cluster of after-school groupies and headed for Meredith's locker.

"Where are we going? I thought we were going to talk to Caroline."

"Not anymore," Elena said. "Wait until we get home. Then I'll tell you why."

"I can't believe it," said Bonnie an hour later. "I mean, I believe it, but I can't *believe* it. Not even of Caroline."

"It's Tyler," Elena said. "He's the one with the big plans. So much for men not being interested in diaries."

"Actually, we should thank him," said Meredith. "Because of him at least we have until Founders' Day to do something about it. Why did you say it was supposed to be on Founders' Day, Elena?"

"Tyler has something against the Fells."

"But they're all dead," said Bonnie.

"Well, that doesn't seem to matter to Tyler. I remember him talking about it in the graveyard, too, when we were looking at their tomb. He thinks they stole his ancestors' rightful place as the town's founders or something."

"Elena," Meredith said seriously, "is there anything else in the diary that could hurt Stefan? Besides the thing about the old man, I mean."

"Isn't that enough?" With those steady, dark eyes on her, Elena felt discomfort flutter between her ribs. What was Meredith asking?

"Enough to get Stefan run out of town like they said," agreed Bonnie.

"Enough that we have to get the diary back from Caroline," Elena said. "The only question is, how?"

"Caroline said she had it hidden somewhere safe. That probably means her house." Meredith chewed her lip thoughtfully. "She's got just the one brother in eighth grade, right? And her mom doesn't work, but she goes shopping in Roanoke a lot. Do they still have a maid?"

"Why?" said Bonnie. "What difference does it make?"

"Well, we don't want anybody walking in while we're burglarizing the house."

"While we're *what?*" Bonnie's voice rose to a squeak. "You can't be serious!"

"What are we supposed to do, just sit back and wait until Founders' Day, and let her read Elena's diary in front of the town? *She* stole it from *your* house. We've just got to steal it back," Meredith said, maddeningly calm.

"We'll get caught. We'll get expelled from school—if we don't end up going to jail." Bonnie turned to Elena in appeal. "Tell her, Elena."

"Well . . . " In all honesty, the prospect made Elena herself a little queasy. It wasn't so much the idea of expulsion, or even jail, as just the thought of being caught in the act. Mrs. Forbes's haughty face floated before her eyes, full of righteous indignation. Then it changed to Caroline's, laughing spitefully as her mother pointed an accusing finger right at Elena.

Besides, it seemed such a . . . a *violation*, to go into someone's house when they were not there, to search their possessions. She would hate it if someone did that to her.

But, of course, someone had. Caroline had violated Bonnie's house, and right now had Elena's most private possession in her hands.

"Let's do it," Elena said quietly. "But let's be careful."

"Can't we talk about this?" said Bonnie weakly, looking from Meredith's determined face to Elena's.

"There's nothing to talk about. You're coming," Meredith told her. "You promised," she added, as Bonnie took a breath to object afresh. And she held up her index finger.

"The blood oath was only to help Elena *get* Stefan!" Bonnie cried.

"Think again," said Meredith. "You swore you would do whatever Elena asked in relation to Stefan. There wasn't anything about a time limit or about 'only until Elena gets him.'"

Bonnie's mouth dropped open. She looked at Elena, who was almost laughing in spite of herself. "It's true," Elena said solemnly. "And you said it yourself: 'Swearing with blood means you have to stick to your oath no matter what happens.'"

Bonnie shut her mouth and thrust her chin out. "Right," she said grimly. "Now I'm stuck for the rest of my life doing whatever Elena wants me to do about Stefan. Wonderful."

"This is the last thing I'll ever ask," Elena said. "And *I* promise that. I swear—"

"Don't!" said Meredith, suddenly serious. "Don't, Elena. You might be sorry later."

"Now you're taking up prophecy, too?" Elena said. And then she asked, "So how are we going to get hold of Caroline's house key for an hour or so?"

November 9, Saturday

Dear Diary,

I'm sorry it's been so long. Lately I've been too busy or too depressed—or both—to write you.

Besides, with everything that's happened I'm almost afraid to keep a diary at all anymore. But I need someone to turn to, because right now there's not a single human being, not a single person on earth, that I'm not keeping something from.

Bonnie and Meredith can't know the truth about Stefan. Stefan can't know the truth about Damon. Aunt Judith can't know about anything. Bonnie and Meredith know about Caroline and the diary; Stefan doesn't. Stefan knows about the vervain I use every day now; Bonnie and Meredith don't. Even though I've given both of them sachets full of the stuff. One good thing: it seems to work, or at least I haven't been sleepwalking again since that night. But it would be a lie to say I haven't been dreaming about Damon. He's in all my nightmares.

My life is full of lies right now, and I need

someone *to be completely honest with. I'm going to hide this diary under the loose floorboard in the closet, so that no one will find it even if I drop dead and they clean out my room. Maybe one of Margaret's grandchildren will be playing in there someday, and will pry up the board and pull it out, but until then, nobody. This diary is my last secret.*

I don't know why I'm thinking about death and dying. That's Bonnie's craze; she's the one who thinks it would be so romantic. I know what it's really like; there was nothing romantic about it when Mom and Dad died. Just the worst feelings in the world. I want to live for a good long time, marry Stefan, and be happy. And there's no reason why I can't, once all these problems are behind us.

Except that there are times when I get scared and I don't believe that. And there are little things that shouldn't matter, but they bother me. Like why Stefan still wears Katherine's ring around his neck, even though I know he loves me. Like why he's never said he loves me, even though I know it's true.

It doesn't matter. Everything will work out. It has to work out. And then we'll be together and be happy. There's no reason why we can't. There's no reason why we can't. There's no reason

Elena stopped writing, trying to keep the letters on the page in focus. But they only blurred further, and she shut the book before a betraying teardrop could fall on the ink. Then she went over to the closet, pried up the loose board with a nail file, and put the diary there.

She had the nail file in her pocket a week later as the three of them, she and Bonnie and Meredith, stood outside Caroline's back door.

"Hurry up," hissed Bonnie in agony, looking around the yard as if she expected something to jump out at them. "Come on, Meredith!"

"There," said Meredith, as the key finally went the right way into the dead bolt lock and the doorknob yielded to her turning fingers. "We're in."

"Are you sure *they're* not in? Elena, what if they come back early? Why couldn't we do this in the daytime, at least?"

"Bonnie, will you get *inside*? We've been through all this. The maid's always here in the daytime. And they won't be back early tonight unless somebody gets sick at Chez Louis. Now, come on!" said Elena.

"Nobody would dare to get sick at Mr. Forbes's birthday dinner," Meredith said comfortingly to Bonnie as the smaller girl stepped in. "We're safe."

"If they've got enough money to go to expensive

restaurants, you'd think they could afford to leave a few lights on," said Bonnie, refusing to be comforted.

Privately, Elena agreed with this. It was strange and disconcerting to be wandering through someone else's house in the dark, and her heart pounded chokingly as they went up the stairs. Her palm, clutching the key chain flashlight that showed the way, was wet and slippery. But in spite of these physical symptoms of panic, her mind was still operating coolly, almost with detachment.

"It's got to be in her bedroom," she said.

Caroline's window faced the street, which meant they had to be even more careful not to show a light there. Elena swung the tiny beam of the flashlight around with a feeling of dismay. It was one thing to plan to search someone's room, to picture efficiently and methodically going through drawers. It was another thing actually to be standing here, surrounded by what seemed like thousands of places to hide something, and feeling afraid to touch anything in case Caroline noticed it had been disturbed.

The other two girls were also standing still.

"Maybe we should just go home," Bonnie said quietly. And Meredith did not contradict her.

"We have to try. At least try," said Elena, hearing how tinny and hollow her voice sounded. She eased open a drawer on the highboy and shone the light onto dainty piles of lacy underwear. A moment's poking through them assured her there was nothing like a book there. She straightened the piles and shut the drawer again. Then she let out her breath.

"It's not that hard," she said. "What we need to do is divide up the room and then search *everything* in our section, every drawer, every piece of furniture, every object big enough to hide a diary in."

She assigned herself the closet, and the first thing she did was prod at the floorboards with her nail file. But Caroline's boards all seemed to be secure and the walls of the closet sounded solid. Rummaging through Caroline's clothes she found several things she'd lent the other girl last year. She was tempted to take them back, but of course she couldn't. A search of Caroline's shoes and purses revealed nothing, even when she dragged a chair over so that she could investigate the top shelf of the closet thoroughly.

Meredith was sitting on the floor examining a pile of stuffed animals that had been relegated to a chest with other childish mementos. She ran her long sensitive fingers over each, checking for slits in the material. When she reached a fluffy poodle, she paused.

"I gave this to her," she whispered. "I think for her tenth birthday. I thought she'd thrown it away."

Elena couldn't see her eyes; Meredith's own flashlight

was turned on the poodle. But she knew how Meredith was feeling.

"I tried to make up with her," she said softly. "I did, Meredith, at the Haunted House. But she as good as told me she would never forgive me for taking Stefan from her. I wish things could be different, but she won't let them be."

"So now it's war."

"So now it's war," said Elena, flat and final. She watched as Meredith put the poodle aside and picked up the next animal. Then she turned back to her own search.

But she had no better luck with the dresser than she had with the closet. And with every moment that passed she felt more uneasy, more certain that they were about to hear a car pulling into the Forbeses' driveway.

"It's no use," Meredith said at last, feeling underneath Caroline's mattress. "She must have hidden it . . . wait. There's something here. I can feel a corner."

Elena and Bonnie stared from opposite ends of the room, momentarily frozen.

"I've got it. Elena, it's a diary!"

Relief swooped through Elena then, and she felt like a crumpled piece of paper being straightened and smoothed. She could move again. Breathing was wonderful. She'd known, she'd known all along that nothing *really* terrible could happen to Stefan. Life couldn't be that cruel, not to Elena Gilbert. They were all safe now.

But Meredith's voice was puzzled. "It's a diary. But it's green, not blue. It's the wrong one."

"*What?*" Elena snatched the little book, shining her light on it, trying to make the emerald green of the cover change into sapphire blue. It didn't work. This diary was almost exactly like hers, but it wasn't hers.

"It's Caroline's," she said stupidly, still not wanting to believe it.

Bonnie and Meredith crowded close. They all looked at the closed book, and then at one another.

"There might be clues," said Elena slowly.

"It's only fair," agreed Meredith. But it was Bonnie who actually took the diary and opened it.

Elena peered over her shoulder at Caroline's spiky back-slanted writing, so different from the block letters of the purple notes. At first her eyes wouldn't focus, but then a name leapt out at her. *Elena.*

"Wait, what's that?"

Bonnie, who was the only one actually in a position to read more than one or two words, was silent a moment, her lips moving. Then she snorted.

"Listen to this," she said and read: "'Elena's the most selfish person I've ever known. Everyone thinks she's so together, but it's really just coldness. It's sickening the way people suck up to her, never realizing that she doesn't give a damn about anyone or anything except Elena.'"

"*Caroline* says that? She should talk!" But Elena could feel heat in her face. It was, practically, what Matt had said about her when she was after Stefan.

"Go on, there's more," said Meredith, poking at Bonnie, who continued in an offended voice.

"'Bonnie's almost as bad these days, always trying to make herself important. The newest thing is pretending she's psychic so people will pay attention to her. If she was *really* psychic she'd figure out that Elena is just using her.'"

There was a heavy pause, and then Elena said, "Is that all?"

"No, there's a bit about Meredith. 'Meredith doesn't do anything to stop it. In fact, Meredith doesn't *do* anything; she just watches. It's as if she can't act; she can only react to things. Besides, I've heard my parents talking about her family—no wonder she never mentions them.' What's that supposed to mean?"

Meredith hadn't moved, and Elena could see only her neck and chin in the dim light. But she spoke quietly and steadily. "It doesn't matter. Keep on looking, Bonnie, for something about Elena's diary."

"Try around October eighteenth. That was when it was stolen," said Elena, putting her questions aside. She'd ask Meredith about it later.

There was no entry for October eighteenth or the weekend after; in fact, there were only a few entries for the following weeks. None of them mentioned the diary.

"Well, that's it then," said Meredith, sitting back. "This book is useless. Unless we want to blackmail *her* with it. You know, like we won't show hers if she won't show yours."

It was a tempting idea, but Bonnie spotted the flaw. "There's nothing bad about Caroline in here; it's all just complaints about other people. Mostly us. I'll bet Caroline would *love* to have it read out loud in front of the whole school. It'd make her day."

"So what do we do with it?"

"Put it back," said Elena tiredly. She swung her light around the room, which seemed to her eyes to be filled with subtle differences from when they'd come in. "We'll just have to keep on pretending we don't know she has my diary, and hope for another chance."

"All right," said Bonnie, but she went on thumbing through the little book, occasionally giving vent to an indignant snort or hiss. "Will you listen to this!" she exclaimed.

"There isn't time," Elena said. She would have said something else, but at that moment Meredith spoke, her tone commanding everyone's immediate attention.

"A car."

It took only a second to ascertain that the vehicle was pulling up into the Forbeses' driveway. Bonnie's eyes and

mouth were wide and round and she seemed to be paralyzed, kneeling by the bed.

"Go! Go on," said Elena, snatching the diary from her.
"Turn the flashlights off and get out the back door."

They were already moving, Meredith urging Bonnie
forward. Elena dropped to her knees and lifted the bedspread, pulling up at Caroline's mattress. With her other
hand she pushed the diary forward, wedging it between
the mattress and the dust ruffle. The thinly covered box
springs bit into her arm from below, but even worse was
the weight of the queen-size mattress bearing down from
above. She gave the book a few more nudges with her fingertips and then pulled her arm out, tugging the bedspread back in place.

She gave one wild glance back at the room as she left;
there was no time to fix anything more now. As she moved
swiftly and silently toward the stairs, she heard a key in
the front door.

What followed was a sort of dreadful game of tag.
Elena knew they were not deliberately chasing her, but
the Forbes family seemed determined to corner her in
their house. She turned back the way she had come as
voices and lights materialized in the hall as they headed
up the stairs. She fled from them into the last doorway
down the hall, and they seemed to follow. They moved
across the landing; they were right outside the master

bedroom. She turned toward the adjoining bathroom, but then saw lights spring to life under the closed door, cutting off her escape.

She was trapped. At any moment Caroline's parents might come in. She saw the french windows lending to a balcony and made her decision in that same instant.

Outside, the air was cool, and her panting breath showed faintly. Yellow light burst forth from the room beside her, and she huddled even farther to the left, keeping out of its path. Then, the sound she had been dreading came with terrible clarity: the snick of a door handle, followed by a billowing of curtains inward as the french windows opened.

She looked around frantically. It was too far to jump to the ground, and there was nothing to grab hold of to climb down. That left only the roof, but there was nothing to climb up, either. Still, some instinct made her try, and she was on the balcony railing and groping for a handhold above even as a shadow appeared on the filmy curtains. A hand parted them, a figure began to emerge, and then Elena felt something clasping her own hand, locking on her wrist and hauling her upwards. Automatically she boosted with her feet and felt herself scrambling onto the shingled roof. Trying to calm her ragged breath, she looked over gratefully to see who her rescuer was—and froze.

"The name *is* Salvatore. As in savior," he said. There was a brief flash of white teeth in the darkness.

Elena looked down. The overhang of the roof obscured the balcony, but she could hear shuffling sounds down there. But they were not the sounds of pursuit, and there was no sign that her companion's words had been overheard. A minute later, she heard the french windows close.

"I thought it was Smith," she said, still looking down into the darkness.

Damon laughed. It was a terribly engaging laugh, without the bitter edge of Stefan's. It made her think of the rainbow lights on the crow's feathers.

Nevertheless, she was not fooled. Charming as he

seemed, Damon was dangerous almost beyond imagination. That graceful, lounging body was ten times stronger than a human's. Those lazy dark eyes were adapted to seeing perfectly at night. The long-fingered hand that had pulled her up to the roof could move with impossible quickness. And, most disturbing of all, his mind was the mind of a killer. A predator.

She could feel it just beneath his surface. He was *different* from a human. He had lived so long by hunting and killing that he'd forgotten any other way. And he enjoyed it, not fighting his nature as Stefan did, but glorying in it. He had no morals and no conscience, and she was trapped here with him in the middle of the night.

She settled back on one heel, ready to jump into action at any minute. She ought to be angry with him now, after what he'd done to her in the dream. She was, but there was no point in expressing it. He knew how furious she must be, and he would only laugh at her if she told him.

She watched him quietly, intently, waiting for his next move.

But he didn't move. Those hands that could dart as quickly as striking snakes rested motionlessly on his knees. His expression reminded her of the way he'd looked at her once before. The first time they'd met she'd seen the same guarded, reluctant respect in his eyes—except that then there had also been surprise in them.

Now there was none.

"You're not going to scream at me? Or faint?" he said, as if offering her the standard options.

Elena was still watching him. He was much stronger than she was, and faster, but if she needed to she thought she could get to the edge of the roof before he reached her. It was a thirty foot drop if she missed the balcony, but she might decide to risk it. It all depended on Damon.

"I don't faint," she said shortly. "And why should I scream at you? We were playing a game. I was stupid that night and so I lost. You warned me in the graveyard about the consequences."

His lips parted in a quick breath and he looked away. "I may just have to make you my Queen of Shadows," he said, and, speaking almost to himself, he continued: "I've had many companions, girls as young as you and women who were the beauties of Europe. But *you're* the one I want at my side. Ruling, taking what we want when we want it. Feared and worshipped by all the weaker souls. Would that be so bad?"

"I *am* one of the weaker souls," Elena said. "And you and I are enemies, Damon. We can never be anything else."

"Are you sure?" He looked at her, and she could feel the power of his mind as it touched hers, like the brush of those long fingers. But there was no dizziness, no feeling of weakness or succumbing. That afternoon she'd had a long soak, as she always did these days, in a hot bath sprinkled with dried vervain.

Damon's eyes flashed with understanding, but he took the setback with good grace. "What are you doing here?" he said casually.

It was strange, but she felt no need to lie to him. "Caroline took something that belonged to me. A diary. I came to get it back."

A new look flickered in the dark eyes. "Undoubtedly to protect my worthless brother somehow," he said, annoyed.

"Stefan isn't involved in this!"

"Oh, isn't he?" She was afraid he understood more than she meant him to. "Strange, he always seems to be involved when there's trouble. He *creates* problems. Now, if he were out of the picture . . . "

Elena spoke steadily. "If you hurt Stefan again I'll make you sorry. I'll find some way to make you wish you hadn't, Damon. I mean it."

"I see. Well, then, I'll just have to work on *you*, won't I?"

Elena said nothing. She'd talked herself into a corner, agreeing to play this deadly game of his again. She looked away.

"I'm going to have you in the end, you know," he said softly. It was the voice he'd used at the party, when he'd said, "Easy, easy." There was no mockery or malice now; he was simply stating a fact. "By hook or by crook, as you people say—that's a nice phrase—you'll be mine before the next snow flies."

Elena tried to conceal the chill she felt, but she knew he saw anyway.

"Good," he said. "You do have some sense. You're right to be afraid of me; I'm the most dangerous thing you're ever likely to encounter in your life. But just now I have a business proposition for you."

"A *business* proposition?"

"Exactly. You came here to get a diary. But you haven't got it." He indicated her empty hands. "You failed, didn't you?" When Elena made no reply he went on. "And since you don't want my brother *involved*, he can't help you. But I can. And I will."

"You will?"

"Of course. For a price."

Elena stared at him. Blood flamed in her face. When she managed to get words out, they would come only in a whisper.

"What—*price*?"

A smile gleamed out of the darkness. "A few minutes of your time, Elena. A few drops of your blood. An hour or so spent with me, alone."

"You . . . " Elena couldn't find the right word. Every

epithet she knew was too mild.

"I'll have it anyway, eventually," he said in a reasonable tone. "If you're honest, you'll admit that to yourself. Last time wasn't the last. Why not accept that?" His voice dropped to a warm, intimate timbre. "Remember . . . "

"I'd rather cut my throat," she said.

"An intriguing thought. But I can do it so much more enjoyably."

He was laughing at her. Somehow, on top of everything else today, this was too much. "You're disgusting; you know that," she said. "You're sickening." She was shaking now, and she couldn't breathe. "I'd die before I'd give in to you. I'd rather—"

She wasn't sure what made her do it. When she was with Damon a sort of instinct took over her. And at that moment, she did feel that she'd rather risk anything than let him win this time. She noticed, with half her mind, that he was sitting back, relaxed, enjoying the turn his game was taking. The other half of her mind was calculating how far the roof overhung the balcony.

"I'd rather do this," she said, and flung herself sideways.

She was right; he was off guard and couldn't move fast enough to stop her. She felt free space below her feet and spinning terror as she realized the balcony was farther back than she'd thought. She was going to miss it.

But she hadn't reckoned on Damon. His hand shot out, not quick enough to keep her on the roof, but keeping her from falling any farther. It was as if her weight was nothing to him. Reflexively, Elena grasped the shingled edge of the roof and tried to get a knee up.

His voice was furious. "You little *fool*! If you're that eager to meet death I can introduce you myself."

"Let go of me," said Elena through her teeth. Someone was going to come out on that balcony at any second, she was sure of it. *"Let go of me."*

"Here and now?" Looking into those unfathomable black eyes, she realized he was serious. If she said yes he would drop her.

"It would be a fast way to end things, wouldn't it?" she said. Her heart was pounding in fear, but she refused to let him see that.

"But such a waste." With one motion, he jerked her to safety. To himself. His arms tightened around her, pressing her to the lean hardness of his body, and suddenly Elena could see nothing. She was enveloped. Then she felt those flat muscles gathering themselves like some great cat's, and the two of them launched into space.

She was falling. She couldn't help but cling to him as the only solid thing in the rushing world around her. Then he landed, catlike, taking the impact easily.

Stefan had done something similar once. But Stefan had not held her this way afterward, bruisingly close, with his lips almost in contact with hers.

"Think about my proposition," he said.

She could not move or look away. And this time she knew that it was no Power that he was using, but simply the wildfire attraction between them. It was useless to deny it; her body responded to his. She could feel his breath on her lips.

"I don't need you for anything," she told him.

She thought he was going to kiss her then, but he didn't. Above them there was the sound of french windows opening and an angry voice on the balcony. "Hey! What's going on? Is somebody out there?"

"This time I did you a favor," Damon said, very softly, still holding her. "Next time I'm going to collect."

She couldn't have turned her head away. If he'd kissed her then, she would have let him. But suddenly the hardness of his arms melted around her and his face seemed to blur. It was as if the darkness was taking him back into itself. Then black wings caught and beat the air and a huge crow was soaring away.

Something, a book or shoe, was hurled after it from the balcony. It missed by a yard.

"Damn birds!" said Mr. Forbes's voice from above. "They must be nesting on the roof."

Shivering, with her arms locked around her, Elena huddled in the darkness below until he went back inside.

She found Meredith and Bonnie crouching by the gate. "What took you so long?" Bonnie whispered. "We thought you were caught!"

"I almost was. I had to stay until it was safe." Elena was so used to lying about Damon that she did it now without conscious effort. "Let's go home," she whispered. "There's nothing more we can do."

When they parted at Elena's door, Meredith said, "It's only two weeks until Founders' Day."

"I know." For a moment Damon's proposition swam in Elena's mind. But she shook her head to clear it. "I'll think of something," she said.

She hadn't thought of anything by the next day of school. The one encouraging fact was that Caroline didn't seem to have noticed anything amiss in her room—but that was *all* Elena could find to be encouraged about. There was an assembly that morning, at which it was announced that the school board had chosen Elena as the student to represent "The Spirit of Fell's Church." All through the principal's speech about it, Caroline's smile had blazed forth, triumphant and malicious.

Elena tried to ignore it. She did her best to ignore the

slights and snubs that came even in the wake of the assembly, but it wasn't easy. It was never easy, and there were days when she thought she would hit someone or just start screaming, but so far she'd managed.

That afternoon, waiting for the sixth-period history class to be let out, Elena studied Tyler Smallwood. Since coming back to school, he had not addressed one word to her directly. He'd smiled as nastily as Caroline during the principal's announcement. Now, as he caught sight of Elena standing alone, he jostled Dick Carter with his elbow.

"What's that there?" he said. "A wallflower?"

Stefan, where are you? thought Elena. But she knew the answer to that. Halfway across school, in astronomy class.

Dick opened his mouth to say something, but then his expression changed. He was looking beyond Elena, down the hall. Elena turned and saw Vickie.

Vickie and Dick had been together before the Homecoming Dance. Elena supposed they still were. But Dick looked uncertain, as if he wasn't sure what to expect from the girl who was moving toward him.

There was something odd about Vickie's face, about her walk. She was moving as if her feet didn't touch the floor. Her eyes were dilated and dreamy.

"Hi there," Dick said tentatively, and he stepped in front of her. Vickie passed him without a glance and went on to Tyler. Elena watched what happened next with growing uneasiness. It should have been funny, but it wasn't.

It started with Tyler looking somewhat taken aback. Then Vickie put a hand on his chest. Tyler smiled, but there was a forced look about it. Vickie slid her hand under his jacket. Tyler's smile wavered. Vickie put her other hand on his chest. Tyler looked at Dick.

"Hey, Vickie, lighten up," said Dick hastily, but he didn't move any closer.

Vickie slid her two hands upwards, pushing Tyler's jacket off his shoulders. He tried to shrug it back on without letting go of his books or seeming too concerned. He couldn't. Vickie's fingers crept under his shirt.

"Stop that. Stop her, will you?" said Tyler to Dick. He had backed up into the wall.

"Hey, Vickie, leggo. Don't do that." But Dick remained at a safe distance. Tyler shot him an enraged glare and tried to shove Vickie away.

A noise had begun. At first it seemed to be at a frequency almost too low for human hearing, but it grew louder and louder. A growl, eerily menacing, that sent ice down Elena's spine. Tyler was looking pop-eyed with disbelief, and she soon realized why. The sound was coming from Vickie.

Then everything happened at once. Tyler was on the ground with Vickie's teeth snapping inches from his throat. Elena, all quarrels forgotten, was trying to help Dick pull her off. Tyler was howling. The history room door was open and Alaric was shouting.

"Don't hurt her! Be careful! It's epilepsy, we just need to get her lying down!"

Vickie's teeth snapped again as he reached a helpful hand into the melee. The slender girl was stronger than all of them together, and they were losing control of her. They weren't going to be able to hold her much longer. It was with intense relief that Elena heard a familiar voice at her shoulder.

"Vickie, calm down. It's all right. Just relax now."

With Stefan grasping Vickie's arm and talking to her soothingly, Elena dared to slacken her own grip. And it seemed, at first, that Stefan's strategy was working. Vickie's clawing fingers loosened, and they were able to lift her off Tyler. As Stefan kept speaking to her, she went limp and her eyes shut.

"That's good. You're feeling tired now. It's all right to go to sleep."

But then, abruptly, it stopped working, and whatever Power Stefan had been exercising over her was broken. Vickie's eyes flew open, and they bore no resemblance to the startled fawn's eyes Elena had seen in the cafeteria. They were blazing with red fury. She snarled at Stefan and burst out fighting with fresh strength.

It took five or six of them to hold her down while somebody called the police. Elena stayed where she was, talking to Vickie, sometimes yelling at her, until the police got there. None of it did any good.

Then she stepped back and saw the crowd of onlookers for the first time. Bonnie was in the front row, staring open-mouthed. So was Caroline.

"What *happened*?" said Bonnie as the officials carried Vickie away.

Elena, panting gently, pushed a strand of hair out of her eyes. "She went crazy and tried to undress Tyler."

Bonnie pursed her lips. "Well, she'd have to be crazy to *want* to, wouldn't she?" And she threw a smirk over her shoulder directly at Caroline.

Elena's knees were rubbery and her hands were shaking. She felt an arm go around her, and she leaned against Stefan gratefully. Then she looked up at him.

"Epilepsy?" she said with disbelieving scorn.

He was gazing down the hall after Vickie. Alaric Saltzman, still shouting instructions, was apparently going with her. The group turned the corner.

"I think class was just dismissed," Stefan said. "Let's go."

They walked toward the boarding house in silence, each lost in thought. Elena frowned, and several times glanced over at Stefan, but it wasn't until they were alone in his room that she spoke.

"Stefan, what is all this? What's happening to Vickie?"

"That's what I've been wondering. There's only one explanation I can think of, and it's that she's still under attack."

"You mean Damon's still—oh, my God! Oh, Stefan, I should have given her some of the vervain. I should have realized . . . "

"It wouldn't have made any difference. Believe me." She had turned toward the door as if to go after Vickie that minute, but he pulled her gently back. "Some people are more easily influenced than others, Elena. Vickie's will was never very strong. It belongs to him, now."

Slowly, Elena sat down. "Then there's nothing anyone can do? But, Stefan, will she become—like you and Damon?"

"It depends." His tone was bleak. "It's not just a matter of how much blood she loses. She needs his blood in her veins to make the change complete. Otherwise, she'll just end up like Mr. Tanner. Drained, used up. Dead."

Elena took a long breath. There was something else she wanted to ask him about, something she'd wanted to ask him for a long time. "Stefan, when you spoke to Vickie back there, I thought it was working. You were using your Powers on her, weren't you?"

"Yes."

"But then she just went crazy again. What I mean is . . . Stefan, you *are* okay, aren't you? Your Powers have come back?"

He didn't answer. But that was answer enough for her. "Stefan, why didn't you tell me? What's wrong?" She went around and knelt by him so that he had to look at her.

"It's taking me a while to recover, that's all. Don't worry about it."

"I *am* worried. Isn't there anything we can do?"

"No," he said. But his eyes dropped.

Comprehension swept through Elena. *"Oh,"* she whispered, sitting back. Then she reached for him again, trying to get hold of his hands. "Stefan, listen to me—"

"Elena, *no*. Don't you see? It's dangerous, dangerous for both of us, but especially for you. It could kill you, or worse."

"Only if you lose control," she said. "And you won't. Kiss me."

"No," said Stefan again. He added, less harshly, "I'll go out hunting tonight as soon as it's dark."

"Is that the same?" she said. She knew it wasn't. It was human blood that gave Power. "Oh, Stefan, please; don't you see I want to? Don't *you* want to?"

"That isn't fair," he said, his eyes tortured. "You know

it isn't, Elena. You know how much—" He turned away from her again, his hands clenched into fists.

"Then why not? Stefan, I need . . . " She couldn't finish. She couldn't explain to him what she needed; it was a need for connection to him, for closeness. She needed to remember what it was like with him, to wipe out the memory of dancing in her dream and of Damon's arms locked around her. "I need us to be together again," she whispered.

Stefan was still turned away, and he shook his head.

"All right," Elena whispered, but she felt a wash of grief and fear as defeat seeped into her bones. Most of the fear was for Stefan, who was vulnerable without his Powers, vulnerable enough that he might be hurt by the ordinary citizens of Fell's Church. But some of it was for herself.

12

voice spoke as Elena reached for a can on the store shelf.

"Cranberry sauce already?"

Elena looked up. "Hi, Matt. Yes, Aunt Judith likes to do a preview the Sunday before Thanksgiving, remember? If she practices, there's less chance she'll do something terrible."

"Like forgetting to buy the cranberry sauce until fifteen minutes before dinner?"

"Until five minutes before dinner," said Elena, consulting her watch, and Matt laughed. It was a good sound, and one Elena hadn't heard for too long. She moved on toward the check-out stand, but after she'd paid for her purchase she hesitated, looking back. Matt was standing by the magazine rack, apparently absorbed, but there was something about the slope of his shoulders that made her want to go to him.

She poked a finger at his magazine. "What are *you* doing for dinner?" she said. When he glanced uncertainly toward the front of the store, she added, "Bonnie's waiting out in the car; she'll be there. Other than that it's just the family. And Robert, of course; he should be there by now." She meant that Stefan wasn't coming. She still wasn't sure how things were between Matt and Stefan these days. At least they spoke to each other.

"I'm fending for myself tonight; Mom's not feeling so hot," he said. But then, as if to change the subject, he went on, "Where's Meredith?"

"With her family, visiting some relatives or something." Elena was vague because Meredith had been vague herself; she seldom talked about her family. "So what do you think? Want to take a chance on Aunt Judith's cooking?"

"For old times' sake?"

"For old *friends'* sake," said Elena after a moment's hesitation, and smiled at him.

He blinked and looked away. "How can I refuse an invitation like that?" he said in an oddly muted voice. But when he put the magazine back and followed her out he was smiling, too.

Bonnie greeted him cheerfully, and when they got home Aunt Judith looked pleased to see him come into the kitchen.

"Dinner's almost ready," she said, taking the grocery bag from Elena. "Robert got here a few minutes ago. Why don't you go straight on back to the dining room? Oh, and get another chair, Elena. Matt makes seven."

"Six, Aunt Judith," said Elena, amused. "You and Robert, me and Margaret, Matt and Bonnie."

"Yes, dear, but Robert's brought a guest, too. They're already sitting down."

Elena registered the words just as she stepped through the dining room door, but there was an instant's delay before her mind reacted to them. Even so, she *knew*; stepping through that door, she somehow knew what was waiting for her.

Robert was standing there, fiddling with a bottle of white wine and looking jovial. And sitting at the table, on the far side of the autumn centerpiece and the tall lighted candles, was Damon.

Elena realized she'd stopped moving when Bonnie ran into her from behind. Then she forced her legs into action. Her mind wasn't as obedient; it remained frozen.

"Ah, Elena," Robert said, holding out a hand. "This is Elena, the girl I was telling you about," he said to Damon. "Elena, this is Damon . . . ah . . . "

"Smith," said Damon.

"Oh, yes. He's from my alma mater, William and Mary, and I just ran into him outside the drugstore. Since he was looking for some place to eat, I invited him along here for a home-cooked meal. Damon, these are some friends of Elena's, Matt and Bonnie."

"Hi," said Matt. Bonnie just stared; then, she swung enormous eyes on Elena.

Elena was trying to get a grip on herself. She didn't know whether to shriek, march out of the room, or throw the glass of wine Robert was pouring in Damon's face. She was too angry, for the moment, to be frightened.

Matt went to bring in a chair from the living room. Elena wondered at his casual acceptance of Damon, and then realized he hadn't been at Alaric's party. He wouldn't know what had happened there between Stefan and the "visitor from college."

Bonnie, though, looked ready to panic. She was gazing at Elena imploringly. Damon had risen and was holding out a chair for her.

Before Elena could come up with a response, she heard Margaret's high little voice in the doorway. "Matt, do you want to see my kitty? Aunt Judith says I can keep her. I'm going to call her Snowball."

Elena turned, fired with an idea.

"She's cute," Matt was saying obligingly, bending over

the little mound of white fur in Margaret's arms. He looked startled as Elena unceremoniously grabbed the kitten from under his nose.

"Here, Margaret, let's show your kitty to Robert's friend," she said, and thrust the fluffy bundle into Damon's face, all but throwing it at him.

Pandemonium ensued. Snowball swelled to twice her normal size as her fur stood on end. She made a noise like water dropped on a red-hot griddle and then she was a snarling, spitting cyclone that clawed Elena, swiped at Damon, and ricocheted off the walls before tearing out of the room.

For an instant, Elena had the satisfaction of seeing Damon's night black eyes slightly wider than usual. Then the lids drooped down, hooding them again, and Elena turned to face the reaction of the other occupants of the room.

Margaret was just opening her mouth for a steam engine wail. Robert was trying to forestall it, hustling her off to find the cat. Bonnie had her back pressed flat against the wall, looking desperate. Matt and Aunt Judith, who was peering in from the kitchen, just looked appalled.

"I guess you don't have a way with animals," she said to Damon, and took her seat at the table. She nodded to Bonnie who reluctantly peeled herself off the wall and scuttled for her own seat before Damon could touch the chair. Bonnie's brown eyes slid around to follow him as he sat down in turn.

After a few minutes, Robert reappeared with a tear-stained Margaret and frowned sternly at Elena. Matt pushed his own chair in silently although his eyebrows were in his hair.

As Aunt Judith arrived and the meal began Elena looked up and down the table. A bright haze seemed to lie over everything, and she had a feeling of unreality, but the scene itself looked almost unbelievably wholesome, like something out of a commercial. Just your average family sitting down to eat turkey, she thought. One slightly flustered maiden aunt, worried that the peas will be mushy and the rolls burnt, one comfortable uncle-to-be, one golden-haired teenage niece and her tow-headed baby sister. One blue-eyed boy-next-door type, one spritely girlfriend, one gorgeous vampire passing the candied yams. A typical American household.

Bonnie spent the first half of the meal telegraphing "What do I do?" messages to Elena with her eyes. But when all Elena telegraphed back was "Nothing," she apparently decided to abandon herself to her fate. She began to eat.

Elena had no idea what to do. To be trapped like this was an insult, a humiliation, and Damon knew it. He had

Aunt Judith and Robert dazzled, though, with compliments about the meal and light chat about William and Mary. Even Margaret was smiling at him now, and soon enough Bonnie would go under.

"Fell's Church is having its Founders' Day celebration next week," Aunt Judith informed Damon, her thin cheeks faintly pink. "It would be so nice if you could come back for that."

"I'd like to," said Damon affably.

Aunt Judith looked pleased. "And this year Elena has a big part in it. She's been chosen to represent the Spirit of Fell's Church."

"You must be proud of her," said Damon.

"Oh, we are," Aunt Judith said. "So you'll try to come then?"

Elena broke in, buttering a roll furiously. "I've heard some news about Vickie," she said. "You remember, the girl who was attacked." She looked pointedly at Damon.

There was a short silence. Then Damon said, "I'm afraid I don't know her."

"Oh, I'm sure you do. About my height, brown eyes, light brown hair . . . anyway, she's getting worse."

"Oh, dear," said Aunt Judith.

"Yes, apparently the doctors can't understand it. She just keeps getting worse and worse, as if the attack was still going on." Elena kept her eyes on Damon's face as she spoke, but he displayed only a courteous interest. "Have some more stuffing," she finished, propelling a bowl at him.

"No thank you. I'll have some more of this, though." He held a spoonful of jellied cranberry sauce up to one of the candles so that light shone through it. "It's such a tantalizing color."

Bonnie, like the rest of the people at the table, looked up at the candle when he did this. But Elena noticed she didn't look down again. She remained gazing into the dancing flame, and slowly all expression disappeared from her face.

Oh, *no*, thought Elena, as a tingle of apprehension crept through her limbs. She'd seen that look before. She tried to get Bonnie's attention, but the other girl seemed to see nothing but the candle.

" . . . and then the elementary children put on a pageant about the town's history," Aunt Judith was saying to Damon. "But the ending ceremony is done by older students. Elena, how many seniors will be doing the readings this year?"

"Just three of us." Elena had to turn to address her aunt, and it was while she was looking at Aunt Judith's smiling face that she heard the voice.

"Death."

Aunt Judith gasped. Robert paused with his fork

halfway to his mouth. Elena wished, wildly and absolutely hopelessly, for Meredith.

"Death," said the voice again. "Death is in this house."

Elena looked around the table and saw that there was no one to help her. They were all staring at Bonnie, motionless as subjects in a photograph.

Bonnie herself was staring into the candle flame. Her face was blank, her eyes wide, as they had been before when this voice spoke through her. Now, those sightless eyes turned toward Elena. "Your death," the voice said. "Your death is waiting, Elena. It is—"

Bonnie seemed to choke. Then she pitched forward and almost landed in her dinner plate.

There was an instant's paralysis, and then everyone moved. Robert jumped up and pulled at Bonnie's shoulders, lifting her. Bonnie's skin had gone bluish-white, her eyes were closed. Aunt Judith fluttered around her, dabbing at her face with a damp napkin. Damon watched with thoughtful, narrowed eyes.

"She's all right," Robert said, looking up in obvious relief. "I think she just fainted. It must have been some kind of hysterical attack." But Elena didn't breathe again until Bonnie opened groggy eyes and asked what everyone was staring at.

It put an effective end to the dinner. Robert insisted that Bonnie be taken home at once, and in the activity that followed Elena found time for a whispered word with Damon.

"Get out!"

He raised his eyebrows. "What?"

"I said, get out! Now! Go. Or I'll tell them you're the killer."

He looked reproachful. "Don't you think a guest deserves a little more consideration?" he said, but at her expression he shrugged and smiled.

"Thank you for having me for dinner," he said aloud to Aunt Judith, who was walking past carrying a blanket to the car. "I hope I can return the favor sometime." To Elena he added, "Be seeing you."

Well, *that* was clear enough, Elena thought, as Robert drove away with a somber Matt and a sleepy Bonnie. Aunt Judith was on the phone with Mrs. McCullough.

"I don't know what it is with these girls, either," she said. "First Vickie, now Bonnie . . . and Elena has not been herself lately . . ."

While Aunt Judith talked and Margaret searched for the missing Snowball, Elena paced.

She would have to call Stefan. That was all there was to it. She wasn't worried about Bonnie; the other times this had happened hadn't seemed to do permanent damage. And Damon would have better things to do than harass Elena's friends tonight.

He was coming here, to collect for the "favor" he'd done her. She knew without a doubt that that was the meaning of his final words. And it meant she would have to tell Stefan everything, because she needed him tonight, needed his protection.

Only, what could Stefan do? Despite all her pleas and arguments last week, he had refused to take her blood. He'd insisted that his Powers would return without it, but Elena knew he was still vulnerable right now. Even if Stefan were here, could he stop Damon? Could he do it without being killed himself?

Bonnie's house was no refuge. And Meredith was gone. There was no one to help her, no one she could trust. But the thought of waiting here alone tonight, knowing that Damon was coming, was unbearable.

She heard Aunt Judith click down the receiver. Automatically, she moved toward the kitchen, Stefan's number running through her mind. Then she stopped, and slowly turned around to look at the living room she'd just left.

She looked at the floor to ceiling windows and at the elaborate fireplace with its beautifully scrolled molding. This room was part of the original house, the one that had almost completely burned in the Civil War. Her own bedroom was just above.

A great light was beginning to dawn. Elena looked at

the molding around the ceiling, at where it joined the more modern dining room. Then she almost ran toward the stairs, her heart beating fast.

"Aunt Judith?" Her aunt paused on the stairway. "Aunt Judith, tell me something. Did Damon go into the living room?"

"What!" Aunt Judith blinked at her in distraction.

"Did Robert take Damon into the living room? Please think, Aunt Judith! I need to know."

"Why, no, I don't think so. No, he didn't. They came in and went straight to the dining room. Elena, what on earth? . . . " This last as Elena impulsively threw her arms around her and hugged her.

"Sorry, Aunt Judith. I'm just happy," said Elena. Smiling, she turned to go back down the stairs.

"Well, I'm glad *someone's* happy, after the way dinner turned out. Although that nice boy, Damon, seemed to enjoy himself. Do you know, Elena, he seemed quite taken with you, in spite of the way you were acting."

Elena turned back around. "So?"

"Well, I just thought you might give him a chance, that's all. I thought he was very pleasant. The kind of young man I like to see around here."

Elena goggled a moment, then swallowed to keep the hysterical laughter from escaping. Her aunt was suggesting that she take up Damon instead of Stefan . . . because

Damon was safer. The kind of nice young man any aunt would like. "Aunt Judith," she began, gasping, but then she realized it was useless. She shook her head mutely, throwing her hands up in defeat, and watched her aunt go up the stairs.

Usually Elena slept with her door closed. But tonight she left it open and lay on her bed gazing out into the darkened hallway. Every so often she glanced at the luminous numbers of the clock on the nightstand beside her.

There was no danger that she would fall asleep. As the minutes crawled by, she almost began to wish she could. Time moved with agonizing slowness. Eleven o'clock . . . eleven thirty . . . midnight. One a.m. One thirty. Two.

At 2:10 she heard a sound.

She listened, still lying on her bed, to the faint whisper of noise downstairs. She'd known he would find a way to get in if he wanted. If Damon was that determined, no lock would keep him out.

Music from the dream she'd had that night at Bonnie's tinkled through her mind, a handful of plaintive, silvery notes. It woke strange feelings inside her. Almost in a daze or dream herself, she got up and went to stand at the threshold.

The hallway was dark, but her eyes had had a long time to adjust. She could see the darker silhouette making its way up the stairs. When it reached the top she saw the swift, deadly glimmer of his smile.

She waited, unsmiling, until he reached her and stood facing her, with only a yard of hardwood floor between them. The house was completely silent. Across the hall Margaret slept; at the end of the passage, Aunt Judith lay wrapped in dreams, unaware of what was going on outside her door.

Damon said nothing, but he looked at her, his eyes taking in the long white nightgown with its high, lacy neck. Elena had chosen it because it was the most modest one she owned, but Damon obviously thought it attractive. She forced herself to stand quietly, but her mouth, was dry and her heart was thudding dully. Now was the time. In another minute she would know.

She backed up, without a word or gesture of invitation, leaving the doorway empty. She saw the quick flare in his bottomless eyes, and watched him come eagerly toward her. And watched him stop.

He stood just outside her room, plainly disconcerted. He tried again to step forward but could not. Something seemed to be preventing him from moving any farther. On his face, surprise gave way to puzzlement and then anger.

He looked up, his eyes raking over the lintel, scanning the ceiling on either side of the threshold. Then, as the full realization hit him, his lips pulled back from his teeth in an animal snarl.

Safe on her side of the doorway, Elena laughed softly. It had worked.

"My room and the living room below are all that's left of the old house," she said to him. "And, of course, that was a different dwelling place. One you were *not* invited into, and never will be."

His chest was heaving with anger, his nostrils dilated, his eyes wild. Waves of black rage emanated from him. He looked as if he would like to tear the walls down with his hands, which were twitching and clenching with fury.

Triumph and relief made Elena giddy. "You'd better go now," she said. "There's nothing for you here."

One minute more those menacing eyes blazed into hers, and then Damon turned around. But he didn't head for the stairway. Instead, he took one step across the hall and laid his hand on the door to Margaret's room.

Elena started forward before she knew what she was doing. She stopped in the doorway, grasping the casing trim, her own breath coming hard.

His head whipped around and he smiled at her, a slow, cruel smile. He twisted the doorknob slightly without looking at it. His eyes, like pools of liquid ebony, remained on Elena.

"Your choice," he said.

Elena stood very still, feeling as if all of winter was inside her. Margaret was just a baby. He couldn't mean it; no one could be such a monster as to hurt a four-year-old.

But there was no hint of softness or compassion in Damon's face. He was a hunter, killer, and the weak were his prey. She remembered the dreadful animal snarl that had transfigured his handsome features, and she knew that she could never leave Margaret to him.

Everything seemed to be happening in slow motion. She saw Damon's hand on the doorknob; she saw those merciless eyes. She was walking through the doorway, leaving behind the only safe place she knew.

Death was in the house, Bonnie had said. And now Elena had gone to meet Death of her own free will. She bowed her head to conceal the helpless tears that came to her eyes. It was over. Damon had won.

She did not look up to see him advance on her. But she felt the air stir around her, making her shiver. And then she was enfolded in soft, endless blackness, which wrapped around her like a great bird's wings.

13

Elena stirred, then opened heavy eyelids. Light was showing around the edges of the curtains. She found it hard to move, so she lay there on her bed and tried to piece together what had happened last night.

Damon. Damon had come here and threatened Margaret. And so Elena had gone to him. He'd won.

But why hadn't he finished it? Elena lifted a languid hand to touch the side of her neck, already knowing what she would find. Yes, there they were: two small punctures that were tender and sensitive to pressure.

Yet she was still alive. He'd stopped short of carrying out his promise. Why?

Her memories of the last hours were confused and blurry. Only fragments were clear. Damon's eyes looking down at her, filling her whole world. The sharp sting at her throat. And, later, Damon opening his shirt, Damon's blood welling from a small cut in his neck.

He'd made her drink his blood then. If *made* was the right word. She didn't remember putting up any resistance or feeling any revulsion. By then, she had wanted it.

But she wasn't dead, or even seriously weakened. He hadn't made her into a vampire. And that was what she couldn't understand.

He has no morals and no conscience, she reminded herself. So it certainly wasn't mercy that stopped him. He probably just wants to draw the game out, make you suffer more before he kills you. Or maybe he wants you to be like Vickie, with one foot in the shadow world and one in the light. Going slowly mad that way.

One thing was sure: she wouldn't be fooled into thinking it was kindness on his part. Damon wasn't capable of kindness. Or of caring for anybody but himself.

Pushing the blankets back, she rose from the bed. She could hear Aunt Judith moving around in the hallway. It was Monday morning and she had to get ready to go to school.

November 27, Wednesday

Dear Diary,

It's no good pretending I'm not frightened,

because I am. Tomorrow's Thanksgiving, and Founders' Day is two days after that. And I still haven't figured out a way to stop Caroline and Tyler.

I don't know what to do. If I can't get my diary back from Caroline, she's going to read it in front of everyone. She'll have a perfect opportunity; she's one of the three seniors chosen to read poetry during the closing ceremonies. Chosen by the school board, of which Tyler's father is a member, I might add. I wonder what he'll think when this is all over?

But what difference does it make? Unless I can come up with a plan, when this is all over I'll be beyond caring. And Stefan will be gone, run out of town by the good citizens of Fell's Church. Or dead, if he doesn't get some of his Powers back. And if he dies, I'll die too. It's that simple.

Which means I have to find a way to get the diary. I have to.

But I can't.

I know, you're waiting for me to say it. There is a way to get my diary—Damon's way. All I need to do is agree to his price.

But you don't understand how much that frightens me. Not just because Damon frightens me, but because I'm afraid of what will happen if he and I are together again. I'm afraid of what will happen to me . . . and to me and Stefan.

I can't talk about this anymore. It's too upsetting. I feel so confused and lost and alone. There's nobody I can turn to or talk to. Nobody who could possibly understand.

What am I going to do?

November 28, Thursday, 11:30 p.m.

Dear Diary,

Things seem clearer today, maybe because I've come to a decision. It's a decision that terrifies me, but it's better than the only alternative I can think of.

I'm going to tell Stefan everything.

It's the only thing I can do now. Founders' Day is Saturday and I haven't come up with any plan of my own. But maybe Stefan can, if he realizes how desperate the situation is. I'm going over to spend the day at the boarding house tomorrow, and when I get there I'm going to tell him everything I should have told him in the first place.

Everything. About Damon, too.

I don't know what he'll say. I keep remembering his face in my dreams. The way he looked at me, with such bitterness and anger. Not as if he loved me at all. If he looks at me like that tomorrow . . .

Oh, I'm scared. My stomach is churning. I could barely touch Thanksgiving dinner—and I can't keep still. I feel as if I might fly apart into a million pieces. Go to sleep tonight? Ha.

Please let Stefan understand. Please let him forgive me.

The funniest thing is, I wanted to become a better person for him. I wanted to be worthy of his love. Stefan has these ideas about honor, about what's right and wrong. And now, when he finds out how I've been lying to him, what will he think of me? Will he believe me, that I was only trying to protect him? Will he ever trust me again?

Tomorrow I'll know. Oh, God, I wish it were already over. I don't know how I'll live until then.

Elena slipped out of the house without telling Aunt Judith where she was going. She was tired of lies, but she didn't want to face the fuss there would inevitably be if she said she was going to Stefan's. Ever since Damon had come to dinner, Aunt Judith had been talking about him, throwing subtle and not-so-subtle hints into every conversation. And Robert was almost as bad. Elena sometimes thought he egged Aunt Judith on.

She leaned on the doorbell of the boarding house wearily. Where was Mrs. Flowers these days? When the door finally opened, Stefan was behind it.

He was dressed for outdoors, his jacket collar turned up. "I thought we could go for a walk," he said.

"No." Elena was firm. She couldn't manage a real smile for him, so she stopped trying. She said, "Let's go upstairs, Stefan, all right? There's something we need to talk about."

He looked at her a moment in surprise. Something must have shown in her face, for his expression gradually stilled and darkened. He took a deep breath and nodded. Without a word, he turned and led the way to his room.

The trunks and dressers and bookcases had long since been put back into order, of course. But Elena felt as if she was really noticing this for the first time. For some reason, she thought of the very first night she'd been here, when Stefan had saved her from Tyler's disgusting embrace. Her eyes ran over the objects on the dresser: the fifteenth-century gold florins, the ivory-hilted dagger, the little iron coffer with the hinged lid. She'd tried to open that the first night and he'd slammed the lid down.

She turned. Stefan was standing by the window, outlined by the rectangle of gray and dismal sky. Every day this week had been chilly and misty, and this was no exception. Stefan's expression mirrored the weather outside.

"Well," he said quietly, "what do we need to talk about?"

There was one last moment of choice, and then Elena committed herself. She stretched out a hand to the small iron coffer and opened it.

Inside, a length of apricot silk shone with muted luster. Her hair ribbon. It reminded her of summer, of summer days that seemed impossibly far away just now. She gathered it up and held it out to Stefan.

"About this," she said.

He had taken a step forward when she touched the coffer, but now he looked puzzled and surprised. "About *that?*"

"Yes. Because I knew it was there, Stefan. I found it a long time ago, one day when you left the room for a few minutes. I don't know why I had to know what was in there but I couldn't help it. So I found the ribbon. And then . . . " She stopped and braced herself. "Then I wrote about it in my diary."

Stefan was looking more and more bewildered, as if this was not at all what he'd been expecting. Elena groped for the right words.

"I wrote about it because I thought it was evidence that you'd cared about me all along, enough to pick it up and keep it. I never thought it could be evidence of anything else."

Then, suddenly, she was speaking quickly. She told

him about taking her diary to Bonnie's house, about how it had been stolen. She told him about getting the notes, about realizing that Caroline was the one who was sending them. And then, turning away, pulling the summer-colored silk over and over through her nervous fingers she told him about Caroline and Tyler's plan.

Her voice almost gave out at the end. "I've been so frightened since then," she whispered, her eyes still on the ribbon. "Scared that you'd be angry with me. Scared of what they're going to do. Just scared. I tried to get the diary back, Stefan, I even went to Caroline's house. But she has it too well hidden. And I've thought and thought, but I can't think of any way of stopping her from reading it." At last she looked up at him. "I'm sorry."

"You should be!" he said, startling her with his vehemence. She felt the blood drain from her face. But Stefan was going on. "You should be sorry for keeping something like that from me when I could have helped you. Elena, why didn't you just *tell* me?"

"Because it's all my fault. And I had a dream. . . ." She tried to describe how he had looked in the dreams, the bitterness, the accusation in his eyes. "I think I would die if you really looked at me that way," she concluded miserably.

But Stefan's expression as he looked at her now was a

combination of relief and wonder. "So that's it," he said, almost in a whisper himself. "That's what's been bothering you."

Elena opened her mouth, but he was still speaking. "I knew something was wrong, I knew you were holding something back. But I thought . . . " He shook his head and a skewed smile tugged at his lips. "It doesn't matter now. I didn't want to invade your privacy. I didn't even want to ask. And all the time you were worried about protecting *me*."

Elena's tongue was stuck to the roof of her mouth. The words seemed to be stuck, too. There's more, she thought, but she couldn't say it, not when Stefan's eyes looked like that, not when his whole face was alight that way.

"When you said we needed to talk today, I thought you'd changed your mind about me," he said simply, without self-pity. "And I wouldn't have blamed you. But instead . . . " He shook his head again. "Elena," he said, and then she was in his arms.

It felt so good to be there, so *right*. She hadn't even realized how wrong things had been between them until now, when the wrongness had disappeared. *This* was what she remembered, what she had felt that first glorious night when Stefan had held her. All the sweetness and tenderness in the world surging between them. She was home, where she belonged. Where she would always belong.

Everything else was forgotten.

As she had in the beginning, Elena felt as if she could almost read Stefan's thoughts. They were connected, a part of each other. Their hearts beat to the same rhythm.

Only one thing was needed to make it complete. Elena knew that, and she tossed her hair back, reaching from behind to pull it away from the side of her neck. And this time Stefan did not protest or thwart her. Instead of refusal he was radiating a deep acceptance—and a deep need.

Feelings of love, of delight, of appreciation overwhelmed her and with incredulous joy she realized the feelings were his. For a moment, she sensed herself through his eyes, and sensed how much he cared for her. It might have been frightening if she had not had the same depth of feeling to give back to him.

She felt no pain as his teeth pierced her neck. And it didn't even occur to her that she had unthinkingly offered him the unmarked side—even though the wounds Damon had left were healed already.

She clung to him when he tried to lift his head. He was adamant, though, and at last she had to let him do it. Still holding her, he groped over onto the dresser for the wicked ivory-handled blade and with one quick motion he let his own blood flow.

When Elena's knees grew weak, he sat her on the bed. And then they just held each other, unaware of time or anything else. Elena felt that only she and Stefan existed.

"I love you," he said softly.

At first Elena, in her pleasant haze, simply accepted the words. Then, with a chill of sweetness, she realized what he'd said.

He loved her. She'd known it all along, but he had never said it before.

"I love you, Stefan," she whispered back. She was surprised when he shifted and pulled away slightly, until she saw what he was doing. Reaching inside his sweater, he drew out the chain he had worn around his neck ever since she had known him. On the chain was a gold ring, exquisitely crafted, set with lapis lazuli.

Katherine's ring. As Elena watched, he took the chain off and unclasped it, removing the delicate golden band.

"When Katherine died," he said, "I thought I could never love anyone else. Even though I knew she would have wanted me to, I was sure it could never happen. But I was wrong." He hesitated a moment and then went on.

"I kept the ring because it was a symbol of her. So I

could keep her in my heart. But now I'd like it to be a symbol of something else." Again he hesitated, seeming almost afraid to meet her eyes. "Considering the way things are, I don't really have any right to ask this. But, Elena—" He struggled on for a few minutes and then gave up, his eyes meeting hers mutely.

Elena couldn't speak. She couldn't even breathe. But Stefan misinterpreted her silence. The hope in his eyes died and he turned away.

"You're right," he said. "It's all impossible. There are just too many difficulties—because of me. Because of what I am. Nobody like you should be tied to someone like me. I shouldn't even have suggested it—"

"Stefan!" said Elena. "Stefan, if you'll be quiet a moment—"

"—so just forget I said anything—"

"*Stefan!*" she said. "Stefan, *look at me.*"

Slowly, he obeyed, turning back. He looked into her eyes, and the bitter self-condemnation faded from his face, to be replaced by a look that made her lose her breath again. Then, still slowly, he took the hand she was holding out. Deliberately, as they both watched, he slipped the ring onto her finger.

It fit as if it had been made for her. The gold glinted richly in the light, and the lapis shone a deep vibrant blue like a clear lake surrounded by untouched snow.

"We'll have to keep it a secret for a while," she said, hearing the tremor in her voice. "Aunt Judith will have a fit if she knows I'm engaged before I graduate. But I'll be eighteen next summer, and then she can't stop us."

"Elena, are you sure this is what you want? It won't be easy living with me. I'll always be different from you, no matter how I try. If you ever want to change your mind . . . "

"As long as you love me, I'll never change my mind."

He took her in his arms again, and peace and contentment enfolded her. But there was still one fear that gnawed at the edges of her consciousness.

"Stefan, about tomorrow—if Caroline and Tyler carry out their plan, it won't matter if I change my mind or not."

"Then we'll just have to make sure they can't carry it out. If Bonnie and Meredith will help me, I think I can find a way to get the diary from Caroline. But even if I can't, I'm not going to run. I won't leave you, Elena; I'm going to stay and fight."

"But they'll hurt you. Stefan, I can't stand that."

"And I can't leave you. That's settled. Let me worry about the rest of it; I'll find a way. And if I don't . . . well, no matter what I'll stay with you. We'll be together."

"We'll be together," Elena repeated, and rested her

head on his shoulder, happy to stop thinking for a while and just *be*.

November 29, Friday

Dear Diary,

It's late but I couldn't sleep. I don't seem to need as much sleep as I used to.

Well, tomorrow's the day.

We talked to Bonnie and Meredith tonight. Stefan's plan is simplicity itself. The thing is, no matter where Caroline has hidden the diary, she has to bring it out tomorrow to take it with her. But our readings are the last thing on the agenda, and she has to be in the parade and everything first. She'll have to stash the diary somewhere during that time. So if we watch her from the minute she leaves her house until she gets up on stage, we should be able to see where she puts it down. And since she doesn't even know we're suspicious, she won't be on guard.

That's when we get it.

The reason the plan will work is because everyone in the program will be in period dress. Mrs. Grimesby, the librarian, will help us put on our 19th century clothes before the parade, and we can't be wearing or carrying anything that's not part of the costume. No purses, no backpacks. No diaries! Caroline will have to leave it behind at some point.

We're taking turns watching her. Bonnie is going to wait outside her house and see what Caroline's carrying when she leaves. I'll watch her when she gets dressed at Mrs. Grimesby's house. Then, while the parade is going on, Stefan and Meredith will break into the house—or the Forbeses' car, if that's where it is—and do their stuff.

I don't see how it can fail. And I can't tell you how much better I feel. It's so good just to be able to share this problem with Stefan. I've learned my lesson; I'll never keep things from him again.

I'm wearing my ring tomorrow. If Mrs. Grimesby asks me about it, I'll tell her it's even older than 19th century, it's from Renaissance Italy. I'd like to see her face when I say that.

I'd better try to get some sleep now. I hope I don't dream.

onnie shivered as she waited outside the tall Victorian house. The air was frosty this morning, and although it was almost eight o'clock the sun had never really come up. The sky was just one dense massed bank of gray and white clouds, creating an eerie twilight below.

She had begun to stamp her feet and rub her hands together when the Forbeses' door opened. Bonnie moved back a little behind the shrubbery that was her hiding place and watched the family walk to their car. Mr. Forbes was carrying nothing but a camera. Mrs. Forbes had a purse and a folding seat. Daniel Forbes, Caroline's younger brother, had another seat. And Caroline . . .

Bonnie leaned forward, her breath hissing out in satisfaction. Caroline was dressed in jeans and a heavy sweater, and she was carrying some sort of white drawstring purse. Not big but big enough to hold a small diary.

Warmed by triumph, Bonnie waited behind the bush until the car drove away. Then she started for the corner of Thrush Street and Hawthorne Drive.

"There she is, Aunt Judith. On the corner."

The car slowed to a halt, and Bonnie slid into the back seat with Elena.

"She's got a white drawstring purse," she murmured into Elena's ear as Aunt Judith pulled out again.

Tingling excitement swept over Elena, and she squeezed Bonnie's hand. "Good," she breathed. "Now we'll see if she brings it into Mrs. Grimesby's. If not, you tell Meredith it's in the car."

Bonnie nodded agreement and squeezed Elena's hand back.

They arrived at Mrs. Grimesby's just in time to see Caroline going inside with a white bag hanging from her arm. Bonnie and Elena exchanged a look. Now it was up to Elena to see where Caroline left it in the house.

"I'll get out here too, Miss Gilbert," said Bonnie as Elena jumped out of the car. She would wait outside with Meredith until Elena could tell them where the bag was. The important thing was not to let Caroline suspect anything unusual.

Mrs. Grimesby, who answered Elena's knock, was the Fell's Church librarian. Her house looked almost like a library itself; there were bookcases everywhere and books stacked on the floor. She was also the keeper of Fell's Church's historical artifacts, including clothing that had been preserved from the town's earliest days.

Just now the house was ringing with young voices, and the bedrooms were full of students in various stages of undress. Mrs. Grimesby always supervised the costumes for the pageant. Elena was ready to ask to be put in the same room with Caroline, but it wasn't necessary. Mrs. Grimesby was already ushering her in.

Caroline, stripped down to her fashionable underwear, gave Elena what was undoubtedly meant to be a nonchalant look, but Elena detected the vicious gloating beneath. She kept her own eyes on the bundle of clothing Mrs. Grimesby was picking up off the bed.

"Here you are, Elena. One of our most nicely preserved pieces—and all authentic, too, even the ribbons. We believe this dress belonged to Honoria Fell."

"It's beautiful," said Elena, as Mrs. Grimesby shook out the folds of thin white material. "What's it made of?"

"Moravian muslin and silk gauze. Since it's quite cold today you can wear that velvet jacket over it." The librarian indicated a dusty rose garment lying over a chair back.

Elena cast a surreptitious glance at Caroline as she

began to change. Yes, there was the bag, at Caroline's feet.
She debated making a grab for it, but Mrs. Grimesby was
still in the room.

The muslin dress was very simple, its flowing material
belted high under the bosom with a pale rose ribbon. The
slightly puffed elbow-length sleeves were tied with ribbon of the same color. Fashions had been loose enough in
the early nineteenth century to fit a twentieth-century
girl—at least if she were slender. Elena smiled as Mrs.
Grimesby led her to a mirror.

"Did it really belong to Honoria Fell?" she asked,
thinking of the marble image of that lady lying on her
tomb in the ruined church.

"That's the story, anyway," said Mrs. Grimesby. "She
mentions a dress like it in her journal, so we're pretty
sure."

"She kept a journal?" Elena was startled.

"Oh, yes. I have it in a case in the living room; I'll show
it to you on the way out. Now for the jacket—oh, what's
that?"

Something violet fluttered to the ground as Elena
picked the jacket up.

She could feel her expression freeze. She caught up
the note before Mrs. Grimesby could bend over, and
glanced at it.

One line. She remembered writing it in her diary on

September 4, the first day of school. Except that after she had written it she had crossed it out. These words were not crossed out; they were bold and clear.

Something awful is going to happen today.

Elena could barely restrain herself from rounding on Caroline and shaking the note in her face. But that would ruin everything. She forced herself to stay calm as she crumpled up the little slip of paper and threw it into a wastebasket.

"It's just a piece of trash," she said, and turned back to Mrs. Grimesby, her shoulders stiff. Caroline said nothing, but Elena could feel those triumphant green eyes on her.

Just you wait, she thought. Wait until I get that diary back. I'm going to burn it, and then you and I are going to have a talk.

To Mrs. Grimesby she said, "I'm ready."

"So am I," said Caroline in a demure voice. Elena put on a look of cool indifference as she eyed the other girl. Caroline's pale green gown with long green and white sashes was not nearly as pretty as hers.

"Wonderful. You girls go ahead and wait for your rides. Oh, and Caroline, don't forget your reticule."

"I won't," Caroline said, smiling, and she reached for the drawstring bag at her feet.

It was fortunate that from that position she couldn't see Elena's face, for in that instant the cool indifference shattered completely. Elena stared, dumbfounded, as Caroline began to tie the bag at her waist.

Her astonishment didn't escape Mrs. Grimesby. "That's a reticule, the ancestor of our modern handbag," the older woman explained kindly. "Ladies, used to keep their gloves and fans in them. Caroline came by and got it earlier this week so she could repair some loose beadwork . . . very thoughtful of her."

"I'm sure it was," Elena managed in a strangled voice. She had to get out of here or something awful was going to happen right now. She was going to start screaming—or knock Caroline down—or explode. "I need some fresh air," she said. She bolted from the room and from the house, bursting outside.

Bonnie and Meredith were waiting in Meredith's car. Elena's heart thumped strangely as she walked to it and leaned in the window.

"She's outsmarted us," she said quietly. "That bag is part of her costume, and she's going to wear it all day."

Bonnie and Meredith stared, first at her and then at each other.

"But . . . then, what are we going to do?" Bonnie asked.

"I don't know." With sick dismay this realization finally came home to Elena. "I don't know!"

"We can still watch her. Maybe she'll take the bag off at lunch or something . . . " But Meredith's voice rang hollow. They all knew the truth, Elena thought, and the truth was that it was hopeless. They'd lost.

Bonnie glanced in the rearview mirror, then twisted in her seat. "It's your ride."

Elena looked. Two white horses were drawing a smartly renovated buggy down the street. Crepe paper was threaded through the buggy's wheels, ferns decorated its seats, and a large banner on the side proclaimed, *The Spirit of Fell's Church.*

Elena had time for only one desperate message. "Watch her," she said. "And if there's ever a moment when she's alone . . . " Then she had to go.

But all through that long, terrible morning, there was never a moment when Caroline was alone. She was surrounded by a crowd of spectators.

For Elena, the parade was pure torture. She sat in the buggy beside the mayor and his wife, trying to smile, trying to look normal. But the sick dread was like a crushing weight on her chest.

Somewhere in front of her, among the marching bands and drill teams and open convertibles, was Caroline. Elena had forgotten to find out which float she was on. The first schoolhouse float, perhaps; a lot of the younger children in costume would be on that.

It didn't matter. Wherever Caroline was, she was in full view of half the town.

The luncheon that followed the parade was held in the high school cafeteria. Elena was trapped at a table with Mayor Dawley and his wife. Caroline was at a nearby table; Elena could see the shining back of her auburn head. And sitting beside her, often leaning possessively over her, was Tyler Smallwood.

Elena was in a perfect position to view the little drama that occurred about halfway through lunch. Her heart leaped into her throat when she saw Stefan, looking casual, stroll by Caroline's table.

He spoke to Caroline. Elena watched, forgetting even to play with the untouched food on her plate. But what she saw next made her heart plummet. Caroline tossed her head and replied to him briefly, and then turned back to her meal. And Tyler lumbered to his feet, his face reddening as he made an angry gesture. He didn't sit down again until Stefan turned away.

Stefan looked toward Elena as he left, and for a moment their eyes met in wordless communion.

There was nothing he could do, then. Even if his Powers had returned, Tyler was going to keep him away from Caroline. The crushing weight squeezed Elena's lungs so that she could scarcely breathe.

After that she simply sat in a daze of misery and despair

until someone nudged her and told her it was time to go backstage.

She listened almost indifferently to Mayor Dawley's speech of welcome. He spoke about the "trying time" Fell's Church had faced recently, and about the community spirit that had sustained them these past months. Then awards were given out, for scholarship, for athletics, for community service. Matt came up to receive Outstanding Male Athlete of the Year and Elena saw him look at her curiously.

Then came the pageant. The elementary school children giggled and tripped and forgot their lines as they portrayed scenes, from the founding of Fell's Church through the Civil War. Elena watched them without taking any of it in. Ever since last night she'd been slightly dizzy and shaky, and now she felt as if she were coming down with the flu. Her brain, usually so full of schemes and calculations, was empty. She couldn't think anymore. She almost couldn't care.

The pageant ended to popping flashbulbs and tumultuous applause. When the last little Confederate soldier was off the stage, Mayor Dawley called for silence.

"And now," he said, "for the students who will perform the closing ceremonies. Please show your appreciation for the Spirit of Independence, the Spirit of Fidelity, and the Spirit of Fell's Church!"

The applause was even more thunderous. Elena stood beside John Clifford, the brainy senior who'd been chosen to represent the Spirit of Independence. On the other side of John was Caroline. In a detached, nearly apathetic way Elena noticed that Caroline looked magnificent: her head tilted back, her eyes blazing, her cheeks flushed with color.

John went first, adjusting his glasses and the microphone before he read from the heavy brown book on the lectern. Officially, the seniors were free to choose their own selections; in practice they almost always read from the works of M. C. Marsh, the only poet Fell's Church had ever produced.

All during John's reading, Caroline was upstaging him. She smiled at the audience; she shook out her hair; she weighed the reticule hanging from her waist. Her fingers stroked the drawstring bag lovingly, and Elena found herself staring at it, hypnotized, memorizing every bead.

John took a bow and resumed his place by Elena. Caroline threw her shoulders back and did a model's walk to the lectern.

This time the applause was mixed with whistles. But Caroline didn't smile; she had assumed an air of tragic responsibility. With exquisite timing she waited until the cafetorium was perfectly quiet to speak.

"I was planning to read a poem by M. C. Marsh today," she said, then, into the attentive stillness, "but I'm not going to. Why read from *this*"—she held up the nineteenth-century volume of poetry—"when there is something much more . . . relevant . . . in a book I happened to find?"

Happened to steal, you mean, thought Elena. Her eyes sought among the faces in the crowd, and she located Stefan. He was standing toward the back, with Bonnie and Meredith stationed on either side as if protecting him. Then Elena noticed something else. Tyler, with Dick and several other guys, was standing just a few yards behind. The guys were older than high school age, and they looked tough, and there were five of them.

Go, thought Elena, finding Stefan's eyes again. She willed him to understand what she was saying. Go, Stefan; please leave before it happens. Go *now*.

Very slightly, almost imperceptibly, Stefan shook his head.

Caroline's fingers were dipping into the bag as if she just couldn't wait. "What I'm going to read is about Fell's Church *today*, not a hundred or two hundred years ago," she was saying, working herself up into a sort of exultant fever. "It's important *now*, because it's about somebody who's living in town with us. In fact he's right here in this room."

Tyler must have written the speech for her, Elena

decided. Last month, in the gym, he'd shown quite a gift for that kind of thing. Oh, Stefan, oh, Stefan, I'm scared . . . Her thoughts jumbled into incoherence as Caroline plunged her hand into the bag.

"I think you'll understand what I mean when you hear it," Caroline said, and with a quick motion she pulled a velvet-covered book from the reticule and held it up dramatically. "I think it will explain a lot of what's been going on in Fell's Church recently." Breathing quickly and lightly, she looked from the spellbound audience to the book in her hand.

Elena had almost lost consciousness when Caroline jerked the diary out. Bright sparkles ran along the edges of her vision. The dizziness roared up, ready to overwhelm Elena, and then she noticed something.

It must be her eyes. The stage lights and flashbulbs must have dazzled them. She certainly felt ready to faint any minute; it was hardly surprising that she couldn't see properly.

The book in Caroline's hands looked *green*, not blue.

I must be going crazy . . . or this is a dream . . . or maybe it's a trick of the lighting. But look at Caroline's face!

Caroline, mouth working, was staring at the velvet book. She seemed to have forgotten the audience altogether. She turned the diary over and over in her hands, looking at all sides of it. Her movements became frantic. She thrust a hand into the reticule as if she somehow hoped to find something else in it. Then she cast a wild glance around the stage as if what she was looking for might have fallen to the ground.

The audience was murmuring, getting impatient. Mayor Dawley and the high school principal were exchanging tight-lipped frowns.

Having found nothing on the floor, Caroline was staring at the small book again. But now she was gazing at it as if it were a scorpion With a sudden gesture, she wrenched it open and looked inside, as if her last hope was that only the cover had changed and the words inside might be Elena's.

Then she slowly looked up from the book at the packed cafetorium.

Silence had descended again, and the moment drew out, while every eye remained fixed on the girl in the pale green gown. Then, with an inarticulate sound, Caroline whirled and clattered off the stage. She struck at Elena as she went by, her face a mask of rage and hatred.

Gently, with a feeling of floating, Elena stooped to pick up what Caroline had tried to hit her with.

Caroline's diary.

There was activity behind Elena as people ran after

Caroline, and in front of her as the audience exploded into comment, argument, discussion. Elena found Stefan. He looked as if jubilation was sneaking up on him. But he also looked as bewildered as Elena felt. Bonnie and Meredith were the same. As Stefan's gaze crossed hers, Elena felt a rush of gratitude and joy, but her predominant emotion was awe.

It was a miracle. Beyond all hope, they had been rescued. They'd been saved.

And then her eyes picked out another dark head among the crowd.

Damon was leaning . . . no, lounging . . . against the north wall. His lips were curved into a half smile, and his eyes met Elena's boldly.

Mayor Dawley was beside her, urging her forward, quieting the crowd, trying to restore order. It was no use. Elena read her selection in a dreamy voice to a babbling group of people who weren't paying attention in the slightest. She wasn't paying attention, either; she had no idea what words she was saying. Every so often she looked at Damon.

There was applause, scattered and distracted, when she finished, and the mayor announced the rest of the events for that afternoon. And then it was all over, and Elena was free to go.

She floated offstage without any conscious idea of *where* she was going, but her legs carried her to the north wall. Damon's dark head moved out the side door and she followed it.

The air in the courtyard seemed deliciously cool after the crowded room, and the clouds above were silvery and swirling. Damon was waiting for her.

Her steps slowed but did not stop. She moved until she was only a foot or so away from him, her eyes searching his face.

There was a long moment of silence and then she spoke. "Why?"

"I thought you'd be more interested in *how*." He patted his jacket significantly. "I got invited in for coffee this morning after scraping up an acquaintance last week."

"But *why*?"

He shrugged, and for just an instant something like consternation flickered across his finely drawn features. It seemed to Elena that he himself didn't know why—or didn't want to admit it.

"For my own purposes," he said.

"I don't think so." Something was building between them, something that frightened Elena with its power. "I don't think that's the reason at all."

There was a dangerous glimmer in those dark eyes.

"Don't push me, Elena."

She moved closer, so that she was almost touching him, and looked at him. "I think," she said, "that maybe you need to be pushed."

His face was only inches away from hers, and Elena never knew what might have happened if at that moment a voice hadn't broken in on them.

"You *did* manage to make it after all! I'm so glad!"

It was Aunt Judith. Elena felt as if she were being whisked from one world to another. She blinked dizzily, stepping back, letting out a breath she hadn't realized she was holding.

"And so you got to hear Elena read," Aunt Judith continued happily. "You did a beautiful job, Elena, but I don't know what was going on with Caroline. The girls in this town are all acting bewitched lately."

"Nerves," suggested Damon, his face carefully solemn. Elena felt an urge to giggle and then a wave of irritation. It was all very well to be grateful to Damon for saving them, but if not for Damon there wouldn't have been a problem in the first place. Damon had committed the crimes Caroline wanted to pin on Stefan.

"And where *is* Stefan?" she said, voicing her next thought aloud. She could see Bonnie and Meredith in the courtyard alone.

Aunt Judith's face showed her disapproval. "I haven't

seen him," she said briefly. Then she smiled fondly. "But I have an idea; why don't you come to dinner with us, Damon? Then afterwards perhaps you and Elena could—"

"Stop it!" said Elena to Damon. He looked politely inquiring.

"What?" said Aunt Judith.

"Stop it!" Elena said to Damon again. "You know what. Just stop it right now!"

15

"Elena, you're being rude!" Aunt Judith seldom got angry but she was angry now. "You're too old for this kind of behavior."

"It's not rudeness! You don't understand—"

"I understand perfectly. You're acting just the way you did when Damon came to dinner. Don't you think a guest deserves a little more consideration?"

Frustration flooded over Elena. "You don't even know what you're talking about," she said. This was too much. To hear Damon's words coming from Aunt Judith's lips . . . it was unbearable.

"Elena!" A mottled flush was creeping up Aunt Judith's cheeks. "I'm *shocked* at you! And I *have* to say that this childish behavior only started since you've been going out with that boy."

"Oh, 'that boy.'" Elena glared at Damon.

"Yes, that boy!" Aunt Judith answered. "Ever since you lost your head over him you've been a different person. Irresponsible, secretive—and defiant! He's been a bad influence from the start, and I won't tolerate it anymore."

"Oh, really?" Elena felt as if she were talking to Damon and Aunt Judith at once, and she looked back and forth between the two of them. All the emotions she'd been suppressing for the last days—for the last weeks, for the months since Stefan had come into her life—were surging forward. It was like a great tidal wave inside her, over which she had no control.

She realized she was shaking. "Well, that's too bad because you're going to have to tolerate it. I am never going to give Stefan up, not for anyone. Certainly not for *you*!" This last was meant for Damon, but Aunt Judith gasped.

"That's enough!" Robert snapped. He'd appeared with Margaret, and his face was dark. "Young lady, if this is how that boy encourages you to speak to your aunt—"

"He's not 'that boy'!" Elena took another step back, so she could face all of them. She was making a spectacle of herself, everyone in the courtyard was looking. But she didn't care. She had been keeping a lid on her feelings for so long, shoving down all the anxiety and the fear and the anger where it wouldn't be seen. All the worry about Stefan, all the terror over Damon, all the shame and humiliation she'd suffered at school, she'd buried it deep. But now it was coming back. All of it, all at once, in a maelstrom of impossible violence. Her heart was pounding crazily; her ears rang. She felt that nothing mattered except to hurt the people who stood in front of her, to show them all.

"He's not 'that boy,'" she said again, her voice deadly cold. "He's Stefan and he's all I care about. And I happen to be engaged to him."

"Oh, don't be ridiculous!" Robert thundered. It was the last straw.

"Is this ridiculous?" She held up her hand, the ring toward them. "We're going to get married!"

"You are *not* going to get married," Robert began. Everyone was furious. Damon grabbed her hand and stared at the ring, then turned abruptly and strode away, every step full of barely leashed savagery. Robert was spluttering on in exasperation. Aunt Judith was fuming.

"Elena, I absolutely forbid you—"

"You're not my mother!" Elena cried. Tears were trying to force themselves out of her eyes. She needed to get away, to be alone, to be with someone who loved her. "If Stefan asks, tell him I'll be at the boarding house!" she added, and broke away through the crowd.

She half expected Bonnie or Meredith to follow her, but she was glad they didn't. The parking lot was full of cars but almost empty of people. Most of the families were staying for the afternoon activities. But a battered Ford sedan was parked nearby, and a familiar figure was unlocking the door.

"Matt! Are you leaving?" She made her decision instantly. It was too cold to walk all the way to the boarding house.

"Huh? No, I've got to help Coach Lyman take the tables down. I was just putting this away." He tossed the Outstanding Athlete placard into the front seat. "Hey, are you okay?" His eyes widened at the sight of her face.

"Yes—no. I will be if I can get out of here. Look, can I take your car? Just for a little while?"

"Well . . . sure, but . . . I know, why don't you let me drive you? I'll go tell Coach Lyman."

"No! I just want to be alone. . . . Oh, please don't ask any questions." She almost snatched the keys out of his hand. "I'll bring it back soon, I promise. Or Stefan will. If you see Stefan, tell him I'm at the boarding house. And thanks." She slammed the door on his protests and revved the engine, pulling out with a clash of gears because she wasn't used to a stick shift. She left him standing there staring after her.

She drove without really seeing or hearing anything

outside, crying, locked in her own spinning tornado of emotions. She and Stefan would run away. . . . They would elope. . . . They would show everyone. She would never set foot in Fell's Church again.

And then Aunt Judith would be sorry. Then Robert would see how wrong he'd been. But Elena would never forgive them. Never.

As for Elena herself, she didn't need anybody. She certainly didn't need stupid old Robert E. Lee, where you could go from being mega-popular to being a social pariah in one day just for loving the wrong person. She didn't need any family, or any friends, either. . . .

Slowing down to cruise up the winding driveway of the boarding house, Elena felt her thoughts slow down, too.

Well . . . she wasn't mad at all her friends. Bonnie and Meredith hadn't done anything. Or Matt. Matt was all right. In fact, she might not need him but his car had come in pretty handy.

In spite of herself Elena felt a strangled giggle well up in her throat. Poor Matt. People always borrowing his clunking dinosaur of a car. He must think she and Stefan were nuts.

The giggle let loose a few more tears and she sat and wiped them off, shaking her head. Oh, God, how did things turn out this way? What a day. She should be having a victory celebration because they'd beaten Caroline, and instead she was crying alone in Matt's car.

Caroline *had* looked pretty damn funny, though. Elena's body shook gently with slightly hysterical chuckles. Oh, the look on her face. Somebody better have a video of that.

At last the sobs and giggles both abated and Elena felt a wash of tiredness. She leaned against the steering wheel trying not to think of anything for a while, and then she got out of the car.

She'd go and wait for Stefan, and then they'd both go back and deal with the mess she'd made. It would take a lot of cleaning up, she thought wearily. Poor Aunt Judith. Elena had yelled at her in front of half the town.

Why had she let herself get so upset? But her emotions were still close to the surface, as she found when the boarding house door was locked and no one answered the bell.

Oh, wonderful, she thought, her eyes stinging again. Mrs. Flowers had gone off to the Founders' Day celebration, too. And now Elena had the choice of sitting in the car or standing out here in this windstorm. . . .

It was the first time she'd noticed the weather, but when she did she looked around in alarm. The day had started out cloudy and chilly, but now there was a mist flowing along the ground, as if breathed out from the surrounding fields. The clouds were not just swirling, they were seething. And the wind was getting stronger.

It moaned through the branches of the oak trees, tearing off the remaining leaves and sending them down in showers. The sound was rising steadily now, not just a moan but a howl.

And there was something else. Something that came not just from the wind, but from the air itself, or the space around the air. A feeling of pressure, of menace, of some unimaginable force. It was gathering power, drawing nearer, closing in.

Elena spun to face the oak trees.

There was a stand of them behind the house, and more beyond, blending into the forest. And beyond that were the river and the graveyard.

Something . . . was out there. Something . . . very bad . . .

"No," whispered Elena. She couldn't see it, but she could feel it, like some great shape rearing up to stand over her, blotting out the sky. She *felt* the evil, the hatred, the animal fury.

Bloodlust. Stefan had used the word, but she hadn't understood it. Now she felt this bloodlust . . . focused on her.

"No!"

Higher and higher, it was towering over her. She could still see nothing, but it was as if great wings unfolded, stretching to touch the horizon on either side. Something with a Power beyond comprehension . . . and it wanted to kill. . . .

"No!" She ran for the car just as it stooped and dived for her. Her hands scrabbled at the door handle, and she fumbled frantically with the keys. The wind was screaming, shrieking, tearing at her hair. Gritty ice sprayed into her eyes, blinding her, but then the key turned and she jerked the door open.

Safe! She slammed the door shut again and brought her fist down on the lock. Then she flung herself across the seat to check the locks on the other side.

The wind roared with a thousand voices outside. The car began rocking.

"Stop it! Damon, stop it!" Her thin cry was lost in the cacophony. She put her hands out on the dashboard as if to balance the car and it rocked harder, ice pelting against it.

Then she saw something. The rear window was clouding up, but she could discern the shape through it. It looked like some great bird made of mist or snow, but the outlines were hazy. All she was sure of was that it had huge sweeping wings . . . and that it was coming for her.

Get the key in the ignition. Get it in! Now go! Her mind was rapping orders at her. The ancient Ford wheezed and the tires screamed louder than the wind as she took off. And the shape behind her followed, getting larger and larger in the rearview mirror.

Get to town, get to Stefan! Go! Go! But as she squealed onto Old Creek Road, turning left, the wheels locking, a bolt of lightning split the sky.

If she hadn't been skidding and braking already, the tree would have crashed down on her. As it was, the violent impact shook the car like an earthquake missing the front right fender by inches. The tree was a mass of heaving, pitching branches, its trunk blocking the way back to town completely.

She was trapped. Her only route home cut off. She was alone, there was no escape from this terrible Power . . .

Power. That was it; that was the key. "The stronger your Powers are, the more the rules of the dark bind you."

Running water!

Throwing the car into reverse, she brought it around and then slammed into forward. The white shape banked and swooped, missing her as narrowly as the tree had, and then she was speeding down Old Creek Road into the worst of the storm.

It was still after her. Only one thought pounded in Elena's brain now. She had to cross running water, to leave this thing behind.

There were more cracks of lightning, and she glimpsed other trees falling, but she swerved around them. It couldn't be far now. She could see the river flickering past on her left side through the driving ice storm. Then she saw the bridge.

It was there; she'd made it! A gust threw sleet across the windshield, but with the wipers' next stroke she saw it fleetingly again. This was it, the turn should be about *here*.

The car lurched and skidded onto the wooden structure. Elena felt the wheels grip at slick planks and then felt them lock. Desperately, she tried to turn with the skid, but she couldn't see and there was no room. . . .

And then she was crashing through the guardrail, the rotted wood of the footbridge giving way under weight it could no longer support. There was a sickening feeling of spinning, dropping, and the car hit the water.

Elena heard screams, but they didn't seem to be connected with her. The river welled up around her and everything was noise and confusion and pain. A window shattered as it was struck by debris, and then another. Dark water gushed across her, along with glass like ice. She was engulfed. She couldn't see; she couldn't get out.

And she couldn't breathe. She was lost in this hellish tumult, and there was no air. *She had to breathe.* She had to get out of here. . . .

"Stefan, help me!" she screamed.

But her scream made no sound. Instead, the icy water

rushed into her lungs, invading her. She thrashed against it, but it was too strong for her. Her struggles became wilder, more uncoordinated, and then they stopped.

Then everything was still.

Bonnie and Meredith were hunting around the perimeter of the school impatiently. They'd seen Stefan go this way, more or less coerced by Tyler and his new friends. They'd started to follow him, but then that business with Elena had started. And then Matt had informed them that she'd taken off. So they'd set out after Stefan again, but nobody was out here. There weren't even any buildings except one lonely Quonset hut.

"And now there's a storm coming!" Meredith said. "Listen to that wind! I think it's going to rain."

"Or snow!" Bonnie shuddered. "Where did they *go?*"

"I don't care; I just want to get under a roof. Here it comes!" Meredith gasped as the first sheet of icy rain hit her, and she and Bonnie ran for the nearest shelter—the Quonset hut.

And it was there that they found Stefan. The door was ajar, and when Bonnie looked in she recoiled.

"Tyler's goon squad!" she hissed. "Look out!"

Stefan had a semicircle of guys between him and the door. Caroline was in the corner.

"He must have it! He took it somehow; I know he

did!" she was saying.

"Took what?" said Meredith loudly. Everyone turned their way.

Caroline's face contorted as she saw them in the doorway and Tyler snarled. "Get out," he said. "You don't want to be involved in this."

Meredith ignored him. "Stefan, can I talk to you?"

"In a minute. Are you going to answer her question? Took what?" Stefan was concentrating on Tyler, totally focused.

"Sure, I'll answer her question. Right after I answer yours." Tyler's beefy hand thumped into his fist and he stepped forward. "You're going to be dog meat, Salvatore."

Several of the tough guys snickered.

Bonnie opened her mouth to say, "Let's get *out* of here." But what she actually said was, "The bridge."

It was weird enough to make everyone look at her.

"What?" said Stefan.

"The bridge," said Bonnie again, without meaning to say it. Her eyes bulged, alarmed. She could hear the voice coming from her throat, but she had no control over it. And then she felt her eyes go wider and her mouth drop open and she had her own voice back. "The bridge, oh, my God, the bridge! That's where Elena is! Stefan, we've got to save her. . . . Oh, hurry!"

"Bonnie, are you sure?"

"Yes, oh, God . . . that's where she's gone. She's drowning! *Hurry!*" Waves of thick blackness broke over Bonnie. But she couldn't faint now; they had to get to Elena.

Stefan and Meredith hesitated one minute, and then Stefan was through the goon squad, brushing them aside like tissue paper. They sprinted through the field toward the parking lot, dragging Bonnie behind. Tyler started after them, but stopped when the full force of the wind hit him.

"Why would she go out in this storm?" Stefan shouted as they sprang into Meredith's car.

"She was upset; Matt said she took off in his car," Meredith gasped back in the comparative quiet of the interior. She pulled out fast and turned into the wind, speeding dangerously. "She said she was going to the boarding house."

"No, she's at the bridge! Meredith, drive faster! Oh, God, we're going to be too late!" Tears were running down Bonnie's face.

Meredith floored it. The car swayed, buffeted by wind and sleet. All through that nightmare ride Bonnie sobbed, her fingers clutching the seat in front of her.

Stefan's sharp warning kept Meredith from running into the tree. They piled out and were immediately lashed and punished by the wind.

"It's too big to move! We'll have to walk," Stefan shouted.

Of course it was too big to move, Bonnie thought, already scrambling through the branches. It was a full-grown oak tree. But once on the other side, the icy gale whipped all thought out of her head.

Within minutes she was numb, and the road seemed to go on for hours. They tried to run but the wind beat them back. They could scarcely see; if it hadn't been for Stefan, they would have gone over the riverbank. Bonnie began to weave drunkenly. She was ready to fall to the ground when she heard Stefan shouting up ahead.

Meredith's arm around her tightened, and they broke again into a stumbling run. But as they neared the bridge what they saw brought them to a halt.

"Oh, my God . . . Elena!" screamed Bonnie. Wickery Bridge was a mass of splintered rubble. The guardrail on one side was gone and the planking had given way as if a giant fist had smashed it. Beneath, the dark water churned over a sickening pile of debris. Part of the debris, entirely underwater except the headlights, was Matt's car.

Meredith was screaming, too, but she was screaming at Stefan. "No! You can't go down there!"

He never even glanced back. He dived from the bank, and the water closed over his head.

Later, Bonnie's memory of the next hour would be mercifully dim. She remembered waiting for Stefan while the storm raged endlessly on. She remembered that she was almost beyond caring by the time a hunched figure lurched out of the water. She remembered feeling no disappointment, only a vast and yawning grief, as she saw the limp thing Stefan laid out on the road.

And she remembered Stefan's face.

She remembered how he looked as they tried to do something for Elena. Only that wasn't really Elena lying there, that was a wax doll with Elena's features. It was nothing that had ever been alive and it certainly wasn't alive now. Bonnie thought it seemed silly to go on poking and prodding at it like this, trying to get water out of its lungs and so on. Wax dolls didn't breathe.

She remembered Stefan's face when he finally gave up. When Meredith wrestled with him and yelled at him, saying something about over an hour without air, and brain damage. The words filtered in to Bonnie, but their meaning didn't. She just thought it odd that while Meredith and Stefan were screaming at each other they were both crying.

Stefan stopped crying after that. He just sat there holding the Elena-doll. Meredith yelled some more, but he didn't listen to her. He just sat. And Bonnie would never forget his expression.

And then something seared through Bonnie, bringing her to life, waking her to terror. She clutched at Meredith, and stared around for the source. Something bad . . .

something terrible was coming. Was almost here.

Stefan seemed to feel it, too. He was alert, stiff, like a wolf picking up a scent.

"What is it?" shouted Meredith. "What's wrong with you?"

"You've got to go!" Stefan rose, still holding the limp form in his arms. "Get out of here!"

"What do you mean? We can't leave you—"

"Yes, you can! Get out of here! Bonnie, get her out!"

No one had ever told Bonnie to take care of someone else before. People were always taking care of *her*. But now she seized Meredith's arm and began pulling. Stefan was right. There was nothing they could do for Elena, and if they stayed whatever had gotten her would get them.

"Stefan!" Meredith shouted as she was unaccountably dragged away.

"I'll put her under the trees. The willows, not the oaks," he called after them.

Why would he tell us that now? Bonnie wondered in some deep part of her mind that was not taken up with fear and the storm.

The answer was simple, and her mind promptly gave it back to her. Because he wasn't going to be around to tell them later.

16

Long ago, in the dark side streets of Florence, starving, frightened, and exhausted, Stefan had made himself a vow. Several vows, in fact, about using the Powers he sensed within himself, and about how to treat the weak, blundering, but still-human creatures around him.

Now he was going to break them all.

He'd kissed Elena's cold forehead and laid her under a willow tree. He would come back here, if he could, to join her, after.

As he'd thought, the surge of Power had passed over Bonnie and Meredith and followed him, but it had receded again, and was now drawn back, waiting.

He wouldn't let it wait long.

Unencumbered by the burden of Elena's body, he

broke into a predator's lope on the empty road. The freezing sleet and wind didn't bother him much. His hunter's senses pierced through them.

He turned them all to the task of locating the prey he wanted. No thinking of Elena now. Later, when this was over.

Tyler and his friends were still in the Quonset hut. Good. They never knew what was coming as the window burst into flying glass shards and the storm blew inside.

Stefan meant to kill when he seized Tyler by the neck and sank his fangs in. That had been one of his rules, not to kill, and he wanted to break it.

But another of the toughs came at him before he had quite drained Tyler of blood. The guy wasn't trying to protect his fallen leader, only to escape. It was his bad luck that his route took him across Stefan's path. Stefan flipped him to the ground and tapped the new vein eagerly.

The hot coppery taste revived him, warmed him, flowed through him like fire. It made him want more.

Power. Life. They had it; he needed it. With the glorious rush of strength that came with what he'd already drunk, he stunned them easily. Then he moved from one to another, drinking deep and throwing them away. It was like popping tops on a six-pack.

He was on the last when he saw Caroline huddling in the corner.

His mouth was dripping as he raised his head to look at her. Those green eyes, usually so narrow, showed white all around like those of a terrified horse. Her lips were pale blurs as she gabbled soundless pleas.

He pulled her to her feet by the green sashes at her waist. She was moaning, her eyes rolling up in their sockets. He wound his hand in her auburn hair to position the exposed throat where he wanted it. His head reared back to strike—and Caroline screamed and went limp.

He dropped her. He'd had enough anyway. He was bursting with blood, like an overfed tick. He had never felt so strong, so charged with elemental power.

Now it was time for Damon.

He went out of the Quonset hut the same way he'd come in. But not in human form. A hunting falcon soared out the window and wheeled into the sky.

The new shape was wonderful. Strong . . . and cruel. And its eyes were sharp. It took him where he wanted, skimming over the oak trees of the woods. He was looking for a particular clearing.

He found it. Wind slashed at him but he spiraled downward, with a keening scream of challenge. Damon, in human form below, threw up his hands to protect his face as the falcon dived at him.

Stefan ripped bloody strips out of his arms and heard Damon's answering scream of pain and anger.

I'm not your weak little brother anymore. He sent the thought down to Damon on a stunning blast of Power. *And this time I've come for your blood.*

He felt the backwash of hatred from Damon, but the voice in his mind was mocking. *So this is the thanks I get for saving you and your betrothed?*

Stefan's wings folded and he dived again, his whole world narrowed to one objective. Killing. He went for Damon's eyes, and the stick Damon had picked up whistled past his new body. His talons tore into Damon's cheek and Damon's blood ran. Good.

You shouldn't have left me alive, he told Damon. *You should have killed both of us at once.*

I'll be glad to correct the mistake! Damon had been unprepared before, but now Stefan could feel his drawing Power, arming himself, standing ready. *But first you might tell me whom I'm supposed to have killed this time.*

The falcon's brain could not deal with the riot of emotions the taunting question called up. Screaming wordlessly, it plummeted on Damon again, but this time the heavy stick struck home. Injured, one wing hanging, the falcon dropped behind Damon's back.

Stefan changed to his own form at once, scarcely feeling the pain of his broken arm. Before Damon could turn, he grabbed him, the fingers of his good hand digging into his brother's neck and spinning him around.

When he spoke, it was almost gently.

"Elena," he said, whispered, and went for Damon's throat.

It was dark, and very cold, and someone was hurt. Someone needed help.

But she was terribly tired.

Elena's eyelids fluttered and opened and that took care of the darkness. As for the cold . . . she was bone-cold, freezing, chilled to the marrow. And no wonder; there was ice all over her.

Somewhere, deep down, she knew it was more than that.

What had happened? She'd been at home, asleep—no, this was Founders' Day. She'd been in the cafeteria, on the stage.

Someone's face had looked funny.

It was too much to cope with; she couldn't think. Disembodied faces floated before her eyes, fragments of sentences sounded in her ears. She was very confused.

And so tired.

Better go back to sleep then. The ice wasn't really that bad. She started to lie down, and then the cries came to her again.

She heard them, not with her ears, but with her mind. Cries of anger and of pain. Someone was very unhappy.

She sat quite still, trying to sort it all out.

There was a quiver of movement at the edge of her vision. A squirrel. She could smell it, which was strange because she'd never smelled a squirrel before. It stared at her with one bright black eye and then it scampered up the willow tree. Elena realized she'd made a grab for it only when she came up empty with her fingernails digging into bark.

Now that was ridiculous. What on *earth* did she want a squirrel for? She puzzled over it for a minute, then lay back down, exhausted.

The cries were still going on.

She tried to cover her ears, but that did nothing to block them out. Someone was hurt, and unhappy, and fighting. That was it. There was a fight going on.

All right. She'd figured it out. Now she could sleep.

She couldn't, though. The cries beckoned to her, drew her toward them. She felt an irresistible need to follow them to their source.

And *then* she could go to sleep. After she saw . . . him.

Oh, yes, it was coming back now. She remembered *him*. He was the one who understood her, who loved her. He was the one she wanted to be with forever.

His face appeared out of the mists in her mind. She considered it lovingly. All right, then. For *him* she would get up and walk through this ridiculous sleet until she found the proper clearing. Until she could join him. Then they'd be together.

The very thought of him seemed to warm her. There was a fire inside him that few people could see. She saw it, though. It was like the fire inside her.

He seemed to be having some sort of trouble at the moment. At least, there was a lot of shouting. She was close enough to hear it with her ears as well as her mind now.

There, beyond that grandfather oak tree. That was where the noise was coming from. *He* was there, with his black, fathomless eyes, and his secret smile. And he needed her help. She would help him.

Shaking ice crystals out of her hair, Elena stepped into the clearing in the wood.

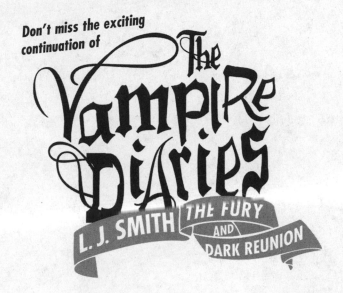

Don't miss the exciting
continuation of

The Vampire Diaries

L. J. SMITH

THE FURY
AND
DARK REUNION

Elena stepped into the clearing.

Beneath her feet, tatters of autumn leaves were freezing into the slush. Dusk had fallen, and although the storm was dying away, the woods were getting colder. Elena didn't feel the cold.

Neither did she mind the dark. Her pupils opened wide, gathering up tiny particles of light that would have been invisible to a human. She could see the two figures struggling beneath the great oak tree quite clearly.

One had thick dark hair that the wind had churned into a tumbled sea of waves. He was slightly taller than the other, and although Elena couldn't see his face, she somehow knew his eyes were green.

The other had a shock of dark hair as well, but his was fine and straight, almost like the pelt of an animal. His lips were drawn back from his teeth in fury, and the lounging grace of his body was gathered into a panther's crouch. His eyes were black.

Elena watched them for several minutes without moving. She'd forgotten why she had come here, why she'd been pulled here by the echoes of their battle in her mind. This close, the clamor of their anger and hatred and pain was almost deafening, like silent shouts coming from the fighters. They were locked in a death match.

I wonder which of them will win, she thought. They were both wounded and bleeding, and the taller one's left arm hung at an unnatural angle. Still, he had just slammed the other against the gnarled trunk of an oak tree. His fury was so strong that Elena could feel it and taste it as well as hear it, and she knew it was giving him impossible strength.

And then Elena remembered why she had come. How could she have forgotten? *He* was hurt. *His* mind had summoned her here, battering her with shockwaves of rage and pain. She had come to help him, because she belonged to him.

The two figures were down on the icy ground now, fighting like wolves, snarling. Swiftly and silently Elena went to them. The one with the wavy hair and green eyes—*Stefan*, a voice in her mind whispered—was on top, fingers scrabbling at the other's throat. Anger washed through Elena, anger and protectiveness. She reached between the two of them to grab that choking hand, to pry the fingers up.

It didn't occur to her that she shouldn't be strong enough to do this. She *was* strong enough, that was all. She threw her weight to the side, wrenching her captive away from his opponent. For good measure she bore down hard on his wounded arm, knocking him flat on his face in the leaf-strewn slush. Then she began to choke him from behind.

Her attack had taken him by surprise, but he was far from beaten. He struck back at her, his good hand fumbling for her throat. His thumb dug into her windpipe.

Elena found herself lunging at the hand, going for it with her teeth. Her mind could not understand it, but her body knew what to do. Her teeth were a weapon, and they slashed into flesh, drawing blood.

But he was stronger than she was. With a jerk of his shoulders he broke her hold on him and twisted in her grasp, flinging her down. And then he was above her, his face contorted with animal fury. She hissed at him and went for his eyes with her nails, but he knocked her hand away.

He was going to kill her. Even wounded, he was by far the stronger. His lips had drawn back to show teeth already stained with scarlet. Like a cobra, he was ready to strike.

Then he stopped, hovering over her, his face changing.

Elena saw the green eyes widen. The pupils, which had been contracted to vicious dots, sprang open. He was staring down at her as if truly seeing her for the first time.

Why was he looking at her that way? Why didn't he just get it over with? But now the iron hand on her shoulder was releasing her. The animal snarl had disappeared, replaced by a look of bewilderment and wonder. He sat back, helping her to sit up, all the while gazing into her face.

"Elena," he whispered, his voice cracking. "Elena, it's you."

Is that who I am? she thought. Elena?

It didn't really matter. She cast a glance toward the old oak tree. *He* was still there, standing between the upthrust roots, panting, supporting himself against it with one hand. *He* was looking at her with his endlessly black eyes, his brows drawn together in a frown.

Don't worry, she thought. I can take care of this one. He's stupid. Then she flung herself on the green-eyed one again.

"Elena!" he cried as she knocked him backward. His good hand pushed at her shoulder, holding her up. "Elena, it's me, Stefan! Elena, look at me!"

She was looking. All she could see was the exposed patch of skin at his neck. She hissed again, upper lips drawing back, showing him her teeth.

He froze.

She felt the shock reverberate through his body, saw his gaze shatter. His face went as white as if someone had struck him a blow in the stomach. He shook his head slightly on the muddy ground.

"No," he whispered. "Oh, no . . ."

He seemed to be saying it to himself, as if he didn't expect her to hear him. He reached a hand toward her cheek and she snapped at it.

"Oh, Elena . . ." he whispered.

The last traces of fury, of animal bloodlust, had disappeared from his face. His eyes were dazed and stricken and grieving.

And vulnerable. Elena took advantage of the moment to dive for the bare skin at his neck. His arm came up to fend her off, to push her away, but then it dropped again.

He stared at her a moment, the pain in his eyes reaching a peak, and then he simply gave up. He stopped fighting completely.

She could feel it happen, feel the resistance leave his body. He lay on the icy ground with scraps of oak leaves in his hair, staring up past her at the black and clouded sky.

Finish it, his weary voice said in her mind.

Elena hesitated for an instant. There was something about those eyes that called up memories inside her. Standing in the moonlight, sitting in an attic room . . . But the memories were too vague. She couldn't get a grasp on them, and the effort made her dizzy and sick.

And this one had to die, this green-eyed one called Stefan. Because he'd hurt *him*, the other one, the one Elena had been born to be with. No one could hurt *him* and live.

She clamped her teeth into his throat and bit deep.

She realized at once that she wasn't doing it quite right. She hadn't hit an artery or vein. She worried at the throat, angry at her own inexperience. It felt good to bite something but not much blood was coming. Frustrated, she lifted up and bit again, feeling his body jerk in pain.

Much better. She'd found a vein this time, but she hadn't torn it deeply enough. A little scratch like that wouldn't do. What she needed was to rip it right across, to let the rich hot blood stream out.

Her victim shuddered as she worked to do this, teeth raking and gnawing. She was just feeling the flesh give way when hands pulled at her, lifting her from behind.

Elena snarled without letting go of the throat. The hands were insistent, though. An arm looped about her waist, fingers twined in her hair. She fought, clinging on with teeth and nails to her prey.

Let go of him! Leave him!

The voice was sharp and commanding, like a blast from a cold wind. Elena recognized it and stopped struggling with the hands that pulled her away. As they deposited her on the ground and she looked up to see *him*, a name came into her mind. Damon. *His* name was Damon. She stared at him sulkily, resentful of being yanked away from her kill, but obedient.

Stefan was sitting up, his neck red with blood. It was

running onto his shirt. Elena licked her lips, feeling a throb like a hunger pang, but which seemed to come from every fiber of her being. She was dizzy again.

"I thought," Damon said aloud, "that you said she was dead."

He was looking at Stefan, who was even paler than before, if that were possible. That white face filled with infinite hopelessness.

"Look at her," was all he said.

A hand cupped Elena's chin, tilting her face up. She met Damon's narrowed dark eyes directly. Then long, slender fingers touched her lips, probing between them. Instinctively Elena tried to bite, but not very hard. Damon's finger found the sharp curve of a canine tooth and Elena did bite now, giving it a nip like a kitten's.

Damon's face was expressionless, his eyes hard.

"Do you know where you are?" he said.

Elena glanced around. Trees. "In the woods," she said craftily, looking back at him.

"And who is that?"

She followed his pointing finger. "Stefan," she said indifferently. "Your brother."

"And who am I? Do you know who I am?"

She smiled up at him, showing him her pointed teeth. "Of course I do. You're Damon, and I love you."

2

tefan's voice was quietly savage. "That's what you wanted, isn't it, Damon? And now you've got it. You had to make her like us, like you. It wasn't enough just to kill her."

Damon didn't glance back at him. He was looking at Elena intently through those hooded eyes, still kneeling there holding her chin. "That's the third time you've said that, and I'm getting a little tired of it," he commented softly. Disheveled, still slightly out of breath, he was yet self-composed, in control. "Elena, did I kill you?"

"Of course not," Elena said, winding her fingers in those of his free hand. She was getting impatient. What were they talking about, anyway? Nobody had been killed.

"I never thought you were a liar," Stefan said to Damon, the bitterness in his voice unchanged. "Just about everything else, but not that. I've never heard you try to cover up for yourself before."

"In another minute," said Damon, "I'm going to lose my temper."

What more can you possibly do to me? Stefan returned. *Killing me would be a mercy.*

"I ran out of mercy for you a century ago," Damon said aloud. He let go, finally, of Elena's chin. "What do you remember about today?" he asked her.

Elena spoke tiredly, like a child reciting a hated lesson. "Today was the Founders' Day celebration." She looked up at Damon, flexing her fingers in his. That was as far as she could get on her own, but it wasn't enough. Nettled, she tried to remember something else.

"There was someone in the cafeteria . . . Caroline." She offered the name to him, pleased. "She was going to read my diary in front of everyone, and that was bad because . . ." Elena fumbled with the memory and lost it. "I don't remember why. But we tricked her." She smiled at him warmly, conspiratorially.

"Oh, 'we' did, did we?"

"Yes. You got it away from her. You did it for me." The fingers of her free hand crept under his jacket, searching for the square-cornered harness of the little book. "Because you love me," she said, finding it and scratching it lightly. "You do love me, don't you?"

There was a faint sound from the center of the clearing. Elena looked and saw that Stefan had turned his face away.

"Elena. What happened next?" Damon's voice called her back.

"Next? Next Aunt Judith started arguing with me." Elena pondered this a moment and at last shrugged. "Over . . . something. I got angry. She's not my mother. She can't tell me what to do."

Damon's voice was dry. "I don't think that's going to be a problem anymore. What next?"

Elena sighed heavily. "Next I went and got Matt's car. Matt." She said the name reflectively, flicking her tongue over her canine teeth. In her mind's eye she saw a handsome face, blond hair, sturdy shoulders. "Matt."

"And where did you go in Matt's car?"

"To Wickery Bridge," Stefan said, turning back toward them. His eyes were desolate.

"No, to the boarding house," Elena corrected, irritated. "To wait for . . . mmm. I forget. Anyway, I waited there. Then . . . then the storm started. Wind, rain, all that. I didn't like it. I got in the car. But something came after me."